Horrors, Inc

By

James R. Vernon

Horrors, Inc. Copyright © 2017

By: James R. Vernon

And

Three Moons Realm Publishing

Three Moons Realm

Cover Illustrations and Design

ISBN: 0996000690
ISBN-13: 978-0-9960006-9-7

CHAPTER 1

"Janitor!"

The man in the cubicle didn't know Eddie's name. Nor did he care that Eddie, who was dressed in unassuming white overalls and pushed around a cart of cleaning supplies for a living, had a master's degree in philosophy and could speak three different languages besides English. All the man cared about was using whatever little power he had to boss around a janitor while he remained figuratively shackled to his cubicle, making calls and typing away at his computer all day.

Eddie would have been the last person anyone would have guessed to be the key witness to the fate of Soladyne Tech, and in all probability, the world. With no friends or family to speak of, the only people that even knew of his existence were those on the first ten floors of Soladyne's headquarters in America. And that was only when they needed him to mop up a spill or change a light bulb.

The rude office worker that had called him over could have figured out Eddie's name, it was embroidered right across the chest of his coveralls after all. After working the same floor for years, Eddie knew the man's name, Mitchal Whitehall, and not because it was displayed outside his cubicle on a thin plastic strip with white lettering. The man had been bossing him around for years. But why should Eddie use his name if the man didn't bother with his?

If Eddie didn't need to deal with people, being a custodian for Soladyne—a Fortune 500 company that seemed to have its hands in everything from pharmaceuticals and electronics to secretive research and development—would have been the perfect dead end job for Eddie. While some people would go nuts spending their days emptying the same old trashcans, cleaning the same restrooms, and wiping up spills, Eddie found the predictability soothing. After spending the better part of his youth being bounced around between foster homes, he welcomed the regular routine, even if it meant putting up with the occasional arrogant jerk.

"Janitor! I'm talking to you."

Eddie turned to look at him, brow raised in question.

"That's right, sport" the man said. "Take your head out of the

1

clouds and actually do your job."

Trying his best to keep a friendly smile, Eddie let go of his cart and moved toward the cause of his growing headache.

"You didn't bother to wipe up my dried coffee rings yesterday. It's distracting. Get to it before you forget again."

Eddie Watson's Rule Number 83: Suffer fools with a smile and wipe down their cubicle with the dirtiest rag from the cart.

Spite kept the man firmly labeled as simply "The Headach" in Eddie's mind. Or if he was feeling more formal, "The Headache on floor six." Eddie selected the terry cloth towel he used earlier in the day to clean the moldy fridge in the break room, dipped it in the dirty water that his mop rested in, and got to work on the stains..

"Would you like me to do your keyboard as well?" Eddie asked with a smile.

"No, but my trash can is practically overflowing. Take care of it."

A simple nod of acknowledgment is all Eddie gave him before grabbing up The Headache's shin-high trashcan and pulling out the bag inside. Apparently in this man's world, two apple cores, half a dozen crunched up wads of paper, and a discarded Redbull Magazine constituted *overflowing*. Depositing the contents in the garbage container in his cart, Eddie returned with the same trash bag even though company policy was to use a new one after each change. But Eddie liked where he was employed. Saving the company five cents while giving the man he disliked the same dirty bag was a win-win in his mind. He was about to return the slightly soiled bag back to its home when the phone on The Headache's desk began to ring, adding its call to the dozen or so other rings going off in the cubicles around them.

"Hold on one sec."

While the man took the call, Eddie leaned down to return the trashcan to its place beneath the desk. An intentionally placed leg came out at the last second to block it. The man looked down on Eddie with an irritated frown while raising a single finger in front of his face and gave it a wiggle.

The Headache was a tiny widget in the massive machine that was Soladyne Tech. Eddie had dealt with people like him from the very first day he started working here three years ago. Since The Headache had no real power at the company, he got his jollies by trying to boss around a custodian. The Headache deserved a kick in the leg, but instead Eddie took a deep breath.

Eddie Watson's Life Rule #23: Don't Make Waves.

Eddie prided himself on being a problem avoider. A single complaint to HR by The Headache wouldn't be a big deal, but all it would take was a couple more from someone else The Headache could recruit and Eddie could come in one morning with his locker cleared out and security ready to escort him right back off the property. Why risk losing a job he was content with just to get the satisfaction of telling the man off? His lips tightened into a thin line of impatience, but that was the extent of Eddie's protest.

"Yes, I know, I know," The Headache said into the phone's receiver. "Big boss coming up to make his monthly appearance." He paused. "You know as well as I do that the guy is a jackass." An even longer pause followed. "Now you're being paranoid.

While Eddie waited, a familiar, friendly tone, like rubber mallets bouncing along the keys of a xylophone, silenced the floor. It was immediately followed by an overly pleasant female voice that chimed over the loudspeaker.

"Good afternoon to our hard-working members of the Soladyne Tech family. Management would like to express its gratitude for all of your hard work. Thanks to your dedication to quality customer service, our company will continue to be a positive influence on society today and in the future. Don't forget to get up every now and then to stretch your legs, and have a pleasant afternoon."

Third announcement of the day. *Two o'clock?* Eddie thought as everyone around him got up to stretch, even those on their phones pausing until they were finished. He, of course, stretched as well. You never knew who was watching, and the company took its routines seriously. The Headache made a show of stretching out while Eddie continued to wait. *Come on, I have four other floors to hit two hours before I can clock out.*

He let out a loud *huff*, which accomplished the desired result. The man stopped his conversation and glared at him for a few moments before rolling his eyes and kicking the small trash can in

Eddie's direction. A quick install of the bag into the trashcan and Eddie hurried to leave floor six—and The Headache—behind him.

The rest of his day was as uneventful as he'd hoped. Cleaning up the microwave on the third floor after someone left a bowl of mac and cheese in too long. Replacing a desk lamp light bulb on seven. Throwing on some plastic gloves to clean up the after-effects of someone's stomach bug. And of course, finishing up his regular job of emptying out the trashcans on all of the floors under his jurisdiction. Eddie also had a few more positive interactions with the employees he worked around. A rotund office worker on seven regaled him with an inappropriate joke involving two female roommates and a broken dryer. A friendly smile from the pretty redhead on floor eight that company policy kept him from exploring further. The best part was being offered a leftover cupcake from a birthday party on floor nine. Chocolate with vanilla icing and rainbow sprinkles. It would have been rude not to partake in the dessert.

Overall it was a fairly pleasant day. When the final announcement came over the loud speaker, Eddie was surprised that the later part of the day had gone so fast.

"Soladyne would like to thank its loyal employees for another productive day. Please make sure not to spend too much time finishing up whatever you are working on. All employees are expected to have checked out of the building before five p.m. We want you to enjoy the rest of your afternoon and come back well rested for another exciting day at Soladyne Tech!"

Eddie was in the elevator before the pleasant female voice had gone through half of its speech. He wouldn't mind fighting the rush so much if it wasn't for the elevator ride. The *Box Of Horror*, as he referred to it, inevitably stopped on each of the nine floors on the way down, while more workers, eager to go home, crammed their way inside. On some evenings, the bodies were packed in so tightly, Eddie felt like the breath of life was being crushed out of his lungs.

And he really didn't enjoy all of the dirty looks he received because of how much room his cart took up. It wasn't the looks themselves that bothered him, it was more about receiving all of that attention. It felt like someone was dropping a fifty-pound blanket over his shoulders.

4

Luck was on his side, and Eddie was able to get to the lobby before the rest of the crowd. An extravagant, two-floored open room, the main lobby of the building looked straight out of a utopian paradise. A large fountain was the centerpiece of the room, surrounded by great ferns and other greenery. Holographic projectors built into the walls shot 3D images of generic men and women in lab coats, holding clipboards and looking important. Soladyne Tech's motto: *The leading company in pharmaceuticals, genetics, computing, and research meant to guide the human race into the future* constantly flashed in the holograms as well, the vagueness of it all the reason Eddie still had no idea what specific products the company actually sold. The only thing that mattered to him was that whatever the company did, it was touted as one of the safest companies that stayed away from animal testing for all of its products.

The silver-colored floor tiles shone as the light flowed through the giant glass front wall, a reflection of the company's stellar reputation. During the right time of day, the tiles sparkled and always seemed polished even though Eddie had never seen anyone working on them. Along both sidewalls, a dozen different glass counters ran the length of the room, each one with a receptionist connected to a particular aspect of the company workforce.

The luxurious ambiance was only marred by the six security guards positioned throughout the room. They were clad in the color of death, from their black helmets with electronic visors all the way down to their steel-toed combat boots. Each wore a utility belt, holding all sorts of nasty anti-personnel equipment. The only body part visible through all of the black was their hands. Both the firearm strapped at their hip and the assault rifles slung over their backs were fingerprint activated. And that was just the brief overview Eddie had received about them the day he was hired.

They were the pinnacle of what someone would expect from a meticulously trained security force. According to upper management, the Soladyne guards were the elite of the elite, plucked from the best police forces and military units across the country. Eddie would have to take their word for it. The most impressive thing he had seen them do is pat down the occasional visitor checking in or out of the building. Nonetheless, even though he had done nothing wrong, knowing they were scrutinizing his every move made him nervous. As he approached the lobby desk, he could feel their eyes on him through their visors. Thankfully, Lizzie, one of the receptionists in charge of checking employees in and out of the building, was much friendlier.

"Hello, Eddie," she said, her wide smile causing her thin-rimmed glasses to tilt a bit to the side and slide down her button nose. She took a moment to fix them and brush a lock of auburn hair from her night-blue eyes. "All done for the day?"

"Yup." He pushed his cart into the designated drop off area and then handed over his elevator access card.

"As talkative as usual, I see. Step up on the scanner, please." She gestured toward the small platform next to the desk. "Any problems or concerns I need to log in your file for administration to address?"

Eddie stepped up and held still as a halo of blue light rose up out of the platform. It traveled up just inches away from his body to the top of his wheat-colored hair. Then it descended, turning into a neon orange before disappearing back into the platform. A moment later a friendly *ding* gave the all-clear and he stepped back down. "I'm a little low on bleach."

"Heaven forbid!" she put on a worried face although her tone dripped with sarcasm. "I'll make sure this crisis is handled before you come in tomorrow or heads will roll."

"Thanks."

Lizzie let out an exaggerated sigh before setting the access ticket to the parking garage onto the counter. "Well, maybe tomorrow you'll be able to manage more than a sentence at a time." She crossed her fingers on both hands. "One can only hope."

"Thank you," he replied, sliding the ticket off the counter. "Have a nice night, Lizzie."

He ignored the shocked expression that sprang to her face as she placed both hands to her cheeks. Lizzie was just being playful, and he knew she wasn't trying to be mean. They had gone through this process together every day for the past three years, not counting the week he was out with the flu and the two weeks last month she was out for an undisclosed illness. During that first year, when Lizzie finally realized that the teasing wasn't appreciated, she kept him for twenty minutes to apologize repeatedly. Since then, he had made sure not to look the slightest bit bothered by her comments. After all, it wasn't her fault that he was socially inept. Despite how uncomfortable her attempts to engage him were, he appreciated that she cared enough to at least try.

Her hearty laughter followed him as he turned to leave. He was able to make it back to the elevators that went to down to the parking levels just as the first group of office workers exited the other set of elevators. A few moments later, Eddie was peddling his bicycle along the sidewalk, dodging well-dressed pedestrians, brushing a hair too close at times, and grimacing at the expletives shouted his way.

Before long, streets lined with high-rises, quirky corner bistros, swanky restaurants, and a sea of men and women in suits transitioned into greasy diners and abandoned storefronts covered with steel bars. Sidewalks showed the cracks of a surface left unmended over the course of decades. Suits and ties were replaced by t-shirts and hoodies, worn by people that lounged against grimy walls or leaned on dilapidated cars. A thin layer of dirt and a variety of liquids seemed to cover everything. Even in the late afternoon, the sun seemed to shy away from this section of the city.

It was the kind of area that the suits avoided, especially if they carried full wallets. Eddie had neither suit nor money to fill a wallet and was generally left alone as long as he made it home before dark. There seemed to be a general understanding between the blue-collar and the no-collar in this section of the city. If you didn't ask questions, or point the law in the general direction of the less-than-legal activities that took place, you didn't became a target of those that found it easier to steal what they wanted as opposed to earning it. When night fell, however, all bets were off. Not being the type of person to carry any kind of weapon, Eddie made sure he and his bike were safely inside the lobby of his apartment complex well before the sun disappeared.

Eddie punched the code into the keypad at the entrance and hefted his bike onto his shoulder before letting himself in. The lobby of the Maserton Apartment Building was vastly dated compared to where he worked. An ancient oriental carpet wound through an open room with old lamps and wall fixtures that casted a faded golden glow. The walls were covered in imitation wood paneling. A few pieces of orange plastic furniture made up a sitting area.

A wide desk sat in front of the office, staffed by the owner's second cousin or something like that, who served as both the building's manager and handyman. The color of everything, from the couches to the chandelier hanging in the center of the room, looked faded and worn.

Eddie waved to the man before hauling his bike to the elevator. A slow and shaky ride later, he was wheeling his bike down the west hallway of the twenty-third floor. The apartment to the right of his was rented by a family of seven that didn't speak English. The woman who rented the apartment to the left had so many late night visitors that even in the cold of winter, Eddie had to run his fan on high to drown out the sounds coming through her wall. Everyone else on the floor was friendly enough, quick to offer some detergent for the building's washers, or roll of toilet paper when he asked, and he was just as quick to keep an eye on their kids or provide a bandage to a wound that he was smart enough not to ask about.

A quick turn of the key, followed by a hard jiggle of the knob, allowed Eddie access to his two-room apartment. Behind the door to his left was the bathroom. To his right was everything else, including the only piece of furniture in the whole place, a sagging black futon. It served as his sofa, bed, and dining room chair. Lugging his bike inside, he leaned it against the crumbling plaster wall. Not wasting any time, he sloughed off his sneakers, and peeled off his sweaty tube socks, lobbing them into the overflowing laundry basket strategically located just outside of the bathroom door. His first destination was the fridge in the tiny corner kitchen. An army of takeout containers greeted him as he pulled open the door. One of the older ones, a serving of orange chicken and rice from a week ago, called his name, and he popped it into the microwave. Hoping the old appliance didn't catch fire again as it tried to heat up his food, he snatched a beer from the fridge before closing the door.

Collapsing onto his futon, Eddie cracked open his beer and gazed out the only window in his apartment. Another day, another dollar. A cliché used too often in the old mystery novels he used to read, but it fit his mood, and in the end, that's all today was—just another day of work in an ever repeating series of days in an uneventful life.

And if he was being honest, Eddie didn't care in the least. A youth spent bouncing around in foster homes, some of which he longed to forget, had made him crave a simpler life as early as his mid-teenage years. And now he had it. Simple job. Simple home. Simple life. Nothing to cause him any more physical or emotional scars. He had finally dispelled the chaos that had surrounded him like a cloud and could live his life in peace.

CHAPTER 2

Eddie hadn't been assaulted or cursed at on his ride into work the following morning, so he was already in a good mood as he stepped off the elevator. He had about ten minutes to spare before the start of the day, but even at 7:50 a.m., the lobby was a zoo of activity. Men and women in suits bustled about, much more so than usual. Twice as many guards stood around the perimeter of the lavish lobby and a few moved among the crowd, batons in hand. One of guards stared him down, the visor following his every move as he crossed the lobby to check in.

Lizzie gave him a tight smile as he walked up to the desk but didn't attempt to engage him in conversation. If the extra guards didn't give it away, the disappearance of her friendly attitude was enough of a sign to tell Eddie something was up.

"You ok, Lizzie?" This was the first time Eddie had ever strived to make conversation in the morning. "Something serious going on?"

He received a withering look in reply. "You really don't pay attention to anything outside of your job, do you?"

"I noticed you were upset."

The withering look remained for a moment more, than she let it go with a sigh. "Yes, you did." An apologetic smile touched her lips as she continued. "I'm sorry. I got reamed out by my manager, who got screamed at by his boss. Everybody is just on edge with the regional manager arriving today."

"Who?"

"The regional manager. Didn't anyone talk to you about this yesterday?"

"No." Eddie suddenly realized that Lizzie looked more official today. Her usually colorful, informal attire had been replaced by an ivory-white pantsuit without the slightest wrinkle or crease. "Maybe I'm not important enough to keep in the loop."

"Doubtful. Like I said, everyone is on edge. Just be careful."

"I will. Thank you." Eddie tried to say more, *wanted* to say more, but instead stared awkwardly for a few moments and then continued on.

After going through the usual security scans and check-in

procedure, Eddie retrieved his cart and started weaving it through the crowd toward the main elevators. Today he had chosen not to wear his overalls and instead changed into a simple pair of black pants and gray shirt with the company name embroidered along the front. *A big wig, huh?* Someone important probably wouldn't get anywhere near the first ten floors above the lobby. Maybe not even the first twenty or thirty. Made sense not to waste time warning a simple custodian. All Eddie would worry about today were the same things he worried about every day: simple things like the bathrooms being stocked with toilet paper or Lizzie remembering to order more bleach for his stock of supplies. Not impressing people ten times above his pay grade. Or the creepy guard that watched him cross the lobby.

Maneuvering his cart onto an empty elevator, Eddie pushed it all the way to the back before accessing the control panel. A quick slide of his security card and the screen lit up, offering him the limited options that his clearance allowed. A few people approached while he was still trying to make his decision, but after a few quick glances at the small amount of room his cart left, they all stepped back to wait for one of the other cars. Before anyone else became impatient enough to join him, Eddie pressed the flashing ninth-floor button on the screen. He looked forward to a peaceful ride in solitude before getting to work.

Just as the elevator doors were sliding closed, a hand shot in between them. The doors opened back up, revealing three men in suits who quickly bustled inside. Despite their formal attire, two of the men were nothing special. They could easily blend in with any of the well-dressed workers in the building, but the third man literally stood out. Not only was he a good foot taller than everyone else in the elevator, the fabric of his suit strained over broad shoulders worthy of a superhero. Black, slicked back hair covered an unnaturally tanned head with pronounced cheekbones and the squared chin that Eddie only thought existed on the faces of comic book heroes. Blue eyes flickered over Eddie and his cart for the briefest of moments and just as quickly dismissed him.

"First stop, Mr. Hinderlight?" one of the smaller men asked.

"Floor six," the tallest man, apparently Mr. Hinderlight, responded in a gruff voice.

11

The other man nodded in acknowledgment and slid his card into the elevator's control panel. The floor Eddie had chosen disappeared from the display as a much broader list of options appeared on the screen. If the man's general appearance and aura of authority hadn't clued Eddie in on his importance, the fact that his underlings had access to every floor except the top three would have done the job. Hinderlight's man pressed the button for the sixth floor and the elevator got on its way.

"What's your name?" Mr. Hinderlight asked. It took Eddie a moment to realize the impressive man was actually speaking to him.

"Eddie. Eddie Watson, sir."

"Eddie Watson." Hinderlight nodded toward one of his underlings. The man pulled out a small touch-screen device and started tapping away at it while Hinderlight continued. "Do you know who I am, Eddie?"

"No, sir." That earned him a disapproving frown from the two underlings but a hearty chuckle from their boss.

"Being a custodian on the lower floors, I don't suppose you would."

There was no condescension in his voice. He said it just as casually as a man might in pointing out the color of the sky. A silence descended on the elevator then, made even more apparent by the happy tones of the music pumping through the speakers. Eddie focused on the steadily increasing floor numbers on the screen.

Three.

Four.

"Tell me something, Eddie." Mr. Hinderlight looked at Eddie as if he expected him to answer any question posed to him without question, but his tone remained friendly. "Would you happen to know a man named Mitchal Whitehall?"

The Headache. Yes, Mitchal Whitehall was his actual name. "Yes, sir."

"Good. Take me to him." Hinderlight pointed with his head toward the underling to his left. "Erik here will take your cart off the elevator and keep an eye on it."

A brief look of surprise touched Erik's face, but he quickly hid it behind a blank expression.

"Of course, Mr. Hinderlight, sir."

Five.

Six.

"Welcome to floor six," the elevator cooed as the doors opened. Eddie stifled a laugh. Anytime he used the elevator, all he received on reaching a floor was a friendly beep. Even the elevator was more pleasant to upper management.

Stepping to the side, Hinderlight gestured to the open doors. "Lead the way, Eddie Watson."

Eddie did as he was told.

A subtle silence followed Eddie, Mr. Hinderlight, and Underling Two as they moved through the maze of cubicles on the sixth floor. The phones still rang, the vents still hummed as they pumped in treated air, but not a single voice could be heard. Heads popped up behind the shoulder-high cubical walls to see what was going on and quickly dropped back out of sight once they caught sight of the impressive man. Mr. Hinderlight ignored them all. Eddie could feel the man's gaze on the back of his head, burning through him toward his intended target. When the floor's team leader stepped out in front of them, it took all of Eddie's self-control not to cringe.

"Hello, Mr. Hinderlight." The man's name was Cliff. Or Clyde. Something beginning with a hard C. The man had never bothered to speak to Eddie. "I'm the chief floor executive—"

Hinderlight raised a hand, which silenced the man, and followed it up with a snap of his fingers. Number Two tapped a few buttons into a handheld device then handed it to his boss. After a quick scan of whatever was on the screen, Hinderlight handed it back before addressing the chief floor executive.

"Calvin Fedlan—"

Ah ha, I knew it!

"Employee here for six years before being promoted to team leader. Hits your recommended numbers every year since, making eleven years of quality service to Soladyne."

"Why, yes," the man stammered, his eyes going wide. "I'm so happy to hear that the company—"

"Because of your exemplary service," Hinderlight continued, "I would like to reward you with some information."

"Information, sir?"

"Yes. According to our records, your wife is cheating on you with
. . ."

Number Two filled in the pause. "David Fannelli. The man who
lives three houses down from yours on the left. They meet at his
house during their lunch breaks from work every Tuesday and
Thursday."

"And today is Tuesday," Hinderlight continued. "Plenty of time
to catch them in the act. You can have today off to do so, and
tomorrow as well to deal with the aftermath. Depending on how
you decide to proceed from here, the company has marriage
counselors or divorce lawyers who specialize in these kinds of
domestic situations."

Apparently, Calvin responded to shocking news by completely
shutting down. He stared at Mr. Hinderlight as if his mind had come
to a screeching halt. At least until Hinderlight spoke again.

"Mr. Fedlan?"

"How . . . um, yes sir. Thank you . . . for the information, sir.
I'll just go get my things."

"Excellent." Mr. Hinderlight watched the man slowly walk away
then turned toward Number Two. "Make sure everything I offered
him is put into the system. Hopefully, he will make the right
decision, but to be fair to the poor man, I want the marriage
counselor available to him and his wife as well."

"Yes, sir."

The slightest smile touched Hinderlight's lips but was gone
before he returned his attention to Eddie.

"As you were, Mr. Watson."

*Eddie Watson's Rule Number 51: If there is a shark in the water,
make sure you're not the one bleeding.*

Eddie did as he was told without question.

They found Mitchal crouched down in his cubical, like a
wounded animal trying to play dead. *Blood in the water.*

"Mitchal Whitehall?" Hinderlight's voice was like the rumble after
a lightning strike.

"Yes." Mitchal was able to risk a single glance up but wilted
beneath the massive man's blue-eyed glare. "That's me." His voice
was barely a whisper.

"The Mitchal Whitehall that said . . ."

Again, Number Two chimed in. "You know as well as I do that the guy is a jackass."

"In direct reference to me?" Hinderlight's hands balled into fists.

"I was just joking."

Number Two took a step forward. "Contract Clause 45.7B: The slandering of upper management, inside or outside of the office, is grounds for immediate dismissal at the offended party's discretion."

"But--"

"And my discretion," Hinderlight spoke right over him, "is that you have fifteen minutes to clean out your desk, collect your things, and exit the building. You've already been locked out of your account and a security guard will arrive shortly to escort you out."

"Sir, I--"

"Did I not make myself perfectly clear?"

It was interesting to see the range of emotions that touched Mitchal's face in the span of a few seconds. Shock changed to anger, anger to fury, and then after he took a good look at the intimidating size of his ex-boss, disgruntled acceptance.

"Fine."

"Excellent. Then we're done here. Mr. Watson, if you would continue to follow me please."

Not waiting for either Eddie or Number Two, Hinderlight began making his way back toward the elevator. He barely got past a single cubical before the other two men were right behind him. Eddie made the mistake of glancing back. Mitchal was glaring at him as if his firing was all Eddie's fault. It was a good thing the man had to be out of the building within the next fifteen minutes. He might not be brave enough to take his anger out on Mr. Hinderlight, but against a custodian? Eddie would make sure to ask Lizzie if the man had been properly escorted out and seen driving away from the premises.

If the room had been silent before, it was like a tomb now. The soft patter of the three men walking on the carpet and the hum of the air conditioning was the only sound. Even the phones seemed to fear making a sound now. When they reached the elevator, Erik was still dutifully guarding Eddie's cart. A smile touched his lips at their return, but it did not last.

"Erik?"

"Yes, Mr. Hinderlight?"

"Mr. Watson here will be accompanying me for the rest of the day. You will perform his duties so that operations on his assigned floors are not interrupted."

"Yes, sir." No pause or look of surprise this time around.

"Excellent. This way then, Mr. Watson."

The imposing man led Eddie and his other underling back to the elevator. Risking a glance back, he found Erik already moving about the office, Windex in hand as he began cleaning the large glass windows that covered some of the office walls. It was strange seeing someone in a fine suit doing Eddie's job, but he was too caught up in everything that was going on to give it more than a second's thought.

Anxiety, like a small worm burrowing inside of his head, made his lip twitch. This was not turning into an average day.

CHAPTER 3

The floor numbers glowed a sharp red as the elevator hummed its way upward.

Twenty-three.

Twenty-four.

"So, Eddie Watson," said Hinderlight as he interrupted Eddie's comforting routine. "Master custodian. Tell me a little about yourself."

Eddie froze. What types of things did someone so high on the corporate food chain want to know about one of the dozens of custodians that worked in the building? His education? His hobbies? Eddie had barely spoken to any of the floor managers while he worked unless they needed him to do something. Now a regional manager wanted to know about him. And how much of his life could be found on the handheld device that Number Two held in his hand? Hopefully nothing from his childhood.

Mr. Hinderlight caught him glancing at said device. "Oh, sure. I could read practically everything there is to know about you from our databases. But a computer fails to capture the nuances you can only get by talking to a person face-to-face. Why would anyone waste time reading *all* about a person when they can skip to the interesting parts that only a more personal conversation can accomplish?" When Eddie continued to hesitate, the large man let out a laugh and placed a reassuring hand on his shoulder. "Come on, now. This isn't a test. Just two men on an elevator." Number Two didn't seem bothered that he wasn't counted among them. "Here, I'll get you started."

Hinderlight snatched the pad away from his underling and gave it a quick glance before handing it back. "Why did you not only get a degree in philosophy, but a Masters at that? Not many jobs out in the real world for a philosophical man."

"Um." An easy question, but Eddie's nerves seemed to have turned his brain to mush. "I don't know."

"You don't know?" He crossed his arms and took on the expression of a man that's just found out that the new car he bought was a lemon. "You put seven years into an education for a subject and you

17

have no idea why?"

Fear cleared the fog that had invaded his mind. "I enjoy figuring things out. Working out problems and finding unique solutions. Discovering the meanings behind the meaningless and unexplainable." He shuffled in place for a moment. "I just like puzzles."

Hinderlight gave a nod, his stony expression softening. "Much better. It's things like that, the personal side to who you are, that isn't listed in your file. If I'm going to have you following me around today, I want to get to know you a little better."

"Following you around, sir?"

Twenty-nine.

Thirty.

Thirty-one.

"Yes. Wasn't my plan, of course. I didn't walk into the building thinking to myself that I should take some low level—" he paused to offer a friendly smile— "low *security* level employee under my wing for the day. But a quick glance at your file peaked my interest. A philosophical janitor with no apparent desire for advancement. Trying to be an average person with an unaverage education. Now why is that?"

Eddie didn't have an answer. This man had already shown he didn't like unanswered questions. Thinking of Mitchal Whitehall's fate, Eddie began to fear that he was in a precarious situation. Would the wrong word put him in the unemployment line tomorrow? The silence that followed only made him more uncomfortable.

Thirty-seven.

Thirty-eight.

Mr. Hinderlight raised a calming hand. "Maybe too tough of a question, although I find it ironic that a young man who likes to find meaning in the meaningless hasn't bothered to turn his inquisitive mind on himself.

"I tried that one time, sir."

"Oh? And what did you find?"

"That Eddie Watson isn't very interesting."

The man exploded with laughter and proceeded to pat Eddie on the back hard enough to make him stumble forward a step or two in the cramped elevator. Hinderlight quickly recomposed himself to resume the conversation.

"Not interesting? I beg to differ. When Eddie Watson's bio came up on the handheld, I said to myself, '*Hinderlight, now there's an interesting young man with the capacity for deep thinking. Getting a bona fide philosopher's perspective on things will help me see the company from a new angle.*' So now, here you are, spending the day as a shadow at my side," he went on like it was a huge honor. "What do you have to say about that, Eddie?"

"Lucky me," Eddie replied barely containing a sigh. "I mean, thank you for the opportunity, sir. But isn't that normally the job of your assistants?"

"You mean Erik and . . . " Hinderlight glanced at the other suited man.

"William, sir." Number Two replied.

"Yes. To put it bluntly, Erik and William were assigned to me and fully understand the weight my position has on their employment. Which makes them . . ." he paused to send William another look.

"Suck-ups, sir?"

That earned a hearty laugh from Mr. Hinderlight. "I would have chosen 'yes-men', but suck ups works as well. I appreciate the straight forward answer, William."

"Thank you, sir."

Forty-five.

Forty-six.

Forty-seven.

"So," Hinderlight continued. "I wanted someone that wouldn't kiss my ass and actually held opinions of his own. Who better than a janitor with a deep background in philosophy?"

Except now I've seen you fire someone for a simple comment from a phone conversation that was clearly being monitored, Eddie thought, *and assign an underling with a higher security rating than I'll ever see to empty trash and wash windows.*

Eddie wiped away a bead of sweat that was sneaking down his temple. "So it was just luck and a whim that got you to invite me along?"

"If you want to look at it that way. I, on the other hand, look at you as more of a project than a tag-along."

"A project, sir?"

"William, psychological exam results on Mr. Watson, please."

Underling Two brought up a page on his handheld and began to read.

"Edward Watson suffers from a strong case of social anxiety possibly brought on by his lack of any strong parental influence or stable home life. He has no close family or friends outside of work."

None of this was news to Eddie, but it still didn't feel good to have one of his phobias read off a computer screen.

"Of course," Hinderlight continued, "I'm not a psychologist and have no intention of trying to cure you in a single day. I figure spending your shift with me and my constant blabbering might help. After all, if you can relax around someone with my authority in the company, spending time with your peers will become a piece of cake." He gave an exaggerated wink. "Especially that cute receptionist you speak to most days."

"Lizzie? I don't--"

"And if you can't relax around me, I'll have to take a more direct approach. You can give the speech I have planned for the end of the day to motivate all of the employees. Just imagine yourself in front of a camera, thousands of eyes staring at your likeness on the monitors in front of them as you give a ten-to-fifteen-minute presentation. Wouldn't that be great?"

Fifty-eight.

Fifty-nine.

The elevator continued to rise, but Eddie felt like he was falling. His nice, average day spiraling out of control. It wasn't until Mr. Hinderlight began to laugh that Eddie realized that he had been holding his breath. He let a gust of air escape his lungs and didn't care how unprofessional he looked.

"Sorry," Hinderlight said in between chuckles. "That was a cruel joke, but I couldn't help myself."

"Welcome to the sixtieth floor," the elevator cooed as the doors opened.

"Alright then," Hinderlight clapped his hands and started rubbing them together. "Let's get this show on the road."

The regional manager strolled out of the elevator, with Eddie and William right behind him. They walked into a low-ceiling lobby ringed by potted plants. Blue slate tiles led past two seating areas with white, leather couches and small, glass coffee tables. At the far side of the lobby, an attractive woman in a gray suit dress, with dark hair pulled into a tight bun, sat behind a steel framed desk with a top made of tempered glass. A guard stationed next to the counter gave them a cursory glance and then returned his gaze straight ahead. The room was covered in light from a multitude of bright white lighting fixtures above them.

As they approached, the secretary gave them a curt nod before speaking.

"Mr. Hinderlight." The woman was all business, her manicured hands neatly folded on the desk in front of her. "We were expecting you thirty minutes ago. Were we misinformed?"

Hinderlight took on a chagrinned expression. "Oh no. Am I in trouble?"

He sounded like a middle school student arriving late to class, which, coming from a man of his size and stature, caught Eddie off guard. By the look of horror on the secretary's face, she hadn't been expecting it either.

"Sir, I in no way meant you were at fault. If my tone made you think--"

"Relax, relax, Miss—" he picked up the silver nameplate that sat on the corner of the desk. "Miss Toner. Just having a little bit of fun. Eddie here has been taking the brunt of my humor so I wanted to give him a break."

"Oh . . ." The woman didn't seem able to recover from her embarrassment.

Mr. Hinderlight casually leaned against the desk. With his size, he still towered over the seated woman. "See, Eddie. This poor girl was doing her best to act nice and official for the big boss. Probably practiced what she would say all morning. Am I right?"

"Y-y-yes," Miss Toner stuttered. "That is true."

"And here I've thrown a wrench into things. But I'm sure Miss Toner can appreciate a little bit of humor and relax."

The faintest smile touched the woman's lips.

"Ah ha!" Hinderlight slapped the table. "I'll take that small gesture as a victory, but sadly I can't press for more. My visit isn't all about entertaining myself. I was told this floor would be my base of operations during my visit?"

"Yes, sir. An office has been prepared." She rose, her smile now a permanent fixture. "This way, please."

Mr. Hinderlight gave a slight bow as he moved away from the desk and then followed after her. The four of them moved out of the lobby and turned down a hallway with glass walls interspersed with mahogany doors. Eddie marveled at the pointlessness of having solid doors when the walls were transparent. As they passed dozens of offices, he was able to see men and women at ornate wooden desks, typing away at computers that would have cost Eddie a few months' worth of paychecks, or speaking on phones as they leaned back in leather desk chairs. The glass and wood muffled most of what was going on inside, but enough sound got through to fill the hallway with a gentle buzz of activity. A far change from the offices on the first ten floors.

One man wasn't having the best of days going by how he was banging his head against the desk. In fact, he was doing it a lot harder than a person would in frustration. *Was that blood on his forehead?* Eddie thought as they passed the office. Just as Eddie was about to mention the injured man, they moved out of view of him and reached the end of the hall. He decided it was best not to question how people behave at the higher levels of the corporation and kept quiet. After all, he had just watched a man get fired for an off-hand comment about a superior. Trying not to think about what he had seen, Eddie focused instead on their destination.

A pair of tall, double doors in the center of a pale gray wall greeted them. Miss Toner slid her keycard through the reader and the doors swung open on their own. She ushered Hinderlight in first, with the rest of the group following right behind. Inside, they found an open office with dark green wallpaper resting above mahogany wooden panels that ran around the entire room. Two small desks sat on either side of the room, each covered in papers and lit by a single desk lamp. A single glass window pane lay square in the center of the back of the room with gray skies and the tops of buildings peeking up over the ledge. Beneath it was a much larger desk, made of polished wood covered in a black lacquer. Other than a lamp that matched the rest of the décor and a dark silver laptop off to the side, the desktop was completely devoid of all clutter.

The secretary closed the doors behind them. "Will this be acceptable, Mr. Hinderlight?"

He took a look around and nodded. "Yes, I believe so. Whose office was this?"

"No one's, sir. It's reserved for the top executives in the company. Ordinary managers aren't allowed to use it."

"Excellent." Hinderlight walked further into the room, his shoes clicking on the small, onyx-colored tiles beneath his feet. Running his hand along the desk, Hinderlight removed his suit jacket and placed it across the back of the chair before moving to the window. "Come here, Eddie. You have to see this view."

Eddie left Underling Number Two and Miss Toner standing by the door to join the other man at the window. He had lived in or near the city for most of his life, but he had never been this high in a building before. Even when he was performing his duties on the tenth floor, any view consisted of looking at the windows or steel of the buildings surrounding Soladyne Headquarters. That wasn't the case here. Looking out across the city, truly seeing it all, took Eddie's breath away. Buildings, short and tall, covered the ground as far as he could see. Besides the green of an occasional park, everything else below him was a sea of brown, gray, and black. Small specks of color moved across the roads below, the vehicles barely visible from this height. The little flashes of color were almost hypnotic.

Either the height or something else deep inside of him brought on the image of the window breaking. He saw himself sucked outside, falling through the sky as the colored specks on the ground grew larger. Cars. People. Gaping in horror as the concrete rushed up to meet him. For the briefest of moments, he was hanging out of the window of one of his old foster homes, the scent of stale beer and the feel of the hand gripping his shirt as it barely held him from falling. A split second later, he was back in Hinderlight's office, feeling dizzy and sick to his stomach.

"So?" Mr. Hinderlight asked. "What do you think?"

"It's a lot to take in." Eddie backed away, putting more distance between himself and the window, and the old memory, but his stomach continued to do flips. "I've never been this high before."

"Ah, have we discovered a new phobia in our custodian?"

Hinderlight tapped on the glass. The low thud of each tap echoed about in Eddie's skull. "Understandable. I grew up in the suburbs. When I got my first job in a high rise, I almost lost my lunch the first time I stared out from only forty floors up."

"Really?"

"No, not really." He let out a laugh as he continued to gaze out the window. "I had already been skydiving twice before I even stepped foot in a building half as tall as this one. But acrophobia is third on the top ten list of fears. It's nothing to be ashamed of, Eddie."

"Thank you."

Eddie's stomach let out a low gurgle.

He thought it was his stomach. But then the gurgle grew louder and he realized that it was coming from behind him, toward the front of the room. Pulling his gaze away from the gray void outside the window, Eddie turned to locate the source of the sound.

Miss Toner stood in front of the door, her head drooped, face hidden behind disheveled hair. Spots of red covered her clothes and dripped from the pen gripped tight in her right hand.

At her feet, William lay prone, a horrible gurgling noise escaping his mouth as blood flowed freely between hands gripped tightly at his own neck.

"What--" Eddie began but halted as the woman, hair still stuck to her face, charged him with wild limbs flailing and the pen in her hand spraying poor William's blood all around.

CHAPTER 4

Eddie tried to move out of the woman's way as she rushed toward him. In his panic, he caught the desk leg with his foot. The room seemed to tilt as he went down. Pain lanced up his right arm, traveling through his shoulder to his back, as he bounced off the desk to the floor. He expected more pain to come when the woman's pen pierced his skin.

But nothing happened.

Panting in fright and confusion, he heard moans and grunts fill the air. His eyes did a quick survey of the room as he tried to make sense of what was happening. The deceased form of William lay across the room. The pool of blood by his neck crept along the tiles, filling in the spaces between each one. Turning his attention toward the increasing sounds of grunts and scuffing, he caught sight of the secretary's heels as they clacked on the ground. Next to them, Mr. Hinderlight's dress shoes shuffled about. Eddie would have thought they were dancing if the horrendous image of the secretary wielding the bloody pen wasn't at the forefront of his mind.

Using the desk to pull himself up, Eddie struggled back to his feet. Miss Toner and Mr. Hinderlight were on the other side of the desk locked in a struggle, with the latter pressed back up against the window. Hinderlight had his sizable hands wrapped around her wrists, trying to prevent her from impaling him. Considering that he was probably triple her size, getting her under control shouldn't have been an issue. Yet sweat was dripping down his temples. Against all reason, the dainty woman seemed to have the strength advantage. Hinderlight's face showed strain, eyes narrowed in concentration and lips pressed tightly together, with the occasional grunt escaping his throat. Every now and then, he forced the woman back for a moment, but just as fast she would slam him back against the window. After the third or fourth time, a small crack appeared in the glass, and slowly spread with each impact.

Miss Toner remained silent other than the clacking of her heels.

Instincts kicked in. Eddie grabbed the heavy lamp off the desk. Hinderlight's eyes flicked over him for the briefest of moments before returning to his attacker. He gave a slight nod. Eddie raised the light and ran into the fray, prepared to knock Miss Toner senseless.

Except he hadn't unplugged the lamp. A few feet short of his mark, the lamp yanked itself out of his hand and sent him off balance. Instead of coming to the man's rescue, all Eddie managed to do was stumble into the struggling pair. His shoulder slammed into the woman's back, giving her the extra momentum she needed to drive the pen into Hinderlight's shoulder, who let out a bellow as the pen pierced through his shirt and into his skin. As Eddie went down, he grabbed the woman's blouse, pulling Miss Toner down on top of himself.

Like a rabid animal, she immediately turned her fury on Eddie. The good news was that her weapon was still firmly planted in the shoulder of Mr. Hinderlight. The bad news was that her fingers were wrapped around his neck, cutting off his supply of air. Miss Toner stared down at him with dead eyes, spittle mixed with blood dripping from her slack jaw. As he buckled and kicked beneath his attacker, he wondered if there was any thought besides *kill* left in her head. Desperate to fling the woman aside, he curled his hands around her wrists. Eddie might as well have been trying to bend solid steel for the little amount she budged. White spots began to burst in his eyes like the Fourth of July. If he didn't get a breath soon, it would be lights out for Eddie. His kicking slowed as the room faded to gray.

A loud *bong* signaled the release of pressure from around his throat. His mouth opened as his lungs sucked in a rush of fresh air. The curtain that had fallen over his vision gave way to the white paneled ceiling above. His eyes drifted to the side where he found Hinderlight standing over him with the lamp, now unplugged, in his hand. Miss Toner lay an arm's length away, her body still except for the slow rise and fall of her chest.

"Thank you, sir." Eddie got out between gasps. He turned to the side to try and rise. "I'm sorry I--"

Eddie cut off as Hinderlight knelt next to the unconscious woman. He lifted the lamp up, and brought it down against her forehead with enough force that the sound of bones cracking filled the room. Eddie flinched. And then Hinderlight struck again.

And again.

And again.

Blood sprayed out like a fountain then fell like crimson rain. It painted the desk. Spotted and spread along the floor. Splattered against Eddie's face and body. All that was left of Miss Toner's face was a pulpy mess.

"Why . . ." The taste of blood on Eddie's lips curdled his stomach and made him gag.

Hinderlight stood, casting the dented and bloody lamp to the side. His body heaved as he took in breath and moved to the window. Each step echoed, sounding heavier than it had as he moved across the room a few moments earlier. He placed his right hand on the fractured glass and braced himself for a few moments until his breathing slowed. When he turned back around, a bloody handprint remained on the glass. With the same hand, Hinderlight yanked the pen out of his shoulder. It dropped carelessly from his grasp and clinked as it hit the floor. He looked at it for a moment then turned his gaze on Eddie.

"I'm sorry, Eddie."

For a moment, Eddie thought he saw something dark in the man's expression. Even with his breathing slowed, the intensity in Mr. Hinderlight's eyes made Eddie glance around for the discarded lamp. Could he get to it before the man? Or would he become the next victim? His limbs felt like rubber, although he had no idea if it was from his recent near-death experience or the residual fear that had stuck around and was now growing.

Some of that fear and shock must have shown on his face as Hinderlight raised a calming hand in his direction. "I'm sorry you had to see that." The large man's shoulders slumped as he moved behind the desk and fell back into the chair. "By the end of today, I might owe you a number of apologies. If you are extremely lucky, you might thank me. No way to know at this point."

"Why did you kill her?" Eddie blurted out. His gaze wandered to the mutilated head of the woman for the briefest of moments before snapping back to gaze in Hinderlight's direction. "She must have been under the influence of something! We could have tied her up until she came to her senses!"

"I don't think it was drugs, Eddie." He looked toward the cracked window. "It might have been something even worse."

"Worse?" His mind ran down a list of things that could have been worse than a deranged woman, strength enhanced by whatever drugs she was on, attacking them. Nothing he imagined even came close.

"Yes." For a moment Eddie thought the man was going to remain cryptic, but then he continued. "Everything you know about Soladyne barely breaks the surface of what lies at the heart of this company. You might have gotten a glimpse of this today."

"Sir." Eddie got to his feet. "What did I see today?"

"I'm not sure yet. If this was an isolated incident, someone will come for the body. Take it to a lab and analyze it. But if this was just the beginning of something else . . ."

Outside, the gray haze had started to lift, letting a few rays of light break through. Instead of providing a comforting glow, it shed more light on the bloody interior of the room.

Eddie moved in front of the desk. "The beginning of what?"

Lost in thought, Hinderlight's eyes grew distant as he stared out the window into the gray haze.

A blaring alarm made Eddie jump. His first thought was that building security already knew what had just taken place. But that was impossible. No one could have found out and reported it that fast. It was just the emergency drill that took place routinely each month. Even with its loud whine, he found a strange comfort in its sound. It was familiar. Something he had heard many times throughout his career at Soladyne. The destroyed head only a few paces from his feet tainted the comfort the alarm provided.

The alarm suddenly doubled in speed. The building seemed to shake as forces came to life. Thick metal shutters descended outside the building, slowly covering the window, depriving the room of natural sunlight and denying access to the outside world. As the room grew dimmer, the electric lamps, as if they had morbid little minds of their own, seemed to focus their light on only the gruesome details. The circular spot of blood on Hinderlight's shoulder left behind by the pen. Miss Toner's mangled corpse. The blood creating an abstract design on the side of the desk.

"This has to be just a drill," Eddie said, reaching for the familiar comfort of hearing the alarm again. "No one knows what happened in this room yet. They can't be related."

Something struck the office doors, sending a booming echo bouncing about the room. Both men froze. Another *boom*, this one hard enough that the doors seemed on the verge of breaking open. Then a moment of silence before it was interrupted by a few muffled yells.

Ending with a scream.

"What is happening out there?" Eddie whispered.

"Nothing good. Do me a favor, William should have a small pouch attached to his belt on his back. Could you get it for me?"

An order. Something to do. It was what Eddie's mind needed. Taking careful steps to avoid the blood spread about the room and to make little noise, he moved toward the fallen man. William's lifeless eyes stared off into the void. His mouth was still twisted in surprise and his hands lay limp atop his throat, hiding the savage wound left behind by the pen. A small blessing, as far as Eddie was concerned. He had already seen more torn flesh and exposed guts than he could handle. One more gross thing would probably empty his stomach.

Eddie went to the dead man's left side, because most of his blood had pooled to the right, and knelt down on a clean spot of tile.

"I'm sorry about what happened to you, man," he apologized to William's corpse. "I hope you've found whatever you believe comes next."

He lifted the back of the man's suit jacket and found a black satchel hooked onto the man's belt. Next to it, poking out of a leather holster, was the handle of a gun. His fingers brushed against the metal handle and for the briefest of moments, he considered taking it. And do what? He had never held a gun in his life. Even if he could hit something with it, could he actually take a life? Doubtful. He left the gun alone and focused on his original objective. It took him a few moments to get it unhooked.

"What's in it?" he asked as he handed it over to Hinderlight.

"Supplies."

After unzipping the container, Hinderlight rooted around for a few moments then pulled out a ivory-colored packet that looked like hand wipes, a small bandage, and a tool that liked like a small hole puncher. After he laid everything out, he gingerly got up out of the chair.

"Help me out of this shirt," he ordered.

Eddie undid the buttons and helped him slide out of the shirt, revealing a chiseled body that could put an Old Spice deodorant model to shame. A carpet of curly black hair covered a chest you might expect to see on a pro-boxer, not a manager who spent most of his time behind a desk. The man looked like he could wrestle an ox, with the ox being at a disadvantage.

Which only made his struggle against the waifish secretary all the more confusing. But that was only one of a dozen questions bouncing around Eddie's mind. He snatched the one that would be easy to answer and went for it.

"Are you going to be all right?" The puncture wound in Hinderlight's shoulder was the size of his thumb, a red crust around the opening oozed blood whenever he moved.

"Yes, yes, I'll be fine." He collapsed back into the chair. "Quick little patch-up and I'll be ready to go."

"Go? Go where?"

Hinderlight grabbed the packets on the table, opened one up, and then began swabbing at the wound with the cloth inside. "We can't stay here. If this isn't a lockdown, then something much worse than a secretary with a pen is probably occurring in the building. An office, even one with an intimidating door like that one, isn't the safest place we could be."

"Wouldn't it be better to stay here, wait for an army of security guards to come find us? They would want to make sure you are safe if this is a real emergency, right?"

The man answered with a laugh, which quickly cut off in a grunt of pain. Once he got himself under control, Hinderlight grabbed the small tool they had retrieved from William's belt, the one that looked like a hole puncher, and rose again. "They aren't coming for me. If we want to be safe, we have to go to them." He looked at the tool in his hand. "You wouldn't happen to have any medical training, would you?"

"No, sir."

"Thought not," he said with a sigh. "Wasn't any mention of it in your file, but I hoped it had just been missed. I'll have to take care of this myself then."

He moved to the shuttered window, close enough to see his own reflection. From where Eddie stood, he could see Hinderlight's eyes flicker over the cracks in the glass for a moment, then focus on the reflection of his injury. He pressed the tool in his hand to the small hole in his shoulder and then pressed a button. A loud *snap* was quickly followed by a grunt of pain from the man. When he pulled his hand away, Eddie caught sight of a small piece of metal that had closed part of the wound.

"Two more should do the job." Hinderlight sounded less than excited about it. "While I finish up, why don't you grab William's gun."

"G-gun?" Eddie stammered.

Hinderlight turned enough to shoot him an incredulous look. "Eddie, things are going to get worse before they get better. I need to know I can rely on you. To know you won't lie or hide things from me. If we can trust each other, we stand a better chance of getting through this alive. If we can't, then we're better off on our own. You can hide yourself in here or take your chances with whatever is happening out there with me."

Click. The object Hinerlight was using to close his injury sounded like the firing of an empty gun.

Eddie Watson's Life Rule #14. When you don't know what to do, do whatever makes the most sense.

At the moment, what made the most sense was listening to the man that had just crushed in another person's head like a ripe melon.

"I'll go get the weapon, sir."

"Might as well drop the formalities Eddie. Just call me Hinderlight. And get the gun."

Moving on shaky legs, Eddie returned to William's body. He unsnapped the holster strap and removed the gun. The weapon felt heavy in his hand. Eddie's philosophical mind wondered if it had been used before. Had taken another life. Multiple lives. His hand shook as he looked at the metal killing machine that fit so snuggly in his palm.

"This will be enough to get us to the security offices on the twentieth floor?"

A third *snap* filled the room before Hinderlight answered. "We're not going to those security offices. We're going to the real ones below the parking garage." Grabbing his shirt off the desk, Hinderlight carefully put it back on as he moved to Eddie's side. He took the gun from his hand and ejected the magazine in one smooth motion like a well-practiced marksman. After a quick look, he returned the full magazine into the weapon. "And no, if shit has really hit the fan, I don't think this will be enough."

CHAPTER 5

Putting a finger to his lips, Hinderlight held the gun up with one hand as he twisted the lock on the door with the other. It gave off a loud *thock* sound that made them both cringe. Both men remained still as they listened for any sign of life on the other side. Silence. Which told them nothing. Unlike the hollow fake wood doors at Eddie's apartment, the office doors could not be taken down by a well-placed kick. These were made of solid hardwood and twice as thick. It would take a battering ram to break them down.

Which was why Eddie cringed when Hinderlight pushed one open enough to peer out.

From his vantage point, Eddie couldn't see out the small space between the barely opened doors. He also couldn't read anything from the other man's face. A whiff of musty copper made him scrunch up his nose, but that came from the dried bloodstains that painted both himself and Hinderlight. Or the two bodies they were just leaving behind in the room. He hoped that was the only blood he smelled. Hinderlight had implied otherwise.

The imposing man crouched to look down the hallway. Despite the wound in his shoulder, he didn't even wince, managing to keep perfectly still. He was like a lion stalking its prey.

"What do you see?" Eddie whispered. In his head it sounded like a shout.

"All clear, at least from what I can see. Maybe the attack on me was an isolated incident. Take a look." He moved to the side and lowered the gun.

Scooting over, Eddie glanced out into the hall. The lights that had lit the hallway from overhead had grown dim, their bright whites changed to a dim red. The long stretch of carpeted floor was as empty as it had been when they arrived. The doors lining the walls were still closed, the glass walls reflecting the red glow of the lights. Ahead, the entryway back into the lobby was shrouded in darkness. Besides the now diminished tone of the lockdown alarm, not a sound could be heard in the hallway. The lack of sound was unsettling in what had been a hallway teaming with activity.

Eddie stepped back and looked to the more confident man.

"What do you think?"

"Keep your head down and try to make as little noise as possible. If there are more people like Miss Toner, it would be best if we avoided them rather than fight. We don't want the attention a gunshot will bring us."

Eddie nodded. It was all he could handle at this point.

"Alright," Hinderlight took a deep breath. "Let's go."

He opened the doors just enough to slide his massive frame through. Which meant Eddie had more than enough room to fit through the double doors. When they were both in the hallway, Eddie turned to close the door behind them but Hinderlight stopped him.

"Best to leave it open," he whispered. "I would prefer to not get trapped in there, but it would be better than being stuck out in the open if things go south and we need a place to retreat."

Made sense. Eddie hadn't even thought about it. He wasn't really thinking about anything. Reacting and following orders from a man that seemed to know what he was doing kept his mind busy so he could not contemplate what was going on around him.

Unfortunately, what he saw next destroyed any chance of that.

What Eddie had thought was just a reflection of the red lights above on the glass walls of the offices turned out to be something horrific. The offices to his left and right were covered in blood. The few pieces of furniture were covered in it. It crawled down the glass like wine left out in the sun, leaving streaks everywhere.

The glass walls cast a red tint on the macabre view inside. In the office to his left, a man lay slumped over his desk, his hair a blotted mess of blood-soaked hair. A computer keyboard lay next to him, its side smashed in, some of the keys broken free and scattered across the desk. In the office to the right, a woman's purple mottled face was pressed up against the glass wall with a computer cable wrapped around her neck several times. Her lifeless bloodshot eyes bulged out of their sockets as her tongue lolled out of her mouth. Deep, bloody gashes covered her clothes. The insides of the offices further down the hall weren't visible, but the red splatters against their walls told enough of the fates of those inside making Eddie want to turn around and lock himself in the larger office behind its thick, double doors.

Hinderlight had other plans. With one finger pressed to his lips, he motioned Eddie onward with his gun. The other man's expression was grim but otherwise seemingly unaffected by the death all around them. Eddie wanted to be sick.

Instead of losing his breakfast, Eddie pressed on. He kept his eyes focused straight ahead. Office windows covered in blood creeped along his peripheral vision but they kept what happened inside a mystery. It also kept Hinderlight, who was trailing behind him, out of his view. In an attempt to block out the massacre, Eddie turned his mind on what he knew of the man. It was baffling to think that anyone would be so unaffected by the carnage spread out around them. Had been so comfortable destroying the head of Miss Toner with such ease and brutality. Eddie had always pictured anyone in management as a pencil pusher, flaunting his power over those below him. Just as The Headache had done to Eddie. Hinderlight was far from that.

Why would a company like Soladyne employ cold-blooded killers as managers?

Up ahead, through the opening to the floor's main lobby, Eddie caught a glimpse of movement out among the lobby furniture. With the lights dimmed so low, he couldn't be sure if it was anything more than a passing shadow. Hinderlight must have seen it too, because he immediately aimed his gun toward the lobby as his thumb pulled back the hammer. When Hinderlight moved up next to him, gun at the ready, Eddie felt the first drops of sweat form on the back of his neck.

Hinderlight took the lead. He pressed his back against the glass walls on the left. After a few steps, he glanced back at Eddie and motioned for him to do the same.

Follow orders, Eddie thought. *Hinderlight will get us through this.*

Joining Hinderlight against the glass wall, Eddie was thankful that all of the carnage seemed to be on the inside of the offices. It was almost strange now that he thought about it. As they moved toward the lobby, he took a closer look at the hallway itself. Not a single thing was out of place. None of the plants had been knocked over. Not a single bloody footprint plastered the rug. Not even a hint of the death and destruction that lay on the other side of the glass walls. It didn't make any sense. How could one or two people slaughter a dozen office workers without a single one running out into the hallway to yell for help or meet their end on the decorative carpet outside? The wrongness of it all tugged at him, but he couldn't figure out what was going on.

More movement up ahead caught his attention. Instead of a blur, these were shadowy humanoid shapes shuffling aimlessly about in the dim light. Upon reaching the lobby entrance, Eddie and Hinderlight crouched together to peer around the edge. Broken light fixtures littered the floor. He could see the shattered panels directly above him of the now useless lights. Had the shuffling shadows destroyed them or something else entirely? Eddie couldn't be sure, but somewhere deep inside the lobby sounded like a dozen people clearing their throats all at the same time, but the noise continued non-stop. Squinting through the darkness at the shuffling forms, he still was unable to discern the details hidden in the shadows. Where they humans, animals, or something that defied imagination? Eddie just wished he could find an answer to one of the dozens of questions bouncing around in his brain.

Hinderlight squatted closer to the entrance, his head moving back and forth as his eyes darted about. He seemed like a cat on the prowl for his next meal. Or maybe it was the other way around and he was the mouse looking for a way past the group of cats stumbling around the lobby. Whichever it was, the larger man seemed to take in everything. When Hinderlight turned, Eddie expected to hear a grand plan for escape.

Instead, Hinderlight pressed a solitary finger to his lips then pointed into the lobby. Eddie followed it, past the shambling shapes, the vague outlines of the couches, ending at the wall opposite them. As his eyes strained and continued to adjust to the low level of light, he realized that he was looking at four sets of double doors. The elevators.

Eddie nodded in what he thought was understanding, but Hinderlight shook his head before holding up his palm out. It took Eddie a second to understand what he meant.

Of course, Eddie thought. *The elevators will be disengaged if there is a lockdown.*

Hinderlight moved his hand until he was pointing to something else at the far corner. At first, Eddie thought the small light on the other side of the lobby was just another lockdown light. Except its red glare wasn't flashing. The light was actually a sign. Stairs. Hinderlight wanted to make for the stairs through the shambling bodies.

"*No way. No how,*" Eddie mouthed the words, vehemently shaking his head. Hinderlight rolled his eyes in response and grabbed a small shard of glass. Before Eddie could stop him, Hinderlight tossed the piece toward one of the other hallways that branched away from the lobby. It hit the wall and shattered into even smaller pieces, clattering as they fell against the wall and landing on the carpet.

Bodies stopped their slow shuffle and stood in place. They swayed back and forth, arms hanging limply at their sides. Haunting moans escaped some of the forms while the rest remained silent. When Hinderlight tossed another shard into the same adjoining hallway, they all turned toward the sound, even more of them calling out that same sorrowful cry. A third piece of glass that made it further into the hallway before breaking got them moving.

Once all of the forms had started shuffling toward the noise, Hinderlight held up three fingers, starting the countdown to *Operation Madness.*

"*Wait,*" Eddie mouthed. "*I'm not ready.*" But Hinderlight was watching the terrors.

Two fingers.

Eddie tensed. *Just have to be quiet,* he thought. *It'll be just like sneaking out of all of those foster homes as a kid.*

One finger.

Eddie took in deep breaths. Focused on the red light of the exit sign. *I can do this.*

The last finger dropped and they crept out into the darkness.

CHAPTER 6

Eddie locked his eyes on Hinderlight's broad shoulders, mimicking his every step as they crept out of the hallway and into the floor's lobby. He marveled at how Hinderlight was able to walk in hard-soled dressed shoes without making a sound. If Eddie was in anything other than sneakers, everyone on the floor would hear him coming. Besides those that were probably murdered by the forms shuffling about ahead of him.

Morbid curiosity made his eyes seek out the shadowy forms that had caused all of the carnage. Even as his eyes adjusted further to the darkness, he couldn't make out much. Although the facial features were indiscernible, Eddie was able to see the outline of their heads as they flopped from side-to-side on rubbery necks.

With the havoc inside the offices, Eddie didn't want to imagine that the shadows in the room had once been people, or that those people had been behind all of that death and destruction. It was easier to think of them as something different, some group of animal or experiment gone wrong. He needed it to be so, needed it so that his slowly crumbling view of the world could be set right. The shadows had to be something less than human, or the world as Eddie understood it no longer made sense.

With his attention focused on the blurred *things* across the room, Eddie hadn't noticed the growing gap between himself and Hinderlight. When he turned his attention back to his capable companion, he was horrified to see that one of the blurs had wandered into the path between them.

It was hard to tell in the dark, but his illusion of the blurs being subhuman was dashed away. What he believed to be a woman stood in front of him, based on the curves of her body and the tangled mess of hair that spread like weeds down past her shoulders. This close, he could make out the person's pressed pants and leather belt, see where the dark blue, buttoned-up shirt puffed out slightly from where it tucked into the pants. Her hands hung at her sides, long fingernails and the back of her hands covered in the same dark stain on the buttoned sleeves at her wrists.

Afraid to move and catch the person's attention, Eddie scanned the darkness until he spotted the silhouette of Hinderlight stalking away from him. A jolt of panic went through him at the thought of getting separated from the only person around who seemed to know what to do. Had Hinderlight ditched him on purpose? Or did he simply not care enough about the lowly custodian to worry if he lost him?

None of that mattered now. He had to move or risk being discovered.

Eddie took a crouched step toward an open spot behind the woman.

A slow moan escaped her mouth and she began to sway faster.

Eddie wished he had kept the gun. Hell, at this point he would have felt better if he had kept the lamp. He froze back in place. The woman twisted about as she swayed, like her top half wasn't sure where to go and her legs were stuck in place. If she spotted him, Eddie was close enough that she could reach him with a simple dive in his direction. Crouched down, there would be little he could do to maneuver out of the way. What would he do then?

The person let out another moan. Deciding to act, Eddie tried taking another step out of her line of vision. His sneaker made a tiny squeak as the rubber sole slid on the tile.

The woman's head stopped flopping about and began a slow turn in his direction.

Eddie tensed, ready to twist about and sprint back the way he came.

A sound of crashing glass echoed through the room. Eddie clamped a hand over his own mouth before he could let out a surprised yell. The swaying form in front of him let out a low moan and began to shuffle off toward the noise. Eddie watched her go, still tense as he waited for the person to turn at any minute and lunge for him anyway. But no attack came. It shuffled along. Bumped into a seat which it pawed at violently until it must have realized the cushioned armrests were not a potential target. Continued on until a few other faceless shapes bumped into it as well. Eddie had expected them to attack each other but a haunting moan of greeting from each was all that followed.

Even though Eddie was crouched down, he was still out in the open and had lost sight of Hinderlight. How could he have been so careless to let him get away? All it would take was a sneeze or an accidental bump into one of those possessed or diseased office workers to end his life. He turned about slowly scanning the room, trying to see any other form that might be a threat in the immediate vicinity. He was clear. No threats. And no Hinderlight. A new panic struck him as the feeling of being all alone in a room full of deranged office workers began to overwhelm him.

Hinderlight's presence had been reassuring, the man's confidence infectious. He had muted the horrors around them and made them seem manageable. Made the forms moving around seem as dangerous as a pack of rabid dogs with broken legs. Now Eddie was alone, fear disabling his legs just as efficiently as broken bones could.

Eddie examined his situation. Fifty floors between himself and the building's main entrance. The possibility of homicidal office workers around every corner. And then there was the little matter of being unable to access the elevators or stairwell without the proper security clearance. His was only good for floors one through ten. Without Hinderlight, he was trapped on the 60th floor. Even if by some miracle he managed to make it to the ground level, the doors and windows were sealed just as tightly as the window in Hinderlight's office. Without Hinderlight, he had no plan at all.

Another moan joined the maddening chorus that echoed at random intervals around the room. It was different, though. Where the others were the mournful and brought about images of grief and loss, this one was different. Forced. The inflection of it almost a question, as if the person wasn't sure if they were actually sad or in pain. A few moments later, Eddie heard the same moan again, this time with more emphasis as if it was trying to get someone's attention.

Across the room, barely visible in the light of the exit sign, crouched Hinderlight. Despite his face being hidden behind a mask of shadows, Hinderlight's broad shoulders and the way he was waving Eddie toward him gave the man away. Relief flooded into him, and Eddie almost reached a hand out to wave back. Common sense quickly returned and he kept his arms at his sides and began to move toward Hinderlight with careful steps. It was slow going, but eventually he found himself at the man's side. Hinderlight grabbed the door handle and inched the door open enough that they could pass through.

On the other side of the door, the stairwell and its metal railing were cast in a dull red glow. While the office workers continued their moans behind them, the stairwell itself was deathly quiet. Hinderlight waved for Eddie to go first. Despite his reluctance, Eddie slid his way through the narrow opening. His eyes darted around as he looked for even the slightest sign of movement. Once he reached the railing, he glanced above and below his floor. Nothing. He would have let out a sigh of relief if there wasn't a mass of zombies just on the other side of the door.

Hinderlight slid around the door and eased it closed. An audible click filled the corridor as the door locked back into place. They both sat motionless, listening for anything. All Eddie could hear was the now muted moans from the other side of the door. After what seemed like an eternity, Hinderlight pressed a finger to his lips once more before motioning toward the stairway down. Eddie was more than happy to put the carnage on the sixtieth floor far behind them.

Down they went, moving slowly, eyes searching the shadows cast by the flashing red lights. Twice they passed floors where moans filtered through the thick security doors. Hinderlight had them move more slowly past those doors to make as little sound as possible. He would then pause at the next floor down and cock his head to the side to listen. Once satisfied with whatever he did or did not hear, he pushed them on again.

It wasn't until they reached the forty-third floor that Hinderlight spoke.

"Let's pause and take a breather," he whispered.

Eddie took a seat against the wall while Hinderlight sat back against the steps. To Eddie, the other man looked completely calm. Even if it was just a front, Eddie wished he could put on the same appearance of confidence.

"What happened up there?" Hinderlight continued. "One minute you were right behind me, and the next you were gone."

"I got distracted and all of a sudden, that person was directly in front of me."

"Distractions might get you killed today. You can't let your mind wander."

Eddie couldn't wait any longer. "Mr. Hinderlight, what the hell is going on? What was wrong with those people? Is it some kind of disease? A virus?"

"I can't be positive."

"But you have an idea. You seemed to know how to handle them."

Hinderlight scratched at his hair, ruffling the perfectly slicked back style and showing the first kink in the man's unshakable confidence. "Soladyne *might* know about a fungus that produces similar symptoms in human beings: increased aggression, aversion to lights, strong sense of hearing but shit vision, and of course the unflattering moans."

"A fungus?"

"Yes, like mushrooms. But incredibly small and thrive in the grooves of the brain. Once they've multiplied enough, they quickly take control of the host's body."

"And then the hosts just run around killing everyone? That many people all at the same time?"

"It *theoretically* could be possible to alter the fungus at the genetic level. Normally, once they take root in a subject's brain, they multiply rapidly, taking over the host in a matter of hours. If some genetic modifier were introduced, it could inhibit the fungi's growth until given some kind of chemical or auditory cue to cause the sudden burst in activity. If that were so, it would certainly point toward some kind of attack by an enemy of the company."

"My God," Eddie shook his head, then immediately regretted it. "Wait, are they contagious? Airborn?" His head began to itch and he scratched at his scalp almost frantically. Was the itching sensation coming from inside his skull?

"No, no." Hinderlight raised reassuring hands. "Even the tiniest bit of light kills it, which is why it causes its hosts to destroy any light source. It would have to be injected into a host. Maybe during one of the buildings annual health checks, which means that some of the building's medical staff are involved."

"But the last building-wide checkup was over two weeks ago."

"I know, and even if they had been infected then, our screening techniques would have caught the infestation as soon as the people left . . . oh no."

Eddie's head still itched but he forced his hands down. "What now?"

"With that many people infected, the only possible way they could have gotten past the lobby is if the scanning systems were hacked. Which means this was planned."

"By who?"

"No idea. Could be a number of different company rivals. This whole situation could be an attack based solely on my visit. Or it could be a smoke-screen for something worse. I won't know until I get in touch with building security."

"And Miss Toner? Do you think she was infected too?"

"I didn't see any sign of contamination in what was left of her skull."

Things started to click and Hinderlight's violent outburst made more sense. "Wait, is that why you bashed her head in? You were looking for signs of the fungus?"

"No, Eddie. I smashed her skull in because she killed William and stabbed me in the shoulder with a pen."

"Oh." *Nope, still a cold-blooded killer.*

"Listen. She might have not been contaminated, but it was clear something was wrong with her. She was homicidal, either because of some other corruption in her mind or because she was on a mission from one of our rivals. Like I said, I don't have enough information about what is really going on here to even guess at the moment. Now if you've rested enough, we should get going."

Eddie let what happened with Miss Toner drop but needed to know more. "Where does the fungus come from? Did Soladyne find it in some hidden part of the world?" An even worse thought crossed his mind. "Did they create it and then have it stolen from one of their labs?"

Hinderlight leaned in, the friendly tone that accompanied most of what he said now completely gone. "How much do you know about what the Soladyne company does? Besides what I've just told you. Which you should immediately forget."

"Nothing." The image of the man bashing in Miss Toner's head popped back up in his mind. "Don't need to know to do my job."

Hinderlight gave a thoughtful nod. "Good. Keep it that way, Eddie. No matter who you see today, don't ask questions. Don't even show the slightest interest. I'm going to do my best to keep you alive through whatever is happening, but if you start asking too many questions, even I won't be able to save you from the Red Suits."

"Red Suits?" An image of Santa Claus dashed through Eddie's mind. "Who are they?"

"See, that's a question. Don't ask those."

Which only created even more questions, but he locked them away. "Yes, sir."

"I told you, just call me Hinderlight."

"Hinderlight. Got it."

Hinderlight opened his mouth to say more, but at just that moment, someone pushed open the door and stepped out. Black slacks, belt, white buttoned-up shirt, and a garish purple- and yellow-striped tie marked him as another common employee.

None of his clothes were covered in blood. Strange how that was becoming the exception rather than the norm.

Hinderlight had the man's collar in his free hand and the gun pressed up under his chin before Eddie had even gotten over the shock of seeing someone new.

"Jesus!" the man yelled, raising both of his hands at the sight of the gun.

"What are you doing in the stairwell?" Hinderlight growled. His eyes were scanning the now terrified man's face. Whatever he was looking for, he didn't seem to find it in the man's close-cut black hair and plain face. Hinderlight lowered the gun, to both Eddie and the new stranger's relief. His hand was still wrapped up in the man's collar as he continued. "During a lockdown, company procedure states that everyone is to remain in place and only use the stairwells if instructed to evacuate."

"I was just sneaking out to catch a smoke." The man's voice trembled. "These lock down procedures can last over an hour sometimes."

"The rules are put in place for a reason--"

Hinderlight cut off as a thud, like a hammer striking one of the doors, echoed from somewhere above them. All three men looked up in unison. The sound hadn't been muffled by a great deal of distance. This had only been from a few floors up. A moment later the sound repeated, this time louder and as if more hammers had been added.

"See?" the stranger asked. "I'm not the only one sneaking out."

One more thud, and then what sounded like a door being ripped from its hinges. The clatter of metal on metal sounded from somewhere above, quickly followed by a new sound. It started as a small patter, then grew into a thundering beat as what sounded like a herd of buffalos began to descend from somewhere over their heads.

"Run!" Hinderlight yelled and pushed the man toward the door that led out onto the floor. He pulled out an emerald-blue card from his pocket and swiped it over the card reader. When the light turned from red to green, Hinderlight swung open the door and ushered the other man inside. Eddie was right behind them as the building seemed to shake from the approaching horde.

CHAPTER 7

In their hurry to get out of the stairwell, Hinderlight practically threw the stranger through the door. Eddie followed close behind. Once through, he slammed the door shut and pressed his weight against it until the sound of the electronic lock engaging clicked through the air.

"It won't be enough," Hinderlight said as he continued to push the man down the hall.

"What?" Eddie looked at the thick steel door separating the floor they were on from the stairwell on the other side. Despite the disbelief that swelled inside him, he followed after Hinderlight.

"There were enough of them to smash through the door above, so it's only a matter of time before they get through that one."

The three hurried down the hallway, Hinderlight pressing the other man forward with Eddie close behind. Unlike most floors Eddie had been on, the stairs on the forty-third floor did not open up to a main lobby. They moved down a singular hall, the thin gray carpet not producing much sound from their steps. They passed office doors and branching hallways but Hinderlight didn't even pause. He drove them deeper into the center of the floor, not even glancing back as he spoke.

"If they are following procedures, anyone on this floor will be sitting quietly in a locked office or bathroom waiting for the all-clear. As long as they are silent, the Infected won't even know they exist. Which is unfortunate for us, of course, as they'll continue to chase us." He glanced back with a bitter smile. "When those things catch us and start ripping us apart, you can be happy in the knowledge that the other people on this floor should be safe."

"Tearing us apart?" the stranger with them replied. "Infected? What the hell is going on?"

"What's your name?" Hinderlight asked as he continued to push the man down the hall.

"Hugh."

"Well, Hugh. Those moans you heard were coming from a group of people infected with something that causes them to turn incredibly violent. Eventually they are going to break through that

46

door, run us down, and kill us in a most horrendous fashion." He paused long enough that even Eddie thought the man had given up hope. Thankfully, the pause must have been for dramatic effect. "If, that is, you keep distracting me while I try to figure out how to keep us alive."

"Infected? What are they? Zombies?"

"No, don't be foolish. These people are fast when stirred and not easily distracted. And they just view anyone not infected as a threat and rip them apart, no brain eating involved at all as far as I know."

"This has to be a joke. Who put you up to this?"

Hinderlight stopped and pushed the Hugh up against the wall. "Honestly, I don't care what you believe. I'm done trying to reason with you. Either find a place to hide or sit out here and see what happens. Eddie and I are going to try to get to the other stairwell. If you can shut your mouth, feel free to follow along, otherwise stay away from us or I'll kill you myself."

Not waiting for the man to give any kind of answer beside the low whimper that escaped his mouth, Hinderlight continued down the hall. Eddie followed quickly after him, casting a quick glance at Hugh. Behind them, the banging got louder as if hundreds of fists were hitting the stairway door. After a few steps, he was relieved as he heard Hugh start to follow behind them. He didn't really know anything about the man besides his name, but Eddie certainly didn't want Hugh to end up like the majority of people he saw on the sixtieth floor.

They continued to move down the hall, Hinderlight making turns seemingly at random. Since this floor was laid out differently than any Eddie had been on, he could only hope that Hinderlight knew where he was going. Eddie still didn't know what to make of the man. As much he wanted to believe Hinderlight's efforts to keep him alive stemmed from pure motives, Eddie didn't entirely trust him. It was clear that the man was keeping secrets. Secrets of a much darker nature than Soladyne's future projects or profit margins. Did Hinderlight need him alive because he was the only witness to what happened with Miss Toner? Or something even more sinister?

Before today, the only dead person he had seen had been on a large screen. One of the few dates he had been on in college, which had been a complete disaster. The woman had been the one to suggest going to see the retro slasher pic about some masked killer running wild at a lake camp. The movie had given Eddie nightmares for weeks, and the rest of the date had ended in an emotionally horrific conclusion.

Escaping into his own thoughts, Eddie almost walked right into Hinderlight. The man had stopped at a T-intersection and was looking in both directions.

"Where the hell are the signs that direct you toward the stairwells?" he asked in a voice filled with contempt. After looking around for a moment more, he rounded on Hugh. "Which way to the other stairwell? I was going in the direction I thought made the most sense but now I'm at a loss."

"I only know about the stairwell where you found me," Hugh stuttered. "My office was right there and I've never had to travel around this floor that much."

Eddie watched as Hinderlight's arms tensed. Did the gun in his hand rise slightly?

"I've met less than a dozen people since I've arrived today," Hinderlight growled, "and so far I've been fairly underwhelmed. After this madness is handled, I'm going to have a long meeting with the human resources department--"

A door burst open only a few feet from where Hinderlight was standing.

He reacted with lightning quick reflexes, swinging the butt of the gun into the chin of the first person through the door, sending him stumbling to the side before crashing to the ground. Before the second person was even out the door, he had the gun aimed right between their eyes.

The woman let out a shriek and backed up against the wall. The man on the ground let out an angry growl before leaping back onto his feet. And froze as Hinderlight aimed that gun in his direction.

"What the hell are you two doing?" Hinderlight yelled, then grimaced and lowered his voice. Somehow it was just as intimidating. "I almost shot both of you."

The man just eyed him up, but the woman filled in the silence around them while the low banging from the far stairwell continued. "We heard voices and figured the drill was just about over."

Eddie had been examining the two as soon as they emerged. He had been worried about them being infected, but now could see they had been enjoying their time hidden away. The woman's blouse was slightly unbuttoned. As was the man's shirt. The button at the top of his pants was secured but the zipper was completely down. Hinderlight either didn't notice or didn't care.

"It's not over and it's not a drill. Get back in the room."

"Who the hell are you?" the man asked. The fact that he was buttoning up his shirt while he said it made it less intimidating than he had probably intended.

A loud crash echoed from far off down the hallway. The two newcomers looked on in confusion.

"Back inside, now!" Hinderlight yelled.

"And if we don't want to listen to you?" the man asked.

Hinderlight's expression darkened. "Your deaths won't bother my conscience."

"We'll take our chances, wacko." The man held a hand out for the woman. "Come on. I know a different room where we can get some privacy and wait out the drill, away from these *assholes*." The woman took the man's hand and sidled past Hinderlight, her eyes locked on his weapon. They both gave Eddie's group one last look before heading off down the hall.

Eddie took some relief in the fact they were heading away from the growing sound of the approaching Infected.

"In!" Hinderlight hissed. He grabbed Eddie by the collar and shoved him inside. Hugh followed close behind and Hinderlight eased the door closed and flipped the lock.

Noting the rectangular table lined with a chair on each side and the flat-panel tv hanging on the wall, they appeared to have found a meeting room. Five stacks of paper were piled at one end of the table as if the room was temping as a sorting station. A wooden file cabinet that doubled as a telephone stand stood off in the corner. Hugh picked up the receiver only to shake his head and return it to the base.

"Dead," he stated and was immediately shushed by Hinderlight.

"No noise from this point on." the larger man whispered. When Hugh opened his mouth to protest or explain himself, Hinderlight raised his weapon and placed a finger from his other hand on his lips. The office worker took the hint and slid into one of the chairs.

A thudding sound, like the rapid beating of a muted bass drum, penetrated the room. It grew louder by the minute. Eddie could feel his muscles tensing. The doors on this floor didn't seem as thick as the ones on the sixtieth floor. By the time the pounding grew to a crescendo outside the meeting room's door, he could hear Hugh hyperventilating beside him. Even Hinderlight's breaths were quickening. Afraid of adding to the noise and giving away their location to the maniacs on the other side of the door, Eddie tried to hold his breath. He could still hear his own heartbeat, pounding as hard against his chest as the footsteps of those in the hallway.

No, he thought, *they are going to hear us.* Even as he thought it, Eddie knew it was irrational. But he had seen what a few of the Infected could do to a person. A hallway of horrors now took up residency in his head. Before today, Eddie had only been in a life-or-death situation once, a memory he wasn't about to relive now. That situation had happened in a flash and been over before he could even give it much thought. His current situation made the possibility of death, a horrible, violent death, a constant possibility.

And the moans and stomping of feet right outside this door didn't help.

A woman's scream overrode everything; the pounding feet, the desperate moans, Eddie's breaths. A man's scream soon joined in, the two mixed together creating a horrible harmony of pain. It seemed to rile up those outside, the thudding of feet increased in tempo while the moans took on a frenzied tone.

Just as fast as they started, the screams cut off in unison. It wasn't until that moment that Eddie realized the thudding of feet and agonizing moans had quieted down. They weren't far, maybe a few doors down. Maybe right around the corner. But they weren't just outside the door anymore. As he waited for his impending death, he hadn't blinked even once. Now that the Infected were passing them on by, their moaning and shuffling feet fading away, he rubbed at his burning eyes in relief. Once he had rubbed the fatigue out of his lids, he looked at his companions.

Hinderlight sat on the floor, leaning against the wall and holding the bloody stab wound on his shoulder. His eyes were closed and his lips were moving although he didn't make a sound. Hugh sat hunched forward in his chair. His eyes were focused on his own hands, which he was rubbing together as if washing them.

Please don't let either of them lose it, Eddie thought. Hugh, he didn't much care about unless the man put them both in danger. It was Hinderlight that worried him. The man had been a rock so far. It was his confidence that had kept Eddie from losing it. If the man lost his grip, Eddie doubted he could hold on without him.

Eddie crouched down next to the man and kept his voice to a whisper. "Are you alright?"

"What?" Hinderlight looked up. "Oh. My shoulder still hurts but I'll be fine."

Not what Eddie had meant, but now he had lost his nerve to ask again. "What should we do?"

"Wait." A light crash echoed from outside the room. "Wait for them to finish with that."

Another crash made Eddie pause. "Finish what?"

"As they calm, they'll turn their attention to destroying the light. If they can do that, and nothing stirs them back up, they'll become as docile as the ones on the sixtieth floor--"

"--And we can sneak out."

"Exactly."

Hugh had stopped rubbing his hands and looked at them with a glimmer of hope in his eyes. "You think we can find the other stairwell and get off this floor? With those things wandering about and the lights destroyed?"

"The Infected won't be able to get to all of the lights and will avoid those areas. Once they are calm, we'll try to figure out where the majority of them have settled. It will be difficult to do in the dark, but if we are quiet and smart about it, we should be able to come up with a way out. If it's easier, we can try and make it back to the original stairwell. We know where that one is, at least, and it's possible that the majority of Infected have moved past us. If not, then we try to find the other set of stairs."

Hugh shook his head vehemently. "If they're calm, why don't we just wait it out here? *Eventually* someone has to come and find us. Every moment we're in lockdown, office workers aren't going home, phone calls aren't being answered, delivery trucks are being turned away. People are going to notice and send help."

"No, they won't." Hinderlight let out a sigh. "The company won't want anyone from the outside world coming into this building, poking around. They'll come up with some excuse: a viral outbreak or some mechanical problem with the lockdown procedure. And with their connections with the government," he shook his head, "this lockdown could go on for days until they are sure it's clear to open things up. That order can only happen from the inside. Our best chance is to get to the safest place in the building, which isn't locked in some barely defendable conference room. We wait until the Infected calm down and then move somewhere safer."

"So we just sit and wait," Eddie said, pulling up a spot on the floor.

"Yes," Hinderlight's confident smile had returned. "We wait and hope that no one else is foolish enough to leave their offices and stir the Infected back up."

It wasn't much of a plan, but Eddie was happy to have one all the same.

CHAPTER 8

Time crawled along in the dim room. Eddie sat at the conference table, watching Hugh in the seat across from him twirl a pen through his fingers like a baton. In an attempt to avoid being overheard by the Infected, the room was devoid of conversation. The only sound was the faintest rustling as Hinderlight circled around the table, hands clasped behind his back, for the millionth time.

After what felt like hours of waiting, Eddie's patience wore out, and he tried to get their leader's attention. First, he tried waving his hands. The boss man didn't seem to notice. Feeling like he had no choice, Eddie picked up an extra pen and threw it at Hinderlight.

It was a good throw. The pen bounced off his left shoulder, barely making a sound as it hit the carpet. Hinderlight stopped pacing and turned with a jerk to look straight at Eddie. Then his gaze went to the floor where he spotted the pen. His expression darkened as he reached down and picked it up. He held the pen up and took a good look at it, then turned his sour expression on Eddie.

Eddie waved him over.

Hinderlight stared a few moments more, then shook his head and shook the pen in his hand.

What? Eddie mouthed.

Hinderlight shook the pen even harder then used it to point at his shoulder. At the bloodstain on his shirt. The bloodstain from where he had been stabbed in the shoulder, *by a pen*, only an hour or two ago.

Shit, Eddie thought. *I'm an asshole.*

Rising from his seat, Eddie moved over to Hinderlight's side. He kept his voice as low as possible when he spoke. "Sorry. I wasn't thinking. I just wanted to get your attention."

"At least give me a few days before tossing something similar to what was used to stab me to get my attention."

"Understandable. What do you think is going on?"

More crashes echoed out in the hallway.

"They're breaking the emergency lights. It's a good sign. Means nothing else has their attention. When it gets quiet again, we'll wait a bit more and then open the door. If I think it's clear enough, I'll signal you and we'll go. Now let me think." He waved Eddie off. "And tell Hugh the plan."

Eddie did as he was instructed, letting Hugh know not only the plan but how to navigate the Infected. The man had a dozen questions which Eddie had no answers to. Eventually, Hugh gave up and returned to his seat, resting his head in his hands. Which left Eddie standing in the middle of the room with nothing to do but think. A dangerous activity.

Eddie Watson's Rule Number 26: If you have to wait to be told what to do, plan ahead to what you think will be expected of you.

Hinderlight would tell them when to move. And they would move. The man had made it clear he had no intention of sitting behind locked doors waiting to be rescued. Eddie doubted the man had ever counted on someone else for his own survival before. He was in a constant state of motion and seemed to just bowl over anything that got in his way. It was an exciting way to live, Eddie was sure, but not one he would ever want to try. Well, he could be a *little* more pro-active. It certainly seemed to work for Hinderlight.

But back to looking ahead.

It was highly unlikely they could make it back to the stairs without running into at least a few of the Infected. Hinderlight wouldn't be frightened in the least, but Hugh was another story. A quick glance was all it took to see the shaking of his hands beneath his head. If he was already tense now, how would he do walking within inches of one of his former colleagues after they'd turned? If Hugh lost it, he could put them all in danger. Hinderlight had already made it clear he was done helping the man. What would he do if Hugh put them in danger?

Eddie looked at the gun still gripped in the larger man's hand.

No way he would use that on Hugh. It would bring the entire mob down on us.

Even so, if Hugh was going to get through this, it would be up to Eddie to not only keep him safe from the Infected but make sure the man didn't make Hinderlight want to murder him as well.

This responsibility was not in his pay scale.

A light tap on his shoulder almost made Eddie jump out of his skin. When he turned, a faint smirk touched Hinderlight's lips for a moment before it disappeared.

"Time to go," he whispered. "Remember to stay low and follow right behind me. Watch our backs in case any of them start moving in our direction from behind."

"What about Hugh?"

"As long as he's quiet and stays out of my way, he can do what he wants."

Moving to Hugh's side, Eddie got the same reaction tapping Hugh's shoulder that Eddie had a moment ago. The man didn't yell out, at least. That was a plus.

"We're going." Eddie said as the man looked up at him. "Stay low and keep a hand on my shoulder. Tap me if you see anything, but otherwise stay as quiet as possible." He wondered if his voice had even a fraction of the confidence that Hinderlight's had.

Hugh nodded and got up, a slight tremble still visible in his hands. All three moved to the door, Hinderlight in the lead. They got low as Hinderlight pressed his ear against the door. Eddie strained to hear anything but could only make out the distant moans of some of the Infected. They had grown more drawn out, as if the action of moaning now was too much effort. He couldn't help but wonder if the moans were caused by the fungus in the people's heads or were the last bit of humanity leaking through as they lamented what they had become.

A slight click brought Eddie out of his internal musings like a cold bucket of water to the face. Hinderlight was opening the door. No more idle thoughts.

Opening the door a crack, Hinderlight peered outside. Then he opened it a little more, the door thankfully quiet on its hinges. After another moment, Hinderlight opened it just enough to get his head through.

From what Eddie could see, the hallway was pitch black. Only the tiniest bit of light escaped from the office to show a fraction of the carpet in the hall.

Hinderlight's body remained still as his head disappeared on the other side of the door. His inaction caused the worst-case scenarios to enter Eddie's mind. Maybe the Infected had decapitated the boss.

Don't be ridiculous, Eddie reassured himself. *Hinderlight would have fallen over by now if he didn't have a head.*

When Hinderlight finally brought his head back into the room, he pressed a finger to his lips then pointed to the left. When both Eddie and Hugh nodded, the larger man held up three fingers.

Then dropped one.

Then another.

Then he was gone, out the door without a sound. Eddie held the door until Hugh took hold of it and eased it shut behind him as quietly as possible. Following Hinderlight's lead, Eddie and Hugh pressed themselves against the wall, inching their way down the hallway behind the boss. Thankfully, it wasn't as dark as Eddie had feared. A low level of light escaped from underneath most of the doorways, letting a faint haze reach up to about knee level. Hinderlight was a few steps ahead of him, the man's back against the wall and his head moving deliberately from right to left. It was impossible to make out his face in the darkness, but Eddie imagined it had the look of a man that dared anything to try and catch him unaware.

Hugh's hand touched Eddie's shoulder, which he was proud to say didn't make him jump, and then the two started moving toward Hinderlight. He started moving as well, and all three made their way back in the direction they had come from. Eddie relied on his ears now more than his eyes, following the shallow breathing of the man in front of him while listening for any sign of the Infected. The twists and turns of the hallways cast the moans bouncing off the walls and made it impossible to be one-hundred-percent sure which direction the sounds were coming from. By the time the group had made their fifth turn, Eddie's muscles ached from being in a state of constant tension.

At their seventh turn, the darkness abated.

Down the hall, a dim red light in the ceiling cast its glow in a small radius around a short hallway. Since the light was still intact, Eddie decided it must have been too high for the Infected to reach. Two doors sat on either side of the hallway, the little amount of light from restroom signs which sat in the center of each made them easier to see.

Unfortunately, light also guaranteed the Infected would be around trying to break them.

Eddie could make out the dark forms of three or four people swaying back and forth just at the edge of the light. They were silent, which somehow made their presence more disconcerting, and all were turned toward the low light. There was no way Eddie's group could pass through the light without being spotted.

Not bothering to turn around, Hinderlight held up a halting hand and placed his weapon on the ground. Eddie and Hugh crouched low, waiting while the boss rooted through his pockets.

From the corner of his eye, he saw Hugh reach slowly for the gun on the floor. Eddie grabbed hold of the man's forearm. Their eyes locked. Eddie studied Hugh, expecting to see violence in his expression. All he picked up from the man was fear. Sheer terror seemed to ooze out of his pores.

Instead of chastising the poor guy, Eddie sent him a sympathetic expression and mouthed the words, "Everything will be okay." Eddie gently eased his hand away from the gun. Hugh didn't resist. Instead his shoulders slumped and he let out a silent exhale. Watching him for a moment more, Eddie turned and glanced in Hinderlight's direction. The man had picked up the gun with his left hand and held something else in his right. There was no way to tell if he had caught any of Eddie and Hugh's exchange, and for Hugh's sake, he hoped the dangerous man had not. Either way, Hinderlight appeared to have a plan as he started to take careful steps toward the light. Unsure what to do, all Eddie could do was watch.

Hinderlight moved with amazing silence and grace, like a barracuda approaching a group of sharks. When he was still a good ten feet away, he stopped and knelt down. His right arm twirled in a slow motion, like he was loosening tense muscles, and then he became still. Eddie counted seven of his own breaths before the man moved again. Hinderlight whipped his right arm up and Eddie caught the glint of light reflecting off of something he threw just before it crashed into an overhead light. The entire hallway fell into darkness except for a very faint glimmer from under the doors.

The shattering glass caused a chorus of triumphant moans from the Infected in the hallway. They shuffled about in place as the broken light made a low tinkling noise as its pieces fell to the ground. A few heartbeats later, when Eddie's eyes had adjusted to the dimness, he could barely make out the nearest Infected swaying about.

Behind them, Eddie started to hear the sound of things being dragged across the carpet. More were coming. Time to go.

Eddie and Hugh moved in unison toward the man. Eddie took his time, making sure each step was quiet. He could barely make out Hinderlight now, and the Infected were only visible because of their constant swaying. It helped that he could still picture where they had been standing before the light was broken. If the Infected had stayed relatively in the same place, he knew where to go to find an opening. Thankfully, Hinderlight was heading in the right direction, or at least the direction Eddie would have gone.

The man moved confidently past the first group of Infected. Eddie found himself holding his breath, and inwardly flinched when he thought Hinderlight brushed up against one of them. The former employee didn't react; it just kept swaying to some rhythm that only it could hear. Just before Hinderlight was about to disappear into the darkness, he stopped and turned back in Eddie's direction.

All right, our turn.

With Hugh close enough that Eddie could feel his breath, Eddie began to move toward the gap with slow, deliberate steps, making sure there was nothing in his way that might trip him up or betray his position. Hugh stayed almost on top of his heels.

Eddie stopped for a moment to work a kink out of his leg, and Hugh smacked right into his back. The two of them fell forward, Eddie catching himself with his hands as Hugh fell on top of his legs. Both managed to keep from letting even the tiniest grunt escape their lips, but their bodies hitting each other and the carpet did make a soft scratching sound.

A questioning moan escaped from the group of Infected directly in front of Eddie, and the swaying bodies slowed. Eddie stayed as still as he could. A difficult prospect while trying to hold himself up with Hugh on top of his legs. His arms burned as he waited for the Infected to resume their swaying. Behind him, the sounds of feet scraping along the carpet continued to grow louder. Just as Eddie's arms felt like they might give out, the Infected resumed their swaying like reeds in a breeze.

It took a moment for Hugh to untangle himself before both of them were up and moving again with Eddie in the front. It was painful to admit, but Eddie's brain just wasn't wired to think on his feet very well. Without Hinderlight, Eddie probably would have stumbled himself into a horrible death by now. As he slowed to move past the first group of Infected, Eddie decided to follow the man's lead no matter what from this point on.

Hinderlight waited long enough to give Eddie a disappointed shake of his head before continuing on. The man moved past the second group with ease and continued on until he was well past the Infected and barely visible. Taking a deep, silent breath, Eddie followed. He had much better luck this time. No stumbles, no noise. Hugh's hand gripped his shoulder like a vice, so that by the time they had made it safely past the Infected, Eddie had to rub the spot in order to restore some circulation back to the area.

But they had made it. Past a group of a little less than a dozen Infected. If this was the most difficult thing they had to do, they might actually have a chance. Hinderlight waved them on, and the trio began to move further down the hall.

Then Hugh coughed.

It was a low sound but in the hallway, it might have well been a thunderclap. The Infected turned toward them in unison. For a moment, Eddie thought that given a few more moments of silence, they would return to their gentle swaying. That hope shattered when a group began to shuffle forward.

Hinderlight was already moving, distancing himself from the Infected. And Eddie and Hugh. Eddie went to move as well but stopped as he saw Hugh frozen in place, his attention on the Infected shambling toward them. Reaching out, Eddie grabbed the man's shirt and gave him a gentle tug. Nothing. Eddie pulled harder, caught between wanting to get the man moving and not wanting to yank him off his feet. The Infected kept coming. How long before their weak eyes spotted their prey? Eddie wasn't going to wait to find out.

Gripping the man with both hands, Eddie dragged him around so that Hugh was facing away from the Infected, and then shoved the man forward. Hugh stumbled a bit, his shoes dragging along the carpet, but then he finally got moving on his own. When Eddie looked back the way they had come, he realized he was screwed.

Three of the Infected lurched toward him, their eyes locked on prey they were close enough to see. Instincts made him grab the handle of the closest door and swing it open between himself and his attackers. To his surprise, three people tumbled out of the bathroom, two in office attire and a third in the body armor of one of the security guards. A tide of relief flooded Eddie at the sight of the guard but vanished as the Infected fell upon them. Screams and yells echoed from the men as they fought off the hands and teeth of their attackers. All Eddie could do was watch the losing battle.

A strong hand grabbed him and jerked him back. Eddie swung a backhanded fist in defense, which smacked against Hinderlight's side. The man didn't even flinch. Instead he yanked again and sent Eddie tumbling away from the melee a few feet away. Trying to keep his balance got his mind working again, and he spotted Hugh moving off down the hall ahead of them and started to follow. He only made it a few feet before glancing back to make sure Hinderlight was behind him. Sure enough, the man with the unflinching resolve was there, waving him on as he approached. Further down the hall, Eddie caught a flash of blue light and heard a buzz of electricity before Hinderlight caught up to him, pushing him on in the darkness.

Not sure how much a stun stick will help, Eddie thought as it dawned on him what the blue light could have been. *But I hope they survive.*

Moans erupted from all different directions as the screaming behind them continued. The floor seemed to shake as the Infected converged on the screaming victims.

Ahead, six of the Infected charged out from around a corner. Before Eddie could even react, Hinderlight was there pressing both him and Hugh back up against the wall. Eddie crouched, fear locking his joints as the Infected thundered past, apparently unaware of how close they had come to new victims. Once they were well enough past, Hinderlight got the three of them moving again.

As their trio moved on toward the stairwell, the screams of the dying seemed to follow them. Guilt welled up inside of Eddie, peaking, as they reached the door to the stairwell and quietly slipped inside. It was horrible to think that his actions had gotten those three strangers killed. Even worse, he felt a bit of relief that their sudden appearance had allowed his group to get away.

Never again, Eddie thought. *If I survive the night, I want to be the reason people were saved, not killed.* He glanced at Hinderlight. *I might not be anything like him, but I'll try my best to be more courageous.*

CHAPTER 9

"What do you mean we're going down to the lobby?" Hugh whispered, his face twisted in confusion. They had moved down the stairwell in silence, the events that happened a moment ago too horrible to recount. "We've reached the twentieth floor. This is where security is stationed. It has to be the safest place in the building."

They stood halfway between the twentieth and twenty-first floor. Eddie and Hugh had taken a seat on the floor to catch their breath, but Hinderlight paced back and forth in front of them. He didn't even look winded.

"Those men are just rent-a-cops in fancy gear." Hinderlight spoke as if explaining something to a child. A stubborn, ignorant child. "They receive more training on how to look intimidating than how to actually hurt or kill anything. You saw how well that one guard did against three of the Infected."

"That was just one man, though. Surely there are a lot more stationed on the—"

"In a real emergency, guards would be sent out to each floor to do a quick sweep. Those are probably as dead as the man we just saw if they ran into any of the Infected. The small skeleton crew that would have remained behind wouldn't offer much protection." He let out a huff. "Even if they had actually been trained for a threat like this."

"But why wouldn't they have been trained?" Eddie asked. "Surely if the company knew something like this could happen, they would at least inform the guards they hired."

"Only a small number of employees in this building know what's really going on inside of Soladyne and its leading competitors."

"So, you're implying that a group of competing companies have conspired together to keep the world in the dark?" Eddie asked incredulously.

"Precisely."

"The dark about what?" Hugh asked, beating Eddie to his next question.

"If we're not careful, you'll find out soon enough. But all you two need to worry about right now is getting to the lobby."

"I still think—"

Hinderlight spoke right over the man. "Eddie, come on. We're going."

Eddie obediently followed. He didn't need to know about any conspiracies or whatever else. Hinderlight had saved his life in the past few hours more times than anyone had ever bothered holding the door for him. The man had his loyalty now even more than his obedience. All Eddie could do was hope that Hugh followed along.

After they had gone two more floors, Hugh caught up with them. He looked disgruntled but didn't say another word as they continued down.

The rest of the trip went without incident. As they approached the doorway to each floor, Hinderlight stopped. He would place an ear to the door for a minute or two and then wave them on. Only once did he place his fingers to his lips and motion for them to crouch down. It wasn't until they had gone down two more floors that he rose and motioned for them to do the same. By the time they reached the doorway to the lobby, Eddie's legs burned and Hugh was openly sweating. Hinderlight paused at the door and listened once more, then motioned for them to take a seat at the far end of the landing. They all sat, huddled close together as they rested and caught their breath.

"I have no idea what we might find on the other side of that door," Hinderlight whispered. "It could be more Infected, or whoever set off the attack in the first place. Or something even worse."

Eddie didn't even want to know what Hinderlight considered worse than the Infected.

"Our main goal," Hinderlight continued, "is to get to the elevators in the lobby."

"The elevators," Hugh repeated. "The ones that don't work during a lockdown."

"They work. You just need high enough security access to work them." He held up his key card. "This will get either of the middle two elevators to work. We just had to get to the lobby where they are stationed during a lockdown."

Hugh just shook his head. "And then we go where? Back up?

Seems counter-productive. We could have just walked up the stairs to wherever you are trying to go."

"No, not back up. Further down. Pass the parking levels to where the real security force is stationed."

"A secret level?" Hugh scoffed. "This is ridiculous. What kind of place is this?"

"Don't you want to be safe?" Hinderlight growled, keeping his tone low. "I'm telling you, there is a lower level and that's where we should be able to find safety. There are extra security measures that make sure nothing infected could go down or come up."

"Security measures like the ones that were supposed to catch the Infected to begin with," Eddie whispered.

"Yes, well, these security measures are all automated. There is no human factor that could allow something to slip by. It's impossible for anything contained below us to come up and vice-versa. You just have to trust me."

"I do," Eddie replied.

"I don't," Hugh said right behind him. "But I've followed along after you madmen so far. Might as well stick around to see this hidden, underground floor."

Eddie thought he caught something in Hinderlight's expression as the man said "floor," but it might have just been how the emergency lighting caught his face.

"Then if you two are properly rested, we should go. Remember, we have no idea what might be out there. Stay quiet and stay close."

Both men nodded.

Hinderlight took the lead as they moved to the door. He took his usual cautious approach, opening a small crack to check things out before sliding through. Eddie was about to follow when Hugh grabbed his arm.

"Do you really believe any of this?" Hugh asked. "Brain fungus. Secret levels. Massive conspiracies. It's all a little crazy. How do we know this isn't just some nerve gas that's turned half the employees here crazy and this Hinderlight fellow is just starting to show signs?"

"The man has earned my trust." Eddie shook Hugh's hand off his arm. "He's kept both of us alive."

"He's kept you alive, you mean. I've just been lucky to be around you when he's decided to be heroic."

"Then I guess you'd better stick close."

Eddie left the man and moved through the door. The stairwell opened up into a long corridor on the other side. A few doors lined the gray walls, but what really caught his attention was the amount of light in the hall. The red emergency lights flashed about the hallway, but they were joined by the comforting white of the normal light panels that ran along the center of the ceiling. After bumbling in the darkness or the blood-colored emergency lights that were a constant reminder of the carnage he had seen so far, the white light was like a beacon of hope. That light not only brought back the thought of the outside world, it also meant the Infected probably weren't around.

Hinderlight reached the end of the hall, the lobby a bright blur beyond him. He was crouched down, the gun held parallel to his hips. Not wanting to get his hopes up, Eddie crouched down as well and slowly approached the other man, Hugh still in tow. When he reached Hinderlight's side, he stopped, not sure if he believed what he was seeing ahead of him.

Despite the metal shutters over the huge windows, the lobby was as bright as ever. Its fountain continued to gurgle clear blue water as if everything was business as usual. The silver-colored floor tiles were pristine and free of dirt and thankfully bloodless. The lush green of plant life filled the room as their leaves fluttered lightly in the breezes created by the air conditioning. Even the glass counters and the scanners next to them looked undisturbed. The only difference that Eddie noted from this morning was that the holo projectors now displayed a large digital lock, which was common for a lockdown. Everything in the lobby instilled a sense of peace and safety. Yet Hinderlight hadn't moved from his spot.

"What are we waiting for?" Eddie asked.

"Quiet," Hinderlight hissed. His eyes didn't leave the lobby. "Don't you see it?"

"See what?" Eddie scanned the lobby again, this time looking for anything out of place. Besides the usually busy room being empty, nothing seemed out of place. "What am I missing?"

"I don't see anything either," Hugh cast a questioning glance at Hinderlight, then rolled his eyes toward Eddie.

"That's because neither of you are looking."

His hand raised, a single finger pointing toward the room. Eddie followed until his sight found a particularly large planter on the opposite side of the lobby. He didn't notice anything off about it or the hint of something hiding in the broken branches and torn leaves.

Hinderlight's hand moved again, this time pointing toward one of the check-in desks. Eddie scanned every inch of its glass surface. The computer seemed undisturbed. The small light and other objects that uniformly adorned all of the check-in desks seemed in their usual place. He could even make out the leather chair behind the desk, carefully tucked in. Eddie looked one more time, then finding nothing, tapped Hinderlight's shoulder and shrugged when the other man looked at him.

"The base," Hinderlight mouthed.

By the front left corner, he finally found what Hinderlight wanted him to see. Even from this distance, Eddie could make out a few red streaks running down the side and collecting in a tiny pool at the bottom.

"Do you think it was one of the Infected?" Eddie whispered.

"You've seen them. Violent. Messy." Hinderlight shook his head. "If even one or two of them had gotten free down here, the room would be in shambles. This is something else."

Before Eddie could ask what, Hinderlight pressed him against the wall with one of his muscular arms. Hugh sidled up to the side of the wall on the other side of Eddie and they crouched in silence. Hinderlight seemed focused on the other side of the room. After a few moments, Eddie caught sight of movement in a small alcove behind one of the desks. A few tall ferns partially hid the space, making it impressive that Hinderlight had caught sight of anything to begin with. Eddie continued to watch as whatever hid behind the plants shuffled about. He caught glimpses of white in between the green leaves but couldn't make much else out.

And then Lizzie stepped out from behind the ferns, brushing off her ivory pants before taking a deep breath and looking around.

Lizzie! Eddie thought. *How could I have not even thought about her this whole time?*

He tried to push himself away from the wall but Hinderlight pushed him back as the imposing man stood and strode directly into the room.

The gun in his hand was pointed directly at her.

"You." Hinderlight didn't shout but the combination of his tone and his emphasis on the word combined with a quick flick of the gun in his hand conveyed the man's aggression just as well. "Who are you?"

Eddie rushed out after him, inwardly flinching as he saw poor Lizzie cower backward. She threw her hands up as she stumbled back a few steps and dropped to her knees.

"Please don't hurt me!" she cried out.

"Quiet," Hinderlight growled before repeating his question. "Who are you?"

"Elizabeth. Elizabeth McClane. I handle check-ins." The poor woman looked on the verge of tears.

"Elizabeth?" Hinderlight was only a few feet away from her now, the gun practically in her face. "You go by Lizzie, correct? You know Eddie?"

"Eddie?" Confusion mixed in with her fear. Eddie winced, hoping it was that same fear that kept her from registering who he was. He pressed the hurt aside and stepped forward.

"Eddie!" Relief flooded her voice as she made to stand. When Hinderlight shook the gun in her face, she knelt back down. Her eyes stayed locked on Eddie though. "Eddie? What's going on?"

"For Pete's sake, Hinderlight," Eddie said as he put a restraining hand on Hinderlight's arm. "She's frightened enough. Take that gun out of her face."

Hinderlight shrugged him off. "Frightened? The question you should be asking is why she is frightened. And of what? The Infected or us?"

"Why would she be scared of us?" Eddie tried moving past the broad-shouldered man but Hinderlight kept himself in between them both. Realizing he wasn't going to get to Lizzie's side, he turned his next question to her. "Where is everyone?"

Lizzie looked back and forth between Eddie and the gun held inches from her face. When she finally spoke, her lip trembled as much as her voice. "I don't know what happened. I took a five-minute break and went to use the rest room. I couldn't have been inside the girl's room for more than a few minutes before I started hearing all of this horrible screaming. Then the alarm started going off, so I locked myself in one of the stalls. I waited, figuring the alarm would stop and someone would come and find me but no one did. When I couldn't stand another minute locked up in that stall, I crept out. That's when I found the entire floor empty and the lockdown shutters covering the only way out."

"Why were you hiding in the bushes?" Hinderlight's stormy expression seemed less than convinced.

"I was creeped out! First by the fact that I heard all this screaming and pictured the worst, only to find the lobby empty. I had been trying to find a phone line that worked or get some information off of the computers but everything was offline. The longer I was out here, the more nervous I got. Then I heard the sound, a strange clicking noise, and lost it. The plant was the closest place to hide."

"See?" Eddie tried once more to get past Hinderlight. This time the man let him. "She's in as much trouble as the rest of us.

Kneeling down at her side, Eddie put an awkward arm around her shoulders. He had never really been good at comforting people, but this seemed like the right thing to do. Lizzie leaned back into his arms, becoming almost like dead weight as she pressed against him. It only made Eddie feel all the more self-conscious as he held her in an awkward embrace.

"Guys," Hugh said from a little behind Hinderlight. With everything else, Eddie had almost forgotten the man was even with them. He was looking toward the lobby entrance and backing away with slow, careful steps. "We should go."

All three turned toward the direction the man was looking. Eddie had expected to see one or two of the Infected but instead, all he saw were the enormous windows that covered the front of the lobby and the gray and dirty bronze of the shutters behind them. A quick glance at Hugh and he realized the man was looking up, higher along the windows. Following his gaze, Eddie still saw nothing.

Until a dirty patch of bronze as big as a bear slid along the glass. Its coloring matched that of the shutters, making it hard for Eddie to believe he was actually seeing something that large clinging to the window panes. A moment later, part of it pulled away from the glass and swiveled forward, leaving no doubt that it was real.

Eddie's breath caught in his throat when the bronze patch opened its eyelids, revealing two sparkling azure eyes.

"Oh God," Hinderlight whispered and swung the gun around to face whatever the hell was staring right at them.

The patch of bronze that seemed off from the rest of the shutters shimmered and grew to a darker shade of brown. Streaks of black appeared, which allowed Eddie to make out the creature's body in its entirety. Larger than a brown bear now that Eddie had a clear view of its size, the creature hung from the glass by four thin legs that somehow defied gravity and kept it attached to the glass. It was as large as a brown bear, with the head of a bat, and large, ridged ears extending as wide as its shoulders. Two leathery wings unfolded from its sides as the creature stared back at them. The wingspan was like that of a small sailplane, at least fifteen to twenty meters across. Its head swiveled about, seeming to take them all in. When its mouth opened, the bottom jaw separated at the center so that the two parts opened up sideways, each lined with rows of tiny, pointed teeth. It looked like an attempt at a horrible grin.

"Run!" Hinderlight yelled as the creature detached from the wall and swooped toward them on its massive wings.

Eddie did not have to be told twice.

CHAPTER 10

The group started to scatter, but Hinderlight's booming voice grabbed their attention.

"To the elevators!"

Eddie took off, Lizzie right beside him. Hugh either didn't hear or care to listen and dove behind one of the desks. Ignoring the man, Eddie focused on the bank of elevators at the opposite end of the lobby. Behind him, he heard the loud crack of gunfire but didn't bother to turn around.

"Get down!" Lizzie yelled right before she crashed into his side and took them both to the floor. A gust of wind pummeled Eddie's face as he hit the ground and everything seemed to go dark.

Except it wasn't darkness. The creature glided just overhead, its four claws close enough that he could see dozens of little suction cups covering the bottom of each. It rose as it passed them, turning in midair before lowering itself to the ground with loud flaps of its wings.

Right in front of the elevator.

The Camouflage Bat let out a screech that pierced the air and felt like needles jabbing into Eddie's skull. He clasped his hands to his ears, saw Lizzie do the same in his peripheral vision, and tried to block out the noise. If he had a dozen pillows to wrap around his head, Eddie still didn't think it would be enough. He gritted his teeth against it and struggled to his feet. Lizzie was already on her feet, and they stared back at the monster a dozen or so yards away. It stared back, its feet shuffling about. And yet, it didn't attack.

"What should we do?" Eddie asked.

Lizzie opened her mouth to respond when a loud *crack* echoed behind them. The creature flinched as if struck and took a few steps backward.

Hinderlight was suddenly at Eddie's side and pressed something into his hand.

"When it dives again, get to the elevator. My card will open it." He paused as the Camouflage Bat let out another ear-piercing shriek that almost made Eddie's knees buckle. When the other man spoke again, his voice was muffled by the ringing in Eddie's ears. "I'll lure him away. Just make sure you keep the door open long enough for me to get inside."

Not waiting for Eddie's response, Hinderlight raised his weapon and fired off two more shots at the creature. The bullets sunk into its chest, but the shots only seemed to piss the creature off. It leaped into the air, its great wings sending torrents of air with each massive stroke. It rose higher and higher, its gaze locked in their direction. When it reached to the ceiling of the lobby, the wings paused and the creature shot down toward them.

Eddie dashed toward the sidewall. When its massive shadow passed by him, he cut in and ran straight to Lizzie as she met him in the center of the room. Two more shots rang out behind him followed by a loud grunt, but his focus remained divided between Lizzie and the wall of elevators. Lizzie ran alongside Eddie like an Olympic sprinter. They slid to a stop in front of the elevator doors at the same time. As he fumbled with Hinderlight's key card, Lizzie's voice urging him on, "Hurry, Eddie. Hurry."

When he finally got the card through the reader next to the elevator buttons, a pleasant *bing* echoed throughout the lobby and the doors opened, revealing the empty car inside.

"Greetings, Mr. Hinderlight," the elevator cooed as they sprinted inside. Eddie spun, prepared to defend himself if need be but was relieved to see the monster no closer than before. Instead he faced an empty lobby. No sign of Hinderlight or Hugh. Even the bat appeared to be gone. How the hell could something that big just disappear?

Camouflage, he thought. *It must be hiding again.*

"Let's go," Lizzie whispered behind him, her breaths coming hard and fast.

"Not without the others," he whispered back. *No one gets left behind.* The doors began to close on him but stopped as he extended an arm out. As the elevator doors opened back up, he scanned the lobby for any sign of movement.

Hugh was easy to find. The man cowered behind the same desk, his head barely peeking out over the top. Eddie waved for him to come to the elevator but the man shook his head.

Now what do I do?

"I have to help him." Even Eddie thought it sounded insane as soon as it left his lips but what else could he do? Lizzie's expression seemed to mirror his thoughts, although she was less nice about it.

"Are you a fucking moron?!"

"Here," he said, handing her Hinderlight's ID card, ignoring the fact that she was probably right. "If that thing gets to us, you go on ahead."

"How do you know I won't use this card as soon as you step out of the elevator?"

Eddie Watson's Rule Number 33: A gift of trust can earn as much if not more loyalty than any monetary bribe.

"Because even though you're scared, we've gotten to know each other over the last three years, and I've come to believe that you're a caring person. I don't think you would abandon anyone if there was a chance of saving them."

"We don't know each other as well as you're presuming," she replied, then let out a sigh. "But I'd like to get to know you better. I'll hold the elevator as long as it's safe enough to do so. Just don't get eaten."

"I'll do my best." He flashed her a smile he hoped would hide at least a little of the fear pounding his heart and took a cautious step back out into the lobby. He looked straight up. No monster there. He had half expected to find it above him, dropping down to crush the life out of him. And to prove that he was a moron, as Lizzie had so eloquently put it. Starting from the ceiling and working his way down, he did a quick scan of the room. No subtle change in color to give the monster away but no Hinderlight either. Which left his first goal of getting Hugh to the elevator. From behind the desk across the room, Hugh's wide eyes pleaded with him to do something.

"*Where is it?*" Eddie mouthed.

Hugh shook his head rapidly. Did that mean he didn't know where it was, or he wasn't going to risk any more movement than that? Eddie asked again and got the same response. The tiniest bit of regret over not leaving the man in the stairwell took hold of him but he shoved the feeling back down. Only positive thoughts. He would get Hugh to the elevator. Hinderlight would magically appear. The creature would fly off and return to the nightmare from which it came. The company would reward Eddie with twice as many vacation days. No, three times as many! All of it possible.

Even if not in the least bit probable.

He took a few tentative steps forward. Nothing. Eddie could feel eyes on him, but they could be the monster's, or Hugh's, or even Lizzie watching from behind him. A quick glance back found the woman standing just inside the elevator, one hand blocking the door, the other hidden behind the wall.

Probably with the card ready to swipe if things go south, he thought. *I don't blame her.*

A few more steps into the lobby. His eyes scanning for the slightest movement or shift in shadow. Not having seen anything that might give him pause, Eddie waved at Hugh to come join him. The man vigorously shook his head. Eddie wanted to scream in frustration but cursed under his breath instead. If Hugh made him walk all the way to retrieve him, Eddie might just kill the wimp himself. After getting him to the safety of the elevator first, of course.

Eddie took only two steps toward Hugh when a snort like the puff of a steam engine made him freeze in his tracks. Movement to his left caught his eye. A muddy brown blur disappeared behind another desk. Hugh must have seen it as well, as the man was gesturing frantically toward the same desk. Eddie waved the man toward him with both hands now and he finally complied, slinking out in a low crouch. He moved toward Eddie, never taking his anxious gaze from the desk where the brown blur lurked. Once Hugh reached him, they both began backing toward the elevator.

Which was why Eddie didn't notice Hinderlight's gun on the ground until his heel brushed it. It moved only a few inches, but the sound of it scraping along the tile in the silent room might as well have been broadcast through a megaphone.

The creature suddenly burst out from behind the desk, a mass of fur, wings, and fangs. It stumbled to the side on wobbly legs and began making its way toward them.

Hugh fled away from the bat toward the elevator. There was no way they would make it now. Eddie grabbed the gun. Maybe he could slow the creature down so at least the other man might make it. The gun felt heavy in his hand as he brought it up to face the charging bat. Then he pulled the trigger.

The first shot almost hurled the gun from his hand. The bullet flew wide. He regrasped the weapon with both hands, took aim, and fired again. He was aiming for the head this time. Instead, he hit the bat's shoulder right where it connected to the wing. It let out a horrible screech, shaking Eddie to his bones, but he kept his bearings and fired again. The third bullet missed as the bat jerked to the side and dove behind one of the desks.

Enough heroics for one day, Eddie thought as he took the opportunity to flee.

Somehow ahead of them, Hinderlight had appeared and was just getting on the elevator, limping on his left leg as he got inside and turned around. He waved them on, the look of fear painting his face pushing Eddie's legs even harder. Hugh was only steps away from safety.

Which made Eddie meal number one. Time slowed.

The creature huffed somewhere behind him.

The elevator door began to close ahead.

The monster's shriek split his skull.

Hugh made it through the door.

Eddie had another six feet left to go. He could hear the bat's mandibles snapping behind him. The image of the worst group home he had been in flashed through his mind. His foster parents were chasing him up the stairs with a lighter and a belt. They finally cornered him in the bathroom. To this day, Eddie could only remember three things about what happened after that. Fire. Pain. Blood.

And then he was turning sideways and through the elevator door. He stumbled and fell against the opposite wall, shooting pain up and down his side. He hit the ground and scrambled up into a sitting position, arms shielding his head, just in time to see the door close completely.

A loud thud echoed in the elevator as something struck the door. When it struck again, a small dent appeared about waist high.

"It's going to get through!" Hugh had backed up against the wall next to Eddie. The man looked as pale as a ghost and seconds away from throwing up.

"Swipe the card again!" Hinderlight yelled. The man was braced in the center of the elevator, arms extended like he was getting ready to wrestle the beast. "Then press the button for the ground floor twice."

"What?" Lizzie paused the card right above the reader. "That's insane. If I press the button for this floor it will just open the door. I'm not giving it access to an easy meal."

The creature struck again, pushing the dent out toward them further and widening it.

"Just do it!" Hinderlight roared.

Lizzie glanced at Eddie and he gave her a quick nod. As she swiped the card down and pressed the button twice, Eddie hoped that Hinderlight had a plan that didn't involve him wrestling the monster.

Without warning, the wall Eddie and Hugh had been leaning against retracted to the side, sending both men falling backward. They landed inside what appeared to be another elevator, except where the original had the welcoming feel you would expect from a heavily traveled elevator, this one had was cold and stark. Hinderlight strode through the opening into the second elevator, Lizzie close behind. As he entered, he pressed the single button on the left side of the secret elevator door. Smiling at the group, Hinderlight stood in the center of the elevator, his arms at his side. Behind him, another pounding opened up the gap between the elevator doors enough that Eddie caught a glimpse of a brown snout sniffing at the air on the other side.

A beam of light shot down from the ceiling, spreading out as it took in every inch of the small area. When it had finished, an androgynous voice came out of some speaker Eddie couldn't spot.

"Welcome, Joseph Hinderlight. You have three unauthorized guests. Are you sure you wish to proceed?"

"Yes," Hinderlight replied.

The elevator began to descend as one last bang followed them down.

"What if it follows us down the shaft?" Hugh asked.

Hinderlight actually laughed.

"The secondary door is much stronger than a normal elevator door. I doubt it will get through. And even if it does, the beast will quickly regret it." When the man didn't explain further, the others looked to voice further concerns but he silenced them with a wave of his hand. "Let's just take a moment to catch our breaths and compose ourselves. We've just been through a very harrowing experience. Please believe me when I say that we are safe, for now, and that our situation should improve once we reach Level One."

His words didn't seem to appease Lizzie and Hugh, but they kept quiet all the same. Eddie had his doubts as well. Learning different languages had given him some insight into how people behave, even if it didn't help him actually interact with them. The fact that Hinderlight was trying to suppress any other questions meant that he had things he wasn't comfortable sharing. But in the end, Eddie decided to put his trust in the man's past actions and not let Hinderlight's reluctance to speak spoil the trust he had in their leader.

With the group settled, even if not happy with being stifled, Hinderlight moved to one of the corners and sat down. It was the first time Eddie could remember the man actually taking a break since the moment he met him. Their de facto leader began massaging his left leg while stretching his neck.

"How did you get around that monster?" Eddie asked, his curiosity getting the best of him.

"Later, Eddie." It was a command hidden behind a friendly smile. "Let me relax."

Silence fell upon the four of them as they descended down the shaft. How fast and deep they were going was difficult to discern. Hugh was holding up as well as Eddie expected. He had slumped against the wall, legs pulled against his body so that his chin rested on his knees. His eyes were locked on some unseen point, and every now and then, Eddie thought he saw the man mumble something.

Lizzie, on the other hand, seemed to be holding it together much better, considering she had almost been mauled by a giant bat creature. She had sidled up next to him, not close enough to touch but enough so that he could hear her steady breaths. Her knees were pulled to her chest, arms wrapped around them as she rested her head back against the wall.

Any time Eddie glanced over at her, she would tilt her head in his direction and returned a friendly, albeit subdued, smile. Sitting in the silence of the elevator car, he was glad for the relative peace and let the moments drift by.

"*Level one*," the secret elevator declared in a cold, female tone unlike the one in the elevators above.

"When the doors open," Hinderlight said as he stood, "keep your mouths shut and don't make any sudden movements." He stepped between them and the door and began smoothing his shirt and pants. He even came close to looking presentable, if it wasn't for the blood and spots of dirt.

The elevator came to a stop. The doors slid open.

And the barrels of six assault rifles stared back at them.

CHAPTER 11

"Don't move!" The voice was like a hammer. Lights flashed into their eyes. Eddie averted his gaze to the elevator floor. "Identify yourselves!"

"Joseph Hinderlight. United States Regional Manager for Soladyne."

"Credentials. Now."

The lights receded, revealing six heavily armed and extremely tense men. Hinderlight took his card from Lizzie and passed it over to a gloved hand. While the man slid the card through a reader on his arm, Eddie took a closer look at the others.

He had assumed they would be wearing matching uniforms, sleek helmets, and com links, but these guys were nothing like the security guards that usually stood at attention around the building. These guys were as diverse as a posse of bounty hunters, each sporting their own style and different weaponry. One man was fully decked out in combat gear minus a helmet while another only wore arm and leg protection, his white Twisted Sister t-shirt a sharp contrast to the armor. Another man wore only a chest protector, his arms bare except for the multitude of different-colored tattoos that ran up both arms. The other three had various levels of protection on different body parts, some of it painted with designs similar to the other man's arms. Physically, they were just as different, ranging from thick and muscular to just thick, with the fully decked out man's armor seeming to hang on what must be a much thinner body.

The way they held their weapons, braced against shoulders, fingers on the trigger, not the slightest tremor in their grip, was all Eddie needed to see to know these men were good at their job.

"Checks out," the man that had taken Hinderlight's card replied. He could have passed for a sumo wrestler with how his body seemed to want to burst out of what pieces of armor he wore. He held out his wrist, a screen faced out toward Hinderlight. "Fingerprint."

"Don't bother," Twisted Sister said, lowering his weapon. The other men didn't follow suit. "I recognize him from an alert I received about a VIP visiting in the building above us. These other three, however--"

"Are under my care," Hinderlight replied quickly.

"You realize you shouldn't have brought them down here. It is a massive breach of protocol."

"When the building is secure, I'll face whatever disciplinary actions The Board feel necessary. Now, can we please move out of the elevator . . ."

"I'm Hafiz Afzal," the man in the Twisted Sister T-shirt replied. "I command Squad K, which you see in front of you. As for moving out of the elevator, *you* may disembark. The others are to remain where they are."

"No, they are coming with me."

Hafiz's face tightened, thin black eyebrows angling down as his eyes narrowed. "In case you haven't noticed, *sir*, we are in a lockdown situation. Not a drill. I can inform you of how serious it is, but not in the presence of a bunch of office workers."

"And I'm commanding you to do that very thing. They've already seen some pretty horrific shit *and* now know about the facility below the main building. Protocol hasn't just been broken, it's already smashed to bits."

"Even so--"

"For the record, I claim full responsibility for these people," Hinderlight said. "If any secrets are exposed in the process, or company laws broken, your security detail will not be held accountable."

"As you wish." Hafiz made a quick gesture to the rest of his team. "Stand down and let them through. Bukowski, get back to the security monitors and keep trying to get a hold of the control station."

Bukowski, the potential sumo wrestler, nodded and trotted ahead of them down the hall. For a man so big, he was more agile than Eddie would have thought. Once he was out of the way, Hafiz motioned for the rest of them to follow. As they did, the rest of the security team encircled them, guns aimed down but fingers still on triggers. Hafiz and Hinderlight took the lead.

"So give me the basics." Hinderlight's voice had lost its friendly tone. "What happened?"

"At 9:42 a.m., we lost direct contact with the control room. One of our men in the room reported through his backup walkie-talkie that it was just a mechanical glitch and they were working on it."

"They don't allow cell phones down here either?" Hugh asked.

Hafiz looked didn't bother to look back, but Hinderlight responded to the question.

"The reason your cell phones don't work in the building above is because their signals are blocked by this facility. Straight phone lines and specially designed radio walkie-talkies are the only way to communicate. One of the many ways we try to protect the security of the facility below the building."

When Hinderlight finished explaining, Hafiz continued. "The last time I heard from him was at quarter past ten. Then all communications, hard lines and radio, went dead. The base's ability to disrupt all communication must have been activated. Not soon after, the lockdown was put in place. The rest of the squads stationed here were sent to sweep the floors and secure the control room, per protocol, while we were left in charge of securing this level. None of the squads have reported back since. Squad K has been holding this level. Unfortunately, the only thing we have access to up here electronically are the elevator monitors. We can tell when one is coming down from the floors above or coming up from the facility's lobby below. Besides that, we are completely in the dark."

"What about the upper levels?" Eddie asked. Hinderlight shot him a look but he continued on regardless. "It's insane up there. The security forces for the main building have no idea what to do."

"What's going on above us?" Hafiz spoke to Hinderlight, ignoring Eddie.

"I'm not sure. I was attacked by a secretary with enhanced strength. I'm not sure where she got it from, but the rest of the floor was crawling with people infected with the Nebun Ciuperca fungus. Other floors were infected as well, and by how fast the people shroomed, I believe it was genetically modified."

"Shroomheads? Which means this was a planned attack." Hafiz rubbed at the stubble on his chin. "That makes sense. Disrupt both above and below at the same time. But to do that, whoever orchestrated this attack must have already had multiple people on the inside. Not as difficult above, but I thought almost impossible down here, especially to have someone in the control room itself. This is troubling news."

"But what about the people trapped up in the building?" Eddie pushed as they continued down the hall. "Why weren't any of the security forces from down here sent up to help or even check on them?"

"The upper levels are low priority. This level must be controlled so that unauthorized personnel—" Hafiz paused in the hallway to glance at Eddie and the others "—don't come down. And more importantly, nothing from The Zoo comes up. That's why Squad K was left in charge here."

That got some laughs from the other security members, although Eddie didn't get the joke.

"Here we are," Hafiz said as they reached the end of the hall. "Last line of defense from what waits below."

They walked into a room filled with computers and monitors, most of which were blank. Bukowski sat in front of one of the few that still had flashing buttons and lights, his girth blocking out most of the screen in front of him. At the other side of the room was a wide, glass window that took up most of the wall, starting at waist height and extending almost to the ceiling. Next to it was an oversized metal door, thick as a bank vault opened wide on its hinges. Eddie peered through it into a dimly lit adjoining room to see plastic boxes and wooden crates haphazardly stacked from floor to ceiling.

"Anything?" Hafiz asked as they entered the room.

"Nothing, sir. No communications. The Zoo's cargo elevators are stuck on the lobby level. Same problem with the personnel elevators. Zero movement. I'm still working on getting a connection to the other elevators in the facility so we can at least track their movement."

"Good. Carry on." Hafiz waved toward the rest of them. "This way. The rest of you will remain in the loading area. To be honest, if everything that happened is an inside job, I don't trust any of you in here."

"Understandable," Hinderlight said before gesturing to the rest of them. "Everyone out."

They filed through the massive metal doorway and into the

adjoining room with the boxes and crates. The room was larger than he had first thought, the ceiling almost two stories, and just as lost in the low light that the few flashing red alarms on the walls provided. Crates, varying from the size of an open laptop to an SUV sat about the room. There was little order to their placement; some arranged in tight clusters while others were stacked almost to the ceiling. The only straight pathway through them ended at a set of elevator doors on the opposite side of the room.

"What's in the crates?" Hinderlight asked.

"Supplies for The Zoo." Hafiz was quiet for a moment, a frown pressing his lips, but then he continued. "Materials and experiments from below." He paused again. "Nothing alive."

Hinderlight glanced around the room, taking everything in. "Is there always this much material moving back and forth?"

"How much do you know about The Zoo, sir?"

"Generalities," Hinderlight replied. "A person at my level is told the basics, shown enough so that we understand it all to be true, and then informed that it is best not to dwell too much on it."

Hafiz nodded "That's smart. Every so often we lose a man or two just because the knowledge or the strain gets to them. I try to avoid thinking about it as much as possible too, but some of the things I've seen--" A shudder ran though him and he didn't go on.

"It's a holding tank for obscure specimens to be studied," Hinderlight went on. "Dangerous specimens."

Hafiz raised a hand. "And let's leave it at that. Be thankful that kind of knowledge is above your pay grade. Some questions are better left unanswered."

"Couldn't be any worse than what we've already seen," Hugh cut in. "We were almost eaten by some kind of giant bat."

"Bat?" Hafiz let out a laugh that held no warmth. "I hope getting eaten by some oversized animal is the worst thing you ever have to come face-to-face with."

"Sir!" Bukowski appeared in the doorway to the security room behind them. "Elevator is on the way up."

"Do you have eyes on the interior?" Hafiz pushed past the rest of them to address the rotund Bukowski.

"No, sir. Camera is still dark."

"Get the others out here then lock the door behind us. You know your orders."

Bukowski nodded. "No matter what happens, that door doesn't open unless you give the all clear."

"Good. Hinderlight?" His eyes locked on the man. "I don't like this. You come down and the elevator comes up. We already know there are people on the inside working to undermine us. You and your people are staying on this side of the door where I can keep an eye on you."

Eddie thought Hinderlight would protest, try to reason with the man so that they, the civilians, could stay on the safety of the other side of the security door. "I agree, Mr. Afzal. We face whatever comes up together. The security of this level cannot be compromised."

Shit, Eddie thought to himself. Hugh was a bit more vocal.

"I don't agree with that one bit!" He pushed past Hinderlight and got right in Hafiz's face. "I'm not a security risk. I handle the purchase and resupply of my floor's office materials. Paper, printer toner. Paperclips, for Christ's sake. And just for my floor! I'm not important enough to be a security risk--"

Hafiz drove the stock of his weapon into Hugh's gut, driving him to his knees. As Hugh stayed there on the ground, wheezing for breath, the rest of the security team sent him disgusted glances. Eddie felt embarrassed for him as the men weaved around him as if he were a steaming pile of shit to be avoided.

"So we're clear," Hafiz said, addressing Hinderlight. "I've deferred to your judgment because you claim responsibility of these *people*. But we do not share the same priorities when it comes to our roles in the company. All I care about is keeping this floor secure and *my* men alive. After I can handle that, then I might concern myself with your well-being. As for these other three, they are your problems. To me, they are already as good as dead."

"Understood. Eddie, pick that man up and get him out of the way." Hinderlight waited for Eddie to do as he was told before continuing to address Hafiz. "Give me a weapon so I can try and keep them safe."

Hafiz looked about to protest, but mumbled something and clicked open the holster on his thigh. "Do you know how to use one of these?" Hafiz asked as he pulled out the gun to hand it over to

Hinderlight.

"I served my country long before I signed up to work for Soladyne." As if to prove it, Hinderlight took the weapon and hefted it in his hand a few times. Then he ejected the magazine, felt the weight of that as well, and then slid it back into the gun. "Full automatic?"

"Semi." Hafiz replied. Was that a touch of respect finally lacing his voice? "Modified from the standard full automatic. Don't fire until I say so. If something nasty is coming up, Kaga–" He motioned toward the man with the tattooed arms "–will identify it first. That way, we'll know where to aim to cripple or kill. And not shoot it someplace that would just piss it off."

"Don't want a repeat of what happened in the Congo," Kaga replied, which got the others chuckling. Except for the one man that was fully decked out in armor. And Hafiz.

"This isn't the time to reminisce like old washed-up football stars," Hafiz barked. "Lock that shit down. Hale, Oshiro, flank on either side. Kaga, Jefferson, join me out front, but keep your distance until we know what we're dealing with."

The men moved without saying a word while Hafiz addressed Hinderlight one last time. "Keep your people back. My men will not hesitate to fire if one of the civilians gets in the way."

Hinderlight nodded. "Eddie, Lizzie. Get Hugh behind that crate right by the security door. I'll be ahead with Hafiz." He turned his attention to the security force leader. "If that is acceptable."

"Can you follow orders?"

"When they save lives."

"Good enough. Then you're with me."

Hinderlight followed Hafiz, Kaga, and Jefferson forward.

Hale and Oshiro disappeared into the shadows somewhere behind the crates.

Eddie picked up Hugh under the arm while Lizzie took the other. Together, they dragged him back behind a refrigerator-sized wooden crate. The metal security door slowly groaned shut. It let out a *clank* as it closed, followed by a series of loud clicks as locks slid into place. Sealing them in a room that seemed to shrink and grow darker by the second.

At the end of the center path, on the opposite side of the room, a pleasant *ding* rang out. All eyes jerked to the elevator. Eddie's breath caught in his throat as the doors slid apart.

CHAPTER 12

Darkness seemed to flow out of the oversized cargo elevator. Darkness and dread. It was more powerful than the fear he had felt while fleeing the Infected, as if every fear imaginable had been crushed together into the size of a golf ball and placed into the center of his heart. It made him want to sprint toward the security door screaming but his feet felt rooted to the floor.

"Exit the elevator with your hands raised!" Hafiz yelled, his gun pointed at the blackness inside the elevator.

No response.

"Last warning! Step out of the elevator. Now!"

A light inside of the elevator flickered for the briefest moment. What Eddie saw in that flicker froze his blood. A towering figure. Scorched skin. A single eye like a cyclops except off to the side.

"Kaga." There was a small quiver in Hafiz's voice now. "Do you have it identified?"

Silence.

"Kaga!"

"The Reaper, sir." Kaga sounded like he was handing out a death sentence. "A level 7E Horror."

"Shit." Hafiz readjusted his weapon against his shoulder. "Weaknesses?"

"None on record. It was only captured--"

The man fell silent as The Reaper stepped out of the elevator and into the light. Standing well over seven feet tall, more a monster than a man, with the requisite humanoid features of arms, legs, body, and head. Besides that, it looked straight out of a nightmare. Clothed only in dirty blue overalls covered in burnt patches, its feet were bare and covered in open cuts that oozed puss. Its thick arms looked as if they had been twisted a dozen times and then released, the skin a mess of ruts and grooves. A thick, heavily scarred neck supported a head that looked like the right half had been thrust into a fire. The skin black and rugged and in some places, burned straight through to the bone. The right eye was gone, the socket a mixture of still smoking skin and bone.

The left eye, iris as black and empty as the elevator behind it, flickered in every direction as it took in the men outside the elevator. What was left of the thing's mouth twisted up into a sickening grin.

"The legs!" Hafiz ordered.

Gunfire erupted in the room. The monster shook as bullets sank into its legs in small explosions of blood. After a dozen or so shots, it fell to its knees. All while not making a sound.

"Cease fire!"

The gunfire cut off. Eddie had put his hands over his ears without realizing it. He let them drop. Beside him, Lizzie had her hands over her mouth, her eyes wide and wet. Hugh was curled into a ball behind them.

Fear drifted about like a heavy mist that filled the room. Eddie couldn't see it, but he could *feel* it flowing out of the monster kneeling at the other end of the room. Its head and body were slumped forward, chest rising and falling as it took in deep, rasping breaths.

"Kaga." Hafiz voice was hoarse as if he were choking on smoke. "Give me something to work with. How did they capture it?"

"Ran it over with a tractor, sir."

"We don't have a tractor. Give me something I can work with."

When Kaga spoke again, he sounded defeated. "It's slow. Besides that, any attempt to study it has led to casualties before any useful information could be discovered."

A laugh filled the room, guttural and horrible, like the groans of dozens of tortured men and women mashed together. The Reaper lifted its head, that ugly grin that only touched the unburnt half of his mouth seeming to stretch its skin. It raised a football-sized fist into the air and smashed it into the ground.

Every light in the room went dark.

And was quickly replaced by the flashes of gun barrels as the loud *pop, pop, pop* of firing weapons filled the room.

Like a bad strobe light, the flashes only made the scene all the more horrible With each flash, Eddie watched as The Reaper started to move, blood as black as the darkness around it spurting out as bullets struck from the front and sides.

Flash.

The Reaper pushed itself up, one knee off the ground.

Flash.

It stood on both feet.

Flash.

It had turned to the left and took a step in that direction.

Flash.

It had moved behind one of the stacks of crates, disappearing from view.

The gunfire in front of Eddie stopped. Flashes still emanated from behind crates to the left and right of the elevator. Then the flashes to his right stopped.

A horrible scream filled the storage room then turned into a muffled yell a heartbeat later. A sickening crunch like a watermelon being flattened filled the room. A few moments later, there was a thud as something dropped to the ground.

Eddie couldn't move. His breath sounded like a hurricane in his own ears, Lizzie and Hugh's breaths sounded just as loud beside him. It had to hear them. Had to be coming for them. His dread painted pictures of what was in store for him. Thick hands grabbing his limbs, digging into his flesh, giant fingers wrapping around his face. Burnt skin smelling of rotten meat covering his mouth and nose. The pressure of his skull caving in under the force of the monster's fingers.

A hand grabbed Eddie's shoulder and he lashed out in a panic. He expected his fist to strike burnt flesh or a disfigured arm, but instead he felt the fine fabric of an expensive shirt.

"Move," Hinderlight whispered and pushed Eddie toward the side of the room. In the darkness, he could vaguely see Hugh and Lizzie moving next to him. They reached the corner of the room and crouched together. Hinderlight had his back to the corner and seemed to look in every direction at once.

"Hafiz and his men are welcome to die here, but we don't have to. We get to the cargo elevator. My card will get us down."

Heads nodded. Tense bodies turned to move but Hinderlight held them back.

On the wall behind them, a light flickered to life. It came from the other side of the glass that looked into the security room. For the briefest of moments, Eddie found comfort in the small amount of light that penetrated the thick glass and made it inside the storage room.

And then The Reaper stepped out from behind some crates and walked right up to the glass.

Hinderlight pushed him again, but Eddie's muscles had turned to mush. He stared at the monster, its burnt side facing him, perfectly lit as it stood inches from the window. Some of the unburnt skin of its cheek drooped down like melted wax, hanging loosely past its chin. It stared into the glass a moment longer, then brought up a fist and smashed it into the glass.

Eddie expected the glass to shatter under the massive blow, but it seemed to flex with the punch and return to its place. The creature struck again with the same result. A low growl escaped its damaged throat and it reared back and delivered a punch like a thunderclap that echoed around the room. And still the glass, or whatever stronger material the window was made of, held fast. The Reaper stood perfectly still staring through the glass, its great body heaving as it took in deep breaths. Then its head slowly turned to look at the thick security door.

A giant step and he was in front of it. Two hands engulfed the handle. The monster's arms bulged as it pulled. A grunt escaped The Reaper's mouth. The door groaned. A low buzz filled the room, like a single fly that's wandered too close to your ear. The buzz grew until it was loud enough to vibrate the crate next to where Eddie and his group were crouched in the corner.

The Reaper lit up, streaks of blue lightning arcing up his arms and flashing all over its body. Smoke poured out of its ears and the empty eye socket. Its whole body locked in place, arms extended as it leaned back and shook. Tiny flames lit up its overalls, and with a pop, its hands released the handle and it flew back against one of the crates. The wooden crate cracked as The Reaper fell on top of it. The smell of burnt flesh somehow mixed in and enhanced the feeling of dread that blanketed the room.

The Reaper righted itself, tiny bolts of electricity still flickering about its body.

Then it turned and looked directly at them.

It took a single step in their direction before the crack of a single shot, right above Eddie's head, broke him out of his stupor. The Reaper's head snapped back, the rest of its body following as it fell backward. The floor shuddered as its massive body crashed to the ground.

"Move!" Hinderlight yelled, and the roar of his voice got Eddie's muscles moving.

The four sprinted together as one, hugging the wall. Eddie swore he could feel the monster breathing down his neck. They got to the far corner and didn't stop, each person bouncing off the wall, crates, or each other as they rounded the corner. Eddie had somehow gotten out in front, his legs straining for even more speed as he expected The Reaper to step out from behind a stack of crates at any moment. The elevator opening loomed ahead of him, the light from the security office hitting the opening like a guiding light.

A body flew across his path from the right and disappeared as it passed into the elevator to his left. Eddie skidded to a halt. The others bumped into him but thankfully had slowed as well. They stood there, all staring at the lighted area, breaths coming fast.

The Reaper stepped out into the light in front of them. It let out another guttural laugh as it stared them down. The dread returned full force, filling Eddie's mind and pressing down on him like an invisible weight. Images of his own death, dozens of them at this monster's hands, filled his head and turned his limbs to mush. Lizzie fell to her knees mumbling something at his side. He heard Hugh begin to scream behind him. Hinderlight stepped forward, gun held high, his arm trembling.

Gunfire erupted, but not from the weapon in Hinderlight's hand. Bullets tore into The Reaper's side, almost bowling it over. It stumbled off to the side, dropping to one knee and raising a twisted arm to shield its head. No matter how many bullets hit it, the thing never went completely down. Eventually the *pop* of gunfire turned into a repeated clicking sound as the barrage of bullets came to a quick stop. At which point The Reaper slowly got to its feet, turned, and began walking toward the source of the gunfire.

Someone gave Eddie a push from behind. He didn't care who it was, Eddie had no desire to go anywhere near where that monstrosity had just been. That feeling of dread had latched onto his very soul, stripping it bare of everything but the overpowering desire to flee. The Reaper was not something a human mind was supposed to see, to comprehend even existed. Anyone that saw it was supposed to die. Flee. Hide. It was all just delaying the inevitable. It was best if Eddie just stood still and waited for--

Something struck his face so hard that his teeth seemed to rattle inside his mouth. Eddie's immediate thought, now that terror wasn't the only thing overwhelming his mind, was that Hinderlight had struck him. He reevaluated that idea as Lizzie slapped him again.

"Move," she whispered with more authority than he had ever heard from her.

Eddie got one foot in front of the other. It was still a struggle, but Lizzie had grabbed his arm and he found some strength from her touch. Together the group moved toward the last stack of crates before the elevator. They stayed huddled close together, drawing strength from each other's presence. Once they reached it, Hinderlight poked his head around the corner to take a look.

And jumped backward as another hail of gunfire was unleashed in their direction.

Over the loud pops of gunfire and pings of ricocheting bullets, Hafiz's voice roared louder than them all. "Just go down, you ugly son-of-a-bitch!"

The barrage of noise continued for a few moments more and then the click of an empty magazine was the only sound that filled the room. Hinderlight poked his head out again then practically thrust Hugh forward. Lizzie had Eddie's arm in her hand again and dragged him out from behind the crates. They hurried toward the elevator. Eddie couldn't help but look in the direction the gunfire originated. The Reaper was struggling to its feet, this second barrage of bullets seeming to have done a bit more damage. With the light of the office behind it, Eddie's eyes saw the monster as a huge shadow that leaked darkness onto the floor. Hafiz faced him, his assault rifle discarded, with what looked like a stun baton in his hand. At its tip, three sickly green lines encircled the black shaft.

Hafiz held the baton at the ready as the monster began a slow, steady gait toward the man. What he hoped to accomplish with the weapon when a hailstorm of bullets couldn't even keep the monster down was lost on Eddie. He silently mouthed the word *run* as Lizzie ushered him onto the elevator. All he could do was watch as the monster continued its slow approach. Light laughter, starting off like the buzzing of locusts grew to the volume of hail on a tin roof, emanated from The Reaper as it closed in on its prey.

Hafiz stood, with all the intensity of a mouse fending off a lion, his grim face lit by the baton in his hand, his head framed in the light coming from behind them.

Eddie's group made it into the elevator, everyone except Hinderlight who moved to the far wall. Even though the back of the elevator was riddled with bullet holes, the soldier who had been thrown, Kaga, seemed untouched by the hail of bullets. He was slumped against the wall. Turning his back on the fallen man, Eddie expected to find the elevator doors closing, blocking off the horror that occurred out in the storage room. Instead he found Hinderlight standing in the opening, his gun raised.

"Close the door, you fool!" Lizzie screamed.

Hinderlight's response was to fire two shots in rapid succession. The back of The Reaper's neck exploded in a dark red mist of blood and bone fragments. The monster immediately crumpled as its legs gave out under it. Unfortunately, only moments after it hit the ground, it was already moving again, flopping about as it tried to get back to its feet.

It was enough of a distraction for Hafiz. The man gave Hinderlight a quick salute, grabbed his discarded rifle, and sprinted to the side. Eddie quickly lost sight of the man behind the crates. It didn't much matter as his attention was on the laggard rise of the The Reaper.

The creature rose like a corpse from the grave and languidly spun around so that it was facing them. Terror slammed into the elevator like a tidal wave as its single good eye fixed in their direction. The Reaper took one slow step on a shaky leg toward them. The next step was more firm. It wasn't until the third step that Hinderlight moved to the side and slid his keycard through the reader on the wall and pressed the only button available to him.

Three long warning bells sounded in the elevator, drawn out long enough that the monster was able to take two steps in between each sound. By the time the two elevator doors started to slide shut, The Reaper was already halfway to them. And it was making better time than the doors.

"It's not closing fast enough," Lizzie yelled as she pressed herself so hard against the elevator wall she looked like she was trying to back right into it. "Do something!"

Hinderlight stepped back to the middle and emptied out what was remaining of his weapon, but his steady aim seemed to have abandoned him as their doom approached. Bullets thudded into The Reaper's chest and arms. It did nothing to impede its approach. It plowed on as the eventual click of an empty weapon signaled the end of their last line of defense. The elevator doors inched closer and closer together. Eddie tried to force them closed by sheer will but to no avail. The monster marched on. It might as well have been death itself, walking with slow, purposeful steps toward them. Even Hinderlight, their beacon of courage, had shrunk back away from the doorway.

The doors were halfway closed. The Reaper was two-thirds of the way there.

Whimpering. Crying. The sounds of a cough that came right before a person dry-heaved.

Only a space a bit wider than Hinderlight's body remained. The Reaper was steps away.

The stench of sweat. The coppery taste of blood inhaled through the nostrils that settled on the tongue. Eddie's senses seemed to heighten as if his mind knew these were the last sensations it would experience, as horrid as they were. Every breath he took felt like a gift.

The space between the doors grew smaller. The Reaper's mangled face came into focus as it looked between the closing doors to its victims on the other side.

A brief hope that the monster was too late.

A massive, scarred hand reached in, stopping the door from closing completely.

At first, Eddie thought the elevator doors would win out. The Reaper got a second hand in, though, and proved him wrong. As machinery ground and groaned in protest, the monster pushed and pulled the doors open until they were wide enough that its entire body could fit through. Eddie could see the entire beast, but what his eyes focused on was the rotten curl of its lips into a horrible grin that allowed black, jagged teeth to peak out.

The barrel of a gun appeared at the side of the monster's head. An explosion of sound ripped through the elevator as the gun fired point blank into the monster's head. Gore exploded into the cargo room and onto everyone inside the elevator. The Reaper's hands slid out from between the doors as it toppled over, its already mangled face now like rotten meat put through a grinder. The security guard in full armor, Jefferson, slid through the doors as they closed. Through the disappearing opening, Eddie caught a glimpse of The Reaper's feet twitching.

Then grow still.

Watched as one mutilated hand grasp a knee and pull itself up behind the door.

And then the doors clacked together. The elevator hummed to life as it began its slow descent.

The five people still conscious all let out sighs of relief.

In the back corner, Hugh doubled over and threw up.

CHAPTER 13

"I need to go back." Kaga's voice was weak, but it still had an air of someone that expected his orders to be followed without question.

The security officer had come to and seemed less than happy about not being murdered up on the security level above with the others in his squad. The rest of the group was spread around the wide elevator, although they all stayed away from the corner where Hugh had emptied his stomach. The smell of bile and blood filled the air, but Eddie would take that any day over the lingering feeling of dread that seemed to dissipate the further down the elevator traveled.

"Not happening," Hinderlight shook his head. "Unless you have a keycard that will get you back up, because you're not using mine."

"Hafiz is the only one with elevator access, and he would never run from his duty like a coward." The large man shot a look at Jefferson as he braced himself against the wall and slowly got to his feet.

"I'm not a coward for wanting to live," Jefferson fired back. "You know what that thing was. We weren't prepared to handle a Horror. We had no chance."

"The odds are *always* against us, rookie," Kaga growled. "But no one ever gets left behind. You've only been with us, what, a month? The rest of K Squad has been out in the real world, in the thick of it facing down and capturing creatures like that for years. You've spent a month pulling guard duty with us in the safety of the lab."

"Yeah, I felt *real* safe a few moments ago," Jefferson retorted.

"You shouldn't feel safe now either. When I'm done with you--"

"Enough!" Hinderlight roared. "Now isn't the time to fight among ourselves."

"Who the hell put you in charge?" Kaga turned his anger on Hinderlight.

"The company *you* work for, the ones that put me in charge of the entire North American division. Which includes you."

"I take orders from Hafiz, not some corporate suit."

"Bullshit."

Hinderlight moved until he was inches from the man's face. Physically, they looked like a perfect match, but after everything that had happened on the floor above, Eddie had an idea of Kaga's training. Hinderlight's past remained a mystery. If Eddie had been a betting man, as much as he liked Hinderlight, his money was on the tattooed security officer, despite his injuries. Considering the way Kaga's nostrils were flaring and his fists were curled at his side, it looked like they were about to find out.

"You want to write me up for insubordination?" Kaga's tone had gone flat. "Put a letter in my file? Go ahead. If you survive long enough to do it."

Hinderlight slammed a forearm into the man's chest, pinning him back against the wall. "I can do worse than put a letter in your file."

Kaga grunted and launched a quick punch into the other man's ribs. Hinderlight barely flinched. Instead, he retaliated by taking a quick step back, then swung his elbow into the tattooed man's temple. That blow did little other than cause Kaga's eyebrows to rise in surprise. It was the follow-up, right hook to the man's chin that toppled Kaga over to the side. He caught himself with one arm, but Hinderlight dropped another punch down across the man's face that brought him the rest of the way to the floor. A few fresh drops of blood joined the already drying bits as they dripped from Kaga's mouth. The tattooed man spit a few more out, then pushed himself back up into a sitting position.

After a moment, Hinderlight offered the fallen man his hand, but Kaga waved it off as he massaged his chin with his other hand. "You're faster than I expected."

"You're sturdier than I expected. Not often a person stays conscious after that combination."

"Happy to disappoint," Kaga paused for a few moments, then offered a blood-streaked smile. "Boss."

"So we're agreed on who is in charge?"

"For now. If we survive this, give me a few days to get back to one-hundred percent, then let's have another go."

"Fair enough." Hinderlight returned the man's smile as he backed up to give him room.

"Where was the help?" Kaga directed the question toward

Jefferson as he rose.

"I was too busy being a coward," the man replied. "Plus, I suppose I understand the chain of command much better than you."

"Asshole." Kaga rubbed his chest, but some of the anger had left his voice. "Alright, *Mr.* Hinderlight. Eventually this elevator is going to reach the main lobby of The Zoo. What do we do from there?"

"Simple. If all of you want to survive, then we have only one chance, *and* we will have to work together. Hafiz said that you lost communication with the main control center, correct?"

"Yes," Kaga replied. "They claimed it was a mechanical failure, but even when radio communications went dark, the general consensus was that someone had taken over The Zoo's control room."

"What if one of those monsters had just killed everyone?" Eddie asked. "Wouldn't that have disrupted everything?"

Kaga shook his head. "Even if a monster had rampaged through the room and destroyed every piece of machinery, walkie-talkies would still be able to send and receive signals and the PA system could have still been used for different locations. If everything is blocked, that means someone is doing the blocking."

"Which means," Hinderlight continued, "we need to regain control of The Zoo's central hub. If we control that, we control not only communications with everyone else in the facility, but also control communications with the outside world. As far as we know, no help is coming. Even if it did, the building is completely locked down and could only be opened to let in reinforcements from the control room. Am I correct?"

"Yes," Kaga replied.

"Then that's our plan. Kaga takes us to the control room, we take it back by force if necessary, lock it down, and call for backup."

Everything was progressing too fast for Eddie to comprehend. Why weren't the others asking the questions that popped up in his mind? He snatched one up and let it tumble from his lips. "Even if we make it to the control room, how could we take it back? We don't have any weapons left that I can see. What if we run into another one of those . . ."

"Horrors," Kaga replied. "The worst of the worst. Horrors are like the monsters and murderers from the worst horror movies.

Except they are real and hard, if not impossible, to kill."

Eddie felt what little security the elevator had provided drain away. "So basically, it would be insane to wander around The Zoo without more weapons."

Hinderlight looked down at his discarded gun and a little wind went out of his sails. Jefferson and Kaga both put hands to their hips and found empty holsters. Kaga didn't even have one of the stun batons strapped to his waist. Jefferson fingered the grip of his, but he seemed less than thrilled with the weapon.

"That might be a problem," Hinderlight said after a few moments more of silence. "Thank you, Eddie for pointing it out. I'm still a little worked up from my scuffle with Kaga. Got a little too gung-ho. We will need more weapons than we have. Any ideas?"

"There is a secondary armory in The Zoo." Kaga replied. "I don't have access to the floor it's on, but I can get us in once we are there."

"That seems foolish, making it difficult for the people that can effectively use the weapons to get to them," Lizzie mumbled.

"Protocols," Kaga let out a pained laugh. "Suits always have to have their rules and safety procedures, no matter how ass backward it is. Or how many times grunts like me file complaints."

"Well, I can get us there." Hinderlight was nodding to himself. "With two trained men and myself, properly armed, we could find a way to take back the control room even against a much larger force."

"I wouldn't mind getting some revenge on the bastards that set The Reaper loose on us," Jefferson said eagerly.

"Another question?" Eddie said, raising his hand then feeling all the more foolish for doing it.

Hinderlight let out a laugh, his overwhelming confidence returned. "Go ahead, Eddie. What else haven't we thought of?"

"What if we run into something like The Reaper once we get down there?"

"We run, of course." Eddie opened his mouth but Hinderlight raised both hands in a calming gesture. "Eddie, don't worry. I understand that my plan does not take into account a great deal of 'what-ifs'. What if those responsible for today are waiting for us when the elevator comes to a stop? What if they were foolish enough to unlock the whole facility and we're walking into a facility that would make even your worst nightmares look like your best wet dream? What if a dozen other possibilities exist that we're not even thinking of that lead to our painful and gruesome deaths?" He let out a chuckle that didn't take the sting from his words.

"These are things that we can't control. The fact that we've survived this long clearly shows that luck is on our side. Maybe we'll waltz right through the facility to the armory without running into a single problem. And maybe whoever was foolish enough to let something like The Reaper free ended up getting themselves killed and we'll stock up on weapons just to find the control room completely unguarded. Or maybe the elevator doors will open and we'll find what's left of the security force mopping up and restoring order."

"Not likely," Lizzie mumbled, but Hinderlight ignored her.

"What I'm saying is, it's good to have a plan. It's even better to know that once those elevator doors open, that plan might go to shit. But at least with a plan, when things do go to shit, we still have a goal to try to get back to instead of running around and guaranteeing we get ourselves killed."

The man made sense. Jefferson and Kaga seemed eager, small, tight smiles touching their lips as their eyes focused on the elevator doors. Lizzie looked less certain, biting her bottom lip as she glanced around the small compartment. When her eyes fell on Eddie, she gave him a confident smile which he returned. Eddie trusted Hinderlight's judgment, which meant if they were going to survive, they all had to work together. Since he had known Lizzie a hell of a lot longer than anyone else in the elevator, she was the best choice for convincing to get on board first. And if he was being honest, he could use the support of someone he had known for years just as much as he needed everyone to be on the same side.

At least he didn't feel as bad as Hugh looked. The man was an unhealthy shade of green, and Eddie hoped he didn't throw up anymore before they could get out of the tight confines of the elevator.

"All right then." Hinderlight's commanding voice interrupted Eddie's thoughts. "Since we don't know what to expect in the facility's lobby, Jefferson, Kaga, and I will take the lead. Assuming there isn't some horrible creature standing just outside the door ready to rip us to shreds, we'll fan out and get a lay of the area. Kaga, Jefferson, you've been on this floor before, correct?" They both nodded. "What can we expect?"

"The lobby is fairly open," Kaga replied. "Anything from personnel to high-level captures pass through on any given day. The higher-ups like to keep it clear and prevent cluttering the room in case something escapes and tries to hide. It also keeps the cones of fire from any direction unobstructed."

"And the layout."

"The room is a pentagon, with this elevator set into its base. The walls to the left and right have access doors to hallways and labs in either direction and loop back on each other. The two remaining walls across from this elevator have elevators that run straight down to the control area and the main containment floors and adjoining labs."

"How do we get to the armory?"

"Take the hallway to our immediate right. About a quarter of the way through the loop will be another set of elevators that go down to the security training gymnasium, medic area, and the secondary armory."

"So that's our first destination, then we loop back to the lobby and head down to the control room. Everybody understand?"

All around the room, heads nodded in agreement.

As if on cue, the elevator let out a series of spaced out *bongs* signaling their arrival.

"Here we go," Hinderlight said as Kaga and Jefferson moved to either side of him.

Hopefully, we are as lucky as Hinderlight thinks, Eddie thought as he readied himself for the worst.

CHAPTER 14

Eddie held his breath as the doors opened. Nothing happened. He continued to hold it as Hinderlight, Kaga, and Jefferson moved carefully out of the elevator into a dimly lit, open room. Nothing happened. His muscles tensed as Kaga and Jefferson moved out of view, each heading toward the two hallways that connected to the main lobby. Hinderlight turned into an indistinct blur the further into the room he moved.

Eddie expected yells, screams, roars. The men to come charging back into the elevator with something out of a horror movie right behind them.

Still, nothing.

When the two security personnel came back into view, Eddie let out his breath loud enough that Lizzie and Hugh both glanced at him. He stepped out to greet the returning men in an effort to hide his embarrassment.

"Nothing," Hinderlight said as he approached. "No blood. No bodies. Couldn't even find a scuff mark on any of the tiles." He scraped the sole of his shoe across the ocean colored tile floor and achieved the required result.

"Left hallway looks clear," Jefferson said.

Kaga shook his head as he joined the group. "Right is clear as well. Which makes no sense. How the hell did The Reaper get on the elevator all by himself? No way whoever is screwing with the facility guided him there without having a casualty or two of their own."

Hinderlight ran a hand through his raven-colored hair. Somehow it remained perfectly in place. "Any chance it got off the elevator from the holding facility and walked straight into ours?"

"Straight it could handle," Kaga replied, "but there's no way it could slide an access card and press the UP button. The Reaper's hands are made for one thing and one thing only—killing. They're simply not capable of that kind of dexterity."

"Another mystery then," Hinderlight shrugged then waved the others out of the elevator. "We won't find the answers standing around here. The right hallway is the quickest way to the armory, correct?" Kaga nodded. "Then let's go. The sooner I have a weapon in my hand, the better I'll feel."

At this point, Eddie didn't think even one of the assault rifles the members of Squad K had used would make him feel safer. He followed along, though, as the entire group left the elevator.

The main lobby was exactly as Kaga had described, a pentagon-shaped room which opened up to almost two stories high. The room was lit by the same emergency lighting as the rest of the building, slowly rotating red lights spaced evenly on the walls a good eight or nine feet off the ground. Above those, twice as many three-bulbed spotlights pointed in every direction. Their lenses were dark, although there was no way to tell whether that was because they shut off during an emergency or had been shut off from some other location. The tiles at his feet were an ocean-blue but took on a purplish tone from the emergency lights the further away they got, spreading out into a wide open room devoid of any furniture or decoration. Where the red lights had only increased the feeling of creepiness in other locations in the building, here, where there wasn't a single place for something to hide, the red haze was almost comforting.

Which meant, of course, that they were going to leave it and enter the tighter confines of a single hallway with closed doors that could be hiding dozens of psychopaths or monsters.

They passed through an open set of double doors into a hallway that was wider than Eddie had expected. Kaga, Hinderlight, and Jefferson took the lead, easily walking next to each other with space between them. A gray carpet spread out ahead of them, tinted red by the light, just like everything else in this cursed place. Solid doors lined both sides of the hallway, with keycard readers attached to the wall next to each one. About half way down the hall, Eddie could see a set of double doors sitting across from each other. Farther ahead, the hallway cut sharply to the left.

"Stick together," Hinderlight said as they started down the hall. "Keep an eye on each other and report *anything* out of the ordinary."

"Should we keep quiet?" Eddie asked.

"I wouldn't go screaming out our location." Hinderlight shrugged ahead of them. "But I don't think we have anything to worry about at the moment. This floor seems pretty dead."

"A poor choice of words." Jefferson turned slightly and glanced at Lizzie. "But a little chitchat might take off some of the edge. Might as well get to know each other."

Lizzie offered him a weak smile that disappeared as soon as the man returned his gaze forward. When she caught Eddie looking at her, she gave a more genuine smile and rolled her eyes.

"I'm less worried about all of you." Eddie tried to keep the annoyance out of his voice. "I'm more worried about what this place actually is for. What we might run into. I know it's all top-secret and hush-hush, but since we might be fighting for our lives at any moment, I think it would make sense for me to know what normally goes on down here."

Ahead, Kaga glanced at Hinderlight, who in turn gave a noncommittal shrug before speaking. "You know more than I do. And at this point, Eddie does have a point. We might be the last line of defense keeping this whole place from coming down around our ears. Might as well let the janitor, secretary, and office worker with a weak stomach in on some things at least. They've already seen some of its darkest secrets."

"You're the boss," Kaga said with a laugh. "It's not like they tell us grunts half the things that go on here, either, but I can probably answer a few questions. And if a higher-up gives the okay, any punishment for whatever I say will fall on him. I'm already in a great deal of trouble for bringing those three down here to begin with." He gestured over his shoulder with his thumb. "No point in worrying about whatever slap on the wrist from The Board is coming now. Ask away, Eddie. I'm as curious as you are to see just how much I *don't* know."

"Why the hell do you keep monsters like The Reaper here to begin with?" Eddie was surprised at the accusation that laced his tone.

Kaga paused, his head tilted to the side. "Because they exist."

Eddie was about to ask for more than that, but the tattooed man continued on his own. "Those things are out there in the world; monsters that defy our understanding of reality, The Reaper being one of the worst. It's classified as a 7E Horror, the 7E denoting a high-kill count and low intelligence."

"And the Horror part?"

"Not self-explanatory enough?" Kaga let out a bitter laugh. "Some egghead's sick joke. Basically, it means the thing can't be killed. You saw how much punishment it took, and we barely slowed it down. I've seen video of a Horror put through a wood chipper, reduced to nothing but a pulpy mess of shredded flesh and shards of bone. The poor fools sent to capture it had no idea it was a Horror, unfortunately. The monster was somehow fully formed an hour later and tore apart half of the squad before they were able to contain it."

"How could that be?" Eddie had never been much of a movie guy, but one of the foster homes he had lived in had them on all the time. Might have been the reason he wasn't there for more than a few weeks.

"No one knows. Probably why the company tries to capture and study them. Horrors follow the same patterns you see in every psychopath movie ever made, although it might be that horror movies were written based on them. I know some Horrors are supposedly older than even the written word. Horrors stalk and kill. Most like to torment their victims. And for whatever reason, they all seem to prefer mutilating women over men."

Eddie glanced at Lizzie, watched as the color drained from her face. "You don't have to scare Lizzie any more than she already is."

"You boys asked the question. I'm just telling you the unfiltered truth, as far as I know it. Besides, there are very strong security protocols put in place when any Horror is involved and brought back to The Zoo."

"They didn't keep that Reaper thing locked away," Hugh said. The man's head looked like it was on a swivel, his eyes glancing in every direction at once.

"Someone had to let it out. Besides, she doesn't need to worry about that one." Kaga's voice grew distant. "It's stuck up on Level One now . . ."

With the rest of his men, Eddie's thoughts filled in the rest.

"Listen, I'm sorry for what happened to your friends--" Eddie began but cut off as Kaga raised a hand.

"Hold up." They had just reached the first set of closed double doors. They were the only ones Eddie had seen so far that had small glass panes set into the metal. Kaga took position along the wall

106

next to the set on the right, while motioning Jefferson to do the same to the set on the left. When both men were in position, they popped their heads in front of the windows. Seeming satisfied, they stepped away from the wall in unison and motioned for the rest of the group to continue.

"Adjoining hallways." Kaga rolled his neck until there was an audible *crunch*. "Good ambush points."

They walked on in silence, the conversation at an apparent conclusion. Eddie glanced at each door they passed. Kaga might have worried about intersecting hallways, but Eddie pictured all manners of monsters ripping through the single doors as they passed and pouncing on him before he could get out a scream. The silence didn't help either so he tried to start up the conversation again.

"How many monsters does this place hold?"

"No idea." Kaga glanced back at him for the briefest moment before returning his attention ahead. "And honestly, I don't want to know. The ones K Squad has brought in give me enough nightmares. I don't need to see pictures and descriptions of everything that they keep locked away down here."

"There are that many?"

"Horrors? No, thank God. But there are plenty of other things out in the world that are only slightly less dangerous. I've seen things out of folktales and urban legends that have made me believe that any story you might think was made up could actually be true."

"No way." Hugh was vehemently shaking his head. "If that were true, the whole world would know about them."

That earned a chuckle from both Kaga and Jefferson, but it was Hinderlight who spoke.

"The world does know. Monsters are reported in tabloids, over-sensationalized so that the stories sound impossible and the witnesses look like backwater jackasses. I know that much, at least."

"Exactly," Kaga continued. "And Horrors are hidden behind tales of your average, deranged serial killers. No one questions it when you say a single psycho caught a group of campers unaware in the woods or the story that a lone gunman massacred an entire movie theater of people. Most just look at it as a chance to push their own political agenda and don't even focus on the people who lost their lives or the cause behind it."

"I still can't believe the truth doesn't get out."

"Then don't, I don't give a fuck." The tattooed man waved him off. "If we get out of here, feel free to go spreading around everything you saw in here. They'll toss your ass into an asylum nice and quick, and if you keep making a stink, the company will send a Red Suit to deal with you."

"That's the second time these Red Suits have been mentioned." Again Eddie pictured jolly men with ivory white beards. "Who--"

"Ok," Hinderlight cut in. "I think we've talked enough about things that go bump in the night."

"You're the boss," Kaga said with a shrug. They had almost reached the turn and the security officers moved ahead and took positions at the corner. Jefferson took the lead, stun baton in hand, his back pressed against the wall. He poked his head around the corner and Eddie could feel the tension build in the group. It deflated as soon as Jefferson stepped out into the hallway and waved them forward.

"It's so quiet down here," Lizzie whispered next to him. Her voice was tense but she offered him a tentative smile.

"I can handle this type of dead." Eddie replied, trying to sound more confident than he felt. "I prefer empty and quiet over fungus-infected drones or unstoppable killing machines."

"Agreed. And don't forget overgrown, invisible bats."

"How could I?" he said with a chuckle of his own.

It felt good to laugh alongside an attractive woman and make light of such a horrible situation. Took the edge off of the tension that had tightened his muscles and strained his mind ever since Miss Toner's attack. As strange as it seemed, being put in this life or death situation seemed to have lessened Eddie's social awkwardness enough that speaking to Lizzie wasn't torture on his nerves as it had been the past few years. If only his life had been threatened multiple times sooner.

Eddie Watson's Rule Number 5: Life throws you the strangest curveballs when you're just trying to be a spectator at the game.

Not wanting the conversation to lull and enjoying his newfound sociability, Eddie pushed on. "All of this certainly wasn't anywhere in our job descriptions."

"Oh really? You didn't have a few pages in your contract about possible mutilation or digestion?"

"No, I guess they don't worry about that with a simple janitor."

She flashed a smile. "I really don't think you're that simple of a man, Eddie Watson."

He felt the blood rush to his cheeks and he let out a small laugh as he turned his gaze ahead. When he saw Hinderlight glancing back at him, a grin touching his lips, he felt the heat in his face double. It was almost a relief when Kaga spoke, allowing him to ignore the mix of happiness and awkwardness he felt.

"We're here," Kaga said.

They had reached a section of the hallway that opened into a sitting area in front of a pair of chrome elevator doors. Cushioned seats sat in the corners and a tall lamp rested behind each. Eddie had expected to see some kind of information board to give a title to the floor and list the floors where the elevator traveled, but the walls were bare. Besides the up and down arrows resting above each door and the familiar card reader in between the doors themselves, there was no other indication of where the elevators went.

"Need your card, bossman." Kaga moved out of the way and made a sweeping gesture toward the doors. "They don't let us grunts go anywhere unsupervised."

Hinderlight let out a noise that sounded somewhere between a laugh and a huff as he approached the card reader. Right beside him, Jefferson moved to his left, hefting the stun baton. He took a defensive posture, his knees bent and the weapon held out at the ready. As soon as Hinderlight slid his card through, the light above the elevator on the right lit up and the door slid open. Jefferson moved in front of it, gave an all clear sign, then stepped aside. The rest of the group piled in, with Jefferson and Hinderlight coming in last.

Eddie expected the elevator control panel to have some complicated array of buttons and screens, but it was the complete opposite. Four different-colored buttons sat along an otherwise blank panel next to the door. He watched as Hinderlight glanced at it, then Eddie raised an eyebrow at the two security men.

"Most places down here aren't labeled," Kaga replied with a smirk. "If you don't know where you are going, the upper management doesn't want you getting there."

"Is this whole place really built to be that secretive?" Hugh asked.

"How would I know?" Kaga replied. "This is the only floor I've been granted access to. Security and capture teams are separate groups from the containment teams that work on the lab levels."

Hinderlight pressed the green button and the doors slid closed. The elevator hummed to life and Eddie felt the shift as they started descending further into the complex.

"My guess is," Kaga continued, "that the majority of the containment team is dead. Which means, the labs are in the hands of whoever took over The Zoo."

Whatever good feelings Eddie had managed to scrape together during his conversation with Lizzie evaporated as the elevator traveled further and further below the earth.

CHAPER 15

A soft bell was the only sound of warning they received as the elevator crawled to a stop. Every time Eddie moved lower and lower into the facility, he wondered if this was how Dante felt as he moved deeper and deeper into hell.

"Lasciate ogne speranza, voi ch'entrate," Eddie quipped, trying to lighten the mood.

"What's that supposed to mean?" Jefferson asked.

"Abandon all hope, ye who enter."

Everybody in the elevator turned to give Eddie an annoyed glare.

"Sorry," he apologized. "Humor is not my strong point."

"Obviously," Hinderlight grunted.

The doors slid open. Kaga and Jefferson moved out of the elevator like a vice team entering the lair of a drug lord.

A large glass window took up most of the wall on the far side of the room, starting waist high and stretching to the ceiling. The floor of the room was a solid piece of concrete with a single drain in the center of the room. Besides that, the floor was bare. The glass against the far wall was flanked by two thick metal doors, both wide open. On the other side of the glass, there appeared to be a number of monitors. Once Kaga and Jefferson seemed content with what they found, they motioned for the others to step out.

"What are those?" Eddie asked, motioning toward the rows of holes that lined the walls to the left and right. They started at knee height and were spread out at even intervals, maybe three or four feet apart, running from one side of the wall to the other.

"Automated gun turrets," Kaga replied.

"All of them?"

"Can't take any chances when this floor houses the bulk of the weapons used by the different security teams. The turrets in the walls will turn anything in this kill box into a mass of ground meat. Then the cleaning crew," he waved at Eddie," janitors like yourself, bag the chunky bits and hose the rest of the mess down into that grate."

Eddie moved toward the center of the room, his stomach turning queasy at the thought of all of those holes pointing gun barrels at him. Looking closer, Eddie could see dried red flakes around the edges of the drain. He shuddered and glanced back at the safety of the elevator.

Kaga looked at him with an amused grin. "Not to worry. I've only heard of one or two occasions where the system accidentally fired on innocent people."

Eddie took a step toward the elevator, feeling only slightly less foolish as he noticed both Hugh and Lizzie do the same.

"Stop it, Kaga," Hinderlight commanded. "They're scared enough as it is."

"The janitor got to spout some nonsense in a foreign language," Kaga said with a not-too-friendly laugh. "We security folks might not be as educated as some of you, but we have our own brand of humor. Besides, those two have been focused on flirting more than they have on being afraid."

"It's not like that," Eddie got out before his nerves silenced him. A quick glance at Lizzie found the woman looking at the ground. The beginning of a smile danced at the edges of her lips.

"I don't care about any of this," Hugh said as he moved toward the door on the right of the glass window. "*I'll* feel better once we're out of this room."

"Not that way," Jefferson said before the other man reached the door. "That leads to the training grounds and med-bay. The armory is through the door to the left."

"Whatever."

Without stopping, Hugh made a sharp turn and moved to the other door. After a quick glance at the walls and the death they held, Eddie followed after him. Before he reached the door, Lizzie was at his side. She offered him a friendly smile as they both passed through into the hallway on the other side. The rest of the group followed close behind. Hugh was standing next to a door on the right wall waiting for them.

"Is it in here?"

"Nope," Kaga replied, walking right past him. "That door goes into the security room you saw through the glass. The armory is further on ahead."

They passed single doors on their left and right. Kaga didn't seem to pay them any mind, so Eddie didn't bother either. The tattooed man seemed more at home on this floor. If the tightly wound security officer let himself relax, then Eddie should feel a bit safer as well. Hinderlight and Jefferson didn't seem to share Kaga's more relaxed attitude and constantly glanced at each door and behind them as they moved down the hall. When the monotony of single doors was finally interrupted by a set of double doors, Kaga made them pause.

"Break room," he said, gesturing with one hand. "Has a small kitchen, tables to eat at, a few cots to catch a quick nap, and most importantly, a fridge constantly stocked with food. I don't know about the rest of you, but I could use a little grub while we're here. What do you think, *Mr. Hinderlight*."

"We should push on to the armory first," Hinderlight began, but paused as his eyes ran over his beleaguered group. "On second thought, a quick trip to raid the break room fridge would be a good idea. No idea what we'll face next. Just enough time, mind you, to put down a quick snack and get some water. Then we're moving again."

"Sounds good to me," Kaga replied with a smile. He pushed open one of the double doors and immediately took a step back.

"Shit," he mumbled as the door swung closed.

"What is it?" Hinderlight asked, the tension in his voice mirroring the same feeling that moved through Eddie's entire body.

"Lost my appetite." Kaga replied, his eyes still on the closed doors. "Best not to go in there if you want to keep down whatever you had for breakfast."

"It's a little late to protect any sensitive stomachs. Open up the doors. I need to know everything that happened down here."

"If you say so. Jefferson?"

Once Jefferson was at his side, both men gripped the handle of the door and pushed it open. Before Eddie could even look inside his nose was assaulted with the coppery smell that had already touched his nostrils multiple times today. Lizzie's gasp and Hugh's rumbling stomach only affirmed what he expected to see inside.

The break room was a mess, plates and cups scattered and broken about the floor, tables overturned, the cots Kaga had mentioned flipped over. And it was all splattered with blood. It took

Eddie a few minutes but he eventually found the source of the red stains that covered the room. A corpse was partially stuffed into the fridge. Its head was hidden behind the door, while the rest of the body slumped in a kneeling position on the floor with multiple slashes across its back. A second body lay in the center of the scattered cots, a socked foot poking out of the green fabric of the overturned beds.

What was worse, along one empty portion of the wall, a message was written in blood.

> *Humans tried to chain me, poke, prod, and degrade me. Now different humans have set me free. So I'll paint the walls with the blood of my former captors with glee!*
> *- J*

"What kind of a sick person would do that?" Lizzie stared at the message on the wall as if it was written specifically for her.

"Probably not a person," Kaga replied. His silence let Eddie paint pictures of what other monsters could have done this.

"Close it off," Hinderlight said in disgust as he returned to the hallway.

"I warned him," Kaga muttered as the rest of them moved back out of the room. The man moved further in and pulled an extension cord out of one of the electrical outlets. Returning to the hallway with the rest of them, he closed both doors and used the cord to tie them together.

"We've started to relax," Hinderlight addressed the group after Kaga had finished. "A mistake that could cost us our lives. From this point on, we approach every door as if a monster is waiting for us on the other side."

He waited until the rest of the group all nodded in unison. "Kaga and I will take the lead. Jefferson, I want you at the back of the group. No more rushing ahead." He paused long enough to send a meaningful glare toward Hugh. "Got it?"

Hugh wilted under Hinderlight's stern gaze, his voice the barest whisper as he agreed with the rest of the group.

Hinderlight glared for a couple seconds longer before returning his gaze to the rest of the group. "Let's go."

The group stayed closer together as they moved down the hall. At each door they approached, Kaga and Hinderlight moved to either side, rattled the handle to make sure it was locked, then made the group wait a few more moments. When nothing burst out, the group continued on. They traversed what was left of the hallway until they reached a large metal door twice the width of the other ones on the floor.

"This is it," Kaga said, moving to the side. "The fact that it is shut is a good sign. Get us in, Mr. Hinderlight."

A quick swipe of his card and a hiss escaped the door that made everyone jump back. Images of a massive snake slithered through Eddie's mind as he readied himself for what lay on the other side.

"It's just the room opening," Jefferson nodded toward the door as it swung languidly inward. "Hermetically sealed. Lots of ammunition and explosives inside."

Everyone gave a nervous chuckle but then quickly stifled it. Their faces returned to the same taut expressions, eyes darting anxiously to and fro as if their laughter had been the *dong* of a great bell, giving away their location to the enemy.

The room on the other side of the door reminded Eddie of a library, the way the metal shelves created corridors just wide enough for a person to walk comfortably between. There seemed to be no rhyme or reason to how the shelves were stocked. Handguns, rifles, ammunition, and dozens of other items Eddie couldn't identify, all squished together, as if whoever stocked the room just shoved the inventory wherever there was an open space. The custodian in him wanted to go around and catalog the items and come up with an organizational system. The rest of his mind kept screaming at him to be on his guard.

"Don't touch anything," Kaga ordered, all of the sarcasm gone from his voice. He moved into the room and paused until the other security member moved to his side. "Jefferson and I will make sure the room is clear and then figure out what weapons you civilians can handle."

"You still think one of them is working with whoever is behind what's going on here?" Hinderlight asked.

"That I don't know. What I *do* know is that I don't want one of them accidentally shooting me in the back of the head."

Kaga and Jefferson fanned out into the room. After a few tense moments of them disappearing into the maze of munitions, they both returned with new assault rifles in their hands, looking more relaxed.

"Room is clear," Kaga replied.

"And defensible," Jefferson added. "We could just set up here. Wait for--"

"You shit-eating coward." Kaga turned on the man, his face twisted in rage. "We don't just sit back and let someone else do our job."

"Our job was protecting Level One. We've already failed at that."

"Don't include me in *your* failure. I was unconscious. You knowingly abandoned your post."

"I saved these people's lives."

"You saved your own. They just happened to be on the elevator that you wanted to use to escape." Kaga jammed a finger into the other man's armored chest. "You've been a skittish little mouse ever since joining our squad."

"Watch who you're poking," Jefferson swatted the other man's hand away. "If you want me to show you that I'm not a mouse, put that gun down. We can settle this right now."

"Both of you are not settling anything," Hinderlight said, stepping in between them. "If you've already forgotten, there *is* something more dangerous than the two of you on this floor. Instead of beating each other up, how about you arm the rest of us and we get out of here."

The two men stared at each other from either side of Hinderlight, which took some effort since he stood at least a foot taller than Jefferson. When neither moved, Hinderlight closed both hands into fists, squeezing them tight enough that Eddie heard the knuckles crack. It was enough to get Kaga to drop his gaze and grunt in disgust.

"Just remember, I don't trust you, coward."

"Likewise."

Kaga let out a huff then turned his ire on Eddie. "You. Any experience with a weapon, ballistic or blade?"

"No," he stuttered, then tried to stand a bit straighter. "I'm a fast learner, though."

"Sure you are." Kaga grabbed a small handgun off the nearest shelf. "Point the nozzle at what you want to hurt and pull the trigger. This holds twelve rounds." He grabbed a magazine and slid it into the handle. "Magazine goes in like this, and unlocks and ejects by pressing here. Take two more magazines from the shelves. Makes sure they are the same and practice loading and unloading the weapon."

Kaga held the weapon out. When Eddie grabbed it, though, the man held on.

"The safety is on," Kaga said, his eyes boring into Eddie's skull. "Keep it on while you get used to the weapon."

"Yes, of course."

Kaga held his gaze for a moment longer then released it and the weapon. "Girl! You're next."

While Kaga turned his attention to Lizzie, Eddie went through the motions of loading and unloading the weapon. After a few slip-ups and a dropped magazine, Eddie got the hang of it. He hefted the gun a few times in his hand, getting a feel for the weight of it. It was lighter than a full jug of bleach, so he figured he could handle carrying it around. Two more magazines fit nicely into his pockets and he was ready to go. He waited as Lizzie and Hugh got a handgun of their own, with the same amount of scorn from Kaga. To his surprise, Hinderlight also grabbed a large combat knife, which he left in its sheath and tucked behind his belt. Kaga and Jefferson pulled a few more things off the shelves that Eddie couldn't identify, handed each of them a pocket-sized flashlight then ushered them back out the door, Kaga pulling it shut behind him.

"Don't want our enemies to have access to all that firepower if we can help it," he said as they gathered right outside the room. "Unless the assholes that are helping them have high enough access to get in, too. In which case we're properly fucked."

Hinderlight shrugged as the man looked at him. "No idea. They very well might."

"Well, here is to hoping they don't. Back to the elevator then so we can continue *your* plan."

The group moved back down the hall, the security officers performing spot checks of every door just as they had on the way up. Lizzie sidled up next to Eddie after a few paces and caught his eye. He read worry in the small squint of her eyes and he thought he knew why.

Something just didn't feel right. Where was the monster that murdered the two guards? Was it hiding down the other hallway? Were there other survivors down that other hallway, trying to keep it from getting to them? Shouldn't their group be looking for more survivors? After all, the more people they had, the better their chances. His mind raced while his stomach churned.

They made it back to the security room without incident, Kaga and Jefferson entering with guns at the ready. The two seemed to have found their confidence again with their new weapons. Hinderlight followed behind them, gun held at his waist. He seemed as cautious as everyone else and Eddie wondered if the man had the same bad feeling as he did. Maybe he could convince Hinderlight to get the security officers to search the rest of the floor for survivors before they left.

As they entered the room, Eddie's eyes panned over to the entrance on the other side of the wall, his mouth open to ask about searching the rest of the floor. Except the door was now closed. As was the elevator.

"Wait," Eddie tried to get out as the others entered the room.

"Welcome, welcome!" a muffled, high-pitched voice announced over a speaker just as the other door slammed closed behind them. "Time to have some fun!"

CHAPTER 16

"What the hell." Kaga spun, the barrel of his gun passing by each of them. Eddie stepped in front of Lizzie, not sure exactly what he could do but feeling the desire to protect her all the same.

"Oh God." Hugh was backing toward the elevator. "What the hell is that?"

An abnormally thin man, donning a white marble mask with slit eyes, an upward pointing nose, and a grin that crossed almost from one side to the other, squatted on top of a security desk behind the glass. His ragged ensemble included a dark crimson tunic, red and gold striped balloon breeches like a court jester might have worn during the Renaissance era. His red jacket cinched at the waist, but the brown leather shoulder armor gave it a more masculine look. The outfit was topped by a strange cap the color of tarnished copper with two points that flipped back like ears. Shoulder length auburn hair spilled out the back, looking every bit as dirty and worn as the man's clothes.

"New friends!" His voice echoed about the room, coming from speakers that Eddie couldn't see. "Five, as far as I can see. Come to play and provide some entertainment for me."

"Kaga," Jefferson said, raising his rifle. "What is that?"

"The Jester," Kaga replied, without looking at his wrist PDA. "A class 4A Horror."

"I remember you!" The Jester rolled sideways, doing a half cartwheel and ending in a handstand. "The man with the tattooed arms. You and your companions shocked poor Jester and made him twitch and shake. Then men in white coats did things worse to poor Jester. Made him suffer and quake."

The Jester's mask changed, the eyes slanting down and the mouth twisting so it looked like it was crying out. It wasn't a gradual change. One moment the mask looked happy, and then it took on a sad look. It was haunting how the mask seemed alive and dead all at the same time. Eddie shivered despite himself and gripped his weapon tighter.

Kaga seemed unaffected by the creature's strange visage. "I remember you, too. Why don't you come out here so we can get reacquainted."

The Jester's mask shifted back to its smiling face. "Why would I do that? Fighting is no fun. We have a chance to play some games. Enjoyment for--"

"Enough of your stupid rhyming," Jefferson cut in.

"You're no fun." The Jester rolled back to a sitting position, his legs folded beneath him. "But if you wish it. Still plenty of entertainment for me to have without being clever with my words. Games, games, and more games."

Hinderlight turned his back on the window. "Or we could just leave."

With purposeful steps, Hinderlight marched over to the elevator and slid his card through the reader. Nothing happened. He tried again with the same results.

"I don't understand," Hinderlight said, sliding the card again. "Why isn't this working? It couldn't have locked me out, could it?"

"Rude to keep calling this one an *it*." The Jester's face shift again, this time both the tiny eye slits and the lips pressed tightly together. "Doubly rude to keep trying to leave. Especially since someone taught Jester how to prevent that."

Rolling backward, The Jester disappeared behind the desks. Eddie watched, waiting for it to return. He heard some movement, and then something popped up. Some*one*. A man, his face pale and covered in small cuts from the top of his bald head down to the day-old stubble on his chin. His simple pleated gray shirt made it difficult to determine what the man's role was in this part of the facility, but at the moment it didn't matter. By his quivering lip and wide, strained eyes, he was clearly in distress.

The Jester peaked out from behind the man's back. "Meet Stan. Stan played with me and lost, but he had so much to say that I decided to keep him around. Showed me what buttons did what. Like this."

The Jester reached around the man and pressed a button on the console in front of him. Lights began flashing inside the room Eddie and his group were in. A loud alarm made everyone press their hands to their ears. By the looks of fear plastered across Kaga's and Jefferson's faces, Eddie could assume what was about to come next. His body tensed as he prepared for the worst.

"Get down!" he yelled, pulling Lizzie to the floor with him. The other civilians followed suit, but Kaga and Jefferson turned their weapons on the glass. The roar of gunfire drowned out the alarm. From his spot prone on the ground, all Eddie could see were shell casings clattering onto the concrete floor. He put a protective arm over Lizzie as the *ratt-tatt* of the guns and the blare of the alarm filled his skull. It seemed to go on forever, the sounds ripping into his ears. Rattling his bones. Battering against his mind. And over it all, the expectation that any minute, the gun emplacements in the wall would open up, filling the room with death.

But the pain of hundreds of bullets tearing into him never came. The gunfire ceased. Then the alarm and flashing light. Eddie glanced up and found Kaga and Jefferson, guns still aimed at the unblemished glass window, their entire bodies shaking. A moment later, when the ringing in his ears was just starting to lessen, The Jester's voice came over the speaker again.

"Well, that was exciting!" It let out a blood-curdling laugh. "So now we understand the rules. Stan here taught me what lovely buttons to push to get my way. Those weapons which give you so much confidence can't touch me in here. You either play my games and *maybe* die, or you refuse to play and I press a button and you absolutely die. Any questions?"

No one responded. Eddie stood and helped Lizzie back to her feet.

"Jester takes your silence as acceptance." It pushed Stan behind him, the man stumbling back out of sight. "Three games we will play, survive all three and you can go free." It raised its hands in apology. "And the rhyming will be kept to a minimum so that poor Kaga does not throw a tantrum. After all, Jester is reasonable."

"First game! Something to get the blood flowing . . . on the inside." It paused to giggle. "A simple trick. A human pyramid, easy enough to do with six people. Three on bottom, a row of two, and our pretty young lady, a rose among the thorns, as its peak."

"That's it?" Jefferson asked. "We just make a pyramid like a bunch of cheerleaders? No hidden catch?"

"Nope. No catching involved at all. Just a little exercise for you and something for me to laugh at. I want to see Kaga down on his hands and knees, it will be practice for when we have some alone time later." It paused to chuckle. "Unless of course, you don't play the game. If that is the case, there won't be a later."

"We'll play," Kaga growled. He moved to the center of the room and waved the others over before getting on the ground. "Come on, let's get this over with."

If you ignored their current situation, Eddie was quite proud of the pyramid they created. He and Hinderlight joined Kaga on the ground as the bottom layer. Hugh and Jefferson took the middle, and Lizzie was the peak. It only took them a few moments to erect their pyramid, but The Jester made them hold it for quite some time before releasing them. Eddie was proud to say his arms didn't wobble once while he helped hold the others up.

"Well done!" The Jester gave two distinct claps before continuing. "But no time for rest. Onto game number two. A guessing game, except I'm doing the guessing. Jester gets three tries to figure out your deepest and darkest fears.

"That's not a game," Kaga said, disgust filling his voice as he approached the window. "I'm familiar with your case file. One of your *gifts* is the ability to read what scares a person the most. You are guaranteed to win this, which doesn't make it much of a game."

The Jester made a *tssk*-ing sound before he replied. "You think you know so much, when you only know fragments of what is real. All of your white-coated men probing and prodding poor Jester." His voice changed as fast as his mask. It looked like it was shouting in rage as the words that came out of it barely contained the anger in its tone. "Jester will dig into the white-coats. Will twist their organs and return the pain done to me a hundred-fold . . ."

It trailed off, its hands rubbing its arms as if lost in the memory. Eddie couldn't be sure, but he thought he saw it shudder. He took a step in its direction, trying to get a better look when the mask shifted again, returning to its look of gaiety.

"But that is fun for later," it continued. "Fun to be enjoyed after we finish playing."

"Playing an unfair game," Kaga replied again.

"Not unfair. Jester is not a mind reader. Truths and lies are as obvious as day and night to Jester, this is true, but a person's fear is like finding your way during a foggy day. Sometimes right, sometimes wrong, the guessing at what can be seen is the fun."

Eddie didn't have any rules for dealing with psychopaths, but he realized if he survived the day, he would have to add quite a few. And he wanted to survive. Wanted *everyone* to survive. "So you have to get all six of us wrong? That doesn't seem likely."

The Jester's mask switched to a smirk. "This one thanks you for the vote of confidence! Such a nice man, but you are right. The chances of that are as slim as what lies between Kaga's legs. Games are no fun if they are not fair, Mr . . . ."

"Eddie."

"Mr. Eddie, what a strange last name."

"It's my first."

"Oh, so informal. Are we friends now, Eddie?" It waved a dismissive hand. "No, best not to be friends yet. I don't want to get attached. It will make your death a sad affair."

The mask switched to a weeping face for a moment then switched back to its happy facade. "As I was saying, the game has to be fair. If I get three or more wrong, I lose. Which is magnanimous of me, I must say."

"And if you win?" Hinderlight asked.

"Simple. I get to kill the ones I guessed correctly and then we move on to our final game."

"Right," Lizzie mumbled at Eddie's side. "Simple."

"Any other questions?" The Jester asked, its mask turning into an inquisitive look. "Then let us begin. I'll start with the smaller of the two men dressed so tight and proper. He wears his fear like a second skin and will be the easiest for The Jester to guess. Step forward and give your name."

"Hugh Reed."

"Boring name for a boring man who probably has a boring fear. Let me take a look at you." The Jester put its mask right up against the glass. It continued to look at him for a moment more, then let out a frustrated sigh. "As I expected. Boring. Bees. A grown man afraid of bees. I don't even need you to acknowledge I'm right, just step back, Hugh Reed."

Hugh did as he was told, his downcast eyes and heavy steps making it clear the monster had guessed correctly. "I'm allergic," he mumbled as he shuffled toward one of the far corners.

"LIAR," The Jester screamed through the speaker. Its mask

mirrored the intensity of its voice. "Do not try to lessen your fear with excuses! It is an insult to the emotion! I ought to end your miserable life right now . . ."

As it raised a gloved hand over the console at its side, Eddie surprised himself by stepping forward.

"That's one point for you," he said, the words rushing out of his mouth. As insane as the creature on the other side of the glass seemed to be, it seemed willing to reason. If Eddie was skilled at anything besides cleaning an office, it was his ability to reason things through to his benefit. "But you have a long way to go to win. Don't ruin the game by throwing a tantrum of your own."

Its hand hovered over the console a moment longer, then it turned its wrist over and shrugged. "You are too right, man known as Eddie. Almost ruined things. Forgive my temper."

The Jester actually bowed its head in apology. Leaving Eddie dumbfounded.

"Um, no problem?"

His response elicited a laugh from the creature. "Good, then we are back to almost friends. Should I try you next?" The Jester shook its head. "No, I'll save you for later. I think I want to try my old acquaintance, Kaga, next."

"Feel free, clown." Kaga placed his weapon on the floor and approached the glass. "I'm not afraid of you, that's for sure."

"Perhaps. Let's see what I remember of friendly Kaga. I would guess you don't fear electricity?" The mask took on a blank expression for a few moments, then returned to its inquisitive expression. "You certainly didn't fear it as your team tried to shock poor Jester into submission."

"No, I don't fear it. And I enjoyed hearing about that." Kaga crossed his arms across his chest and smirked. "*And* that counts as your first guess. You asked it in the form of a question."

"Clever." Its tone disagreed with the statement. "A shame you didn't use that same intellect to NOT get stuck in a pillbox by someone you shocked into a drooling mess."

"Some*thing*," Kaga fired back. "Just because you look like a human being doesn't make you one. You are just some horrible creature that enjoys killing helpless people!"

The Jester leaped to its feet, clapping happily as it spun in a slow circle. "There it is! There it is!"

"What are you blabbering about?" The sudden shift seemed to catch Kaga off guard, his voice a mixture of anger and confusion. "There what is?"

"What you are afraid of, of course. Anger is often caused by fear, and I could see the picture of both clear around you as you worked yourself up." The Jester stopped moving and squatted, resting its elbows on its knees. "You don't fear something like me. What you really fear is something like me getting a hold of your family. Burning, drowning, or flaying them like you've seen done to countless, nameless victims in the past." Its mask twisted into an ugly sneer. "You have a wife and a daughter, if I'm not mistaken."

"YOU DON'T EVER TALK ABOUT THEM!"

Eddie could only watch as Kaga charged the window. He pounded his fists against the glass, each blow sending a hollow thud around the room. Jefferson moved to restrain him and caught an unintentional elbow to the eye for his trouble. Hinderlight had better luck, getting behind the man and slipping him into a full Nelson hold. Kaga struggled against him, but Hinderlight got him back. When the huge man finally relaxed, Hinderlight let him go. The administrator's wound must have opened again as the bloodstain on his shirt looked damp. Eddie glanced around, saw the shock written on the others' faces. All the while, The Jester stood at the glass and smiled.

"Not to worry, Kaga," it said after the commotion had calmed down. "Jester doesn't take revenge on the families of those that were behind this one's hurt and humiliation. All of the pain and torture are saved for you."

"Whatever, you sick fuck," Kaga grunted. He turned his back on the glass, grabbed his discarded rifle, and marched into the opposite corner from Hugh. Once there, he sat and began fiddling with the weapon while mumbling to himself.

"Poor loser," The Jester sighed, its mask mirroring the sound. "Another point for Jester. Two to zero. Not a good start for your little group."

"Why don't you give me a try," Hinderlight strode right up to the window. "The name is Joseph Hinderlight, and I know exactly what wakes me up in the middle of the night in a cold sweat. What haunts--"

"Clowns!" The Jester shouted.

Hinderlight smiled. "No."

The Jester shrugged and tilted its head to examine the man. "That was just a quick guess. You seem like the type that faces their fears head on. Thought you strutting up here trying to look tough was because you feared people that dressed similar to Jester."

"Not even in the slightest."

"Fair enough, fair enough. Jester will put a little more effort into it."

Except The Jester seemed to do the opposite, laying down across the top of the console, one leg crooked at an angle, his head resting in one of his gloved hands. He lounged there, staring at Hinderlight while the intimidating man stared right back at him. Eddie found it interesting to watch. Hinderlight stood stoic, barely moving as he stared down what Kaga claimed was a dangerous Horror on the other side of the glass. The Jester certainly didn't seem that terrifying. If anything was like a restless child. It shifted about, letting out little grunts as it changed positions. It sat up multiple times, only to tap at the glass while its mask shifted expressions, before flopping back onto its side. The fifth time it repeated the same motion, Hinderlight let out a laugh.

"Having a bit of trouble?"

What sounded like a low growl barely registered over the speaker.

Hinderlight crossed his arms across his chest. His smile widened. "Is there some kind of shot clock we can use? I don't want to sit here all day while you stall--"

"Scorpions!"

Hinderlight's laugh was louder this time in reply, a great, infectious thing that made Eddie smile and want to join in although he didn't know the joke.

"Scorpions?" Hinderlight said as his laughter calmed. "I spent years as a soldier fighting in the desert, laying in the sand while scorpions and other ugly desert creatures crawled all over me. I've *eaten* scorpions. They certainly don't keep me up at night."

"So nothing desert related," The Jester mumbled, sounding a bit defeated. "That's fine. This one still gets one more guess."

"Do we have to wait as long as we did for your second guess?"

"No. Just give Jester a little time."

"Absolutely. Take a little bit of time. After all, you didn't use up any time when you wasted that first guess."

The Jester's mask flashed an expression of embarrassment for the briefest moment, then took on a blank expression as it stared at Hinderlight. It had gotten up off its side, sitting on its knees, its body rigid and its lackadaisical posture all but gone. Moments stretched on as the two mental combatants fought on while their bodies remained still. In the end, it was The Jester that broke the silence once more.

"I don't know." Exasperation was clear in its voice. "Drowning?"

"Not even close." Hinderlight's grin spread from ear to ear.

"What is it then?" The Jester sounded almost desperate in its plea.

"Sorry. That's not part of the game. You guessed, you were wrong, so you don't get to know."

"Fine, be that way." The Jester's mask took on a pouting expression. "Jester didn't want to know anyway."

"Sure."

Hinderlight had already turned his back on the glass. He walked past Eddie, whom he patted on the shoulder a few times and took a seat near the elevator doors. Eddie's confidence was bolstered from that reassuring pat. And the cocky smile the man now wore as he watched The Jester continue to pout. It had turned so that its back faced the group, shoulders slumped, its hair spilling out of its hat and down its back.

"Do you think it's given up?" Lizzie asked at Eddie's side.

"Doubtful," Eddie replied, his eyes watching The Jester closely. There was something about it that intrigued him. It seemed too . . . human.

"Ok," The Jester's high-pitched voice interrupted Eddie's thoughts. It had spun back around. "A minor setback but Jester is ready to resume the game. Might as well move on to the security officer this one doesn't know. What's your name, fully armored man?"

"Rory Jefferson."

"Well, Mr. Jefferson, let's take a good look at you, all decked out in your armor." The Jester seemed to take him in with a glance and then waved him off with a dismissive wave of his hand. "Too easy. Jester *sees* darkness around you. *Feels* weight pressing in. *Smells* carved wood and churned earth, even through the glass. Obvious that this one most fears being buried alive."

The Jester sat back on its haunches, a pleased look appearing on its mask.

"Nope," Jefferson replied. "Not my darkest fear."

"Of course it is!" The Jester leaned forward. "Unless it isn't . . . " Its mask shifted into a confused look. "Jefferson isn't lying, so The Jester must be wrong. But the pictures and things Jester senses remain the same. Something similar then?"

"Feel free to keep trying."

"Maybe Jefferson's fear is burying someone alive?"

"Are you supposed to be good at this? It sounds like you're stuck."

"This one just—" The Jester paused, his mask screwing into a look that was partial confusion and partial disgust. "Jester doesn't understand. This one's intuition is saying 'buried alive.'"

It was strange, hearing a creature that was supposed to be as deadly and dangerous as the monster that attacked them on the security level sound so lost and confused. Kaga had made it clear that the Horror was a murderer. The tattooed man had shown nothing but contempt and anger toward the thing, but Eddie was struggling to see the monster in what appeared to just be a strange man with a bizarre mask and a dark sense of humor.

"Make your last guess." Jefferson voice interrupted Eddie's musings.

"Jester doesn't know," The Jester replied, his voice a growl of frustration. "Earth worms?"

Jefferson chuckled. "Worms?"

The Jester waved him away. "Flukes happen. No big deal. Two points for Jefferson's team and two for Jester. Keeping the score close makes it more interesting anyway. Shall we move on? I think I'll try my almost-friend Eddie next."

Eddie stepped forward. Lizzie pressed a comforting hand on his shoulder as he passed her and stood in front of the glass.

The Jester's mask returned a friendly smile, the first friendly one as far as Eddie could remember. When it spoke, its voice sounded like a parent instructing their child about life.

"Not to worry, almost-friend Eddie. I won't make a joke of whatever fear I find. And if your group loses this game, I promise your death will be quick. Instantaneous compared to what I plan to do to Kaga."

It said the last part loud enough that the other man must have heard him, but Eddie didn't turn to look. He couldn't drag his eyes away from looking at The Jester's porcelain mask. In all honesty, deep down, he was afraid of a lot of things. Each of his foster homes had gifted him with some kind of phobia. A foster mother that kept threatening to burn the house down whenever he left his room a mess. A foster father at a different home that locked him in a pitch-black basement whenever he had company over. And that was just the tip of the iceberg. Eddie's curiosity wanted to know which of the many things that haunted his dreams his subconscious considered the worst.

"Eddie, my boy," it continued. "Jester wanted to save you for later because it knew your darkest fear from the moment you appeared. The distance you keep from the others, how you flinch when any of them raise their voice, your awkward reactions when the pretty girl touches you. Jester would gamble a good amount of coin that Eddie lives alone, goes straight home from work, and avoids as many people as possible. This one would even guess that Eddie doesn't even know more than a handful of names of those that live around him. The simple explanation for these behaviors is that your deepest fear is to be around other people.

"But Jester is not simple. This one sees deeper. Sees the small looks Eddie casts at his companions, searching for acknowledgment. Secretly desiring to fit in even as he struggles to keep those around him from seeing the fear he has just being with them. To Jester's insightful eyes, this one sees the deepest fear of almost-friend Eddie is that he will enjoy growing close to people, but that those people will eventually turn on him."

"No, that can't be true," Eddie began, but even as the words left his mouth, he realized that The Jester was right. His past was, well his past, but bouncing around from one messed up foster home to the next had done its damage to how he interacted with people. When he had finally gotten out on his own and went to college, he lasted all of a half a semester in the dorms before he had to get an apartment on his own. He graduated and got his Masters but did so by keeping his head buried in books and his body locked away in his place. For the longest time, he had blamed his studies for his antisocial behavior.

This one creature had given Eddie more insight about his own problems than any long dead philosopher had ever revealed to him.

"Look on the bright side." The Jester's pitying expression on his mask matched his tone. "Life or death situations always bring people together. Even if Eddie ends up getting on that elevator and leaves this one safely behind, there are a lot worse things than Jester locked away in this place. Well–" It placed a hand to its cheek. "–*supposedly* locked away in this place. Who knows what else the ones that let this one out released from their cages as well."

"Wait," Hinderlight said, moving in front of Eddie so that the larger man was just inches from the glass. "The people that let you free. Who were they? Why did they let you go?"

"No idea, nor does this one care. If Jester ever finds out, this one will bake them a cake, but for now, we have a game to play. And your team is losing three to two." It pressed its face against the glass and waved toward Eddie. "Not your fault of course, almost-friend Eddie, but Jester will need you to move so that the lovely lady that's been hanging on your arm can take her turn."

Eddie stepped back, offering what he now realized was an awkward smile to Lizzie as she stepped forward. The one she returned was friendly, but Eddie thought he saw the slightest twist of pity in the angle of her mouth and squinting of her eyes. He shook his head as he moved besides Hugh and took a seat. It didn't dislodge the sudden anxiety he felt.

The Jester sat crossed-legged as Lizzie approached. "Name, please!"

"Lizzie McClane."

"Well, Lizzie, it's do-or-die time. I get this right, you and three of your companions are mine for the slaughter. If this one is wrong, you're all one step closer to leaving poor Jester alone on this floor."

"I understand." Her voice sounded surprising calm for having not only her life but Eddie's and a few of the others in her hands.

"My first impression . . ." he trailed off.

"Yes?"

"Is that you should be careful with poor Eddie. He doesn't look it, but this one feels like he is a bit fragile, and since the two of us are almost friends, Jester feels the need to look out for him."

"I'll keep that in mind."

"Good. Now back to the game at hand." The Jester stared at her for a moment. A moment that stretched as the monster shifted about in place, its mask slowly changing from inquisitive to annoyed. "Something strange is confusing this one. Are Ms. McClane and Mr. Jefferson related in some way?"

Jefferson smiled and shook his head. "First time I've ever seen her."

"Same," Lizzie said with a shrug. "I didn't even know he worked here until a today."

The Jester seemed less than pleased with both responses. It kept shaking its head and when it spoke, its voice sounded subdued.

"I cannot read this one. Not at all."

"So then you give up." Hinderlight grinned.

"For Ms. McClane, yes I do. Both telling the truth but Jester swears there is a connection there nonetheless. A mystery your companions can attempt to unravel. This one enjoys games more than mysteries, and our game ended in a tie. A very interesting turn of events."

"Interesting isn't the word I'd choose if I was a complete loser." Kaga said, approaching the glass. "And you said three wrong counted as a loss for you.

"That is true. Can't kill any of *you*. But there has to be special consequences for a tie."

Before anyone could say another word, The Jester flipped backward off of the console, landing on its feet. It reached down and yanked the forgotten Stan up in front of him. The Jester stared at them, the slits representing its eyes slanted down. Poor Stan stared at them through the glass, mouthing the words *Help Me*.

"Wait a minute," Eddie said, taking a step forward. It was all he was able to say.

Blood splattered against the window as The Jester's white-gloved fist burst through the chest of poor Stan. Right next to the glass, Eddie could only look on in horror as pain crossed the man's face for the briefest of moments. As blood filled his mouth, Stan's eyes rolled back and his body twitched as it hung suspended on The Jester's arm like a fish on a hook. After a few more horrible seconds, The Jester retracted his hand and Stan's corpse dropped back out of view.

"You monster!" Lizzie sobbed from behind Eddie. He moved back and put a comforting arm around her.

"Yes," The Jester replied. Its mask had taken on a blank expression, short, thin horizontal lines representing both the eyes and mouth. "Jester is exactly what you all *think*."

"You didn't have to kill him." Eddie had to raise his voice to speak over Lizzie's sobs.

"Don't bother trying to understand *it*," Hinderlight said in disgust.

Eddie couldn't help it. It spoke and acted like a regular human being even if it wasn't one. The Jester wasn't like The Reaper. It had intelligence, a sense of humor, even if it did lean more toward the darker side. What made it just as homicidal as The Reaper?

"You didn't have to kill him," Eddie repeated as if the words could take back the deed. "You don't have to kill at all. No one *has* to kill."

"Is that so?" The blank face remained, although now a few drops of blood marred the otherwise pristine surface of the mask.

"It is. I have no idea what you are, but you have to want more than to just murder people."

"Everyone has a little murderer in them, almost-friend Eddie."

"I don't believe that. Years of debating and writing papers on philosophy has led me to one conclusion."

"Ohhhh, you're a thinker. And what have you determined during your philosophical musings. In your *few decades* on this planet?"

"Eddie Watson's Life Rule Number One" he replied, still holding Lizzie tight against him. "Everyone born on this world, no matter how nervous they may make me, has the inherent capacity to choose good over evil."

The Jester stared at him, its head tilted to the side, the two pieces of fabric drooping back on its hat. When it spoke, the mask kept its blank expression.

"Final game, then you get to leave. Ready?"

"Whatever," Hinderlight replied. "Let's get this over with."

The Jester leaped back up on the desks, its mask pressed against the glass. "Rushing, rushing, rushing. Just want to leave poor Jester."

"Go ahead," Eddie said, releasing Lizzie as he moved toward the glass. "One more game, then you promise to unlock the elevator and let us go?"

"Jester promises to the one called Eddie. Promises to the philosopher, the one that has never been rude. A simple game and then you can go."

"Alright," Hinderlight said, stepping forward. "What game do you have for us next? More questions? Riddles this time?"

"No, this game is simple. Straightforward. A decision." It paused and Eddie could almost swear it was doing it for dramatic effect. "You must choose one in your group to die."

CHAPTER 17

"Not happening." Eddie stormed up to the glass. "What did I just say?"

The Jester's mask smiled back at him. "Almost-friend Eddie said that everyone *doesn't* have a little murderer in them. There are six people here, and Jester would bet at least one of them does."

"So you're saying," Jefferson began as he moved up close to the glass. The way he held his rifle at the ready threw up warning signals for Eddie. "That we just have to kill someone and then you'll let us go?"

"You can't possibly be thinking--" Hinderlight began but cut off as Jefferson swung the barrel of his gun in the man's direction."

"Quiet, suit. I'm talking to the monster right now." Jefferson kept the gun trained on Hinderlight but his eyes went to The Jester. "Is that all? Just one person dies?"

"Yes, but before Jefferson gets all trigger happy, this is not a matter of who can kill first. This one doesn't want some chaotic firefight. After all the fun we've had, Jester doesn't want more of Jefferson's group than needs be to bite the bullet." It gave a little chuckle. "If you'll excuse the saying.

"There must be a decision, a consensus by the group. Five must vote to kill the sixth. Once it's clear the group has come to a decision, Jester will give you permission to execute your choice. Only when I've given you permission, though. Don't want anyone with an itchy trigger finger ending the game too early."

"That will never happen," Eddie said, stepping up to the glass. "We're not going to *murder* anyone. No one is going to make that choice."

"If you do not choose, there will be . . . unfortunate results."

"How unfortunate?" Hugh asked, the gun twitching in his hand.

"Very unfortunate." The Jester gestured to the wall on the left, and then the right, taking in the rows of small gun turrets. By the looks on everyone's faces, they understood what the creature was implying.

"Then, if there are no more questions–" The Jester took a seat at the center of the glass "–we can begin. Choose who dies so the rest of you can live. Feel free to take your time. Jester knows this might be a tough decision. Unless Eddie is wrong, of course, and you all don't mind seeing a single person killed so you can live."

"This is madness," Lizzie said, stepping back from the group. "We can't just murder one another."

"We're not murdering each other." Hugh put his back toward the wall. "Just one person is going to die."

"No, we're not doing this." Eddie moved toward the center of the room, slowly turning as he tried to address everyone. "This monster wants us to turn on each other, be a murderer like itself. But we're better than that. We're not killers."

"I am," Jefferson replied. "Pretty sure Kaga is as well. You don't get a job like ours without a little blood on your hands."

Kaga's shrug was enough to confirm Jefferson's statement. Not exactly what Eddie wanted to hear the men admit but he continued. "Even so, we still have a chance to be better--"

Hugh strode forward. "*It* doesn't care if we're better people. If we don't do what it wants, we're all dead. I don't know about the rest of you, but I'm not ready to die down here like some cow awaiting slaughter."

"I have to agree." Kaga had moved closer to the group. "This thing doesn't care about your morals because it doesn't have any. If we have a chance to live here, we have to take it. We're voting."

"Should we do a secret vote?" Hugh asked. "Write a name down on paper and put them into Jefferson's helmet?"

"That's the coward's way," Hinderlight replied. He frowned and looked at everyone in turn before continuing. "If we're going to do this, if each of us is going to choose a person to kill, they are going to do it to the person's face."

"Fine with me." Jefferson moved right in front of Hinderlight. "I choose you."

"Step back," Hinderlight ordered.

"Or what? You can't kill me without a vote. In this room, you're not even a big boss. You've got no power right now."

There was a tapping on the window. The Jester's high-pitched voice sounded amused as it spoke through the speaker. "I only said that you couldn't kill each other. Feel free to get physical, slap each other around, so to speak, if it helps you reach an overall decision."

The words were barely out of The Jester's masked face when Hinderlight struck. He grabbed Jefferson's rifle with his left hand and shoved him with his right. The force of the blow made the security officer stumble back, his hand releasing the weapon. To Jefferson's credit, he recovered after two steps. As Hinderlight tossed the rifle to the side, Jefferson retaliated with a quick combination of blows. Hinderlight was able to block the first two, but Jefferson slipped the third under his defenses and caught the larger man in the side of the stomach.

Hinderlight winced from the blow, his body bending into it. He blocked a roundhouse aimed at his head, then launched an uppercut that clipped the other man's chin. Jefferson's eyes glazed as he stumbled backward again, but he kept his feet. It was clear, though, even to Eddie that Hinderlight had just gained the advantage.

Jefferson brought his arms up just in time as Hinderlight stepped forward and began raining down strikes of his own. Each punch wrenched one of Jefferson's arms to the side, but he quickly got it back up in place before Hinderlight's next blow. Hinderlight was driving him back toward one of the side walls, to the point where Kaga had to move out of the way. Eddie expected the other security officer to step in, but he just watched as Hinderlight drove Jefferson closer to the wall.

With nowhere else to go, Jefferson tried to strike back but it ended up being his downfall. As Hinderlight knocked one of his hands to the side, the security officer dropped low and tried sending a punch into the other man's ribs. It connected, but Hinderlight didn't even flinch this time. Instead, the larger man used the opening to swing a fist upward into Jefferson's unprotected face. It caught him square in the cheek. With the wall directly behind him, Jefferson's head had nowhere else to go but smack against it.

This time, his eyes rolled back and he slid down the wall, ending the fight.

Except Hinderlight didn't stop.

He continued his onslaught, most of his punches striking or glancing off of the man's helmet. A few did get through, and Jefferson's face grew red as Hinderlight split the man's lip and bloodied his nose.

"He's going to kill him," Lizzie shouted, which broke Eddie out of the shock he had been in when the fighting first erupted.

Eddie rushed forward and tried to restrain Hinderlight, but he might as well have been trying to hold back a raging gorilla. All he managed to do was lessen the impact of the man's punches on the unconscious Jefferson.

"Help me," he yelled. He had expected Kaga to rush to his partner's aid but it was Hugh who appeared at his side. Between the two of them, they were able to overpower Hinderlight enough to pull him away from the downed man. With no target for his anger, Hinderlight seemed to deflate in their arms. Eddie still held him for a bit longer to make sure he was indeed finished before letting him go. Once free, Hinderlight stalked off and pressed his hands against the wall, his body heaving as he took in deep breaths. Eddie followed after him. When he got to the man's side, he saw his shirt had gotten damp again around his wound.

"Your shoulder," Eddie began, moving to his friend's side. "It's bleeding again—"

"Of course it is." Hinderlight's voice was so laced with contempt that Eddie shrank back from it. "Instead of letting it heal, I have to keep putting one idiot after another in his place. I'm getting tired of dealing with people that have no idea the scope of what is going on here."

"Would it help--"

"No, just back off for a bit, Eddie. Let me calm down and catch my breath."

Eddie did as he was told, returning to the group. Kaga was kneeling at Jefferson's side, carefully shaking the man. When he finally regained consciousness, he took a slow look around before speaking.

"Where was the support, Kaga?" Jefferson mumbled. He had a far away look in his eyes and his battered face was pale.

"As far as I'm concerned," Kaga replied, "if you want to get in someone's face, you better be able to back up your blustering."

"I'll remember that." His eyes were starting to clear as he spoke. "Let me just sit here a second without you breathing all over me."

"Whatever you want." Kaga rose and took a few steps back.

"Well, that was exciting!" The Jester's voice echoed around the room. "For a second, I thought you were going to let Mr. Hinderlight kill Mr. Jefferson. Which would have been unfortunate because then you would have broken the rules of the game and I would have killed you all."

"Would hate to make you do that," Lizzie muttered.

"It doesn't matter," Eddie shook his head. "We're not going to just kill someone to please you."

"Never said it would please this one," The Jester said, tilting its head to the side. Its mask wore a confused expression. "We're just playing a game. A game that came from your naive belief that everyone in the room would have the same morals as yourself."

"You're saying it's the custodian's fault we're playing this game?" Hugh asked. "His yammering is what caused all of our lives to be in jeopardy?"

"No, no, no." The Jester waved him off. "You would have played something that put all of your lives at risk regardless. Jester just picked this game to test his little beliefs."

"It doesn't matter," Eddie replied. "I'm still not voting."

Hinderlight moved back toward the group, his calm demeanor seeming to have returned. "Let's not speak in absolutes, Eddie. Morals aren't bulletproof, and I certainly am not ready to just give up. One thing at a time. Let's see if at least the majority of the group can decide on someone to sacrifice to this sick fuck."

"Language!" The Jester placed two hands against a mask that looked mortified. "There are ladies present."

"I'm not--" Eddie began but Hinderlight cut him off.

"Again, let's see if the majority can agree on someone first. Then we'll see about convincing the rest." The stout man turned around and took in everyone with his steady gaze before continuing. "I vote for Jefferson."

Jefferson flipped him off but remained silent.

"I vote for Eddie," Hugh's eyes shot downward as Eddie turned a surprised look in his direction. "If you're not going to vote and get us all killed, you're the logical choice. If everyone else votes for you, it won't matter if you vote or not."

"What the hell, man."

Kaga stood. "I vote for Eddie as well." He shrugged as Eddie looked at him. At least he had the courage to return Eddie's gaze. "Sorry. Nothing personal. The spineless man just made a good point, though. And I'm certainly not voting to kill a woman."

"Screw you," Lizzie retorted. "Don't use my gender as an excuse to vote for Eddie."

The outburst just earned her a laugh from Kaga. "Alright, *Princess.* Who do you vote for then?"

"If I have to vote," Lizzie said as she gave Eddie a look that held a strength he had never seen from her before, "it certainly won't be for Eddie. I vote for Jefferson."

"Bitch," Jefferson replied. Eddie almost went after the man, but kept his cool as Jefferson continued. "I'd happily see you or the big boss sliced and diced, but I'm not going to waste a vote on either of you. I vote for the janitor as well."

"Three to two," The Jester said. "Eddie is in the lead, but he could tie it up with a simple vote for the already beaten up and bloody Mr. Jefferson."

"I told you I'm not voting." Eddie shook his head, unable to fathom how things had gotten so bad. Would they really vote to kill him? He only had Hinderlight and Lizzie in his corner, but for how long?

"So," Jefferson struggled to his feet. "If the janitor doesn't vote then he doesn't count for the total. Which means three out of five of us are voting for him. Looks like a majority to me, *Mr. Hinderlight.*"

"And I said it would be up to the majority to convince the rest. And Eddie could still change his mind . . ." Hinderlight looked at Eddie, his eyes wide and lips pressed into a tight frown.

"No," Eddie replied.

"Listen," Hugh said, showing more backbone than Eddie had seen the entire time since they had met. "The two of you–" he motioned toward Hinderlight and Lizzie "–have known Eddie longer than the rest of us. I can understand it would be hard to turn on him. But we *will* all die."

"This doesn't seem right," Lizzie mumbled.

"Or you could change your vote," Hinderlight countered. "Vote for Jefferson."

Kaga waved off the idea like he would a nagging fly. "Wouldn't make sense. Believe me, I have no love for this man," he motioned toward Jefferson, "but in case you forgot, once we get out of here, we are still a few rungs down on the food chain for anything else that might have gotten free. Given the choice between a moral custodian and a ruthless, but combat-trained security member, I have to side with the man that might keep me alive."

"Even if he might shoot you in the back?" Hinderlight asked.

"If I had some monster trying to butcher or torture me, I might prefer a bullet to the back of the head. Would Eddie be able to do the same? To put one of us out of our misery if some creature was ripping us apart?"

"No," Kaga continued. "I didn't think so. I'm not switching my vote, it doesn't seem like that guy–" He motioned toward Hugh. "–is changing his, and I'm positive Jefferson isn't about to vote for himself. If you want to get out of this alive, you and the lady will have to switch."

Jefferson picked up his rifle. No one made a move to stop him. Eddie did not like how things were going at all. Each member of their little group except for Eddie had a weapon in their hand. They stood in a circle now around the room. Eddie could guess why. Even with The Jester's rules, he had no desire to have his back to another member of the group.

"So?" Jefferson asked. "What's it going to be? Are we all going to die here or can you two toughen up and realize that Eddie is the best choice to sacrifice?"

Kaga and Hugh were both looking to Hinderlight. Eddie had Lizzie's attention. The woman looked torn. Her smile had been replaced with pursed lips and her muscles seemed to tense as if she were preparing to run. It was a horrible situation and Eddie wished he could say something to her. Part of him wished he was brave enough to offer up his life so that the others could live. All he could do was keep repeating to himself that giving in now to The Jester's game would be like giving up a large part of who he was, who he wanted to be. He wasn't ready to do that or to die.

"I don't think--" Lizzie began, but Hinderlight spoke right over her.

"No. Even if she changes her mind, I'm not budging. You're right in saying I've known this man longer than the rest of you. I've also promised him that I'm going to do everything in my power to get him out of here alive. If I can't fulfill that promise, then I'd prefer to die here along with Eddie. We might all be going to hell, but I'm at least going with a lighter conscious than I came to work with today. I'm not voting."

"You have to be kidding me," Hugh threw up his hands. "You're going to let us all die to save the janitor?"

"I'm not voting either," Lizzie replied, glancing at Hinderlight first, then Eddie, and finally rested her gaze on The Jester. "Three people not voting means your game is over. We're not going to murder anyone. You'll just have to do your own dirty work."

"As you wish," The Jester replied. It raised its hand up high over its head, then brought a single finger slowly down until it pressed something on the console.

A warning buzzer filled the room and shook Eddie's teeth. Warning lights flashed, creating a strobe effect in yellow. The room erupted in chaos, everything appearing in slow motion to Eddie.

Jefferson unholstered the handgun at his side in one smooth motion.

Lizzie screamed and dropped to the floor.

Kaga and Hinderlight started to move.

Hugh pounded on the elevator door.

The barrel of Jefferson's gun aimed at Eddie's head.

Kaga's shoulder slammed into Eddie's side, taking him off his feet.

Gunfire erupted in the room.

And then it was over. With Kaga on top of him, Eddie couldn't see anything. He heard Kaga's heavy breathing. Someone whimpering. A struggle and a grunt that sounded more in pain than angry.

Kaga rolled off of him, giving Eddie the opportunity to see that neither of them were hurt. He looked for the others. Lizzie and Hugh were cowered down at opposite ends of the room. Hinderlight had Jefferson pinned face down, both of the security guards arms twisted behind his back.

No one had been shot.

The warning buzzer stopped. The flashing lights stopped. Hugh stumbled forward as the elevator door opened in front of him.

"Game's over." The Jester's voice was filled with amusement as it echoed over the speaker. "Eddie was right. Jester was wrong.

Eddie's group wins and is free to go. Have a pleasant trip!"

CHAPTER 18

Everyone stood in silence as the elevator slowly rose back toward the floor of the main lobby. Eddie couldn't help but notice a considerable distance placed between himself and everyone else. What was there to say? People had been willing to murder each other. People had *tried* to murder each other. Eddie couldn't bring himself to even look at Hugh or Jefferson. Thankfully, the group had decided it was a better idea to keep all of the deadly weapons out of the man's hands. Hinderlight had his assault rifle strapped to his back and now carried two handguns. They had left Jefferson with a stun baton and a more sturdy steel baton to defend himself. Eddie didn't trust the man, but at least now he had to watch out for being struck in the back as opposed to being shot. As far as Kaga was concerned, Eddie had mixed feelings. The man had voted for him to die as well, but then saved him in the end. And now they had to pull back together because they could step off the elevator and face something just as maniacal as The Jester. Or worse, some mindless killing machine like The Reaper.

Eddie was still trying to figure out how the team would function again when the elevator sounded its friendly tone, signaling their arrival back on the main floor of the facility. As everyone filed out, Jefferson and Kaga taking the lead with their assault rifles, Hinderlight put a restraining arm on Eddie's shoulder. Lizzie glanced at him, her mouth parting slightly, but she turned and walked out with Hugh right beside her. Eddie and Hinderlight filed out last, walking a few paces behind the rest of the group as they started back toward the main lobby.

"Keep your eyes on Jefferson," Hinderlight whispered, never taking his sights off the man's head. "There's something not quite right with him."

"That goes without saying."

"It's more than that. I've never interacted with any of the security forces that work in the less savory areas of our company, but he doesn't seem like the other security personnel we've run into here." He paused. "Plus, what The Jester said keeps running through my mind. I know that creature couldn't figure out my fear either, but he admitted defeat with me. With Jefferson and Lizzie, he seemed confused. And he mentioned that whatever was confusing him felt exactly the same with both of them."

"You can't possibly think--"

"I'm not sure what to think at this point. Maybe it's just The Jester's games, making me doubt the others. All I know is that I trust you. So just keep your eyes on the others and let me know if you see anything strange."

"Hinderlight . . ." Eddie struggled to get out the words.

"I know," he replied, giving a friendly smile. "I told you I'd make sure you made it through this. Couldn't turn my back on you because of some psycho in a mask and a bunch of strangers."

"Thanks." The word didn't even begin to express Eddie's gratitude.

"Just remember what I said. We are far from out of this."

Eddie nodded and the two hurried on to join the group. Everyone seemed much more on edge. There was no banter, no friendly looks. Kaga and Jefferson moved to check the doors while everyone else seemed to focus on the floor in front of them. The silence in the hallway, peaceful before, now seemed like the calm before a storm. Horrors waited behind each doorway. Lurked right around the corner in the hallway. And each moment they didn't appear, it just made the tension in the group build.

They had made it around the bend and were just passing the set of double doors leading into different hallways when Hugh broke the silence.

"So are we going to talk about what happened down there?"

"I'd prefer not to." Lizzie glanced back at Eddie then turned her eyes back to a spot in front of her.

"We should keep quiet." Kaga rattled the handle of the door he was checking before moving on. "Didn't we do enough talking in front of that creature?"

"I don't want to brush it off like nothing happened," Hugh replied. He rubbed his hands together nervously as he glanced around at everything except his companions. "We were talking about murdering each other. And you know what? I don't think I should feel guilty about wanting to survive."

"Then don't." Hinderlight was glancing around as well, but there wasn't the slightest shake to his step or his voice. "No one cares if you feel guilty or not. Just keep it quiet until we've gotten to the lobby's elevator."

"You know what?" Hugh's voice began to rise as he spoke. "I'm sick of following everyone else's orders while no one listens to a damn word I say."

"Quiet, you idiot," Kaga growled.

"No! I'm tired of taking orders. I'm tired of this freak show! I'm tired--"

All around them, doors flung open. People in jet-black robes stepped out into the hallway, their faces and hands hidden in the fabric they wore. Some of Eddie's companions let out a yelp of surprise. They all moved back and bunched together, weapons raised as they formed a tight cluster facing out. The men that surrounded them made no further move once they had entered the hallway, but their very presence oozed malevolence. At least two dozen of them faced Eddie's group. They stood wordlessly, arms folded into the sleeves of their robes.

Eddie pulled his gun as well, everything he had said in front of The Jester bouncing around his mind. Could he use the weapon? Kill someone even if it was in self-defense? But how would that make him any different from Jefferson and Hugh, who had wanted to kill *him* for the exact same reason?

"Back up!" Hinderlight yelled.

Kaga spun left and right, the sight of his weapon resting on one black-robed figure for a moment before flicking to the next one. "Who they hell are all of you?"

A single person stepped forward out of the mass of robes as if emerging from the shadows themselves. Nothing visually distinguished him from any of the other robed figures, but when he spoke, his tone was gruff and clearly male, and held the air of authority.

"We are the ones that have taken this place." He opened his arms to indicate all of those gathered with him. "We are the bringers of change. This facility is ours now."

"Like hell it is," Kaga said, training his weapon on the man.

"We have the control room and have isolated the majority of your security force. Put down your weapons and we will take you all alive. If you resist, one of our more zealous acolytes might accidently murder you, which would be most unfortunate."

"Or we could just empty a few dozen bullets into all of you and see how much blood those robes can soak up. When the last of you falls, we will be on our merry way," Kaga replied.

"Try." The man's voice had gone deathly cold.

Kaga looked at the man a moment more. A *click* filled the air. *Click, click, click.* It took Eddie a moment to realize the sound was Kaga trying to fire his weapon. Trying and failing. A chorus of *clicks* filled the hallway as the rest of his group tried to use their guns with the same result.

"Your weapons are useless against us," the man continued. "Come quietly so that we may determine if any of you are who we need."

"Who you *need*? We don't even know who you are," Hinderlight asked.

"And you don't need to, but we need to know you. There is something we want deep below. Even with our taking of the main control, we still cannot gain access to it."

"And if none of us can give you access to whatever you are looking for?"

"You will be detained until we find someone who can. We have no desire to waste lives unnecessarily."

Eddie wasn't sure if he believed the man.

"Hell with this," Kaga grunted, his views instantly clear. He spun his weapon, readjusting his grip on the rifle stock so that he held the weapon backward. The stock of the weapon struck the nearest robed man in the side of the head with a loud *thwak*. No one else moved as the man crumpled to the ground in a heap.

"Gun's still good for something," Kaga joked.

And then the hallway erupted into chaos.

The robed men surged into them, a tidal wave of black that threatened to drown them. Eddie lost sight of Jefferson and Hinderlight almost immediately, and then a gloved fist just missed his face and glanced off his shoulder. Eddie began swinging wildly with his useless weapon. Each time the metal struck something soft, it sent a shudder up his arm. He didn't have time to see who he hit or the damage he had done. Hands grabbed at him. Fists seemed to strike from every direction. At one point, Eddie thought he saw Kaga's tattooed arms swinging away in the crowd, but he quickly was swallowed back up by the mass of robes. And still Eddie continued to fight, knocking hands away, trying to keep fists from striking his face. There was no rhyme or reason to Eddie's defenses; he just flailed about trying to stay free.

And then Lizzie was there. She struck a man from the side with her weapon. By the expression on her face, she was just as surprised as Eddie at her own actions. She continued to look surprised as she grabbed Eddie's hand and yanked him out of the mass of flailing bodies. She beat a path through the black robes which seemed to part at her ferocity. At one point, Eddie actually thought they were going to get free from the mob. They burst through the pack and emerged into a relatively clear area. But more doors opened and at least a dozen more black robes stepped into the hallway.

"What now?" Eddie asked, his hand tightening on the useless gun it held.

"Change comes from the pain within," Lizzie said as the men circled them.

"What?" Eddie asked but didn't have time to hear if she answered.

The men rushed them. Eddie did the only thing he could do. He swung his weapon. Tried to kick out legs. Even bit the errant arm or hand, although he couldn't bring himself to bite down hard enough to do any real damage. All the while he tried to hold tight to Lizzie while she did the same.

But the blows still came. A punch to the back. A kick to the shin. A backhand that snapped his head to the side and brought the coppery taste of blood to his lips. Eddie tried to move forward, to get out of the mob and pull Lizzie along with him. Covering his face with the useless gun in his hand and dropping his shoulders, he barreled straight in the direction he believed was the one they had been going in. Grunts and shouts followed him so he shouldered people out of the way. The blows against his body seemed to increase. Each one felt like it bruised bone and organ alike. But still he pressed on. Just when he thought his legs would give out, he broke out of the mass of black-robed bodies. Elation filled him as he glimpsed the end of the hallway and the lobby beyond it within reach.

Until Lizzie slipped from his grasp.

Eddie spun, lashing out with both hands, his feet, whatever he could, but Lizzie was gone. Swallowed up in a mass of black.

"Lizzie!" he yelled, then struck a hooded face as a man at the end of the mob turned and reached for him. "Lizzie!"

No reply, just the grunts of fighting men.

He was about to rush back into the fray when a hand grabbed his collar and yanked Eddie backward. He stumbled but was able to pivot and swing his weapon at his attacker. A hand caught his wrist.

"You have to stop that," Hinderlight said as he dragged Eddie a few more feet until he was able to get his feet under him.

"Sorry--"

"Just get to the elevator," Hinderlight said, then stumbled as well.

Eddie caught him, which was a struggle to do with the much larger man. It also gave him a clear view of Hinderlight's face. Various fresh cuts marred his checks and chin, and the bridge of his nose looked askew.

"But Lizzie," Eddie began as he struggled to right the man.

"If they took her, she is still alive. We can come back for her." His hand tightened on Eddie's shoulder. "I need your help *now*."

Amidst the madness around them, Eddie couldn't tell if it was a command or a plea. It didn't matter. More robes had noticed them on the fringes and were moving to intercept them. As much as it pained him, they had to move. Had to leave the others, including Lizzie, behind.

Eddie balanced himself on Hinderlight enough to kick the first robed man that reached them and then got moving. He ran down the hall as fast as his bruised body would let him, battered muscles screaming in protest. Hinderlight was right beside him, the man's face a mess but his eyes alight as he stared straight ahead. Each door ahead of them was a potential ambush point, but it was also a milestone. Twelve sets of doors away from the lobby and hopefully the escape of the elevators. Eddie's heart pounded against his chest as they ran.

Eleven doors. Ten.

Ahead, one of the doors swung inward and another black-robed man stepped out. Eddie threw the useless gun in his hand as hard as he could. It struck him right in the chest, causing him to stumble backward into the office. Eddie didn't even bother to see if the cultist was still on his feet as they passed.

Nine.

Legs pumping, his lungs felt like tinder just about to catch fire. *Eight. Seven.*

"They're coming," Hinderlight wheezed beside him. Eddie didn't bother to look back. Didn't think he could keep his feet from stumbling if he took his eyes off his goal.

Six. Five. Four.

This close, he could see the dimly lit lobby more clearly. Where the hallway carpet ended and the tiles began. From there, how far to the elevator? Could he keep up this pace?

Shouts echoed behind them, none of them friendly. Hinderlight's breathing sounded like a fan running out in the rain.

He would make it. They both will make it.

Something stepped into the dim light where the hallway reached the lobby. A single man, almost as big as Hinderlight.

"Plow . . . through him," Hinderlight barely got the words out. *Three.*

Eddie tensed his shoulders, braced himself for the impact. *Two.*

The man began to wave them on. Eddie could see the tattoos that ran from his wrists and disappeared under the armor covering his shoulders.

"Come on!" Kaga yelled as he continued to wave.

An ally was the only thought that crossed Eddie's mind. The words seemed to add strength to his legs and hope in his heart. He raced past the last remaining set of doors and into the lobby. Kaga had already started running toward the elevators by the time Eddie and Hinderlight crossed the threshold, and they followed him as he sprinted across the empty room. They moved unobstructed across the ocean-blue tiles, their soles making a slapping sound as they struck the hard floor. Kaga reached the elevator first, then spun and waited for them.

Of course, Eddie thought. *He doesn't have an access key.*

At this point, whether the man had waited because he didn't

have the key or because he actually wanted to help didn't matter to Eddie. He was there, another number on their side against the mob in pursuit.

Eddie reached the elevator next, slamming into the wall as he struggled to slow down. His shoulder hit, sending a small lance of pain down his side, but it was nothing compared to the aches in his muscles or the burning in his lungs. Hinderlight reached them last, the man's legs giving out right before the elevator. He crashed to the ground, rolling a few feet before coming to a stop inches from the elevator.

"The card!" Kaga yelled.

Hinderlight's breaths sounded more liquid than air, but he managed to extend an arm, the card grasped in his hand. At the other side of the room, black-robed figures burst out of the hallway. There were dozens of them, their sleeves flapping as they ran like injured crows.

Kaga snatched the card from his hand and swiped it down through the reader. Immediately the doors came to life and opened, the inside all chrome handrails and reflective steel, twice as large as a regular elevator. A light flashed above the doors while a friendly warning bell filled the lobby. The sound just seemed to incite the mob into more frenzy as they approached.

"Help me get him in," Kaga grunted as he grabbed one of Hinderlight's arms.

Eddie got to his feet and grabbed the other, despite the protestations of his body. With two great heaves, they got him onto the elevator. Kara's fist smacked down one of the buttons on the console next to the door and the elevator let out another tone in reply. Both men faced the oncoming horde as the elevator door slowly slid shut. Eddie couldn't see any of the faces of the robed people as they approached, but they seemed to let out a collective screech of rage as the door finally shut. Once Eddie felt the elevator start to move, he let himself relax. He dropped to the floor, panting into his hands as he brought them to his face. Beside him, Hinderlight let out the occasional raspy breath.

"Can't wait to see what we have to go through next," Kaga said as he, too, joined Eddie and Hinderlight on the ground.

Now that he was safe for the moment, all Eddie could think

about was the feeling of Lizzie's soft hand as it slipped through his fingers.

CHAPTER 19

"Your boss looks like he is in bad shape." Kaga was sitting with his back against the wall of the elevator as it hummed its way downward. His head tilted back so that he was staring at the ceiling. A thin cut stretched from his left ear across his cheek, and the edges of both of his eyes looked puffy. Blood stained the crisscrossing tattoos on his arms, but Eddie couldn't see any cuts in the designs. Despite how he looked, though, Kaga was in considerably better shape than Hinderlight.

The regional manager still lay where they had left him, his blackened eyes closed, the wheeze of breath sounding ragged as it flowed through his busted nose. His shirt was damp with sweat and the red stain by his shoulder seemed moist and stuck to his body.

"Do you have anything to help him?" Eddie asked. "An emergency first aid kit or something like that?"

Kaga nodded. "A few things in an emergency pack. I'm not a doctor, though. Oshiro is our squad's medic . . ." He trailed off for a moment, then frowned and continued on. " . . . *Was* our squad's medic. We're all taught how to perform basic field dressings, but I'm far from the best at it."

He detached a small bag from his belt similar to the one Eddie had gotten off of Hinderlight's bodyguard. Kaga emptied its contents onto the elevator floor, revealing similar supplies as well: alcohol wipes, bandages, the small tool used to seal cuts. It also had gauze, small clamps, a small tube, a number of vials each one a color of the rainbow, and a single needle. He glanced at the supplies, then at Hinderlight and shook his head.

"If we're going to do this right, it can't be rushed. And we have no idea what's going to be waiting for us at the bottom of this ride."

Kaga pushed himself up and off the wall and swiped the access card through the reader on the inside control panel before he pressed a button labeled Stop. Low alarm bells began to toll as the elevator slowed to a halt.

"There, that should give us some time."

Kneeling back down, Kaga took a closer look at Hinderlight's face and body. "Nose is busted, that's obvious. I'm not seeing any deep lacerations on his face." Moving his gloved hand down to Hinderlight's shirt, he let it hover over the blood stain on his shoulder. "Is this new? Part of the stain looks like it's been dry for a while but the rest is damp."

"He got stabbed by a pen earlier today."

"A pen?" Kaga let out a low whistle. "This guy is full of surprises. Help me take off his shirt so I can get a good look."

Eddie complied, unbuttoning Hinderlight's shirt and pulling his uninjured arm out of its sleeve. When Kaga tried to take off the other sleeve, the shirt stuck near the wound.

"I was afraid of that," Kaga said, motioning toward the area. "Blood has dried onto the wound, whatever bandage he had on it, and the shirt. Going to have to rip it off of him. Hold his arm down to provide counter-weight and in case he wakes up. I'm bruised enough; I don't need him adding more."

Eddie did as he was told, pressing both hands down on the man's shoulder. He could feel Hinderlight's lungs as they struggled to take in air. Kaga gripped the side of the shirt, took a deep breath, and yanked at the fabric. What sounded like duct tape being torn off filled the elevator. Hinderlight let out a soft moan but his eyes remained closed. With the shirt no longer stuck to the man's shoulder, Kaga pulled off his sleeve and tossed the shirt aside.

With Hinderlight now undressed from the waist up, Eddie was appalled to see the state of the rest of the man. Hinderlight's body looked as if it had been trampled. Circular shaped bruises covered most of his torso, each one a different shade of purple ringed by dark brown. The rest of his skin looked pale and drawn, exposing the outline of his ribs. The wound on his shoulder looked even worse. Whatever had sealed it was now torn away, leaving the puncture wound exposed. The skin around it was red and looked like it was swelling with a greenish fluid oozing from it.

While Eddie looked on, Kaga began to probe the man's body with his hands. Hinderlight let out a low groan but otherwise remained motionless.

"At least one rib is bruised," the tattoo man said, his attention focused like a laser. "Might be broken. Nothing to be done about that either way. No way to know if he is bleeding internally, although if he was, there would be nothing I could do about that either. This stab wound on his shoulder is about the only thing I can attend to with the supplies I have, and that's just to close it up and redress it. It looks infected."

"Can you do anything with those?" Eddie waved at the various vials.

"No, those aren't meant for fighting infections. Might be able to find some antibiotics on one of the lower floors, but he'll have to tough it out until then."

"Alright."

Eddie watched as Kaga set out everything he needed. The man glanced at it all then got to work.

"So, Eddie," Kaga said as he began wiping at the wound. "How does a simple guy like you get dragged into all of this?"

"Just wrong place, wrong time, I guess."

"Has to be a bit more than that. You're a janitor, right?"

"Custodian."

"Sorry. *Custodian.* How did you end up in the company of someone so high on the corporate food chain?"

"It's a long story."

"Well, we have time. And it will help me work if we're talking. Let's hear it."

"Ok." So Eddie went on to explain the day. His chance elevator ride with Hinderlight and the coincidence in knowing the man he wanted to fire. Being brought up to the office on the sixtieth floor and then the attack by crazy Miss Toner. Their narrow misses with the Infected and finding Hugh. Ending with barely escaping the huge bat creature in the main building's lobby. By the time he was done, Kaga had finished cleaning and bandaging Hinderlight's puncture wound.

"That's one crazy story," Kaga replied as he fastened the bandage in place.

"Tell me about it. I came in today expecting to clean some restrooms, Windex some windows, and then head home to my boring apartment. Not get chased down by some giant, camouflaging bat creature." He glanced toward Kaga's wrist display. "Any idea what that was called? I feel like it should have a name."

"Let me check." Kaga pressed the screen a few times then shook his head. "No chameleon-bat hybrids in the database."

"How is that possible? I thought the company knew about every monster, psychopath, and urban legend that existed."

"I don't know, I'm just a grunt, remember? Maybe it's something no one has ever seen before. Or maybe it's been classified for some reason and I just don't have access to it. All I know is that it's not in *my* database."

"If you hunt them, why wouldn't you have access?"

"Who knows why the members of The Board do what they do? Who even knows what their motivations are for capturing all of these things?"

"You don't think they do it to keep people safe?"

"Did you feel safe running from The Reaper or playing The Jester's sick games? I certainly didn't."

"But they were *supposed* to be locked up, right?

"That's right. Locked up. Instead of thrown into a twenty-ton steel safe and dropped in the middle of the Atlantic Ocean. Between you and me, and I guess this guy–" Kaga waved at the prone Hinderlight. "If the company cared so much about human lives, they would have buried, sunk, or launched into space every single thing they captured, from the little fairies all the way up to the Horrors like The Reaper."

"Wait." Eddie was sure he heard the man wrong. "You have fairies. Pixie dust and wings and all?"

"Well, yes and no. These aren't your Disney variety, all tiny and sprinkling their pixie dust all around. The real things belong in an H.R. Giger painting."

"I can't believe . . . " Eddie began, then let out a laugh. "I've seen enough that I should start believing, shouldn't I?"

"Yes, you should. We'll be going into the heart of the facility now. There is no telling what else has been set free or able to get out in all of the confusion. Just remember, even a creature that appears cute can turn down-right nasty after being locked away, poked, and prodded. Don't trust anything nonhuman. In fact, don't trust any*thing* or any*one*."

"Got it."

Eddie was about to ask another question, but the way the man had said the last statement bothered him. The start of the conversation, although appearing innocuous, was beginning to feel more like an interrogation than a way to pass the time.

"You're been probing me, haven't you?" He didn't bother to hide the surprise and anger in his voice. "You still don't trust me?"

"I don't *know you, custodian.*"

"You say that like you think I'm more than what I appear to be."

"All I know is, you and this big-wig show up, you claim to have gone through hell, *we* go through more hell, and yet somehow the two of you are still alive. I'll admit I underestimated Hinderlight. The man is clearly trained in hand-to-hand and the use of firearms, and isn't afraid to literally throw his weight around when someone crosses him. And maybe since they tell someone in his position a little of what goes on here, they train him too. Or he trained himself. Dozens of reasons he could have those types of skills, and I could spin my mind in circles figuring out if they are legit reasons or ones I should be worried about.

"You, on the other hand, are a *janitor.*" Kaga waved away Eddie's correction before he could utter it. "If you want to dress up your job and give it a fancier name, that's your business, but you *are* a janitor. Claim to be one, at least. How you could have survived this mess is beyond me, even with Hinderlight's help. And the fact that you happened to get on the elevator at the precise moment as Hinderlight at the beginning of the day, somehow gained his trust, and have been following him deeper and deeper into the building, learning about things that the majority of the people above have no idea about makes me wonder. You're either incredibly lucky, or you've had some outside help. If it's the latter, that would point to you being a part of whatever is going on today."

"I'm not one of those black-robed guys. They kicked the crap out of me too," Eddie struggled to explain himself.

"And yet you somehow got free. From a mob of people."

"So did you, and Hinderlight. And Lizzie was the one to pull me free of the mob. They would have taken me too if not for her."

"Except she *was* taken and you weren't."

Eddie threw up his hands. "What the hell do you want from me? I have no idea why I'm still alive. All I wanted for most of the time I've been running around, trying not to shit myself as one monster after the next hops out and tries to eat or dismember me, is to get the hell out of here."

"And now?"

"Now I want to make sure that Lizzie and Hinderlight get out of here as well." He paused, a frown spreading across his face as he tried to control his anger. "And Hugh and Jefferson if we can manage it."

"Really?" Kaga looked genuinely surprised. "After those two were ready to kill you to save themselves?"

"You took their side too."

"And I'd do it again in a life or death situation like that. Does that make me a bad person? Well guess what, I don't give a fuck. Since I've been at this job, I've seen enough horrible shit to shed every compassionate bone in my body. Easier not to care about one of your teammates when he might be torn apart the next time you go out on a mission. Or have even worse done to him or her. All I care about is loyalty and survival, and if we're being honest with each other, you haven't shown me a reason yet to be loyal toward you and you sure as hell don't contribute much to my own survival."

The final words struck a blow that would have staggered Eddie if it had been physical. Instead, this shock destroyed any illusions of himself as being useful. He had seen himself as a vital member of the group. The voice of reason and compassion during their confrontation with The Jester. The one person looking out for everyone else in the group. What a joke. Hinderlight was looking out for him because of some mixture of pity and guilt. That was the only reason why he was alive, survived this long. In the back of his mind, he had seen himself as more useful than Hugh, but that had been an illusion as well. All of his philosophies and ideals made him no better than the coward he had seen in the other man.

He was useless.

His expression must have mirrored his mood as Kaga seemed to wince from the sight of it. "Want me to take a look at you?

"I'm fine."

"Doubtful. We all took a beating. Stop pouting and let me take a look."

The truth in the man's words embarrassed him. "I'm fine. Bruised and sore, and a bit rattled with everything that's happened so far, but otherwise fine. Thank you, though."

Kaga shrugged and sat back. "It's your body. Don't try to tough it out, though, if you are really in pain. Let me or the boss man know."

"I will." He looked over at Hinderlight. "Should we try to wake him?"

"If we're going to get moving, then yes."

"We should. We have to stick to Hinderlight's plan while trying to figure out how to free Lizzie, Hugh, and Jefferson. If they are still alive. We can't help anyone if we just hide out on the elevator. Let's get Hinderlight up and make sure he can move on his own, then start the elevator back up. Do you think you *can* wake him?"

"I can try." Reaching down, Kaga gently began probing the man's face. His fingers settled on the man's nose, each hand gripping one part of the separated cartilage.

"Wait--" Eddie tried to get out.

There was a sickening crunch as Kaga reset Hinderlight's nose. The larger man's eyes shot open and he let out a groan that could have rivaled any of the monsters they had seen. His eyes fluttered closed, but he brought a hand up to gingerly probe at his face. Whenever his fingers brushed anywhere near his nose, his faced scrunched up, which then elicited another moan. This happened a few more times before he finally spoke.

"Did we all make it?"

"No," Kaga replied even though his eyes met Eddie's. "Although I don't *think* anyone was killed.

Hinderlight opened his eyes at that point. His gaze fell on Kaga first, and he gave the man an appreciative nod. When he turned his head and spotted Eddie, relief bloomed in his expression. His bruised eyes seemed to relax and a tired smile touched the corner of his lips. It just reinforced Eddie's feeling of uselessness. Hinderlight never expected him to survive without him. All he was to the man was a burden that he tolerated because of some strange sense of responsibility.

"Glad to see our stalwart custodian made it. I wasn't really with it during our mad dash for the elevator and wasn't sure what was memory and what might have been hallucination or wishful thinking. You as well, Kaga." He closed his eyes for a moment before continuing. "I would choose you over that Jefferson fellow any day. I have the sinking feeling if I was passed out in front of that man, I'd never wake back up."

Kaga let out a half laugh, half snort. "I considered finishing the job the mob started, but you know–" He waved toward Eddie. "–witnesses."

"Lucky for me then. I helped get Eddie free."

More than helped, Eddie thought, *and payed the consequences for it.*

"So we think the others are alive," Hinderlight continued, "but probably captured. Any idea who our attackers were, Kaga?"

"No. I deal mostly with monsters. We don't get briefed on gangs or cults unless they are going to be a hindrance. I was actually hoping you might have an idea."

"Nothing pops to mind. Besides the robes, I didn't really have much else to go on, though. It's true, upper management gets briefs on all of the occult and potential threats to the company, but as many as we hear about, we're warned that twice as many are hiding in the shadows of society. Has there been a larger number of people moving in and out of the facility recently?"

"Not that I've noticed. If people gain access to the security level in between the building and The Zoo, I don't pay them much attention. They either have to be let down from the control room or have security card access. Hafiz and Bukowski were the ones that paid attention to people coming in and out when it was our squad's shift on the security level. The rest of us were there just in case something happened."

Hinderlight grimaced, although it wasn't clear if it was from the lack of information or from his injuries. "So we have no idea if the group we ran into has been slowly trickling in or if the majority got let in today after they took The Zoo's control room."

"Yes, although the bigger question is how some fanatical group could infiltrate a high security facility like this one in the first place." Kaga was looking directly at Eddie while he spoke. He returned the man's gaze with a hard look of his own. While he might feel useless at the moment, Eddie didn't appreciate being lumped in with a bunch of thugs in black robes. "If it's a small group, we might have run into the entire batch of infiltrators already."

"Doubtful. Even if they were brazen enough to come out in the open, it would make sense not to bring out the ones that infiltrated the company, just in case they needed to use them again."

Hinderlight began to push himself up, but his arms wobbled and he slumped back down. "I might be more injured than I thought."

"Which might be a problem if we intend to wrestle the control room back into our possession." Kaga moved to his feet and began to pace back and forth. On the small elevator, it only took a step or two before he had to turn. "And I was being literal with the word, wrestle. I lost my firearms in the scuffle, and I didn't notice any weapons on either of you two."

"No," Eddie replied. "I dropped mine."

"Same," Hinderlight joined in. "Both the rifle and my handgun. All I have left is one of those combat knives."

"Well," Kaga said, throwing up his hands. "It's not like they would be useful anyway against the robed ones. If those men have the ability to stop guns from working, it would explain how they took the control room without raising any alarms and why my team never heard from any of the other security teams. Without the use of their weapons, even a highly trained squad could easily be overwhelmed by a mob like the ones that assaulted us."

The memory of the guns failing to work rushed back to the forefront of Eddie's mind. "How the hell did all of our guns happen to misfire all at the same time? I'm far from an expert, but it seems unlikely that should happen."

"Magic," Hinderlight and Kaga said in unison, then shot glances at each other.

"You have to be kidding me," Eddie said. "Monsters I can accept, mainly because I've seen them. Magic, though? I didn't see any of the robed men waving their hands around or shooting lightning bolts from their eyes."

"It doesn't work that like," Kaga replied.

"For the most part," Hinderlight said. "There are many different types of magic, and just like the monsters and the cults and all the other things that seem out of story books, we don't even know all of them. The only consistency about magic is that the stronger the concentration, the more likely that technology, chemical reactions, even the laws of physics, time, and space go a little wonky."

"Which means?"

"Basically," Kaga replied, "the more magic in an area, the more likely anything manmade will fail. So, either one of those men did something subtle to magic the guns into not working, *or* one or more of them were so powerful that they just knew the guns wouldn't work around them."

"This has been very educational, I'm sure." Hinderlight tried to rise again, this time getting up into a sitting position with his back to a wall. "But irrelevant. We need to keep moving forward. Our goal was the control room. Whether we have guns or not doesn't matter. We *have* to take that control room back. If we have that, we can slowly take the facility back."

"Agreed." Kaga crossed his arms in front of his chest. "Except we circle back to the point that you are in no condition to help out. That leaves me and the janitor."

"Custodian," Hinderlight muttered. His attention had turned to the different-colored vials on the ground. "The honey-colored vial. Give me that. It will be enough to get me going."

"Not a chance. Since you specifically picked the honey, then I'll assume you know what it does. And the side effects associated with it."

"I do. We'll either have the control room well before the side effects take effect or we'll be dead."

"That may be true--"

"Then don't argue. Just give it to me."

"You do realize that out of everything we've done, this is the most foolish. Those vials are only supposed to be used as a last resort."

"This is. *Give it to me.*"

Kaga looked at him, glanced over at Eddie, then shrugged and picked up the vial and the syringe. "Your funeral."

Hinderlight extended his left arm. "Convenient that you both have already undressed me." Kaga grunted as he filled the syringe with the viscous honey-colored liquid. "Does it need to go into a vein?"

"No. You ready?" A quick questioning glance at Hinderlight, who nodded in response, and then Kaga slid the tip of the needle into the man's arm. He pressed until the entire contents of the syringe went into Hinderlight, then removed the needle and wiped the edge on his pants before slipping the cover back on it.

For the first few moments, nothing seemed to happen.

Hinderlight sat with his back against the wall, his eyes closed. He took deep breaths, the rasp in each one painful for Eddie to hear. He was about to ask if whatever in the vial was working when Hinderlight opened his eyes and got to his feet. Eddie expected him to wobble or struggle as he rose but the man seemed fine. Eddie's initial thought was that the vial had to contain some kind of super drug that healed all injury.

Except the rasp in Hinderlight's breath was still there. Alert eyes looked out from behind puffy skin and a swollen nose. His upper body was starting to turn splotchy colors as it began to bruise. The man might be on his feet but all the injuries still appeared to be there.

"How do you feel?" Eddie asked.

"I don't feel anything." Hinderlight rotated his head until an audible *crack* escaped his neck. "That's the point of the drug."

"And the side effects?"

"Not something to worry about," Hinderlight said dismissively. "Now, where is my shirt?"

Kaga had remained crouched and was stuffing the medical supplies back in his pouch. He paused to snatch up Hinderlight's shirt and toss it up.

"Alright." Hinderlight slipped the wrinkled and bloody designer shirt back on. "Both of you ready?"

"Yes," Kaga replied, as Eddie repeated the same.

"Then get us moving."

Kaga rose and pressed the stop button again. The warning tones shut off immediately and the elevator hummed back to life as it began its descent. Kaga favored them with a wide smirk.

"Let's see what kind of a shit show we can get into next."

CHAPTER 20

Eddie expected the control room floor to have the same setup in terms of security as the armory level, which is why he was surprised when the elevator doors opened and he found a quaint little lobby instead. A square setting of four couches facing each other sat in the middle of the room on an old Oriental rug. A single check-in desk sat against the far wall, bookmarked by two hallway entrances. Tall ferns grew out of finely decorated pots in each corner of the room, their vibrant greens turned violet by the blue flashing emergency lights. The whole scene looked more like the lobby up in the main building, albeit a much smaller version, as opposed to the entrance to one of the most important parts of the facility.

"Hmm . . . it's quiet," Hinderlight commented, which almost made Eddie jump. The man was right. The hum of the elevator was the only sound that could be heard.

Eddie had been expecting some kind of resistance. Some horrible new beast to flee from or fight. At the very least, a single black-robed guard watching out for his fellow crazies. Eddie had also been expecting a destroyed room from whatever battle had ensued when the robed men took the floor. Instead, everything seemed calm and in order, minus the lack of people.

Of course, so had the main lobby upstairs right before they had been attacked by a giant, camouflaging bat.

"They don't need guards," Kaga said pointing up at the far right corner of the room. A small security camera sat suspended upside down from the ceiling. "The whole floor is monitored. The control room can see everything, so if any of those robed bastards are inside, I don't think we're going to get the drop on them."

"Alright," Hinderlight said before taking a quick look around before addressing Kaga. "How many different ways can we gain access to the control room on this floor?"

Kaga grimaced and rubbed at the stubble on his chin. "I don't know."

"What? How can you not know?"

"I've never been on this floor before. They only let squad leaders come down, unless there is an emergency. As long as I've worked here, there hasn't been one, so . . ."

"They can see our every move and we don't even know how to get to the room," Hinderlight finished, his tone a mixture of surprise and disgust.

Eddie only shared the man's surprise. "You can't just look up the floor plan on your wrist-thing?"

Kaga shook his head, a rueful expression painting his face. "Security forces aren't granted that kind of information. We're taught how to use the elevators, under our squad leader's supervision, of course, and that's about it. Like I've said, we're given very limited access and information in terms of the facility. Our job is more focused on capturing the things that go bump in the night."

"That's . . . fine," Hinderlight got out between clenched teeth. "We'll just improvise. Be ready for the ambush I'm sure the robes are setting for us." His voiced dropped as he continued. "It's not like we have any other options."

Hinderlight waved them forward and they exited the elevator. The larger man took the lead, moving better than either of his companions. Eddie marveled at how much healthier the regional manager appeared. While the man moved on with his usual confident gait, Kaga and Eddie limped along behind him. It was a good thing that they had given up on a stealthy approached. It was an effort for Eddie to put one foot in front of the other without wincing. He could use a shot of that orange concoction himself.

They moved unaccosted through the lobby, with Hinderlight pausing at the reception desk. A simple piece of furniture, the wooden desk had a scattering of papers on its surfaced and what looked to Eddie to be a high-end desktop computer connected to a monitor larger than any tv he could afford. Hinderlight tapped at the keyboard for a few minutes, then swiped the whole thing aside with an annoyed grunt.

"Whole thing is locked down." His voice was closer to an animal's growl than a human's. "Just once I'd like something to go right for us for a change."

"Maybe we'll get to the control room and find that they've all killed each other," Kaga said, capping his statement off with a grim laugh. "That would be a pleasant surprise."

"Or maybe they couldn't find what they were looking for and left," Eddie added.

"Would you two take this seriously." Hinderlight was looking down the hallway, a hand to his head. He itched at his raven-colored hair for a few moments as he stared into space. When he spoke again, his voice had the tone of a man barely suppressing his rage. "We'll just continue on. Keep our eyes out for traps and any sign of which direction to go to reach the control room."

"You're the boss," Kaga replied.

They followed the man as he moved down the hallway, Eddie staying between them. The hallway itself was painted a drab gray with an equally bland tan Berber carpet. They passed a number of solid wooden doors, Hinderlight pausing to examine each room to check for employees or a possible ambush. All they found were empty offices, single restrooms, and storage closets. Eddie tensed up each time a door was opened and barely had time to relax before their leader was checking another. Kaga followed along behind, allowing Hinderlight to check the rooms while his attention seemed to be everywhere at once. The security officer was always moving, although with the jerky movements of an injured man. Occasionally, he would double check a room or idle in front of a hallway intersection, but for the most part, he hung close to Eddie's back, his hand hovering near the knife in his belt.

Eddie hoped the motion was because of his fear of attack and not because of Kaga's lack of trust in him.

After a few turns and having to backtrack upon reaching a dead end, the weight of the silence on the floor began to wear on Eddie's nerves. When the simple click of Hinderlight opening one of the doors made him flinch, Eddie decided to break the silence.

"For such a large facility, it's been pretty devoid of people."

"Not counting the black-robed ones," Kaga muttered as he glanced behind him. "And who knows how many of those were employees."

"Even so, we haven't found anyone hiding." He paused as a shiver ran down his spine. "Or that many bodies."

"Saw enough bodies on the armory floor," Kaga growled. The man's hand rested on the hilt of his knife. When Eddie glanced at it, Kaga raised an eyebrow at him and gave a curt nod before continuing. "When the lockdown began, most were probably in the lab levels above and below us. Reasonable to assume that's where most of them still are at the moment. Hopefully, they're making sure all of our detainees stay locked up nice and tight."

"But what about this floor? I would think a floor as important as this one would be staffed by a lot of people. We've checked a few dozen offices so far and have found nothing."

"How the hell should I know? Maybe they all moved to a different floor. Maybe the black robes took them and sacrificed them all to some dark god." Kaga narrowed his eyes. "Why all the questions?"

"Don't you find it strange?"

"What I find strange is your hundreds of questions."

"I'm just--"

Eddie cut off as he walked into Hinderlight's back. The man had paused at a corner and was poking his head around the side.

"Quiet," he hissed, glancing back for just a moment to cast an angry look at both Eddie and Kaga. When he returned his gaze to the side hallway without any further explanation, Eddie felt a mixture of apprehension and curiosity. Crouching down, he moved along the wall until his head was level with Hinderlight's waist and he could look around the corner himself.

For most of the adjoining hallway, nothing seemed out of the ordinary. It was at the end where the hallway took a sharp right, that Eddie caught sight of what had made Hinderlight pause.

A pair of double doors, as thick as Eddie's arm, barely hung from their hinges, swaying slightly as if they would fall off at any moment. By the misshapened doors and the way they hung outside in the hallway and not in the room itself, it looked like something had broken out. The doorway was a good hundred paces away, so he couldn't see what lay beyond it. What he could make out, though, were the dried stains splattered against the destroyed doors and adjoining walls.

"I think we found the control room," Hinderlight kept his voice low. "Kaga. Do you think all of that was done by one of the security teams?"

"Doubtful." The man walked out into the middle of the hallway to get a better look.

"Don't you think you should hide?" Eddie asked.

"Why?" The security officer waved him off. "There is nothing in the hallway and we have to go down it eventually. If there are some black robes waiting in ambush, I want them to know I'm ready for them. If some*thing* else broke through that door, I'd rather have it come charging out of that room while we're all the way down here."

Eddie gestured toward the doors. "Why would you think something that got loose from this facility did all that?"

"Simple. If one of the other security teams or the black robes did that, the doors would be blown *in*. Pretty obvious that isn't the case."

"Well then." Hinderlight joined Kaga in the hallway. "Maybe you were right and they all ended up killing each other. That would make things a whole lot easier."

"Unless they royally fucked up the control room."

"Let's hope not." Hinderlight turned and waved Eddie forward. "Come on. Kaga is right, best to barge ahead and see what we have to deal with."

Eddie Watson's Life Rule Number 9: If you know you're about to walk into a hurricane, don't worry about finding an umbrella. Get the hell away from the hurricane.

Eddie pushed the thought to the back of his head as he followed after the two other men. Hinderlight and Kaga each took a side of the hallway, both men checking doors now at a faster pace. Not bothering to be stealthy, the men slammed or kicked open the doors. Eddie stayed a step or two behind, flinching with each crash of the doors. The other two men would take a quick glance inside and then turned their attention back to the destroyed doorway at the end of the hall. When nothing came charging around the corner, they would visibly take in deep breaths and move on to the next door.

When they finally reached the end of the hallway, Eddie's already frazzled nerves were at their breaking point. If something did come charging out of control room now, there was a good chance that his heart would give out long before whatever had destroyed the door and bloodied the walls could even reach him. Kaga and Hinderlight seemed less afraid as they stepped out into the adjoining hallway. As soon as both men were in front of the open doorway, they stopped dead in their tracks. After a few

168

moments, Hinderlight covered his eyes and began to rub his forehead. Kaga looked away and spit in the carpet.

Since neither men were giving him an update, Eddie moved to join them, The coppery smell of blood and decay struck his nose as soon as he got close to the destroyed doorway. There was much more blood than he had originally thought, and the door looked like something had punched a few dents into it before they finally got out.

"Do you see any sign of what destroyed the door?" Eddie asked from a few feet back from the men.

"Blood trail leads off down that hallway." Kaga gestured toward the patches of dried blood on the wall and carpet, then to his right in the direction of the adjoining hallway. "Either something very big was bleeding or covered in a lot of blood after it busted out of the doors."

"That's reassuring," Eddie mumbled as he approached the door. His mind began to come up with pictures of werewolves and vampires and any other movie monster that his one set of foster parents made him watch when he was six. Despite adding more nightmares to his ample repertoire, those foster parents had been the least scarring of the different families he had lived with. At least as far as he could remember. Memories of his childhood were foggy at best. As he approached the destroyed doors, Eddie wondered if memories of this day would become cloudy with time as well.

One glance through the open doorway wiped out any thoughts of his past or of ever forgetting this day.

Bodies lay strewn about the octagonal room, dressed in both the black robes of the occultists and the normal office wear of the employees. Large chunks had been taken out of body limbs that Eddie could see, while other corpses had giant, bloody rents running down their chest or back. Some looked like they had died trying to scramble over the various rows of control panels and monitors. Others had died while crouched underneath them, their bodies rolled up into balls that had done little against whatever large instrument had been used to slice into their bodies. Even more littered the various steps that led past the rows of consoles and down to the center of the room.

The middle of the room looked like it had once been a wide, open floor, with the lowest row of consoles around it forming a perfect rectangle. Now, it was covered by a large pile of bodies, maybe twenty to thirty people piled together. Bloody track marks covered the floor where the bodies had been dragged from wherever they had died over to the pile. And it wasn't just office workers that made up the gruesome mound of bodies. Black robes were also thrown into the heap, with no obvious reason why some were chosen and others had been left wherever they had died.

"They must have ushered the whole floor into this room," Hinderlight said at Eddie's side. "And then whatever came out of this door got them all at the same time."

"This would explain why the black robes were having trouble finding whatever it is they are looking for." Kaga paused as he returned his gaze to the carnage inside. "If they lost control over this room, it would make it much harder for them to move around."

"That's why they must have wanted me," Hinderlight agreed. "Or more specifically, wanted my level of elevator access. They're stuck in the lobby."

"Good. Let them stay stuck up there, the bastards." Kaga emphasized his words by kicking a robe-wearing corpse.

Eddie was less than relieved. He had been scanning the mass of dead bodies scattered around the room. With some in pieces, it was hard to get an accurate count of the devastation. He settled on counting what he thought were complete bodies. Then stopped once he reached the forties. Even if some of the deaths had been caused by the black robes, whatever killed the rest had to be something horrible. And unless it also knew a way to get around the security measures on the elevator, it was still on the floor somewhere.

"We're not safe here," Eddie muttered.

"What?" Hinderlight asked. Kaga's eyes fell on him too, making him pause before answering.

"Whatever did this is still around." Eddie gestured about. He could have closed his eyes, spun around, and pointed and he still would have been aiming his finger at a body. Or a part of one. "We can't stay here."

"Except we *have to*, Eddie. If we control this room, we can start taking back control of the facility. Get word to the outside world. Lift the lockdown when it's safe." Hinderlight placed a hand on his shoulder. It was probably meant to be reassuring, but after what Kaga said, it just made Eddie feel like a placated child.

"Boss man is right." Kaga said and moved in through the doors. "But so is the janitor. Let's see if we can get this place locked down in case whatever walking blender killed all these people decides to come back."

"You're right. I'll try to see if the door is salvageable, or if I can at least barricade it."

Kaga let out a grim chuckle. "Hope you can make it stronger than whatever busted through it the first time."

Hinderlight responded with a grunt and moved off toward the doorway.

"Come on, Eddie." Kaga gave him a not so gentle push forward. "Let's see if we can get some of the blood cleaned off one of these consoles and try to bring some order back to this place."

The smell was even worse as they walked into the room. It reminded him of the one home he lived at as a child that was right around the corner from a slaughterhouse. If they had been outside, instead of who knows how deep underground, they would probably be choking on flies as much as they were the stench. As they moved further into the room, Eddie had to stop twice to keep from vomiting. As strange as it was, Eddie began to be thankful for the overwhelming smell of the room. It took all of his willpower and focus to keep from throwing up, which kept his mind away from the horrendous loss of life that surrounded him. Part of him feared that if he was able to sit and process the death toll, it might reduce him to tears. Which was the last thing he needed to do in front of the other two men.

Kaga seemed unperturbed as he moved about the array of bodies and electronic equipment. Every so often he would pause at a console, a small glimmer of hope lighting up his eyes. He would then swipe off whatever blood or body part half obscuring the monitor and clack away from a few moments on the keyboard before smashing his fist down on it and muttering a curse.

Behind them, Hinderlight began his work on the door. Clanks and groans of metal on metal filled the air, mixing in with Kaga's grunts and growls. When the tattooed man had effectively broken his fifth keyboard, he rounded on Eddie.

"Blasted things are either broken or have their security access locked. Instead of standing there with your thumb up your ass, help me try and find one that still has the operator logged in. Or start searching the bodies for some kind of access code."

Eddie hadn't realized he had just been standing still until Kaga turned his ire on him. Not wanting to anger the man any further, or start digging through corpses, he moved over to the row of consoles next to Kaga and got to work. To keep his nerves and stomach from doing summersaults, Eddie did his best not think about the things he was removing from the tops of the consoles. Crimson stains were just partially dried blots of jelly. Appendages were tightly rolled stacks of paper towels. As he tried and failed to find an unlocked console, he let his mind focus on the sounds Hinderlight was making as he worked. Clanks. Clicking noises. Screeches. He had finished a whole row without any luck trying to distract himself with the sounds and illusion of doing simple janitorial work.

It was when he crouched down at the next row of consoles near the center of the room that he realized the only sounds Hinderlight was producing now were the strange clicking noises. Like a rusty pair of scissors opening and closing. Except the scissors had to be much larger than your average pair to produce such a loud noise. Curiosity made Eddie look for Hinderlight more intently.

Except Hinderlight wasn't by the doorway. Eddie glanced around but couldn't find the man, and yet the sound continued to grow louder. He was about to rise and ask Kaga if he knew where Hinderlight was when the clicking sound seemed to hit its peak.

And then, by the mangled and bloody door, the noise's origin poked its head around the doorway. Something new to add to his growing list of nightmare material.

CHAPTER 21

Eddie saw just the head first, a massive thing that was mostly a gray beak and deep blue and purple feathers. Two pale green eyes sat at the end of the beak, which was covered in pinpoint whiskers. Its head swiveled around a bit on an elongated neck, which wore a thick black collar with the end of a broken chain attached, before the rest of it walked into the room. Roughly the size of a grizzly bear, its body looked like a turtle with the bottom half of the shell removed. Light purple leathery skin ran from the top of its neck down its torso, ending in a stubby tail. Its back was covered in some kind exoskeleton shell studded by sharp, bony protuberances. Massive, muscular arms ended in long, hooked claws covered in triangular bone spurs. The whole thing was held up by thick, elephant-sized legs, also covered in feathers, that ended in what a chicken's foot might look like if given an over-abundance of growth hormones.

"Freeze," Kaga whispered from the other side of the console where Eddie crouched, his voice hoarse. "A Khurobak. Don't make a sound."

The man sounded so sure of himself that Eddie did just that, frozen in a half crouch near one of the bodies. The smell made his eyes water and stomach churn but he remained still. His eyes locked on the new monstrosity that had appeared.

The head, extended out in front of the Khurobak's body, swiveled back and forth a few times. The eyes, devoid of irises, never blinked and its beak kept opening and closing slightly as if it was tasting the air. After a few tense moments, the beak dropped toward the nearest corpse and the monster's two large claws sank into either end of the body with a sickening *thunk*. The giant beak dipped and clamped down on the leg of what looked like one of the office workers. The sharp edges of its mouth sliced through clothing and flesh as easily as a hot knife through butter. When its head rose again, blood dripped from its beak and its mouth moved in a chewing motion. Letting out a loud gurgle, it threw its head straight up in the air, neck extended, and began gulping down its meal. Its throat bulged as a large chunk of office worker slid down. When it

173

had finished, it dropped its head and took another bite.

Eddie's already sore body ached as he tried to stay perfectly still and watch the Khurobak. The monster, just like the giant bat, was as impressive to behold as it was terrifying. Things like The Jester and The Reaper at least appeared human, and Eddie could apply his basic understanding of what existed in the world toward them, but creatures like this defied everything he knew. He knew he should be afraid. Knew he should be shaking in fear, especially with all of the carnage the creature had probably wrought all around him. But he stared at it with a vast sense of wonder, similar to the first time he had seen a documentary about great white sharks. While a large part of him wanted to crawl under the other bodies and hide, there existed a part that wanted to walk right up and run his hand over the lilac feathers and feel the grooves in its indigo shell.

Something struck his cheek and fell against his chest as it fell. Eddie clamped his hands over his mouth to suppress the surprised yell that almost gave him away. Looking down to see what hit him, he found a severed finger rolling to a stop not too far from his side. When he looked back up, Kaga slowly and deliberately mouthed the words *"Blind"* and *"Hunts by sound. Move to far wall. QUIETLY."*

Eddie dipped his head in understanding. Turning his back on the monster in the doorway, which was a feat of bravery in itself, he began to make his way down the aisle toward the wall. Each step had to be carefully placed. Bodies and appendages littered the small path in between the consoles, as did overturned chairs and smashed electronics. Each one was a trap, a potential alarm to alert the creature that a fresh meal was slowly creeping away. He kept his breaths as quiet as possible, trying to keep calm while his heart thudded against his chest.

Despite his worries, they met at the wall without incident. Crouched at the edge of the consoles, Eddie found some courage in the other man's presence, especially with the combat knife gripped tightly in Kaga's hand. A quick look around found no sign of Hinderlight. Eddie turned to find the Khurobak slurping down another bite. When it had finished, it reared back and sunk its hooks into one of the more fully appendaged corpses near the door with a loud *thunk*. Stepping carefully, it began to turn itself around until its stubby tail pointed into the center of the room, then began stepping backward, pulling the body along behind it.

"Start moving toward the door," Kaga mouthed.

Without waiting, Kaga began a slow climb up the path between the wall and the rows of consoles. Eddie moved behind him, his eyes locked on the man in front of him. Every instinct told him to watch the monster instead. His mind began painting pictures of turning around just as the Khurobak sliced its hooks down into his back. The smell all around him mocked him with his probable fate, to become just another piece of meat to add to the creature's food pile.

No, Eddie thought, pushing the thoughts from his mind. *I'm not going to be the scared little mouse Kaga expects.*

Pushing down his fear, Eddie made his muscles relax as he navigated the various body parts strewn about. Because he was focused on what *might* happen to him, he was determined not make a careless mistake. Eddie would follow the man in front of him and they would make it out of here without the Khurobak even seeing them.

Except Eddie was so focused on avoiding body parts that he failed to see the one Kaga was just about to step on.

Kaga's foot kicked a dismembered limb, which rolled out ahead of him. It threw him off balance and he reached out to catch himself on one of the nearby consoles. Which wouldn't have been a problem if he hadn't been holding a knife already. Metal smacking metal let out a ringing note. It might as well have been a dinner bell.

Eddie turned to see the Khurobak swing its head in their direction. Its hooks releasing the body it was dragging and stepped up onto a nearby console. Still a good five rows away. The feathers on its neck ruffled and it let out what sounded like a mixture of a turkey gobbling and an eagle screeching. When it had finished, the Khurobak tilted its head to the side and perched perfectly still.

Eddie hadn't moved. Barely breathed. Maybe if they kept quiet, it would dismiss the noise it heard and go back to feeding.

The Khurobak let out another horrible noise, then hopped to the next row of consoles. Or at least it tried. The monster fell short, smashing into the control panel and knocking one of the screens to the ground.

Kaga grabbed the closest body part, what looked like a leg in a gray pair of slacks, and leaned back as if he were going to throw it.

"Go," Kaga growled.

Eddie's gaze locked ahead as he sprinted up the stairs. He had only made it a few steps, his feet sounding thudding against the floor, before Kaga was at his side.

Their only saving grace was that the Khurobak seemed confused on which noise to go after first. Eddie heard the leg strike a console, knocking things off with a loud clatter. An even larger crashed followed as the Khurobak went after the sound. Eddie didn't bother to look back until both he and Kaga had reached the door.

Seeing the beast's beaked head pointed in his direction made Eddie immediately wish he hadn't looked.

Kaga headed away from the corridor they had come from to get to the room. Eddie hesitated for a moment, but then ran back the way they came. He might have a better chance of survival with Kaga, but he knew the other way, remembered where the dead ends were and which turns to make to get back to the elevator. He sprinted as hard as his injured body would allow down the long hallways and sharp turns until he almost ran right into Hinderlight.

"Where . . ." Eddie gasped as he stumbled to a halt.

"I went back to one of the supply closets we passed to get some tools to help work on the door. What--"

Hinderlight cut off as the Khurobak came crashing around the corner.

"Holy shit!" Hinderlight said and fled back in the direction of the elevators. Without time to think, Eddie did the same.

They raced down the hallway, Hinderlight taking lefts and rights as fast as he could. Eddie kept with him, but got completely turned around as they seemed to take the first branching hallway every time. He had no idea if Hinderlight knew where they were going or was just trying to lose the creature. The latter didn't seem to be working as Eddie continued to hear the monster crashing along behind them, just out of sight.

"Maybe we can trap it in the elevator," Eddie got out as they ran. "If you can get us back there."

Hinderlight looked like he was about to shake his head as he ran but instead spoke. "Yes," he finally got out. "Let's try. This way."

They ran on down the maze of hallways. Now, with a specific goal in mind, Hinderlight made less turns. He paused for the briefest moments to get his bearings before rushing on. With every pause, every long corridor they sped down without turning, Eddie caught a glimpse of what pursued them. Beak, hooks, feathers and all. It was relentless in its pursuit, always seeming to stay right on their trail.

Eventually, one turn led into a hallway which led to the lobby of the floor. The sight of the open area, its couches, and the possibility of survival, added new life to Eddie's legs. He pumped them as hard as he could, catching and almost passing Hinderlight as they ran into the room. Within seconds, they were across the carpeted floor and at their goal.

It wasn't until Eddie and Hinderlight were in front of the elevator door that they realized the flaw in their plan. The door was big enough for the monster to get in, except with the monster this close on their heels there was no way someone would be able to lure the Khurobak inside without getting caught in it as well.

"This isn't going to work," Eddie said between pants of breath.

"I know. Sorry, Eddie." Hinderlight had his attention on the creature. "I need to lock down the control room, which means trapping or killing that beast. Keeping us both alive at this point would be impossible."

Before Eddie could respond, Hinderlight swiped his keycard through the reader. The monster let out a howl that echoed through the room as the elevator door opened. Hinderlight grabbed Eddie by the collar and swung him around. Caught off guard, all he could do was flail his arms like a fool. With a strained grunt, Hinderlight launched Eddie into the elevator. He slammed sideways into the back wall, all of his breath whooshing out of his lungs from the impact before dropping to the floor. Eddie tried getting up, even as he struggled for breath. All he managed was to get on his hands and knees, his elbows shaking as he pushed himself up enough to look out of the elevator. Hinderlight was standing there, his arm extended toward the card reader on the outside.

"Survive," Hinderlight said, his eyes half shut and a grimace crossing his face. Then the man slid his arm up and the elevator began to close. To Eddie's credit, he made it halfway across the floor before the doors closed completely. He heard shouting and growls. Something banged against the door. Then silence. Silence that lasted three hundred breaths. Eddie counted each one, as he remained on his hands and knees, hoping that Hinderlight would open the door. That he and Kaga would give the all clear and pick him up, as they had in the past. But they never came.

And Eddie, for the first time since things had gone to hell, found himself alone.

CHAPTER 22

Eddie Watson's Life Rule Number 981: Get busy livin', or get busy dying.

Alright, that was a line from Shawshank Redemption. One of the few movies that Eddie actually enjoyed. The line certainly fit in Eddie's current situation though. Stuck on an elevator. Allies gone or dead. Cultists, monsters, and the unkillable Horrors loose in the building. He had two options. Sit around in the elevator and hope to be rescued *or* try to figure a way out and do something with what was left of his considerably shorter life span.

...you sure as hell don't contribute much to my own survival.

Kaga's words lit a fuse in Eddie that he didn't even know was there. He had helped people today, even without the training and overwhelming confidence the other two men had. All while he stayed true to who he was as a person. Eddie might not be able to do as much as the other men, but he could still do *something*.

Eddie Watson's Life Rule Number 19: Small victories lead to greater successes.

And that first victory was finding a way out of the elevator. He went to stand, but his body screamed at him for making the effort. Soreness from his previous beating mixed in with a sharper pain in his side from getting tossed into the elevator wall did not want him to rise. So his first victory came from forcing his body to stand when it felt like he had been put through a tenderizer. With that accomplished, he turned his attention on escape.

The most obvious solution was to try the elevator buttons first. When the three of them had first pulled Hinderlight into the elevator, Eddie hadn't paid much attention to the array of control buttons. Seven different colored buttons ran in a vertical line, each one an oval as long as Eddie's finger. Kaga had smacked the second from the bottom, the emerald colored one, which meant that was for the control room floor. That one he would leave alone. If Hinderlight thought it better to try and take on that monster without him, Eddie would respect his decision. That left six other buttons to press. Since Kaga had said that all of the elevators had unlabeled, colored buttons to make sure that only the people that belonged on the elevators knew where they were going, Eddie picked one at random. A bright orange button right in the middle.

Nothing happened. He pressed a different button. Still nothing. Eddie pressed each button in turn, except for the emerald one, without any effect. Not even a warning buzzer. He hadn't really expected the elevator to move without an access card but hoped it would at least take him back to the lobby. It was doubtful the black robes would have just been standing around waiting for someone to come up after all, and he would have gladly taken his chances with a human foe as opposed to the other things that were *supposed* to be contained in the facility.

Or The Zoo, Eddie thought, *as Kaga kept calling it.*

But the name of the place wasn't going to get him out of the elevator.

"Access hatches," Eddie mumbled to himself. "Every elevator has some kind of access hatch."

The floor was a solid piece of laminate designed to look like off-white tiles so it probably wasn't underneath that. The ceiling was made of mirrored panels, each one more than wide enough to fit a person through. He couldn't make out any variation from where he was standing, but they were his best bet. Eddie just had to get onto something so he would be tall enough to examine them. The side of the elevator had thin, brass handrails, not the best step ladder but he would take what he could get. Using the corner to help him balance, Eddie was able to climb onto a handrail. If he pressed his hands along the ceiling, he could keep himself up and examine about half of the panels for a way out. Which he did and found nothing. Not letting himself feel defeated, Eddie got down and tried the other side.

"Success!"

One of the panels in the back corner unhooked from a latch as he pressed it up, swinging it down to reveal an opening to a square hatch. Eddie had expected with his luck to find it locked, but the small handle turned easily and with a single shove, swung upwards and away with a light squeak. Darkness greeted him through the opening. Not a single light stood out as a beacon in the shaft above. Thankfully, he still felt the small bulge of the flashlight he had taken from the armory in his pocket. When he brought it out and clicked it on, the small light did little to combat the darkness above. But at least it was something. From his vantage point, the small beam of light illuminated the elevator cable as it stretched up and disappeared above him.

For a long time Eddie stood there, perched on the handrail with the light shining into the darkness. His mind created all manner of creatures that could be hiding just out of reach of the light. Ready to snatch him up and drag him into the shadows, never to be seen from again. But one image overrode the others. Hinderlight's pitying glance.

Anger and determination pushed aside his fear. Putting the flashlight between his teeth, he reached out and gripped the edge of the opening. His arms strained as he attempted what might have been his first actual pull-up in years. Even so, he got his chin above the opening, one arm and then the other. With muscles screaming at him, Eddie pulled the rest of his body out and onto the top of the elevator. He turned onto his back and was immediately greet by the vast darkness above him. His fingers snatched the flashlight out of his mouth and he pointed the meager light upwards.

Nothing descended upon him. He swung the flashlight around, checking all four corners of the square elevator shaft, flashing it at every metal beam that provided support for both the shaft and the elevator. Still nothing. He lay there in silence, using the weak light to unveil as much as it could while he listened. When the only sound that reached him was his heavy breaths, Eddie finally let himself relax. Sitting up, he did a slow pan around the walls of the elevator shaft until he found what he was looking for. A metal ladder stretched up into the darkness on his left, a good two feet between both the elevator and the wall. A way up and hopefully a way out.

Another small victory.

Eddie got up and moved onto the ladder. A small voice inside his head told him to glance down at the space between the elevator and the wall, but he couldn't bring himself to do it. Heights had never been an issue for him, but there was something unnerving about the thought of staring down into the dark nothingness. Best to just focus on going up. Placing the light back between his teeth, Eddie began to climb.

Except as he moved, he found it more and more difficult *not* to

181

look down. He only made it a few rungs before he began looking back at the soft glow of light exiting the elevator hatch. As weak as it was, it was certainly more inviting than the darkness above. But if moving up was equivalent to moving forward, upward he would go.

He passed a number of small, rectangular vents as he climbed, large enough for a man to crawl through, stretching off into the building. Eddie didn't have a phobia of enclosed spaces either, but he would prefer not to find himself wedged into the tight space. He continued climbing, looking for a better way out of the elevator shaft. Once the elevator was far enough down that his light no longer could reach it, he stopped looking. The small amount of light that shot upward from the opening still provided a small sense of comfort.

At last his meager flashlight found a large break in the wall above him. Climbing a few more rungs, he caught a glimpse of an outer elevator door. *An escape!* If he could get it open, of course, but it still offered a ray of hope, a destination with a way out of the oppressive darkness. He climbed up until he was right next to it, reached over, and touched the metal. Maneuvering himself to the edge of the ladder, he wrapped his legs as tight as he could around the rungs and then stretched out until his fingers were wedged into the seam of the doors. Making sure he had a strong hold of both the opening and the ladder, Eddie pulled with all his might. Grunting and groaning with the effort, Eddie strained against the door, his muscles protesting.

He couldn't even get the metal doors to shudder the barest fraction of an inch.

Feeling slightly defeated, Eddie maneuvered himself back fully onto the ladder and rested his head over a rung, facing down as he caught his breath. Which is how he noticed the weak ray of light from the elevator hatch go dark for a few seconds before returning to its faint dot of light.

Eddie climbed down a few rungs and aimed his light into the darkness below. He was too high for his weak light to reach the elevator, but he still saw the light coming out of it through the hatch. Had his mind played a trick on him? Maybe he had blinked without realizing it, an involuntary movement that had blocked out all of the light. Except something was making the hairs on his arm stand on end.

And he no longer felt alone.

The light of the flashlight only went so far, but he began to scan the walls as far down as it would reach. Metal beams and bolts greeted him. Shadows danced around as he tried to search as much of the shaft as he could with the light, moving it until they disappeared, reappearing on the other side as the light ran along the wall.

Except for one shadowy form that stood out from the rest of the elevator shaft, a few dozen feet down. It sat in the beam from Eddie's flashlight for a time before disappearing behind one of the thicker girders on the opposite side of the shaft. Eddie kept the light on that spot, again not fully trusting his eyes.

Nothing moved. A thought occurred to him and he moved the beam up a few feet, waited five breaths, then quickly brought the light back to the original spot.

Eight golden eyes reflected the light back at him, four on each side of a head the color of the metal all around it. With Eddie's full attention on the creature, he could make out the ends of eight legs wrapped around one of the four-foot wide beams used to steady the elevator. Furry mandibles rubbed together as it stared back at him with eight golden hexagons. He could almost feel it studying him before the head disappeared back behind the girder.

Eddie no longer wanted to be in the elevator shaft.

The elevator door wasn't an option. That just left one of the vent openings he had passed during his climb. There was one a few rungs down. It was large enough for him but not large enough to fit whatever body could hold up the head of what still hid behind the girders. Sticking the flashlight between his teeth, Eddie moved down the ladder as fast as he dared, doing his best to point the light toward the creature. With each step he expected the creature to rush out at him, but the light seemed to keep it behind the girder. When Eddie had moved far enough down, he clung to the ladder with one arm and reached backward and felt around until his fingers touched open space. He was about to turn and pull himself into the opening when the barest whisper of a sound, like velvet against metal, drew his attention. He pointed his light up toward the same girder to a spot directly across from him.

Again the light found eight golden eyes watching him, measuring him. The creature must have moved straight down behind the girder. Silently. A predator hunting its prey. It stayed longer in the light this time before disappearing behind the girder again.

Eddie wasn't about to wait to see what it did next. He swung himself around to the opposite side of the ladder and reached across with both hands to the vent. Pushing off with his legs, he practically dove through the opening. The impact knocked the flashlight free from his hand and he heard it clatter as it fell down the side of the shaft. But his real concern was for his calves and feet as they still dangled outside of the vent like meaty worms. Using his elbows to propel himself the rest of the way in, Eddie began to crawl as fast as he could away from the vent opening. His elbows, knees, and head banged against the pliable metal walls but he ignored the pain as he kept going. His only thought was to get as far as he could.

A dull, scraping sound took up behind him.

Something touched his right foot. Hooking it. Eddie felt the pressure of his foot being squeezed, the intensity increasing until Eddie was sure he wouldn't be able to easily shake free.

And then it started to pull.

Panic struck as he let loose a yell. He kicked at whatever held him but it wouldn't let go. It pulled, slowly, methodically, dragging him back toward the vent opening. Eddie flailed about, kicking, trying to grab onto something. The smooth metal walls gave his fingers nothing for purchase. And still, it pulled him as he twisted and turned, no rush or frantic movements, just the steady motion of drawing him closer and closer to the elevator shaft.

Suddenly, his impending doom cleared his mind somehow. Instead of picturing the chittering maw that awaited him, Eddie's mind went back to his adolescence. A memory long forgotten but filled with the same fear he now felt. Trying to escape and hide. Crawling under a porch. A hand grabbing his foot, trying to pull him back. His shoe coming free and then escape. Hiding until a police officer found him and brought him away.

Eddie stopped his frantic jerks and focused. Free foot to opposite heel. A strong push. His shoe came free and shot away, as did whatever still had a hold of it. An angry chittering rose up behind him and the soft scraping returned, but Eddie was already moving. Crawling as fast as he could on bruised elbows, pressing off with the sole of his still shoed foot while the other slipped around as he tried to gain purchase. He continued to crawl until the scratching either stopped or was too far away for him to hear. He then collapsed onto his stomach, his face pressed against the metal, breaths coming hard and heavy.

Another gruesome death averted.

Another small victory achieved.

Which left him panting, alone, and with only one shoe as he crawled ahead in the cold darkness of the vent.

CHAPTER 23

"Alright Eddie," he said to himself, "which way this time?"

This was the seventh cross-junction he had reached since crawling around in the tight metal confines of the vent. Seven cross-junctions, four T-junctions, two forced left turns, and three forced right turns. Twice, he had crawled right into a sharp downward slope that had him sliding down, faster than he would have liked, coming to a stop as his hands and then his face smacked into the vent as it leveled out again. The first time the thud of the impact echoed all around him, Eddie had worried about bringing some other monstrosity crawling through the vents to find him. He had lain as still as a dead mouse, his ears straining as he waited to hear even the tiniest ping of something else moving through the vent. Had waited as fear twisted his gut and made the hairs on the back of his neck stand on end. Waited until the fear drained away and he realized that it was actually hunger that gripped his stomach and the circulating air in the vent that caressed his neck. At that point, he allowed himself to laugh and began crawling again. When he came crashing down the second time, he let out a curse and kept moving.

Eddie did all this without even the smallest ember of light.

And a missing shoe.

"Think I'll try going straight this time."

His voice echoed eerily in the small confines of the vent. After that, Eddie decided to keep speaking to a minimum.

Crawling along, with only his thoughts to accompany him, Eddie's mind began to wander. He blocked thoughts of the horrors he had seen, those that might lay ahead, and instead focused on the ones from his past. Those that he hadn't completely blocked from his memory.

Thirteen different families had taken him in through his early youth and adolescence. Thirteen homes that passed background checks and filled out all of their paperwork perfectly. Thirteen sets of parents that displayed to the authorities in charge of his case a wholesome desire to add him to their family. Eddie had gone into each one as if starting his life anew, and each one had ended in some form of tragedy or abuse. When the smoked cleared, he would be whisked away and sent back to the group home for boys.

When he let his mind explore the dark reaches of his past, Eddie always went back to the first family he remembered. He had been six at the time, happy to be out of the group home and seeing the world as if for the first time. His foster parents, the Hendersons, had seemed as normal as their name. They had visited Eddie six times during the whole process of adoption, talking about how wonderful their life would be once he came home with them. How excited their older son, Bailey, was to gain a little brother. Only a month after going home with them, Eddie had woken in a hospital surrounded by nurses, and men and women in nice brown and black suits asking him questions which he answered with his throat raw and his voice sounding like a croaking frog. The Hendersons had been there as well, answering questions, glancing back and forth between Eddie and what he had later found out were social workers.

The biggest surprise to Eddie while he lay in the hospital bed, connected to all forms of monitors, had been the first time he had heard the Hendersons lie. Lie to protect their real son. Thankfully, the social worker must have seen through their nervous smiles and forced concern. Eddie was taken straight from the hospital back to the group home. He never saw the Hendersons again. Except in his nightmares. He would be staring up from underneath the water, his head banging against the bottom of the bathtub, Bailey's arms securing him in place. Everything distorted by the splashing water except for Bailey's cold brown eyes as they stared down. In his nightmares, though, Bailey's parents were always there as well, staring down and not moving to help.

Eddie would wake up just as he felt his lungs begin to burst and the water rush into his mouth as he tried to take in a breath. He would wake to a coughing fit, in his own apartment instead of a hospital bed. It would take him a few moments to remember where he was before he could calm down. Even in his late twenties, that nightmare still returned the most, even though he couldn't even remember the first names of his first foster parents. Just Bailey's.

Lost in thought, Eddie fell victim to another downward slope in the vent. He slid down this one just as fast as the others, bracing himself for the eventual impact. Pain lanced up his arms as they struck the thin metal, accompanied by a loud gong. The force of his body coming to an abrupt stop folded Eddie up on himself. When the ringing in his bones stopped, he unfolded himself until his body was horizontal and gave his aching arms the chance to recover before he started moving again.

Lying there in the darkness, body aching, allies taken by strange men in black robes or probably torn to shreds by some oversized, hook-limbed chicken, things looked fairly bleak. He had no weapon, no backup, and no right shoe. Then again, he had survived so far.

"Small victories, right?" Eddie pushed himself up onto his elbows. "Let's see if I can get out of this stupid vent."

Despite the protests of his muscles, Eddie began crawling along again. There had to be a way out that wasn't back into the elevator shaft with the giant spider. A maintenance hatch. Vents into a bathroom or office. Or more preferably, a break room stocked with food and water. He just had to make one lucky guess at the next intersection. The thought drove him onward.

Until at last, he saw the faintest ray of light illuminating the vent further ahead.

At first, he thought it was just his mind playing tricks on him, telling his eyes what it expected to see despite the darkness. As he crawled forward, the image remained. He could start to make out where each section of the vent was welded together. The bolts that held it in place. And most importantly, the origin of the meager light that fought against what had been a neverending procession through darkness. The light invigorated him, pushed him forward. Even when he reached its source and found a thin grate no wider than a toaster, his excitement remained. It looked down into a room, which meant it was possible he could find another grate, in another room, that might be big enough for him to kick out and crawl through.

Eddie was about to move on but curiosity got the better of him and he placed his face right up against the grate so that he could get a good view of the room below. The room was the size of your average living room, except devoid of any furniture or defining features. The floor was a good ten feet below him, pure white, like a bleached bone left out in the sun. The walls were the same color, devoid of decoration. The only discernible break in the sterile white was a single door placed on the left side of one of the walls and a long glass window waist high, a few feet tall and spanning the rest of the wall from the door to the far corner.

What really caught his eye, though, was what resided inside. A woman appeared to be curled up in the corner, her long, coffee-colored hair covering most of her body. She wore a tan leather shirt that hung from her shoulders but still managed to show the curves that marked her as a woman. The leather looked old, not the type women wore walking the streets of the city; this was more frayed and untreated. She wore shorts made from a similar material which left her calves and feet bare. The woman's skin was a sickly, tawny color and almost blended in with the outfit she wore. Something struck Eddie as odd about the huddled up woman, besides the fact that she appeared to be locked in a stark white room, but he couldn't put his finger on it. Still, she was the first person he had seen in a while. Feeling secure in his vent high above her, Eddie decided to see if she was ok and what she knew.

"Hello," he called through the grate. "Are you ok?"

The woman lifted her head slightly, but her face was still hidden behind the mass of hair. Eddie heard what might have been a sniffle from her, but then she curled up into a tighter ball.

"It's ok." He tried to make his voice as friendly as possible. "I'm not going to hurt you. Couldn't even if I *did* want to. I'm stuck in the vents above you."

Her head perked up at that, the hair rustling like chocolate waves as she swung it aside with a flick of her neck.

Which revealed a face more feline than human. Almond shaped eyes, irises as black as fresh ink stared up at him from deep inside her face. A brown, triangular nose wrinkled a few times and sniffed at the air, the whiskers coming off of her muzzle twitching. Where Eddie had thought her skin a sickly color, on closer inspection he realized that it was fur, and not skin, that held the tawny color. It covered everywhere Eddie could see, from her neck, down to her hands and long-clawed fingers, even her feet, which looked like a strange combination of a human foot and paw.

Her appearance took him aback for a moment, all of his previous encounters with otherworldly creatures making him pause. Except her eyes reflected back an intelligence that he hadn't seen in the other creatures. An intelligence and sorrow.

"Um....hello." The words sounded foolish as they left Eddie's mouth.

"Gado, detsadoa?" Despite her feline features, the woman's voice was clearly human, even if her words were foreign to him.

"I don't understand. Do you understand me?"

She tilted her head to the side. "Goliga."

"Is that a yes? No?" Eddie would have banged his fists on the vent in frustration if they weren't already sore from doing that exact same thing as he crawled around in the dark. "I don't suppose you'll be able to help me much."

The woman let out a sigh and curled back in on herself. "Nulisgediyvna."

"I'm sorry, I don't understand—"

"Wena!" It came out halfway between a growl and roar with a mixture of anguish and pain thrown in for good measure. "Wena!"

Even though he couldn't understand her, he got the gist of what she wanted from the dismissive tone of her voice. Eddie took one last look at the woman, locked away with nothing but the clothes on her back, and then started to crawl on. Was this how all of the things detained were treated? He could understand that kind of treatment would be acceptable for a killing machine like The Reaper or a psychopath like The Jester. The woman, despite her appearance, seemed to be in complete despair over her situation. Was that her life now, forever locked away unless whoever worked here decided to run some tests on her?

If Eddie was being honest, he had even felt a moment of compassion for The Jester anytime it mentioned the torturous experiments they performed on it. Only a moment, though. The Jester had murdered someone right in front of him and the rest of his group. But was the feline woman just as dangerous?

For the first time since the madness of the day had begun, Eddie wasn't running from his life or worrying about where the next attack would come from. It was here, in the relative safety of the venting system, that he began to question the motivations and ethical practices of Soladyne Tech. From the things Hinderlight had said, Eddie had been under the impression that the company protected the common people from the monsters that apparently existed in the world. Conducted research and made use of their finds to better humanity. But was this the cost? Locking away intelligent creatures, regardless of whether they were a danger or not? And what kind of experiments did they perform? Were they humane or the type no government would allow done even on animals? From what The Jester had said, it seemed more likely the latter.

As Eddie crawled along, the light coming from the woman's cell fading behind him, questions and doubts began to infect his mind. He tried his best to push it out of his head. Focus on the task ahead. Find a way out of these stupid vents. But hundreds of hours combing through the philosophies and ideals of mankind's greatest thinkers had hardwired his brain. Everything he had learned while getting his education made him lean toward believing there was a much darker side to the corporation than he had been shown. And now, unsupervised by Hinderlight or anyone else that might want to keep the truth from him, he had the chance to discover if his gut feeling about Soladyne was correct.

Eddie had two objectives now. Survive, of course still being the first, but the second was to find out as much as he could about the company and the things held down here in the facility.

Neither of which changed his short-term goal of getting out of the blasted vents.

Thankfully, it wasn't long until he noticed more light coming from the next T-junction. A few moments later, he was crawling toward another vent, the growing light pouring through giving him hope. But it wasn't just light that reached his senses. The strong aroma of freshly brewed coffee drifted through the tight space, making his stomach growl with apprehension and his mouth water. If there was coffee, then there might be food as well. Doing his best to contain his excitement, Eddie increased his pace until he reached the covered opening. Sure enough, he found a vent large enough for him to fit through if he could get it free. A quick glance in found comfortable looking couches, a table with surrounding chairs, countertops with a microwave, and a sink sitting next to a silver, two-door fridge. Anticipation of finding what wonderful treats might lay inside made him raise his hands, ready to beat at the grate until it came free.

Instead, he froze as voices began to speak below.

Angling himself so he could get a better look around the room, Eddie's heart sank as he spotted two men standing in black robes, their heads uncovered. Despite the fact that they both had to be a part of the cult, the worst part was what they each held.

A cup of coffee and a mouth-watering, cream-filled doughnut.

CHAPTER 24

"Damn, these are good," one of the robed men said, his mouth half full. "That was a good idea, Carl, finding a break room and getting something to eat."

"Sure," Carl replied as paused to take a sip from his cup. "I mean, why rush around rounding up all of the scientists on this floor? It's not like they're going anywhere."

"A valid point," the other man replied before stuffing his mouth with more doughnut.

Eddie stared down at the men, feeling a bit disappointed. Not just over the inability to get a doughnut for himself, but the appearance of the men without their hoods.

They looked normal.

No scary tattoos or facial deformities. No dark murmuring or praying to some long forgotten god. They didn't toss about magical spells as Hinderlight had warned. These were just two average Joes, standing around, having a conversation while they slacked on their duties. If not for the clothes, they could have been custodians like him on their break.

It was disappointing, but also at the same time, a relief. Without their numbers, the robed men were no longer one of the many things in the facility that Eddie had to fear.

That wasn't to say he thought he could take on the two below him, unfortunately. Hinderlight, or Kaga, or any of the other security personnel could probably handle the two without breaking a sweat. All Eddie could do was lie in the vent and listen, while hoping they got bored and left so he could find a way to remove the grate, climb down, and find something to eat. So that's what he did, lay there and listen.

After taking another sip, Carl waved the doughnut in his other hand to take in the entire room. "Surprised we didn't find any scientists in here. If I was somewhere that went on lockdown and might be holed up for hours, this would be the first place I'd head to."

"I don't know about that," the other man replied. "As soon as I heard any kind of alarm, the last place I'd want to go for security was some break room with a less than secure-looking metal door. Have you seen some of the things they keep down here?"

"Yes, Beck. I looked in a couple of the rooms. Many were empty. The first one I found that wasn't made me wish I could scrub the image of what I saw from my mind."

"I know! I saw this one thing—"

"No, don't tell me. I don't want to know. We see enough weird stuff with this cult. I don't need to add anything else to my nightmares."

"Suit yourself," Beck said with a shrug. "So what should we do now? We haven't heard anything since our fellow brothers took that...what was it called?"

"Khurobak."

"Yeah, that *thing* to the control room. What if it got loose and killed everyone?"

The second man let out a laugh. "Why would they risk something like that? Obviously if our *brothers* didn't think they could control it, they would have left it locked up."

"Maybe. I just don't understand why, if they needed to kill a bunch of people, they didn't just do it themselves instead of using that ugly chicken thing."

"Khurobak," Carl replied. "And it is part of the ritual for Voltozas. Weren't you listening when the Master was giving out instructions?"

"I kind of blanked out after I heard the word 'mutilation.'"

Carl let out a sigh. "That monster had to eat a certain number of people and then be killed itself. It's just one of the many requirements for the ritual."

Eddie repeated what he heard over and over again in his mind. *Voltozas. Ritual.* He had no idea what any of it meant but it might come in handy. To someone.

"Whatever," Beck replied. "Just as long as we receive the rewards we've been promised."

"Exactly. Just think about the end goal. Eternal life. Becoming more than human. All the things promised in the brochure and during the high priestess' rants. We just have to wait our turn is all, after those above us in the ranks get their rewards first."

"You mean the fanatics?" Scorn laced Beck's voice as he

continued. "Chanting and praying. Cutting themselves up. Let them have their rewards first. I'm not about to go mutilating myself when we're all going to be rewarded the same way. Half the stuff they say sounds like gibberish anyway."

"Watch what you say. It would be dangerous if any of those *fanatics* heard you speak like that."

"Yeah, yeah. You have to admit, though, that they seem a bit nutty. Hell, I wouldn't have even believed half of the shit they preached about if they didn't have that creepy ass giant bat hanging over them while they did it."

"True," Carl replied, "and now we're in a facility surrounded by things a hundred times worse if you believe the warnings we received. Can you imagine if even a fraction of these things got loose—"

A screeching noise, like when you hold a live microphone too close to a speaker, cut him off as it filled the air. The vent system only seemed to magnify the sound, and Eddie had to clamp his hands over his ears as it seemed to drill right into his brain. The sound cut off almost as soon it began, but the ringing remained in Eddie's ears. The man's voice that replaced it was slightly distorted like from a speaker.

"Attention, those still alive in The Zoo. My name is Joseph Hinderlight." Eddie silently cheered. *"This is not a drill. Our facility has been infiltrated by unidentified assailants. These men and women are dangerous and have been in control of the entire facility. That has come to an end. I am re-establishing the company's control and then, as we gain more intel on the intruders, we will begin to purge this threat from every level. For now, if your location is secure, remain where you are.*

"Now, for those in the black robes. Your pet chicken monster is dead. We have regained the control room, which means your movements are again restricted. Reinforcements are on the way to the building. My suggestion to you is to give up now, peacefully, before you make things worse for yourself. This is your one and only warning."

There was a pause and for a time static filled the air. When Hinderlight's voice returned, it sounded strained.

"Finally, I want to speak directly to my missing companion. I

pray you are still alive. If so, find your way back to the control room. Although we are secure here, we could still use your assistance as we move forward.

"That is all."

"Well, that's not good," Carl said as Hinderlight's voice cut off. "Maybe things aren't as under control as we believed."

"I think our little break is over." Beck raised his hood so that his head disappeared back into the darkness of the robe. "Let's finish what we were supposed to do and get back to the meet-up point on this floor with the rest of the group."

"Agreed."

Carl emptied what was left in his cup into his mouth then tossed it aside. Securing his own hood, the man took a step then paused. "Crap. Almost forgot the security pass card. I put it down next to the microwave."

"Well, get it then, you—"

A bang echoed below him. Eddie tensed as he watched both men swing around in the same direction.

"They weren't going to let anything else out on this floor, right?" Carl's voice trembled as he asked.

Beck's voice dropped so low that Eddie barely heard his reply. "No. Other than the scientists we were supposed to find, we should be the only ones left on this floor. There shouldn't be anyone around to let anything free."

"Could the scientists have opened up one of the cells?"

Before the other man could answer, a crash as loud as a thunderclap filled the room. Both men leaped back as slivers of metal fell to the floor about them. Beck let out a yell that got cut off as what looked like a huge centipede crashed into him. Carl dove to the side as the other man was enveloped by an endless number of dark orange and brown body segments, each one the size of a love seat. Two pairs of legs sprouted from each segment, thin almost translucent appendages that seemed to move with a mind of their own, stabbing and scrambling over whatever they came into contact with as the body squirmed across the floor where Beck had been just a moment before. Eddie was able to count close to thirty-five segments before the tail finally came into view. As it slithered on, only a bloody mess remained of Beck.

196

The other man didn't wait to join his friend. Carl sprinted out the door while the giant centipede slithered around the room. The insect seemed oblivious to the other man as it coiled around and brought its head back over the pile of chunks that had been Beck. Eddie couldn't bring himself to look away until the creature had finished its meal. When it slithered on with its multitude of legs, not even a drop of poor Beck remained. But the creature didn't seem satisfied. It circled the room a few times and then tore into the fridge.

So much for getting a meal, Eddie thought. *I'll have to look elsewhere.*

With an even louder grumbling stomach, Eddie left the bloodied room behind and continued his journey through the vents. Despite his hunger, he couldn't help but feel his spirits lifted. Hinderlight was alive, and Eddie assumed by the man's confidence over the loud speaker that he had Kaga still with him as well. Eddie had tried not to think about what had happened to the man after he had tossed Eddie into the elevator, but deep down he had assumed the man had finally met his match. It was a relief to find out he had been wrong and that there were still people alive trying to gain control of the facility.

That didn't mean he believed everything Hinderlight had announced. Before being chased out of the control room by the Khurobak, the place had seemed unsalvageable. Hinderlight and Kaga may have the skills to fight off monsters, but that didn't mean they were all that tech savvy. Kaga had seemed more like the type to repeatedly smash a computer until it worked the way he wanted or stopped working completely. If they had been able to get things working as they had claimed, that was wonderful, but Eddie wasn't going to hold his breath. And he certainly wasn't going to sit and wait for the cavalry to arrive.

Plus, he had information now that Hinderlight could use. The Khurobak had been part of some ritual that had gone wrong. Except, did it? The monster still seemed to feast on a number of people, even if the cultists hadn't intended to be counted among them. And if Hinderlight killed the Khurobak, then he finished that part of the ritual for them. That still left whatever artifact for summoning the Voltozas that the men had been talking about. It was all gibberish to Eddie, but Hinderlight and Kaga might have a better idea what it all meant. More importantly, they might know how to keep the cultists from achieving their goals.

Eddie just needed to get out of the god-forsaken vents. If he had actually been paying attention to where he was going instead of thinking about what he wanted to be doing, he would have noticed when the vent ahead of him slopped down again. For the fourth time, Eddie went sliding down, letting out a yell as he sped toward the bottom. This time, when he came to an abrupt stop, he didn't get his arms up in time and a good deal more of his face struck the bottom than he hoped. The impact dimmed his vision while a sharp pain lanced from his forehead down his spine.

As he lay there, trying to get his wits to return, the sound of voices reached his ears once again. Even though his body ached and he felt exhausted, Eddie picked himself up and began to crawl toward what he hoped was someone who could help him.

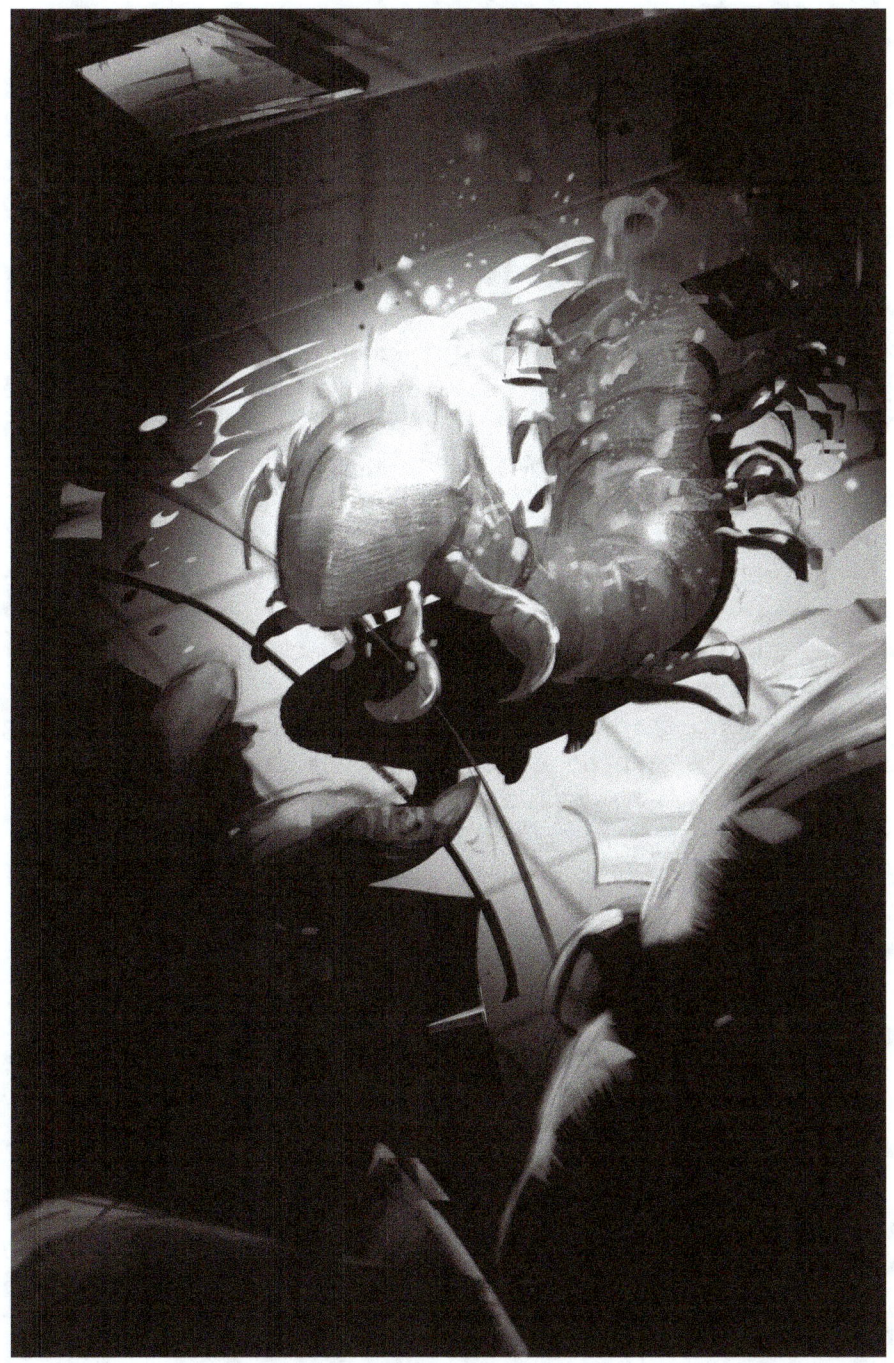

CHAPTER 25

Relief flooded Eddie as he stared down into a restroom and found three men and two women, dressed in white lab coats instead of the intimidating black robes of the cultists.

"Remember, they're *Voltozas* cultists," Eddie mumbled to himself. The name could be important. Maybe the scientists might know. He just had to figure out a way to introduce himself without freaking them out.

The five men and women were all dressed in similar fashion. They wore all white, from their unadorned lab coats, plain, white dress shirts and pants, even their sneakers, which were wrapped in the same coverings he had seen doctors and nurses wear in hospitals. The only thing different about each of their attire was the style and color of their hair and the different glasses each of them wore. At the moment, four out of the five were sitting in a circle on the black tiled floor, while the fifth, a woman with fiery red hair cut short with spiky tips, stalked back and forth in front of the bathroom stalls.

"How long are we going to stay locked in this disgusting bathroom?" the redhead asked. Despite her flamboyant hair color, the deep lines by her eyes and corners of her lips marked her as older than she appeared. Possibly the oldest of the five.

A man with thinning black hair whose features showed hints of Asian descent responded. "You heard the announcement. This isn't some run-of-the-mill lockdown drill. We're under attack. The *intelligent* thing to do is stay here until someone retrieves us."

"Besides," the second woman joined in as she brushed an errant blond strand of hair out from in front of her glasses. She had petite features and her complexion almost matched her attire. "You know everything in this facility, including the bathrooms, are kept immaculately clean."

"Yes, yes," the black haired man replied. "The janitorial staff makes sure even the bathrooms and break rooms are kept as sterile as possible. I myself have written three emails to our human resources department commending the work they do."

The redhead let out a laugh. "I'm sure HR printed out and framed each one, Melvin."

"Indeed," Melvin replied with a knowing nod of his head. Even though Eddie caught the sarcasm that laced the redhead's voice, Melvin apparently missed it.

The blonde woman took the break in the conversation to speak. "Should we even be talking this much? We don't want to attract any attention to ourselves. Just because that man said they were getting things under control doesn't mean we aren't still in danger."

"Niara is right." The second man to speak, an African-American gentleman with a close-cut black beard with hints of gray and a completely bald head, rose to stand. "The infiltrators might be on this floor, or even worse, they've let out some of our test subjects."

"Bah!" The red head dismissed him with a violent wave of her hand. "No one would be foolish enough to let out any of the things we keep locked up down here, Charles. After decades of research, we haven't been able to find a way to control any of the ones we've caught. I doubt a bunch of wackos in robes could just stroll in here and start bossing one of our subjects around."

"Ingrid, that Hinderlight fellow mentioned some chicken monster..." Niara began but Ingrid cut her off.

"He could be talking about anything. More than likely, these infiltrators brought in a monster they had well under their control from outside of the facility. None of our subjects are loose, and I doubt they would be whatever these infiltrators are after, anyway."

Melvin shook his head. "Even so, if the majority of us believe we should remain quiet, that is what we should do."

"This isn't a democracy," Ingrid replied. "As the senior researcher present, the protocol is that in a lockdown situation where multiple people are sheltering together, the employee with the most seniority is placed in charge." She paused and stared at every member of the group until they nodded in acceptance. "Good. Then my first order is that I don't give a shit about how much noise we make. If we're lucky, we'll attract the attention of one of the security teams and they can escort us somewhere other than the women's bathroom."

A stupid idea popped into Eddie's head as the woman finished her rant. He needed these people if he was going to get back to the control room, and they would be safer with Hinderlight. If they continued to shout at each other, it was only a matter of time before the wrong people found them. Or the wrong thing. Eddie just needed to avoid a power struggle with the red-headed woman named Ingrid.

"Hello," Eddie called through the vent. Any of the five that weren't already on their feet leaped up at the sound of his voice. They frantically looked around, even the one man that had remained silent the entire time, until Eddie spoke again. "Up here in the vent. I'm security officer Watson and I'm here to rescue you. I'll be right down."

Eddie thought he had made his voice sound official but wouldn't know if they believed him or not until after he got down. Crawling forward until his feet rested over the grate, Eddie flipped around and started striking the metal as hard as he could with his heel. In the cramped confines of the vent system, he didn't have a whole lot of room to get much momentum, but he repeatedly struck the cover as fast as he could. He was beginning to sweat by the time he felt the grate begin to give. After a dozen or so more strikes, one of the corners broke free. Eddie put his all into the last couple of hits, and the second corner of the grate swung away to open up beneath his feet.

"Watch out," Eddie called as he flipped back onto his stomach and shimmied until his legs swung down out of the vent. He continued to lower himself slowly until he only hung from his fingers. A quick glance reassured him that none of the scientists were directly below him, and then he let go and dropped the remaining distance. He landed easily enough on the tile floor, his knees bending to absorb the impact, before he straightened to address the men and women in the room.

"I just want to say—"

Eddie was cut off as hands seized his arms. Someone kicked out the back of his knees. He would have fallen if he wasn't already being held up. Instead of allowing his face to strike the ground, however, his captors dragged him forward and pressed him not so gently face-first against the nearest wall.

"Who are you?" It sounded like Ingrid, but with his face squished up against the wall, all Eddie could see was presumably Charles as he strained to hold onto Eddie's left arm.

"I told you." Eddie's words slurred as he tried pull his head off the wall enough to speak. "I'm a member of security."

"Except you're not dressed like any security officer I've ever seen," Ingrid said from somewhere behind him.

"And he didn't defend himself very well," Melvin said. He had a hold of Eddie's right arm. "I would think a member of the security team would be able to handle a couple of scientists."

Both made valid points. Eddie tried to picture the brief amount of time he spent with Squad K before The Reaper had appeared.

"If you've seen enough of us," he countered, "then you know we all don't dress the same. I was cut off from my equipment anyway when the lockdown was put in place."

"It is true some of the squads are a little lax in their attire," the woman named Niara said. "Squad K in particular. That doesn't explain why he is completely weaponless. Those muscle heads always have at least a knife or two on them at all times."

"I had weapons," Eddie replied, "but I lost them trying to escape from some of the monsters that got loose. That's how I ended up in the vents."

"I told you subjects could have gotten loose," Charles said. Eddie felt the man's grip loosen on his arm. "It makes sense that whoever was trying to infiltrate the facility would set a number of subjects free to create chaos."

"Except," Ingrid said, "they would have no way to control them. The infiltrators would be just as much at risk as the rest of us if they let any of our subjects out."

Eddie tried to wrestle back control of the conversation. "As far as I know, they only intentionally released one monster to help perform some ritual. Something went wrong because the creature, a Khurobak, killed what looked like all of the employees working on the control room floor *and* the cultists that let it free. It smashed up the majority of the computers too."

"See," Ingrid said with a smug tone, "I told you they couldn't control any of our subjects."

"That's what you're focused on?" Melvin released Eddie's arm and rounded on the woman. "Mr. Watson just said that dozens of people died and you want to gloat about being right."

"Nothing we can do about those people now. I'm not about to cry over people I've never even met."

"You're worse than the things we keep locked up. It's no wonder your team has the highest casualty rate out of our whole department." Melvin's tone continued to rise the more he spoke. "You put all of those below you at risk just so you can reap the accolades for the discoveries *their lives* buy for you."

"Don't be ridiculous." If Ingrid was insulted or ashamed by the accusation, Eddie couldn't tell from her tone. "People die in the name of the experiments we perform down here all the time. You're just jealous that my team actually learns things from their sacrifices."

Charles released Eddie's other arm and stepped between the two. "You both need to calm down. This isn't the time or the place for this."

Eddie was losing control of the situation. Fast. He had to rein in this group before they either killed each other or brought something down on them that killed them all. *What would Hinderlight do?* The memory of the disagreement between Kaga and Hinderlight leaped to mind.

"Enough!" Eddie got in between them and pushed everyone apart. "I didn't just tumble through four floors of the ventilation system just to watch the lot of you squabble over things that don't matter when we need to focus on survival."

"Don't matter?" Melvin rounded on him. "Of course some grunt would say that. You barely have enough intelligence to pull a trigger, let alone know what we risk our lives for every day." The scientist was getting more heated with every word and was sticking his finger in Eddie's face. "All you really are is just some ignorant jackass with about the same understanding of what goes on here as your average janitor."

Eddie's right fist connected squarely with Melvin's left cheek. The blow made the man stumble backward until he smacked up against the wall. Everyone else, including Eddie, stood gaping. As far as he could remember, that was the first time he had ever lashed out at anyone. Not wanting to lose his opening, Eddie mentally shook himself and spoke.

"Don't ever get in my face again." He pointed a finger at Melvin, who had a hand to the side of his face. "As a security officer, my job is to keep everyone safe. Don't for a moment think that I'll tolerate any insubordination. Questioning me at the wrong moment might get all of us killed. The next person that steps up to me like that—" he swung his hand around until he had pointed to everyone else in the room "—will be left behind. Do I make myself clear?"

He got a few mumbled acknowledgments.

"Do I make myself *clear*?"

Each person replied with a solid "yes."

"Good. Then if there are no more interruptions, I can come up with a plan." Eddie waited to make sure no one spoke. And to try and organize his thoughts. He hadn't realized how much effort it took to try and act tough. "Our main objective is to get the five of you back to the control room. It's the most secure room and you might be able to assist them in fixing the damaged consoles."

"That sounds reasonable," Ingrid replied.

"First things first, then," Eddie said as he took the whole group in with a gaze. "Names. You all can call me Eddie. During my time in the vent, I caught most of the rest of your names." He looked at each person as he repeated them. "Ingrid, Niara, Charles." He paused and gave his best intimidating stare to the man he had struck. "Melvin. The only person I haven't heard even speak is . . ."

"Trevor," Ingrid said with a sigh. She gestured toward the third man, who at the moment was cowering behind one of the bathroom sinks. Out of all of the scientists, he seemed the most out of place. A handsome man with chiseled features, ruffled dirty blond hair, and deep blue eyes that peered out a pair of thin-rimmed glasses, Trevor looked more like a model than a scientist. He also looked frightened out of his mind.

"He doesn't speak much, does he." Eddie made it more of a statement than a question.

"That's because he can't," Melvin replied. His tone was laced with anger, but he wasn't looking at Eddie. "Why don't you tell him why, Ingrid?"

"Just one of the many accidents that have occurred in the facility—"

"Accident?" Melvin growled. He glanced at Eddie then took a

deep breath. When he spoke again, his voice was strained as he clearly tried to hold in his anger. "One of *your* test subjects cut out his tongue."

"Working in close proximity with any of the test subjects has its risks."

"Especially if you ignore all of our safety protocols." Melvin's voice sounded on the edge of breaking.

"Trevor agreed to the experiment," Ingrid replied. "And The Jester had been fairly passive all day—"

"Wait," Eddie cut in. "Did you say The Jester?"

"Yes." Ingrid gave a little smile. "You've heard of it? That creature is one of my favorite subjects. So human looking but clearly otherworldly. And quite insane."

"Heard of it?" Eddie shook his head. "I've seen it. Was forced to play its demented games."

"It's . . . free?" For the first time since Eddie saw the woman, her unshakable demeanor melted away. "Out of its containment cell?"

"Yes."

Melvin let out a grim laugh. "What's the matter, Ingrid? Picturing what might happen if The Jester gets you alone in a room?"

"Shut up, Melvin."

"Poor Trevor had only been working here for a couple of weeks when The Jester took his tongue," Melvin continued. "You've been torturing that creature for years. Just imagine what it wants to do to you."

"They were just experiments . . ."

Ingrid trailed off, her eyes wide as she stared at the floor. Her body had started shaking, not a great deal, but enough for Eddie to notice. He couldn't afford to have her lose it now.

"It doesn't matter," Eddie said before Melvin could get in another word. "The Jester is locked down in the armory, which isn't even connected to this part of the facility. What we need to worry about right now is getting to the control room. I don't suppose any of you have access to the main elevator?"

Ingrid continued to stare at the ground, while Melvin watched her with a twisted smile. Charles and Niara both swung their gazes back and forth between the two. Out of everyone, Trevor appeared to be the only one that was even looking at him. The man shook his head, then crouched lower behind the sink. *Is this what trying to be a leader is like?* Eddie thought. *Every person focused on themselves instead of what needed to be done?* He was beginning to understand why Hinderlight had gotten frustrated so easily. Despite his best efforts, Eddie felt his own anger rising.

So for the first time in his life, he let it out.

Planting his feet, Eddie lashed out with a kick at the nearest stall. The strike produced a loud bang, followed by a smaller one as the door crashed into the inside of the stall. Everyone in the room jumped. As the sound stopped bouncing around inside the room, all eyes turned back on Eddie.

"Do I have your attention?" Eddie didn't wait for them to respond. "Because that's the last time I'm going to try and get it. You all need to pull your heads out of your asses and realize how bad of a situation we are in. Most of the security teams are gone. The few people we are in contact with have a tentative hold on the control room at best. A pack of cultists are running around doing who knows what, and monsters are running loose in the facility killing whoever they come in contact with.

"All of this is going on and the lot of you are squabbling like a bunch of children. From this point on, you have two options. Either fall in line, pay attention to *everything* I say, and stop your petty bickering, or I'll toss whoever causes me a problem in with the nastiest creature I can find. Do I make myself clear?"

Five heads with the same frightened expression nodded in unison.

"Good," Eddie let out a long exhale. He used the pause to compose himself. Not just from the anger, but from the satisfaction he felt. So this was what it felt like to be assertive. And having everyone look at him wasn't making him uncomfortable. It was liberating. Eddie made himself lock eyes with each person in turn before continuing. "Then let's get to work."

CHAPTER 26

"Al right." Eddie had begun to pace around the bathroom as soon as he had gathered as much information from the scientists as he could. He tried to strike an imposing stature but it was difficult to do while limping around with only one shoe. The rest of the group lounged around in what space they had. "We're on the fourth floor of what you call the Living Containment sub-levels. Since you all only have access to the secondary elevators that connect the four floors of this section, we need to find an access card that will allow us to use the main elevator in order to get back to the control room level.

"We basically have two options, most of which will rely on luck. We can try and find one of the four floor leaders since they are the only ones with the access cards we need. The second option is trying their offices first and hoping they left their cards there before the lockdown started.

"Which has a very slim chance of working," Charles said with a flippant wave of his hand. "Obviously, the company doesn't post the schematics for any of its systems for the employees to peruse. I don't even know what fail safes are in place. Any attempt to tamper with the control panel could lead to the elevators being completely locked. Or worse, the doors might open without the elevator there."

Eddie shuddered. "No, we don't want that. I've seen what lurks in the elevator shaft."

"You've actually seen it?" Niara's head perked up. "The Mega-arachnid?"

"A fitting name," Eddie replied with a shudder. "And just its head. Eight beady eyes that stared directly into my soul. Not something I wanted to see while climbing a barely lit elevator shaft."

"Her kind can be a little intimidating," Niara continued. "I haven't seen the current one since she was a child, but even when her mother died and they dragged the body out, the corpse was frightening in and of itself."

"Wait, you mean you purposely put them in..." Eddie paused and raised his hands, "Never mind. It's not important. Let's say hot-wiring the elevator is a very last resort. We'll focus on our other options instead. Does each of the floor supervisors have an office on their assigned floor?"

"Yes." Ingrid rested her hand on the wall, then quickly pulled it away. With a look of disgust she moved to the nearest sink and began vigorously washing her hands. "Erich Graf is the head of this level. His office is at the far end of the floor."

Eddie nodded. "That's where we'll start then. Hopefully, Erich is hiding inside of his office. If not and we can't find his access card, we'll start working our way up. Is there any chance there could be other scientists hiding out on this floor? If so, we should gather them up as well."

"Doubtful," Charles replied. "This floor is a fairly new addition to this section of the facility. Most of the cells are empty. The majority of the subjects are on the first three floors where the experiments are performed on them."

"All right then. If this level isn't used as much and there are people here, they would be better off staying wherever they are hiding."

"As would we," Melvin mumbled loud enough to be heard.

"Except *we* have a job to do. Is everyone ready?"

When all five nodded their agreement, Eddie moved toward the exit. He hoped the fact that these five were still safe and sound behind a door with a simple bolt lock meant that the rest of the floor was monster-free. Maybe the fourth floor remained untouched by all of the chaos. Or the scientists could have just been extremely lucky so far. Eddie hoped it was the former as he opened the door and led them outside. The group exited the bathroom into a stark white hallway that mirrored the containment cell he had seen earlier. The bathroom entrance sat at the top of a T-junction. A single continuous light source ran along the center of the ceiling, about two feet wide, that lit every corner and made shadows nonexistent. A few doors were visible in each direction but nothing else.

"Which way?" Eddie asked.

Ingrid motioned straight ahead. "That hallway leads to the

honeycomb of containment cells on this floor. Erich's office is on the other side."

Without another word, Eddie took the lead and led them down the hallway. Most of the other scientists stayed behind him, except for Ingrid. The confident woman walked side by side with him, her face stern and eyes hidden behind the rims of her glasses. There was something about her that made him nervous, but Eddie couldn't put his finger on it. She didn't bother to hide the fact that she thought herself above the rest of them; her haughty attitude had only vanished for a moment at the mention of The Jester before it quickly returned. He felt judged whenever her eyes fell on him, and although she appeared to defer to him at the moment, he didn't doubt that she was constantly trying to stay three steps ahead of everyone in the group.

Despite his worries about the woman, she remained quiet as they reached the end of the hallway. The path branched off at that point to run diagonally to the left and right. Eddie could see a number of doorways in either direction before the hallways split again in more directions.

"Which way?" Eddie asked.

"Is this your first time in one of the Living Containment levels?" Charles asked.

"Yes." Eddie made sure to keep his answers short.

"Strange," Ingrid said as she gestured to both hallways. "All of the floors are built in the same design. A honeycomb of crisscrossing hallways that all lead to a collection of labs and the floor supervisor's office at the far end. I would have thought you would have visited one of the floors while delivering a captured creature at some point during your employment."

"I haven't been an employee for very long. I've spent most of my time in training." Eddie's mind raced as he tried to recall anything the members of Squad K had said that he could use. "The squad I was assigned to has mostly been stationed in the facility. I wasn't allowed on the two capture missions they went. 'Too green' I believe was the reason they gave each time."

Ingrid gave a huff in reply, which Eddie used to change the subject. "If the direction doesn't matter, we'll take the hallway angling to the right."

"As you wish," Ingrid replied.

Eddie started walking before she could say more. This new hallway looked similar to the previous one, except that the doors lining the walls looked like they were made of a much stronger material than the others. Each one also had a small screen next to it that had dancing rays of light bouncing across it. The image reminded Eddie of the screen saver he had on his old laptop. He was about to touch the screen when Charles grabbed his hand.

"Not a good idea. The access panels for the containment cells are fingerprint activated. Anyone that touches one of those panels without the proper clearance gets a powerful enough shock to leave them twitching on the ground."

Eddie carefully pulled back his hand. "And only scientists have access?"

"To occupied cells on this floors, and only the scientists that are assigned to study live specimens. Researchers from other sections of the base wouldn't have access to these cells. Technically, scientists from other areas wouldn't even have access to these floors without clearance from a floor leader."

"Come on," Ingrid said. The woman had moved ahead further down the hall. "Since this is the largest floor, the cells stretch on for quite some time. We shouldn't be wasting time explaining things to a security grunt." She gave Eddie a hard look. "Especially one that should already know how things work around here."

Eddie returned a frown of his own. "I don't claim to remember everything from training," he lied, "but I do need to know things like this now. If you've forgotten, the facility is still under attack. Based on what Charles just told me, if creatures were let out purposefully, it could have only been accomplished by someone who already had access. That's important to keep in mind."

"Why? Do you believe one of *us* is a part of this grand conspiracy?"

"You can't think that," Niara placed a hand on his shoulder, her eyes wide with concern.

"I assure you," Charles joined in, "the five of us have been together since the lockdown first started. No one has had the chance to perform any underhanded deeds."

Eddie shrugged off Niara's hand and raised his own in a calming gesture. Anxious faces stared back at him, so he put on his best smile. "No, no. I wasn't accusing anyone. I just want to have all the facts lined up so I can give a thorough report to Mr. Hinderlight when we make it back to the control room. That's all."

"Then can we continue on?" Ingrid began tapping her foot. "Like I said, we have some ground to cover."

"Lead the way," Eddie replied.

The group continued on, Ingrid in the lead now with the other scientists not far behind. Eddie took up a position in the back as they walked down the repeatedly branching hallways. Describing the containment area as a honeycomb was more accurate than he had expected. Eddie quickly lost his orientation as they took a multitude of turns, and he had no idea how Ingrid was deciding when to go left or when to angle right. The woman certainly seemed focused on her destination.

The real reason he wanted to stay back was to keep an eye on the five. It was one thing to say he didn't suspect any of them, but the more he learned, the more he started to become wary of anyone he didn't really know. Even if he believed that they had all been locked together the entire time, that didn't mean one or more of them hadn't been working for the cult of Voltozas prior to this. He or she could still be lying low in case they were needed at some other time. If that were so, the person or people were probably too good at keeping their secret to slip up now, but Eddie would keep his eyes on all of them just in case.

Eddie was so wrapped up in his thoughts that he almost didn't notice the group had stopped in front of one of the cells.

"I have to be sure," Ingrid was saying to the rest of the group. "Mr. Watson must have been mistaken."

"Weren't you the one that said we shouldn't waste any time?" Melvin asked.

"This isn't a waste of time. Can any of you say you haven't at some point experimented on The Jester?" Ingrid looked around, but no one returned her gaze. "That's what I thought. I want to know if he really is free, and if so, what moron let him out."

Ingrid placed her fingertips on the panel and it immediately sprang to life. Multicolored circles appeared on the screen, their meaning lost on Eddie. It reminded him of the face of a Rubik's cube, except that the buttons were arranged in a ten by ten grid. Any time Ingrid pressed one of the buttons, the entire grid changed in combination. Her fingers began to fly over them so fast that the colors blurred. After less than a minute of the impressive light show, she stopped and stepped back. An electronic voice greeted her from the panel.

"Hello, Dr. Ingrid Westburg. Please state your request."

"Open cell viewing window."

With a hiss and click, a large section of the wall next to the door slid an inch or so back and then dropped into the wall. A transparent surface lay on the other side, which gave a clear view into the room beyond. Bright white walls enclosed a single square room. The inside was completely devoid of furniture or anything else besides a tiny grate high above the floor. Eddie remembered all too clearly what the view was like from that height. By the scowl on Ingrid's brow and small tremble in her lip, she really had expected The Jester to still be in the room.

"Who released subject 3024A?" Ingrid asked.

"Error. Information corrupted."

"When was the subject released?"

"Error. Information corrupted."

Ingrid balled her hands up into fists. When she spoke again, her voice was strained. "Diagnose cause of error."

"Unknown. Multiple connection failures. Main control hub damaged."

Ingrid struck the control panel and placed her head against the glass. The other scientists seemed taken back by her outburst. Trevor even jumped when Ingrid spoke. "This is much worse than I thought."

"Why?" Eddie asked.

Ingrid turned her head enough so that she was partially facing him. "Because it means everything you've said is true."

"You didn't believe me?"

"I believed you thought what you were saying was true, but you're just a security grunt. A rookie at that. I thought that you might have been a bit confused. Possibly over exaggerating."

"Sorry to disappoint you," Eddie replied dryly. "Can we continue on now?"

"Yes, of course." Ingrid made no move to push herself off the wall. She slumped against it, her attention still on the inside of the empty cell. Eddie watched as Melvin took a step toward her, expecting him to take advantage of her momentary weakness. Instead, the man just shook his head and turned his attention to Eddie.

"I know the way," he said. "I'll take the lead."

"And her?" Eddie asked as he gestured toward the distraught scientist.

"I'll get her moving," Niara replied.

They all waited as Niara moved over to Ingrid. The blond put her head close to the other woman's and began speaking in a hushed tone. Eventually, Ingrid nodded and pushed herself off the wall. Niara put an arm around the taller woman's shoulder and lead her away as Melvin began to move further on. The others followed along except for Trevor. The mute man hurried over to the glass and peered inside one last time, then sprinted ahead to walk with the two women, leaving Eddie and Charles to bring up the rear.

"Don't let her personality bother you," Charles said as he walked along at Eddie's side. "Ingrid is one of our top team leaders."

"She doesn't seem like someone who works well with others."

"What you see as an abrasive attitude, the higher-ups see as an efficient and dedicated team leader. Ingrid's team is highly regarded among all of the lead scientists on each floor, and they have had a number of important breakthroughs with our subjects in recent years. I wouldn't be surprised if she was promoted to lead scientist whenever the next position becomes available."

Eddie glanced ahead. Ingrid was still being led by Niara, her shoulders slumped and her head lowered. "If you ask me, she kind of seems like a pompous jerk, and Melvin certainly doesn't seem to have any love for her. I'm surprised he didn't start in on her as soon as she realized she had been wrong."

"It's true Melvin and she butt heads on a daily basis. If I was being honest, most of the other scientists steer clear of her if they can. But working down here, locked away from the rest of the world and surrounded by such horrors, you can't help but feel a bit of camaraderie with your fellow scientists. Even bitter enemies can show each other some compassion in the worst situations."

"This whole day has certainly been trying for everyone," Eddie replied.

"I'm not talking about these cultists or whoever attacked the facility and caused all of the chaos. I was talking about The Jester's escape. You said you've seen it, correct? How would you describe it?"

"Insane. Cruel. Manipulative. And underneath all of that, very angry."

"Well, Ingrid has spent the better part of her time as a team leader focused specifically on The Jester. Experimentation. Biopsies. What some might consider torture."

"Torture? On a living creature?"

"On a monster. This isn't like testing perfumes on baby rabbits. Everything locked away here would murder each and every one of us. Or eat us. The research we do goes toward figuring out the safest ways to stop or kill these creatures if need be."

"If you say so," Eddie replied. The Jester certainly seemed like the very definition of evil and had no trouble murdering the poor man it had captured. On the same token, though, it had let all of them live. Did something like it still deserved to be poked and prodded? What about the cat-like woman he had seen? She seemed intelligent. And sad. Were the scientists performing the same horrible experiments on her as well?

"Well," Charles continued, oblivious to Eddie's inner turmoil. "The Jester certainly holds grudges, and out of all of us, has made obvious its hatred of Ingrid. How would you feel if you just found out a monster like that was free?"

Eddie let the question hang in the air. Thankfully, Charles took his silence as empathy for Ingrid's fears. And Eddie did feel for the woman. He certainly wouldn't want any of the monsters he had seen so far to not only want to kill him but to also have a personal grudge as well. But if Ingrid, and the rest of the scientists that worked here, had no problem slicing and terrorizing the monsters they caged, were they really any better than the creatures they captured?

The question clung to Eddie's mind as they continued on in silence. As he struggled with the morality of what was happening in the facility, he began to miss the simple hypothetical questions from his philosophy classes. Unfortunately, none of them had prepared him to deal with the ethical treatment of mystical creatures and monsters. He continued to ponder the questions that had been raised all the way to the lead scientist's office. And whether or not he could continue to support the company that had provided him with a peaceful life up until today.

Or if there was some way he could bring the whole thing crashing down.

CHAPTER 27

Eddie shelved his convicted view of the facility as they entered Erich Graf's office. Whether or not the torture of living creatures needed to be brought to light had to wait. Survival came first, otherwise, it wouldn't matter if he decided the company was evil or good. And that survival depended on getting them all back to the main control room. When everyone is safe, Eddie could ponder if he could do anything about the experiments that went on in The Zoo.

And he desperately needed another pair of shoes.

His footwear was only a minor issue compared to his slowly growing concern that one of the men or women with him might be working for the cultists.

Making it safely to the control room wouldn't be enough to ensure their survival if he brought back someone that was secretly aligned with the cult of Voltozas. Eddie made a show of looking around the room but in reality, watched each person as they moved about the office.

The scientists were searching through file cabinets, pushing aside the piles of papers on the large desk at the back of the room, even looking under the multitude of laptops that covered the conference table in the middle of the room. Ingrid moved about slowly, occasionally checking a drawer or lifting a folder, but she spent most of her time staring off into space. After hearing Charles's opinion on the harsh redhead, Eddie was starting to feel more empathy for the woman. The more he thought about it, the more he could see his own social ineptitude mirrored in the woman. Her inability to socialize translated more toward hostility, while his caused more of an avoidance of social situations, but they came from the same place. That, added with the fact that she had worked in the facility the longest out of the five, made him suspect her less.

The others were more of a mystery. Trevor moved about the room like a jittery squirrel. If anyone made the slightest sound, the young man spun around to find the source of the noise. He did that more than he did any actual searching. Eddie wouldn't be surprised to see Trevor sprint out of the room if someone clapped their hands together. Out of everyone, he was the only one that had a motive to betray the company and Eddie wouldn't have blamed him. To be put in a dangerous situation in the name of science and then have your tongue cut from your mouth? If that didn't scream motive, Eddie didn't know what did.

After Trevor, Melvin and Niara had spoken to Eddie the least. He watched them both for a few moments as they searched different areas of the room but found nothing. The only thing he had noticed about Melvin was his disdain for how Ingrid ran her team. It didn't seem like a good enough reason, though, for the man to turn his back on the company. Niara, on the other hand, seemed to enjoy what she did. Or maybe she enjoyed the creatures she worked with. Anytime she spoke about any of the monsters, Eddie had noticed a demeanor change to the point it looked like she was seconds away from fawning. It was possible that if she felt some infatuation with the things held in the facility, she might be against how they were experimented on. But if that was reason enough to make her guilty, then the same could be said about Eddie. Letting some cult invade wouldn't really help all of the creatures get free, though, so her empathy for the monsters wasn't that strong of a motive either.

That left Charles.

Charles had taken a seat at the main desk at the back of the room and was typing away on the keyboard, his fingers flying over the keys while he squinted at the screen in front of him. Out of the five scientists in Eddie's new group, Charles had seemed the most open to talking to him. At this point, the older man might be his best source of information. Making a show of looking around, Eddie made his way over to the back of the room.

"What are you doing?" Eddie asked as he looked over Charles's shoulder.

"Trying to break into Dr. Graf's email." Charles glanced back over his shoulder. "Not for nefarious purposes, of course. I'm hoping I can figure out his schedule for today. If we don't find his card here, it would be helpful to know where he was supposed to be when the lockdown occurred. That way, we can limit our search to that floor instead of blindingly going from one level to the next, hoping to run into him or one of the other lead scientists."

"Makes sense. Any luck?"

"Some. The man is a bit eccentric, and as you can tell by the state of his office, not very organized. His login password was easy enough to figure out, though. The man is obsessed with the old television show, *Quantum Leap*. Have you ever seen it?"

"I don't watch a lot of TV. Don't even own one, to be honest."

"Good for you. A complete time sink, if you ask me. I only watch the news on occasion. Being locked away down here, you start to lose your connection to the rest of the world. I like to see what is going on above the facility, both the good and the bad. Makes the work we do more meaningful."

"By work, you mean the unregulated experimentation on captured creatures."

"A narrow explanation of what we do. Certainly not one I would expect from one of the men that actually does the capturing. They do inform you of what your job requires when they hire you, yes?"

"Oh, yes of course," Eddie stammered. Why did he feel like the one on the defensive? "But it's sold more on the idea of protecting innocent people from the dangers they don't even know exist. They don't exactly tell us what's going to be done with the creatures once they are captured."

"And that you do know what is done, it makes you question your job?"

"Yes." Eddie winced even as the word left his mouth. Then got mad for wincing. "Not that I don't see the importance of it all." He let out a laugh that even a deaf person could tell was fake. "But my opinion doesn't much matter. I'm just a grunt here to do a job, not examine the ethics of the whole situation."

"Perhaps." A small smile crept into Charles's expression. "Then again, you seem different from any of the grunts I've met."

"Oh?" Eddie could feel the sweat start to drip through his thinning hair. "I'm sure we're all different in our own ways. We are plucked from all over the world, after all."

"True, true," Charles continued to type away. "Don't mean to give you the third degree. Talking just helps me focus, believe it or not."

"It's not a problem. Just not used to people asking my opinion."

Which is true, Eddie thought. *How often does someone ask the janitor for his thoughts?* "I find—"

"Found something," Charles said, interrupting him. The others gathered around to look at the monitor as he continued. "Looks like there was some big meeting scheduled right around the time of the lockdown on the second floor. The memo was sent this morning, so it must have been some last minute decision. It's just labeled as 'important meeting' but it came from the first floor supervisor and was sent to not only the other floor supervisors but all of the team leaders as well."

Charles glanced over his shoulder with a confused expression. "You were one of the recipients, Ingrid. Why didn't you go? Or even mention it when we spoke about figuring out where Dr. Graf might be?"

"I was busy," Ingrid replied, some of the steel returning to her voice. When the rest of the group continued to stare at her, she let out an exasperated sigh. "I already had some experiments scheduled for subject 1225A, and I wasn't about to put them on hold for some random meeting. If it was important enough for me to be there, they would not have thrown it together at the last minute. I would probably still be performing my experiments if I hadn't been dragged into that bathroom by the rest of you."

"You were wandering around in the middle of a lockdown," Melvin said as he shot her a scowl. "If it had been because of an escaped monster, you could have led it right to us." He paused to take a breath. "But that email does explain why I hadn't seen my team leader at all before the lockdown."

"Same," Niara joined in. "Usually Dr. Helfor has my team gather at the beginning of the day and have each person give a report on what they had planned for the day, but she sent out an email this morning cancelling and told us to get right to work."

"Wait," Eddie jumped in. "So all of the floor supervisors *and* team leaders were all meeting in the same place? Do random meetings of that size happen often?"

"They are uncommon," Ingrid replied, "but not unheard of. The lack of information about what the meeting would entail was strange, now that I think about it."

"Convenient might be a better word." Eddie began to rub at his chin. "It would make sense that this meeting might have been put together so that the cultists could have all of the important people already gathered in one place."

"Which means the first floor supervisor could either be a part of this cult or allied with them." Melvin was nodding as he spoke. "Any number of people involved in that meeting could be. Which doesn't bode well for us."

"Except," Eddie said, "I overheard two of the cultists not long before I found you. It sounded like they had been cut off from the rest of the group, which makes sense since the main control room was littered with as many cultists' bodies as it was normal-looking office workers. It's possible the cultists never got around to collecting all of them before they lost control of the facility. It's our best bet to find an access card that would get us back to the main control room."

"And what if we do find them all still there?" Melvin asked. "There are a total of twenty different team leaders that work on the Living Containment floors. By what we were just saying, more than likely at least a few are secretly working for this cult. It would be foolish to risk bringing that many people with us without knowing who we could trust."

"I know." Eddie moved around to the front of the desk so that he could face the rest of the group. "We'll have to leave them there."

Eddie could see the protest begin to rise on some of the scientists' lips and quickly cut them off with a raised hand. "It's not the best solution, I know, but we can't risk losing the control room again. The only thing we can do is warn them that we think there could be some hidden conspirators in the group. That way, they will be on their guard, and it might actually flush some of them out."

"He's right," Ingrid said, much to Eddie's surprise. "The control room has to be protected at all costs. We can't risk bringing the wrong person and letting the cultists gain control again. After all, from the sounds of it, it was pure luck that our security team got it back in the first place. I don't think we want to rely on Mr. Watson to take it back again if it is lost."

"Thanks." Eddie ignored the barb. "If there is nothing else we can accomplish here, we should get going. The faster we find the lead scientists, the better."

He winced as he took a step toward the door. "Before we leave, did anyone happen to find an extra pair of shoes?"

***

As they walked back through the containment area, Eddie sported a new pair of shoes they had found in a gym bag that were only slightly larger than what he normally wore. It had been difficult for him not to ask to look in on some of the cells as they walked through the multitude of corridors. A morbid part of him wanted to see what other strange and interesting creatures were locked up this deep underground. The other part wanted to see if there were any as intelligent as The Jester or that cat-woman he had seen. To ask them about how things really were and how they were treated. None of which a security officer for the company would do. So instead, Eddie kept his mouth shut and his eyes open as they walked along the quiet halls of the fourth floor.

They reached the sub-elevator that connected the Living Containment levels without incident. Despite constantly being on the lookout for the next monster attack or sudden appearance of cultists, Eddie appreciated this short respite from constant danger. Despite their little quirks, the scientists were much less intimidating to be around than Hinderlight and the real security officers. Eddie would also be lying if he said he didn't like the sense of accomplishment he felt in leading this small group. It was a shock to realize it, but acting like a leader not only felt more natural than he had expected but also helped him interact with other people much more than he usually could. If Lizzie was here, he would almost consider this time as pleasant.

But Lizzie was in the hands of the cultists.

A fact that escaped him while he fled up the elevator shaft and crawled through the vents. It hadn't returned while he played at being a security officer and leader. It came back to him now as he stepped into an elevator similar to the one he had escaped onto right after she had been taken. Guilt slithered into his mind and grabbed hold. He had been so focused on his own survival and what the company was doing that he had forgotten about one of the few people he could consider a friend.

As the doors closed and the elevator started to rise, Eddie pushed all thoughts about the company's ethics and how the monsters were treated from his mind. He had to focus on the human lives first. Those threatened by whatever the cult of Voltozas had planned, the rest of the people locked away in The Zoo, and especially Lizzy.

And if there was time, maybe he would try to save Jefferson, too.

CHAPTER 28

"So how do we approach this?" Charles asked as the elevator rose.

"Carefully," Eddie replied. "And quietly. As far as I know, the majority of the cultists are stuck on the main floor. But I did see a couple on the third floor looking to round up scientists, so even though we didn't run into any on the fourth, it doesn't mean there might not be stragglers on all of the other ones."

"And what do we do if we run into any of them?" Niara asked.

"If they don't see us first, we avoid them if we can. Get to the maze of containment cells. Shouldn't be that hard to keep away from them with all of the different branching hallways in the containment area."

That seemed to send everyone into their own thoughts. They rode the rest of the short trip in silence, each person standing stock still until the low *ding*ing sound announced their arrival. When the elevator door opened on the second floor, Eddie took the lead with Charles at his side and the others close behind him. The group moved along the corridors of offices and labs without issue and arrived at the single corridor marking the beginning of the honeycomb hallways of the creature containment area. The conference room where everyone had been scheduled to meet was, of course, on the other side.

"What if another one of the creatures has gotten out?" Melvin whispered.

Eddie had been wondering the same thing. The image of the large centipede-like creature engulfing and devouring the cultist on the third floor was foremost in his mind.

"Avoid it, if we can," he said, addressing the whole group. "If things suddenly go really bad, we scatter and try to get back to the elevator.

Niara looked less than pleased with the plan. "And if we're cut off from the elevator, too?"

"Try to lose whatever is chasing you until you can get back to the elevator."

"What if we can't?" she pressed. "You know, there are some subjects on this floor that I feel I have good relationships with—"

Ingrid snorted. "You can't be serious. These things are monsters. Monsters that we've experimented on. Whatever you may *think*, any of these things would turn on you in a second if you set them free."

"Not all of us perform invasive experiments on our subjects." Niara crossed her arms. "I take a more humane approach, and my team leader, Dr. Wetzel, supports my—"

"Dr. Wetzel is a quack. The only reason he still holds a position here is because of his family's relationship to one of The Board members."

"That's not true. Dr. Wetzel is a brilliant—"

Eddie cut her off before the argument grew worse.

"Enough. We're NOT letting anything out of its cell." He made sure his tone matched his conviction on the subject. "Even if one of your monsters likes you, Niara, it doesn't mean it wouldn't attack the rest of us. We rely on ourselves only to watch our backs."

"I have a suggestion." Charles raised his hand. "We do have some tools in the labs that are considered dangerous. Electrical cattle prods. Both metal and laser scalpels. Bone saws. And quite a few chemicals that would cause serious damage to the skin of both man and beast. Most of it is locked up, but as a team leader, Ingrid has access."

"That's a good idea," Eddie said after taking another glance down the hallway. "I hope we won't have to defend ourselves but it's better to be prepared. Just the scalpels and cattle prods, though. Let's steer clear of carrying around dangerous chemicals. Do you want to lead the way, Ingrid?"

"Very well." The cold woman had regained most of her composure after they had left Dr. Graf's office. Eddie wasn't sure if he preferred the harsh yet focused side of her or the subdued but distracted version. "The closest lab with the supplies you seek is this way."

Ingrid led them back the way they had come to one of the many unmarked doorways. Opening the door, she ushered them inside before closing it behind them. Inside, Eddie found himself staring at a macabre mixture of a modern lab and a torture chamber.

The room was dark ivory. It reminded Eddie of some of the white undershirts he still wore after years of repeated washes. Darker splotches marring the walls were stains that had sunken too far in to be removed completely. The tiled floor was a similar shade of faded white, but no amount of washing had completely cleaned the grout. Dark stains of red had leeched into the white material, making it impossible to erase the evidence of everything that was done in the room. And from the equipment, it looked like a lot. While stainless steel cabinets and counters lined the walls, the latter covered in various test tubes and beakers, the majority of the room was furnished with either cages or examination tables. The thick metal bars of the cages looked as if they could contain even the mightiest animal while the cage sizes ranged from small enough for a rabbit to large enough to hold a young elephant. The stark metal tables also varied in size and shape. The only similar aspect that they all shared were the different thick leather straps and metal chains that hung from their sides or were bolted to the floor all around them.

Eddie tried not to think about what was done to the creatures once they were placed onto those tables. "Where are the weapons?"

"Scientific tools, you mean," Ingrid replied. She moved across the room to one of the cabinets on the far side. While most had simple latches to open the doors, the one she stood in front of had a card reader. A quick swipe of a card she produced from her pocket opened it up and she pulled open the two large doors that took up most of the cabinet. "Dangerous tools, yes, but still just tools."

"I don't see how a cattle prod is a scientific tool," Niara murmured but clamped her mouth shut after Eddie shot her a hard look.

Each person took a turn at the cabinet, choosing their "tool." Despite her comment, Niara chose one of the cattle prods, a thick rod almost as long as her arm with a yellow cap at the end and two copper-colored prongs. Both Melvin and Trevor grabbed cattle prods as well. Charles armed himself with a set of scalpels, a few going in his pocket while he gripped one tight in his left hand. Ingrid chose what looked like a small pen light and then stepped aside to allow Eddie his turn. He chose a set of scalpels for himself, although he only took two—one to keep at the ready and one for backup. With their choices made, they left the room and returned to the hallway leading into the containment area for that floor.

Charles took the lead this time, with Eddie at his side. The rest of the scientists followed close behind, except for Niara. She hung a little bit further behind, casting furtive glances around every now and then, biting at her nails. By the time they had taken their fifth turn through the maze of hallways, the woman looked on the verge of freaking out. Which worried Eddie. He tapped Charles on the arm so that the man stopped. Eddie approached the fidgety woman.

"Is everything ok?"

She blinked a few times, then gave a half laugh. "Of course. Why?"

"You just seem worked up about something."

"Nope. Nothing at all. Just nervous like everyone else, I suppose."

Eddie glanced at the rest of the group. Each looked like a tightly wound spring, arms at their sides, shoulders hunched forward, even the slightest movement jerky and short. Niara, on the other hand, seemed like she couldn't stop moving.

"Are you sure?" he asked.

"I just . . ." she began then took off down one of the adjoining hallways.

"Wait—" Eddie began but the woman was moving too fast and he wasn't about to yell after her.

"Just let her go." Ingrid shook her head. "Niara has always been a bit off, going on and on about how we should change how we treat the subjects."

"No," Eddie shook his head. "We stick together. Let's go."

He was surprised when the others didn't put up a word of protest and just fell in behind him. They followed after Niara, down twists and turns that only further disoriented Eddie. How the scientists could keep track of them, especially when all of the doors had nothing to distinguish one from the other, he had no idea. Eddie kind of understood the need for secrecy, even inside a secret base, but not having a single label on rooms holding dangerous creatures seemed foolish. Even negligent. When they finally caught up with Niara, she was standing in front of one of the doors, typing away at the control panel.

"I just wanted to make sure he was ok," she said as they walked up to her. "It will only take me a second."

"Check on who?" Eddie asked.

Ingrid spoke before Niara got the chance to respond. "This is such foolishness. If you were on my team, I would have had you transferred out of this division as soon as you showed the first sign of forming an attachment with one of the subjects."

"What?" Eddie said but then grew silent as the cell's viewing window began to open. Everyone moved toward the window, except Ingrid. The redhead rolled her eyes and turned her back on all of them.

At first, as Eddie looked inside the bare white room, all Eddie saw was a large stone, black as tar, the size of a two-seater couch and covered in some slick resin, resting in the corner. Then Niara tapped on the glass.

A huge, canine head lifted up from behind what Eddie now could see was the creature's body, its short, pointed ears shooting up. It had a short muzzle and sniffed at the air with four nostrils instead of two. Dark purple eyes stared back at the window for a few moments, then it pushed itself up on legs as thick as paint cans and padded over to the window, the four pointed claws on each paw clicking loud enough for Eddie to hear it even through the window. At its full height, it looked more the size of a lion than a dog, its eyes staring back at them with an almost quizzical look.

"Where the hell did that come from?" Eddie whispered in awe. "I want to make sure I never go there."

"He's not as dangerous as he looks," Niara said, placing a hand to the glass fondly.

"And not from this world," Ingrid grunted. "Now that you've seen your little pet, can we go?"

Eddie spun around. "Not from this world?"

Ingrid smirked at him. "You thought everything we keep contained in this facility came from earth? Came from this dimension?" She let out a gruff laugh. "They really don't tell you grunts much, do they?"

"I guess not," he said, trying to rein control over his surprise. The others didn't seem to pay attention to the exchange. Except for Charles. The man was looking at him with that half smile and mischievous glint in his eyes. Eddie rushed on. "We should get going now. We've spent too much time here already."

"Alright." Niara didn't attempt to hide her disappointment as she began pressing the keys on the control panel. With much less enthusiasm than when she arrived.

"Leaving?" a voice said from not that far away. A voice Eddie recognized. One that sent a chill down his spin as the memory of the robed man flashed across it. It was the same voice he had heard from the leader of the cultists.

Everyone turned to face the voice and was greeted by a mass of black-robed bodies that took up the hallway. They had gathered at the point where the hallway branched off in different directions. Effectively limiting where Eddie and his group could go. As one of the cultists stepped forward, he waved his hand and seven or eight broke away from the group and disappeared into the other hallways.

"Surprising to find a group of scientists wandering around," the man continued. "Especially after Mr. Hinderlight's little announcement. You should have listened to the man's instructions."

Eddie should have been afraid. Even though the number of men in front of him was less than the mob that had caught them unaware on the first floor of the facility, they were still outnumbered three-to-one. If he had to guess, the cultists that had left were even now circling around to cut them off from the other direction.

But instead of fear, all he felt was anger. These were the people that had caused all of the death and destruction in the facility. Had infected the innocent and oblivious people that worked in the main building above. Had let loose a stream of horrible monsters for some unknown end. These were the people that had taken Jefferson and Lizzie. At least most of the monsters killed because it seemed like second nature to them. What these *people* had done, they had all done without the slightest thought to the lives they were ruining. And ending.

"Where's Lizzie?" Eddie asked, his fingers tightening around the scalpel in his hand.

The leader of the group didn't respond. Eddie was about to ask again when the hooded figure let out a chuckle. "Now I recognize you. You were with that other group on the first floor. One of the few to get away. I would have thought you would be holed up in the control room with that Hinderlight fellow. Not sure how he retook the control room. We should have had a few dozen of our people in there. Any chance you know how he was able to do that?"

Eddie ignored the question and repeated his own. "Where is Lizzie?"

"I'm guessing you're talking about the woman that was with you?" The man brought both hands up and slowly pulled back his hood. Pale blue eyes stared at Eddie from deep within a marble-white face. The man was devoid of hair from the top of his head down to his chin, his face gaunt and angular as if his skin barely fit over his skull. When he spoke again, Eddie caught sight of yellowed teeth behind his thin lips. "Oh, don't you worry. She is being well taken care of. I can take you to her if you wish."

"How about you just tell me where she is and we'll find her on our own." Someone gasped behind Eddie. He glanced back to find that the other cultists had already circled back around behind them. A quick count put their numbers around twelve. Still two-to-one odds, but better than if they faced the larger group.

Then he noticed Niara's fingers still pressed against the control panel.

"Oh no," Eddie mumbled as the cell door slid upwards and open.

CHAPTER 29

Complete and utter silence. No one moved. It seemed no one even breathed. Eddie couldn't be positive, but he imagined that all eyes, whether peering from behind glasses or from beneath hoods were focused on that open door. And the sound coming from inside the room.

Click. Click. Click.

Eddie's immediate instinct was to flee. Barrel through the smaller group of cultists and get as far away as he could before the black beast inside took its first steps of freedom in who knows how long. Fleeing now, though, would take him right past the open door. If the creature—the Hound he decided to call it—saw him running, it might decide Eddie was the first thing it would hunt with its newfound freedom. That, and the fact that he now felt a sense of responsibility for the scientists he had tricked into believing he was some kind of security officer, kept his feet locked firmly in place.

Click. Click. Click.

The Hound's massive head emerged first, purple eyes blinking rapidly as its great muzzle sniffed the air. Its ears perked up, two black triangles with the slightest touch of pink on the inside, barely visible as they tuned into the hallway. Hot steam escaped its nostrils with every breath, each exhale like an industrial fan. A black, oily liquid ran down its fur, coalescing in drops hanging off its body but refusing to fall. It was as if the great beast sweat darkness.

Click. Click. Click.

Only Niara seemed unafraid as the Hound stepped out into the corridor. While those around her shook with the effort of trying to stay perfectly still—Eddie included—the pale scientist extended a friendly hand toward the animal. Toward the monster.

"What the hell—" Ingrid whispered then cut off as the monster turned its large purple eyes in her direction.

"It's ok," Niara cooed, though it was hard to tell whether her words were toward the Hound or Ingrid.

The Hound watched Ingrid for a few more moments then returned its attention toward the other woman. Eddie risked a glance back at the cultists. Not a single one had moved. The only one with his hood down, the creepy bald man with skin as white as the walls around them, had both of his arms raised as if to hold back the throngs of black robes behind him. Their leader's face was blank, but his pale blue eyes were locked on Eddie instead of the beast behind him. As if letting out one of the many monsters had been his idea.

Pulling his gaze away from the cult leader's eyes, Eddie returned his full attention to said monster. The Hound had clicked its way on clawed paws within a few feet of the pale scientist. It stood rigidly, head tilted to the side as it looked at the scientist's hand extended in front of it.

"It's ok," Niara cooed again to the great beast. "You remember me, don't you?"

A low growl escaped its mouth as the Hound lowered its head. Its great maw opened to reveal two rows of razor sharp teeth. Still Niara didn't flinch. She even smiled. Eddie felt like he was going to throw up. The Hound's mouth spread wide and its stubby tail gave a wag as it closed the remaining gap between itself and the scientist.

Click. Click.

And then the great beast licked Niara's hand with a thick pink tongue.

The pale woman smiled at first at the friendly gesture. Then frowned as if trying to figure out some great mystery.

The frown broke wide as she began to scream.

Eddie watched in horror as the woman held up her hand, a smoking mess of melting flesh and tendons. Before the second scream had escaped her lips, her bleached white finger bones appeared, waggling as the tissue melted off of them like popsicles left out in the sun, before they succumbed to whatever chemical was in the saliva of the black Hound and began to dissolve themselves. Niara dropped to her knees as her hand disappeared into a smoking puddle of goo in front of her. Melvin retched on the floor. Trevor and Charles began to flee.

And that's when everything really went to shit.

The Hound pounced on Trevor before the mute man had gotten even a few steps away. Its massive body pinning him to the floor.

Red stains appeared instantly where the beast's claws dug into the squirming man's body before the Hound's massive maw clamped down on Trevor's shoulder. A hiss like a thousand snakes filled the corridor as his lab coat and then the shoulder itself began to melt away where the Hound's mouth held tight. A tumult of screams rose over the now fading moans of Niara as both scientist and cultist alike fled for their lives. Except as Eddie watched the other scientists sprint away from the carnage around him, some of the cultists actually ran toward him from both directions, makeshift clubs and broken pipes clutched tight in their hands.

Fight or Flight.

Only a moment to decide.

Niara had toppled onto her side, eyes rolled back. Trevor's thrashing had become weak. The Hound feasted. The black robes were coming. Eddie had two scalpels, their blades no larger than his thumbnail.

Flight it is.

He took off, forcing himself not to look at Trevor or the Hound as he passed them. Three cultists barred his way, but their attention was clearly focused on the carnage behind him. Eddie didn't slow. Hands grabbed at him weakly. Feet tried to trip him up. But Eddie made it through and kept going. Screams followed him as he ran, echoing in every direction. Images of Niara and Trevor repeatedly flashed across his mind. One moment they were whole, the next they were disfigured and dying, just as he had left them. Guilt and fear mixed into a sickening combination that made him want to throw up one moment and sob the next. And still he ran.

Left. Right. Right. Straight.

There was no thought to the directions he took in the catacomb of hallways. Away. That's all that mattered. Away until the screaming stopped or until one lucky turn brought him somewhere he could hide, or better yet, the corridor back to the elevators.

Right. Straight. Left.

Whenever his body screamed at him to slow down or his lungs begged for rest, Eddie would glimpse a black blur down an adjoining hallway. Cultist. Hound. It didn't matter. It might as well have been Death itself stalking the halls. Eddie pushed on. The screams followed him, keeping him company. They rose and fell like the ocean tide; start low, crescendo to a high, drop off again, and then disappear for the briefest of seconds before a new one began. Sometimes they seemed close by, other times he barely heard them over his own hoarse breaths and the slap of his soles on the tile floor. But they were always there.

Straight. Left. Right.

As he rounded another corner, Eddie had only a second for his mind to comprehend the black clothed forms before he crashed into them. *Oofs* and grunts filled the corridor as the wind was knocked out of lungs and bodies fell about the floor. Eddie had only the barest moment to collect his thoughts before a hand wrapped around his throat. He lashed out with a kick, all instinct, and the hand dropped away as his heel made contact. Another hand grabbed his arm, but somehow he found one of the scalpels in his hand. A quick slash, the feeling of the blade finding resistance, and then he was free.

A figure in white appeared above him, offering a feminine hand. He took it, the grip like iron as he was pulled back to his feet.

"Run!" Ingrid yelled and Eddie complied.

A hand grabbed at his leg but he shook it off and then he was on the move again, Ingrid in the lead. The woman led him through the twists and turns of the hallways with more confidence than Eddie felt. While he had changed direction on a whim, Ingrid paused at each juncture for a split second before choosing where to turn. What her destination might be and to what end, he had no idea, but the smallest sliver of confidence began to worm itself back into his stomach. If the woman had a destination, then she had a plan. If she had a plan, then they had a chance.

Except nothing was that simple.

The pair was halfway down a hall when a pack of cultists rounded the corner. The group paused just before unintelligible shouts echoed down the hall toward Eddie, followed closely by the cultists themselves. Eddie and Ingrid spun and took off back the way they had come, Eddie now in the lead. Blind chance again controlled the direction they headed as Eddie chose which way to go. If Ingrid disagreed with his choices at any of the junctions, she kept it to herself. The only sound she made was the wheeze of her breaths and the occasional grunt. A quick glance back found her attention focused on his back, her expression pained as she pressed on. And the cultists still behind them, not gaining ground, but not losing any either.

After Eddie's fifth or sixth turn, they made it most of the way down a hallway before two cultists stepped into their path. Both brandished blunt objects, impossible to identify as Eddie's vision blurred and his body screamed in rebellion. Dropping his shoulder, he hoped his momentum would drive a wedge large enough for himself and Ingrid to plow through without slowing down too much.

A black shadow flashed in front of the cultists. In its wake, one of the cultists reappeared sprawled out on the ground and the other cultist was gone. Eddie didn't slow as he raced past the down man. Kept his eyes straight ahead as he heard the playful growling and awful screams coming from the corridor opening to his right. He pumped his legs as hard as he could. Turned at each intersection. Only risked a glance back whenever his breathing was too loud to hear Ingrid's own panting. Then, after he felt he had put enough turns between the Hound and his diminished group, Eddie sprinted straight. They raced down hallways, cell doors flying past. Peering ahead, he thought he could make out an end to this hallway, four or five junctions down, where it made a sharp turn to the left. He hoped a single option meant the end of the cell block. They must have passed more than three dozen cells on either side of them by the time Eddie reached the end and skidded around the turn.

And ran straight into a dead end.

Two cell doors were the only things that broke up the walls to either side of them and a single door sat at the far end.

"You've managed . . . to get us trapped," Ingrid scoffed as she bent over and pressed both hands to her knees. "The only thing . . . behind that door . . . is a bathroom."

Not feeling the need to respond, Eddie turned back the way they had come. Just in time to see seven black-robed cultists come racing into the cross section of hallways they had just left. For a moment, Eddie thought they might have kept going, that the cowls of their robes might hide the fact that Eddie and Ingrid were down the hall to their left. Of course, luck *wasn't* on their side at this particular moment as one of the cultists in the middle of the pack turned, saw them, and shouted something that made the rest of the group stop. Before they started moving again, Eddie had Ingrid's arm in his hand and was dragging her toward the lone doorway at the end of the hall.

"I said—" Ingrid panted at his side but he cut her off.

"It'll have a lock on it, won't it?

She nodded and he felt no need to explain further.

The door did have a lock, evidenced by the fact that it wouldn't open as Eddie yanked on the handle.

"Now what?" Ingrid gasped. She had bent over again and leaned against the wall.

"We can either fight or give up and let them take us," Eddie replied as he tried to catch his own breath.

"You might have the training to take on seven people with a small knife but I haven't been in a real fight my entire life."

"So we just give up?

Ingrid straightened up. "No." Reaching into her pocket, she pulled out the laser scalpel from her coat pocket. "We hurt as many of them as we can, then hope they still want to take us alive."

"I can live with that," Eddie replied. He gripped his own scalpel tight in his hand and turned toward where the cultists would soon appear.

"For as long as we have left *to* live," Ingrid said as she stood at his side.

And it was at just that moment, as the pair braced themselves for a final stand, that the bathroom door opened behind them.

CHAPTER 30

"And what do we have here?" A new, high-pitched voice asked as the door opened up.

It took a moment for Eddie to recognize it, but not Ingrid. She lashed out with her laser scalpel, the tiny blue light on the end the only sign that the high-tech device was even on. A brown leather-gloved hand caught her wrist and gave a little twist. Ingrid let out a pained squeak and dropped her weapon before yanking her arm free. Both she and Eddie backed away from the door, Eddie not caring as much about the cultists behind them anymore.

"What an odd pair," The Jester said as it stepped out into the hall. "Almost-friend Eddie and—" The Jester's voice remained jovial but its mask twisted into an expression of rage "—farthest-from-a-friend Ingrid."

Ingrid's voice came out almost a whisper as she bit off each word as if she had repeated them dozens of times before. "I've told you to call me Dr. Westburg."

"You have!" The Jester responded, the lips of the mask shifting into a smirk, the ridges of the eyebrows rising. "Hundreds of times you've said those words. While Jester has been shackled to a table." Its voice grew colder with each sentence. "After being shocked into a blubbering mess. While your cronies stand around jotting things down on their electrical notebooks. And you've sliced into this one's body. Again. And again. Removing little pieces of Jester and placing them under microscopes. Hacking off body parts just to time how long it takes them to grow back." A knife appeared in its left hand, as if materializing from the air itself, a wickedly curved blade half the length of Eddie's forearm and made of a strange, cobalt blue metal. "This one has remembered each and every time you've come a-calling on poor Jester, *Dr. Westburg*."

To Eddie's chagrin, or possibly his relief, the seven cultists that had been chasing them chose that moment to appear around the corner. They paused for a moment as they took in the scene and then one of them stepped forward and pointed the end of a pipe toward the three of them.

"Good. Three more prisoners for the High Clerk."

The Jester tilted its head back and stared at the ceiling for a moment while letting out an exaggerated sigh. When it turned its attention back toward the cultists, annoyance was clearly displayed on its mask.

"Are any of you the same black-robed fools that set Jester free?" Robed heads twisted around to look at each other, a few offering up shrugs. "This one assumed not. Jester would suggest *you* fools stop interrupting the nice reunion this one is having with Eddie and *Dr. Westburg.*"

"Listen, freak," one of the men replied. He stepped forward, brandishing a metal pipe. "All three of you are coming with us, even if I have to bloody up that stupid clown suit you're wearing."

"Oh my," Ingrid murmured.

"Clown suit?" The Jester turned to Eddie, mask twisted into a confused expression. "Did that wretch just infer Jester was a clown?" Things were happening way too fast for Eddie's mind to keep up. His brain was still waiting for the knife in The Jester's hand to start cutting into Ingrid and then himself. He only managed to open his mouth and get out an indistinct noise. The Jester looked at him for a moment more, rolled its head in disappointment, and turned its attention on Ingrid. "Did *you* hear that fop infer that Jester was a clown?"

"Yes." The words came out barely above a whisper. Ingrid eyes were squeezed shut.

"Hey!" the cultist called as he slammed the edge of his pipe against the wall for emphasis. "Are we doing this the easy way or the hard way?"

"How droll. We'll do it *the hard way.*" The Jester replied, its tone laced with sarcasm. It reached out with its free hand and caressed Ingrid's cheek, which made the woman shiver as her eyes remained shut. Then it turned and gave a weird combination of a bow and curtsy to Eddie, head bowed as it crossed its legs and dipped into a half squat so that its knees poked out at the sides. When The Jester raised its head again, the expression on its mask could only be described as one of maniacal glee.

The robed men must have missed the multiple mask transformations as they began approaching, pipes and other blunt objects held at the ready. Their leader shook his hood free, revealing a tan man with a tightly trimmed goatee.

"You're going to regret this, freak." He went so far as to smack his pipe in his hands a few times.

"Over the years, there are many things Jester regrets." The monster practically skipped toward the seven men. "But over seven more deaths, Jester shall hardly fret."

The cultist at the front smirked at The Jester's rhyme. When the two were close enough to touch, the cultist swung his pipe at the side of The Jester's head. All it touched was air as The Jester ducked underneath the blow. The cultist swung again, a backhanded strike this time that also missed its mark. This only seemed to anger the man as he began attacking with a fury, side swipes, overhead chops, even solid stabs with the blunt object. All of which came close to striking The Jester but always just missing their mark.

"A clown this one called me," The Jester taunted as it dodged yet another series of blows. "An insult most grave. Now, to sate my anger, it's his tongue this one ultimately craves."

"Stand still, you little—"

The Jester stepped to the side of a blow and drove its knife up into the skin beneath the man's jaw. The sickening sound of ripping flesh filled the hallway as the monster grabbed inside the man's mouth with its free hand and began twisting the blade about with the other. All while the cultist gurgled on his own blood. Time seemed to slow as The Jester routed around in the man's mouth until with a jerk of its hand, the man's tongue came free, spraying blood all about the corridor. It removed the knife from his jaw with a flourish and the cultist crumpled to the floor, bubbles of crimson fizzing out of his mouth.

Unaffected by the carnage at its feet, The Jester placed the bloody tongue against the lips of its mask and began to flap it about toward the other cultists. "Who's next for trying it *the hard way.*"

The cultists turned their robed heads toward their fallen companion in unison. The man thrashed about weakly, hands gripping the destroyed mouth and jaw as if they could hold back his life as it seeped through his fingers. As the man fell still, and to the complete bafflement of Eddie, they all attacked.

The Jester laughed as he danced delightedly in place.

As the cultists reached it, the monster moved with the elegance of a ballet dancer. Every prance and pirouette graceful, almost beautiful, as if the carnage that followed wasn't turning into a dance of death.

A twirl to the right left behind a cultist gripping his face as blood poured through his fingertips.

A handspring to the left dodged a blow strong enough to crack a skull. Using its momentum, The Jester planted a dropkick to another cultist's face with a sickening crunch of cartilage. The impact stopped the monster in its tracks as it fell onto its back with a loud thud. If the impact slowed The Jester down at all, it didn't show as the monster immediately rolled out of the way of a stomp aimed at its mask. Its expression was one of pure joy as it kept rolling along the ground like a child in a field on a summer's day.

The Jester barreled through the cultist it had just struck, then two more after that before tumbling back to its feet. Three remained, including one with a horrible slash down his face from the monster's previous attack. They tried to tackle it as it rose but ended up only crashing into each other. It would have been almost comical except that The Jester dipped and drove its knife into the necks of two men before spinning out of the way as the third tried to brain it.

That's when Eddie thought The Jester had made its first mistake.

It spun into the waiting arms of one of the cultists, the large man's hood falling backward to reveal a snarling brute of a man with three short, black Mohawks topping his head. The man let out a growl as he wrapped two thick arms around the monster, pinning him as he lifted The Jester into the air. The man and the monster were face-to-face, the cultist's face strained from the effort of containing the monster, while The Jester's mask still wore its overjoyed expression.

"Kill it!" the man yelled and two cultists rushed to oblige.

Before they could strike, The Jester lashed out with a knee that struck the large man square between the legs. The cultist let out a howl and relaxed his arms enough that the monster twisted and dropped down out of his arms. It was at that moment the other two cultists reached them and The Jester was lost from view among the three men.

The sound of ripping cloth was heard and a moment later, all three cultists fell away from The Jester. It was down on one knee, a knife now in each hand as it extended its arms. It rose as the three men hit the ground, the front of their robes a mess of blood and intestines. Eddie watched in horror as all three pawed at their stomachs as if to reposition the organs back into their bodies.

And just like that, the fight was over, leaving a scene that would have fit into the bloodiest of horror movies.

Behind him, Ingrid hacked and possibly threw up. Eddie couldn't be sure. He couldn't look away from the gruesome scene.

Seven bodies lay strewn about the hallway. The three that had been disemboweled had stopped their useless efforts, either from lack of energy or the realization that nothing could save them. Blood flowed from their stomachs as their bodies twitched in their last glimmer of life. The two that had received cuts to the throat were facedown, pools of blood expanding slowly out from beneath them. Their black hoods still covered their faces, the robes wet with what little blood they could absorb. Of all the bodies, the cultist that had spoken was the worst, his face a crimson mask, mouth wide from the scream he could never produce with his destroyed jaw and missing tongue.

Which left one man alive. The one that The Jester had sliced from chin to scalp. The survivor struggled up onto his elbows, and that's when the monster reached him. Two knives slammed into both of the man's temples, his skull seeming to offer little resistance.

Blood spurted. Eyes rolled back. Body twitched and then fell limp.

Leaving Eddie and Ingrid alone with The Jester.

Its mask flashed with an expression of wide-eyed wonder and overwhelming joy turning into squinting eyes and a soft smile of contentment as it pulled the knives out and rose.

"Now that is what this one calls a good massacre." The Jester began to saunter back in their direction, blood dripping from the blades it still held, onto its faded, multicolored tunic, and down fitted pants. It left red, pointy boot prints with each step. "With those rude people properly silenced, we can now resume our

242

conversation. Or more specifically, Jester can have one *last* conversation with *Dr. Westburg*."

"No." The words surprised Eddie as they left his lips. Despite the bodies, blood, and viscera painting the hallway behind the monster, something in Eddie made him want, no, *need* to stand up for the defenseless woman. By the expression that appeared on The Jester's mask, it was surprised at his sudden defiance as well.

"Almost-friend Eddie." The Joker's tone was as full of pity as its expression changed to match it. "Very noble. Jester would expect no less, just from knowing you this brief amount of time. Still, you need to move so that Jester does not need to slice you to ribbons on the way to exacting sweet revenge on the good doctor."

"I can't let you kill her." It was an effort for Eddie to keep his voice and body from shaking in equal measure. He grasped at the faintest hope that he might convince The Jester to stay his blade. "You let the group I was with earlier go without harm. Why can't you do the same here?"

"This isn't another game like before." The expression on The Jester's mask had gone as flat as its tone. "This isn't about Jester's amusement. This is a simple matter of revenge." Its leather gloved hand squeaked as it tightened around the handle of the curved blade in its grip. "This one is going to take the *good Dr. Westburg* back into that bathroom and let her experience the barest fraction of pain that she delivered upon Jester over the years. She won't survive long enough to know the full extent of what she did to him, but Jester will do its best to show her as much as her frail human body can handle in a short amount of time."

"Ingrid would still be hiding out with some of her fellow scientists if not for me. She's my responsibility now. I can't just step aside and let you kill her."

"Really?"

The word had barely reached Eddie's ears when suddenly, The Jester was right in his face, its mask mere inches from touching his nose. This close, he could see a spider web of minuscule cracks covering the entire surface of the marble-like material. The coppery smell of blood overwhelmed his nose, but underneath that was something else. It was almost floral.

The knife blade that suddenly appeared and pressed against his nose smelled decidedly worse.

"Jester sees a lot has changed since the armory." The Jester's emotionless voice chilled Eddie to the bone. "A follower has become a leader. A philosopher has turned into a defender of the amoral, of those that torture the defenseless. This one supposes that in your view, torture in the name of science is acceptable if it's on a monster like Jester."

"I never said I agreed with what—"

Eddie was cut off as the blade disappeared from view and a sharp sting bloomed across his left cheek. The blade felt warm, almost hot, against his skin. A trickle of that warmth began to move down his face. But it all faded as Eddie stared into The Jester's eyes.

Not the painted lines or subtle bumps that appeared on the mask that were a mock representation of eyes. Human eyes, teardrop shaped with sharp gray irises that held the faintest hint of gold, filled with an intensity that Eddie had never glimpsed in the eyes of another human being.

"Your eyes..." Eddie began but trailed off as coherent thought left him.

"What?" The Jester jerked its head back as if it was struck. "What are you blabbering about?"

"I . . . didn't know you had real eyes. And gray, such a unique color . . ."

The knife dropped from The Jester's hand but it was quickly snatched out of the air before it reached the tiled floor. It sat down for a moment. Its mask now featured two small lines where the eyes should be and a single longer line for the mouth, the edges turned down to a barely noticeable degree. Despite its blank expression, Eddie could still picture those eyes. They continued to face his direction for what could have been a heartbeat or an eternity before finally speaking again.

"Very well." The Jester tilted its head to the side and gave a slight shrug before standing. "Consider it a gift, *friend* Eddie. Or maybe *loan* would be a better word." The Jester extended its neck to the side so it could see around Eddie's legs. "A loan this one might choose to collect on at any time. Less likely the longer we remain friends. More likely if Eddie ends up sacrificed by these

244

weirdos in black robes or murdered and eaten by one of my many roommates. But for *this* moment, Jester swears not to use these knives to explore every organ in that fire-headed woman's body." It held out both knives on shaking hands toward the woman. "Despite how every nerve in this one's body screams for your blood. And as a show of good will, this one will even escort you to the elevator on this floor."

"I'll take it," Eddie exhaled a breath he hadn't even realized he had been holding.

"What," Ingrid gasped from behind him. "You can't trust that, that *thing.*"

"I don't need to." The words rushed out of Eddie's mouth as the expression on The Jester's mask turned sour. The image of the creature's eyes danced across his mind but he quickly suppressed it. "If it wanted, it could kill us at any time. But I've also seen it keep its word, no matter how twisted those words might be."

"I'm not traveling with—"

"And how are you going to stop-" Eddie paused. He'd been about to call the creature a monster. Instead, he took a deep breath and tried to adjust his thinking. "The Jester? If it wants to come with us, there isn't much we can do about it."

Ingrid's mouth opened, and by the look in her eyes, it seemed like the woman was about to tell him exactly what she expected him to do. But at that exact moment, The Jester placed an elbow on Eddie's right shoulder and leaned against him. Again he smelled the faintest floral scent mixed in with the overwhelming smell of blood. As Ingrid worked her mouth without making a sound, Eddie did his best not to cringe at The Jester's touch. After a few more moments, the scientist closed her mouth into a hard line and stalked off past the two of them. After she had left them, The Jester's elbow pressed hard against his neck as its mask leaned in close to his face.

"Let's go." The Jester's high-pitched voice was like nails on a chalkboard this close to Eddie's ear. It twirled both knives in its hands until one seemed to vanish. The other stopped spinning and pointed to the corpses only a few feet away. "All of those dead bodies are already starting to produce a not-so-flattering smell."

And that's how Eddie found himself walking down a hallway

littered with corpses, accompanied by a scientist, and a Horror with a creepy mask, dressed up like some jester from the medieval ages.

CHAPTER 31

"You do realize it's going to kill us," Ingrid whispered from Eddie's left.

"*You* do realize," The Jester chuckled in its high-pitched voice to Eddie's right, "that this one is standing close enough to snatch your pretty red hair and gag you with it until you show some manners."

Eddie would have laughed if he wasn't imagining how The Jester might give such a lesson. "How about the two of you refrain from talking to each other. That way, there won't be any misunderstandings."

"I *wasn't* talking to *it*." Ingrid's voice was laced with vitriol. "I was talking to you, which I suppose is worthless. For a security officer, you seem to prefer making nice with our subjects."

Eddie would have loved to respond with a witty comeback, but he was too busy worrying about what The Jester might do if Ingrid said the wrong thing. *When* Ingrid said the wrong thing. He wished she would go back to being the frightened, distracted woman she had turned into when she had first heard about The Jester's escape. The red-head scientist had actually become human enough that the other scientists had refrained from taking advantage of her show of weakness.

That fear had somehow passed. Now she seemed snooty and angry, with more of the latter directed specifically at Eddie. It was beyond him how the woman could suddenly discard all of that terror she had shown earlier and focus enough to look upon him in such an aggressively negative . . .

Of course. Eddie couldn't believe he had missed it. He glanced over at Ingrid as they walked.

"What?" she asked as she returned his look with a deep-set frown. Despite the anger in her eyes, they twitched after every couple of breaths. As they walked down the hallway, her hands opened and closed repeatedly at her sides. The hallway itself was cool, almost cold, and yet Ingrid had beads of sweat taking up residence across her forehead. If Eddie had to take a guess, Ingrid was probably handling her fear by turning it into anger. And taking that anger out on Eddie since she couldn't unleash it on The Jester. Which meant that if he wanted to keep her from losing it, he had to weather whatever attitude she directed his way.

This whole being a leader thing was getting more difficult by the second. Even more unfortunate was the fact that Ingrid didn't seem to be able to get very far without feeling the need to unload on him again.

"Since you clearly can't stand up for yourself, do you at least have a plan?" At first, Eddie thought she was talking about what they needed to do, but then Ingrid's eyes shot toward The Jester. He decided to pretend like he hadn't noticed.

"We should still try to find the other scientists that were supposed to be on this floor."

"Gone." The Jester said without missing a beat.

"What? You mean dead?"

"No," The Jester spoke as if to a child. "If this one meant dead, this one would have said as much. The scientists are gone, herded like cattle off to the elevator by a large group of black robes."

"When?"

"Not too long ago. Jester did not notice the good Dr. Westburg among the group so decided to see if she was hiding somewhere else."

"So we were too late." A massive setback, but not the end of the world. "Well, then we can at least look for the others that were with us. In all the chaos, it's possible that they got away." He paused, some of the confidence leaving his voice. "Except Niara and Trevor, of course."

"Yes, well that foolish woman should have known better than to let one of the subjects out. How she could have trusted such a nightmarish creature is beyond me."

Again the woman was hitting a little close to home with The Jester walking within striking distance of them both. It made it even worse that Ingrid was smart enough to be able to choose her words to do exactly that.

"Doesn't mean either deserved to die."

"Trevor?" The Jester's mask lit up with a surprised expression. "That handsome fellow that gifted me his tongue?"

"Gifted?" Ingrid stopped and turned to face the Horror. "You ripped that poor young man's tongue out. He hadn't even done anything to you. He was a new recruit!"

The Jester faced her and answered with a shrug. "Trevor was one of your little minions. That day, this one would have preferred the queen bee herself, but Jester takes what Jester gets."

"Enough!" Eddie hadn't meant to shout, but the two had pushed things far enough and part of him wanted to test this amnesty that The Jester seemed to offer. After all, Eddie couldn't walk on eggshells around it forever, and he couldn't exactly trust it not to change its mind at the slightest outburst. "Ingrid, stop pushing buttons. If The Jester has decided *not* to kill us, then it is stupid to continue antagonizing it. Whatever happened in the past we can't change now, and dwelling on it with death possibly around every corner won't help us survive the present."

"But the things it has done—"

"Don't justify the things you've done to it, and vice-versa. *Let. It. Go.*"

Ingrid crossed her arms in front of her chest and turned her back on them with a huff. She remained quiet, though, so Eddie took that as a victory.

Which left the Horror. Its arms were also crossed but The Jester's mask wore an overly smug expression.

"So much rage in the one with red hair. With the looks she gave you, Jester is surprised she didn't respond with a—"

"Same goes for you." Eddie turned on The Jester. The hairs on the back of his neck began to rise, his body warning him of the danger of his actions even when his mind pressed forward. "I appreciate the help you're offering, but if you are truly sincere about aiding us, then you need to stop trying to rile her up."

"This one has barely said a few sentences to that woman. The one that deserves to have her skin stripped and eyes plucked—"

"That's what I mean," Eddie rushed ahead before The Jester could put any more horrible images in his mind. "You can't keep tossing out offhanded threats about what you might do to Ingrid. The two of us are already stressed enough about what's going on and how we're going to survive without you making constant reminders of the cruel things you have dancing around your head."

After a moment's pause, The Jester responded with "Very

well." The mouth on its mask twisted into a pout. "Almost-friend Eddie takes away much of this one's fun. Jester will no longer mention its desire to hang the red-headed scientist upside down by her ankles and skin her like a rabbit."

Eddie stared at The Jester with his best disapproving glare. While trying not to think about what The Jester could do to him.

"That was the last promise . . . I mean threat." The Jester gave a curt nod as if that sealed its words.

"I . . . hope so," Eddie stammered, surprised at The Jester's quick acquiescence. He tried to read something from The Jester's posture or expression that might hint at what it was actually thinking, but The Jester just looked back at him with a grin that stretched almost completely across its mask. Could he really trust something everyone else saw as a monster to behave?

"Stare any longer, and this one might just blush bright enough that it shows through its mask."

Eddie ignored the comment and directed his next question toward them both. "Can we go now?"

"Fine," they said in unison. Ingrid glared at the Horror as their words overlapped. A small tongue appeared on The Jester's mask, pointed toward the woman. Inside his head, all Eddie could do was groan. He would just have to hope for the best. He started moving again and the other two fell in behind him, which of course made him uncomfortable. He was starting to feel more like a teacher escorting two fighting students to the principal's office as opposed to an actual leader. It certainly didn't help the already stressful situation. Thankfully, the feeling only lasted until they reached their first intersection. Eddie signaled Ingrid to take the lead as the woman seemed more comfortable in the twists and turns of the labyrinth of cells. She gave him a curt nod as she moved ahead, only taking a few moments to look around before leading them off down a hallway to the right. Eddie fell in a few paces behind her with The Jester walking close enough that they could have held hands. He tried not to think about the Horror as they moved among the stark white hallways of the facility.

Then they turned a corner and found what was left of Melvin and Charles.

The corpses of the two men were torn up, bits and pieces of

each strewn about the hallway. Their heads, with Melvin's thinning black hair and Charles's bald head and small beard, were the only things that remained relatively untouched. Besides the fact that they were no longer attached to their bodies.

From the mass of other bodies, it was hard to determine which limbs belonged to whose, especially when there was an equal number of black- clothed body parts as white cloaked ones. If the sight wasn't bad enough, the smell of burnt flesh and blood assaulted Eddie's senses. Ingrid covered her mouth with her hand and quickly turned away. The Jester readjusted its pants.

"We'll go another way," Ingrid mumbled through her hand. Eddie didn't risk opening his mouth and just nodded.

Seeing what was left of poor Charles and Melvin was a sobering reminder that the monstrous Hound was still somewhere on the floor as they detoured in a different direction. Sobering and frightening. Yet, with all of the things Eddie could have been worrying about as they traveled the hallways of the hidden facility, there was one thing unnerving him more and more. At first, he thought it was a combination of everything that they had been through since reaching the floor, but when he really focused on this growing feeling of unease, it seemed to point to The Jester.

A quick glance found The Jester's mask focused ahead, but Eddie still felt like he was being watched. His mind kept drifting back to the sight of those sharp gray irises staring back at him. How did it even see through that creepy changing mask? Did it see anything at all, or did The Jester perceive in some mystical way that Eddie couldn't even comprehend? So many questions that lay way outside of Eddie's realm of understanding. Philosophy allowed for an open mind with a great deal of questions but very few answers.

Of course, The Jester had shown a tendency toward *not* killing him, even after his little admonishment, so maybe one or two questions for the Horror might not put him in any *more* danger.

"When I saw your eyes—" Eddie began but The Jester's hand shot up, a single waggling finger extended to silence him.

"Whatever Eddie *thought* he saw, forget it."

"But—"

"*Forget it.*"

Even without Eddie's knowledge of how dangerous The Jester was, its tone held enough warning to scare off someone twice as big as Eddie. He shut his mouth before it got him into any more trouble. Despite the questions that struggled to escape his lips. The mask made The Jester appear just like many of the other monsters, but was *it* really *an It*?

"What are you?" It took a moment for Eddie to realize his mouth had vocalized his thought. It took less time than that to regret the blunder. Thankfully, the question didn't seem to anger it.

"A Horror is what the scientists labeled this one, so a Horror is what this one must be." It let out a laugh but its mask was the picture of contempt.

"I'm not asking how they see you. I've seen plenty of other Horrors that only seem motivated to kill or eat anything they come across. By the fact that I'm still alive after running into you twice, it's obvious that you are different. I'm just curious what makes you . . . *you*."

As The Jester's mask morphed into a blank expression, Eddie realized he might have gone too far. When it spoke, its flat tone only reinforced his concern.

"Do you hope to learn about Jester just as the scientists wish to learn? Start with questions first, then move on to items that cut, shock, and burn?"

Despite the mental red flags that rose with The Jester's words and rhyme, Eddie pressed on. And if he was going to press on, he might as well be bold about it.

"I thought we were *almost* friends. Wouldn't that mean we should *almost* know a little about each other? You've already figured things out about me. It's only fair that I know a little more about you."

The Jester was silent for a stretch of time. Long enough for Eddie to regret being so bold. Long enough for his mind to return to the scene of The Jester's massacre just a few hallways behind them. Long enough for him to glance down at the bloody knife still clutched in The Jester's hand. Almost long enough for him to jump when The Jester finally did reply, but thankfully Eddie kept his feet on the ground.

"Eddie is a clever one, using this one's words and twisting them into a shape he can use. Clever and bold." It paused for a moment before letting out a laugh. It sounded genuine enough that Eddie let himself relax a bit as it continued on. "But also true. This one laid out Eddie's fears in front of what Jester guesses were mostly new acquaintances. And the cute woman. Not very polite at all. Jester will be open with Eddie as long as the questions do not require complicated answers."

Eddie wasn't sure what that meant exactly, but he took it as a positive sign. He would try and keep the questions simple. "Do you have a name besides Jester?"

"Yes."

Eddie waited until it was clear The Jester wasn't going to say more. "What is it?"

It dismissed him with a wave of a hand. The one that didn't hold the knife, which Eddie took as another positive sign. "That requires a complicated answer."

"Alright." Eddie racked his brain for what *wouldn't* require a complicated answer. "Did I see your real eyes?"

The Jester shrugged, but Eddie noted a distinct tension in the Horror's shoulders. "Perhaps. Or Eddie is an excellent guesser."

"Has anyone else ever seen them?"

"Not to this one's knowledge."

"But you do have a human face behind that mask?"

"Complicated. Enough about what lies behind the mask. Ask this one something else."

Eddie couldn't stop the frown on his face, but he did as he was asked. There was one question that he was curious about above all of the others anyway.

"Alright. Don't take this the wrong way, but why would something like you want to be friends with a person like me?"

It turned then, its mask wearing an expression Eddie hadn't seen on it before. He couldn't put his finger on the emotion The Jester was trying to display, but if he were to guess, it would be confusion. "Complicated," It finally replied. Eddie was about to ask another question but the creature continued on. "If nothing else, Jester has nothing to fear from a simple janitor."

Eddie cringed at the exact same moment that Ingrid spun around, her expression a mixture of surprise and outrage.

"A *janitor*!" she shrieked. "You're nothing but a janitor?!"

The Jester's mouth had changed into a smirk. "Whoops. Sorry for letting the cat out of the bag."

Eddie ignored The Jester and raised his hands in a calming gesture toward Ingrid. "That is true, yes, but—"

Ingrid continued on right over him. "I've been following some foolish janitor? You have some nerve lying to us like that. Niara and Trevor might still be safe in the bathroom if you hadn't convinced us to leave, convinced us by lying about who you really are."

The words hurt as they had the ring of truth to them. Even so, Eddie still believed he had made the right call. "You were no more safe in that bathroom than out here. The cultists would have eventually found you—"

"So you say. Or they could have only been concerned with those they tricked into meeting together. The little group I was in charge of might have been left alone until these cultists were eventually routed out of the building."

"No," Eddie shook his head, some of his resolve returning. "I was with possibly the last remaining security force for most of my time in the facility. They were easily outnumbered, and that was just by the cultists. Throw in whatever Horrors had gotten free and their chances of getting things under control on their own looked pretty grim. Things *still* look grim. You might have been safe in that bathroom for a bit longer, but for you to assume that eventually things would just work themselves out is foolish. Two people are trying to hold the control room for the facility *and* get whatever they can back up and running. *Two people.* If we're lucky, they'll be able to get a line out to the outside world and *eventually* Soladyne might send reinforcements.

"Except by then it could be too late. These cultists have some kind of ritual they want to perform, and from everything I've seen in this facility already, whatever they're planning has got to be even worse than what you have locked away. I don't know about you, but I would rather be out here struggling to survive with the off-chance that I might be able to help those in the control room figure out a way to stop them. The old me might have tried hiding out in some bathroom while everything goes to shit, but I'm starting to get used to being in the thick of things."

Eddie knew he was getting through to the woman as her expression slowly shifted from outrage to doubt. He just needed to drive home his point and he might actually win her back. A smile started to touch his lips, but he kept it under control. It wouldn't do if he tried to put on a confident smile and it faltered,

"Instead of sitting on our hands, we can actually do something. Get you and whoever else we can find *and trust* to the control room, get things running again, and figure out the best way we can put a stop to these—"

"A puppy!" The Jester squealed, its gloved hands clapping together in excitement.

The sharp pitch of The Jester's voice knocked Eddie out of his momentum, and it took his brain a moment to register what The Jester had actually said. Before he could even look over Ingrid's shoulder, though, Eddie knew what he would find.

Standing in the hallway ahead of them, head down and teeth bared, was the Hound.

CHAPTER 32

"Don't turn around," Eddie whispered. His eyes remained locked on the Hound while hoping Ingrid obeyed him. The large beast looked on the verge of charging them, its thick leg muscles tense, black head dropped low, and short ears pointed up. Eddie wasn't well versed in dealing with wild animals. He had never even had a pet gerbil as he was bounced from foster home to foster home. But from what little he did know, the worst thing to do was make any sudden movements.

"Here, puppy!" The Jester yelled, walking past the two of them.

Yup, we're dead, Eddie thought. Down the hall, the Hound hadn't moved. Maybe The Jester's distinct lack of fear was making it cautious. Or it could just be allowing the fool to get closer so it would have less of a chance to run and hide. Either way, The Jester continued toward it.

"Here, boy!" The Horror went as far as to make kissing noises. Then to the complete bafflement of Eddie, it stowed its knife away somewhere near its waist.

"Should we run?" Ingrid whispered.

"Not yet," he whispered back. "The Jester has its attention now, but if we run, it might decide to go after us instead."

"If the Hound goes after The Jester, maybe we'll get lucky and it will choke on its arm or leg and we'll be rid of both threats."

A possibility. One that certainly *might* take a lot of the pressure off the two of them. The Jester was a wild card, to be sure, and just because it seemed to be on his side at the moment didn't mean it wouldn't turn on them later. One wrong word, and Ingrid and he could find themselves on the end of The Jester's knives. For all Eddie knew, this was all just another one of its twisted games. Lull them into a sense of security or worse, dependency, and then pull it all out from under them.

Except Eddie had seen something in The Jester's eyes. Its real eyes. Not the dead eyes of The Reaper, but eyes filled with emotion. There was something to this Horror that made Eddie relax around it the more time it stayed in his company. Again, it might just all be some sick ploy, but Eddie's gut was telling him that for the moment at least, The Jester was an ally.

Which meant he didn't want to see it get mauled by the Hound.

"Jester," Eddie said with a harsh whisper. "Get back here."

"What?" Jester shouted back without turning.

"What are you doing?"

"Going to see the puppy, of course! Look how cute it is with its oily fur and pretty purple eyes."

Eddie moved with slow, deliberate steps around Ingrid so that he was between her and the beast. "It's dangerous. That's what killed Niara and Trevor. And who knows how many of the cultists."

"So it bit the hand that experimented on it. Completely understandable." Jester continued moving toward the Hound, all the while motioning for the beast to come closer. "And if it ate cultists, then it did Eddie a favor. Sounds like a good boy to Jester." The Jester placed its hands on its knees and waggled its head toward the creature. "Who's a good boy? You are, aren't you!"

The Jester was close enough now to the Hound that the animal could reach him in two giant bounds of its muscular legs. The Horror continued to coo at the beast while the Hound began to growl louder and louder. Why it hadn't attacked already was beyond Eddie. The beast could change its mind at any moment, though, so Eddie had to come up with a plan. The problem was, should his plan involve trying to help The Jester or should he just try to save Ingrid and himself and let the Horror take care of itself?

Hands gripped Eddie's shoulders and it was through pure force of will that he didn't leap out of his skin. The next moment, Ingrid's face was practically nuzzled against his cheek.

"Why are we still here," she whispered, her breath tickling his neck. "That creature is focused on The Jester. Now is our chance to sneak away."

It only took Eddie a moment to decide. "No. We have to help it if the Hound attacks.

"You have to be kidding me." Eddie flinched as her nails dug into his shoulders. "I thought you were getting buddy-buddy with that Horror just so it wouldn't change its mind and kill us. But you're actually concerned about it." The nails dug deeper. "You are a complete moron."

"Maybe. But it's too late now anyway."

The Jester had reached the animal. It crouched down in front of the Hound and extended a friendly hand toward the beast. All Eddie could picture was poor Niara, her face twisted in agony as the Hound's saliva melted her hand down to nothing. The Jester claimed to be able to heal itself, but it had been talking about the pokes and prods from the scientists. Did its strange powers allow it to heal from everything? Eddie believed he was about to find out. The Hound took one long look at The Jester's extended hand. Its four nostrils sniffed at the glove and then continued up the arm. Drops of saliva dripped from its mouth, narrowly missing The Jester's hand and arm. Where the drops hit the ground, small wisps of smoke rose. When it had finished sniffing The Jester's arm, it pulled its head back and stared at the Horror with its large purple eyes.

Then it whimpered and slunk away in the opposite direction.

The Jester's shoulders slumped and when it turned around, Eddie watched as the lips on its mask drooped into a pout.

"Well, that was anticlimactic," Eddie whispered just before something struck him in the back of the head. He stumbled forward, the shock of the blow causing his loss of balance more than the small amount of power behind it. Flailing his arm out, his fingers caught hold of a door panel. Muscles strained as he swung himself into the wall instead of falling face first onto the tile floor. Before he had even gotten his bearings, Ingrid was in his face.

"That was the last time I let you put *my* safety in jeopardy because of some twisted concern for that Horror." She was practically screaming at him, her hands waving about as if she had lost control over them. "I believed you a fool before but followed because I at least believed as part of the security team you had some knowledge of what was going on and what needed to be done."

"I do have an idea of what's going on. Everything I've said so far—"

"Could just be more lies. For all I know, maybe *you're* working for this cult as well."

"Doubtful," The Jester said. It moved toward them, a sad expression still frozen on its mask. "Jester would know if Eddie lied, and so far, the only lie this one has detected was that he was part of the security force. Besides," Jester leaned against the wall and crossed its arms, "Eddie would not look good in all black."

"The word of a Horror means nothing to me," Ingrid replied even though her attention was still locked on Eddie. "The Jester could be backing your story just to confuse me even more."

"I—" Eddie barely got the single word out before Ingrid stuck a finger in his face.

"I'm done with you. I'm getting on the elevator with *my* keycard, going back down to the fourth floor, locking myself back in the bathroom, and waiting for the real security force to deal with these interlopers. You have fun stumbling around with that loaded weapon—" her finger moved to aim at The Jester "—pointed at your own head."

The Jester's mask shifted into a look of mock surprise. It even went as far as to place a hand against its cheek. "A horrible accusation. Jester does not use weapons that need to be loaded."

Ingrid glared at the Horror.

"Besides," The Jester continued. "She slows us down. Let her go. I'll be content if some other monster finishes the good doctor off."

"No, I need her," Eddie replied while locking eyes with the woman. "And more importantly, I trust her. We have to get her to the control room so that she can help pull this place back together and stop whatever the cult has planned."

"*Fine*," The Jester said with a sigh as it took a few steps toward the woman. "Let this one remind Dr. Westburg that it is because of this *janitor* that this one has decided to not to open up Ingrid's insides and play a tune with her intestines. If you wish to head off on your own, Jester will give you a marginal head start before this one comes after you."

Ingrid took a few steps back, her eyes going wide as the fear of the Horror finally clawed its way out of wherever she had tried to hide it. Eddie could use that fear to get her to do what he wanted.

Except that wasn't the kind of person he was.

"No. If she comes with us, it has to be by her own choice."

"Why?" Somehow The Jester had produced one of its knives without Eddie even noticing. "Bullying is a great deal more fun."

Eddie shook his head. "That's not who I am. She either comes of her own free will or she can try being on her own. I won't have her follow me out of fear."

"Boring," The Jester replied, but the knife disappeared just as quickly as it had appeared. "This one will be disappointed on the day Eddie's chivalry and morals get him killed."

"Hopefully that won't be for a long time," Eddie replied then turned a pleading look toward the woman. "The people I can trust are few and far between, especially since I am just a janitor and shouldn't even be down here. Which is why I'm asking you to stay with me. I'm begging you. Let me get you to the control room where you can do some good. Pretty much the only way I know how to help."

It was a shot in the dark, but it was the only shot he had. If Ingrid abandoned him now, he wouldn't just lose her access card and be stuck on this floor. Eddie would lose one of the few chances he had since this whole nightmare had begun to do some good. All he could do now was hope that the woman saw the important role she could still serve in getting the facility back under control.

"I'll follow you to the facility's control room," Ingrid finally replied. Eddie let out a relieved breath as she took another moment to readjust the glasses on her face. "For now. But I won't follow blindly, and I certainly won't have my opinion ignored."

"I understand." Eddie tried put on a friendly smile. "Thank you."

She waved off his thanks. "Just get me to the control room. If I am able to help once I get there, *then* you can thank me."

"Excellent." The Jester clapped its hands together and pranced around in a circle. "The band is sticking together. Lead the way then, *Dr. Westburg.*"

***

The rest of the trip through the maze of corridors went without incident. They didn't spot the Hound again. The creature was either lost somewhere else on the floor or making an effort to avoid The Jester. Ingrid made sure not to pass through the same hallway where Niara and Trevor had met their end. They hadn't noticed any other corpses as they moved, which meant that it was possible that the Hound didn't leave any of its meals behind. Even so, Eddie didn't think Ingrid would do very well if she found more of what was left of her fellow employees, and he certainly didn't want to give The Jester an opportunity to comment about them.

Eddie had expected to run into some of the cultists again at some point, but no one else seemed to be wandering the hallways, or at least none that they traveled through or passed. While the lack of enemies was a relief, Eddie couldn't help but wonder what they were up to now. He was still in the dark about what the cult's mysterious ritual was all about. As far as he knew, Hinderlight still didn't even know that much.

"Here we are," The Jester said with a slight bow in front of the elevator doors. "Safe and sound. As promised."

"Thank you," Eddie said, unsure what to do next with the creature. "What will you do next?"

"Oh, this one doesn't know. Lots of fun to be had while things are a mess. Jester could go find some more of the black robes to play with, thin the herd so to speak. Maybe find the puppy and offer it an arm or a leg, try to make friends."

Eddie couldn't decide if that image was funny or horrific. It was a testament to what he had experienced so far that the former was even an option.

"Well . . . have fun with that."

To his surprise, The Jester offered him a gloved hand. Eddie hesitated for the briefest of moments before taking it. The glove's material felt surprisingly soft against his palm, but The Jester's grip was as hard as steel.

"Then this is where I leave you."

There was no warning as The Jester plunged the knife directly into Ingrid's chest. The woman screamed and threw up her hands, but the Horror stabbed and slashed, a series of attacks that happened too fast for Eddie to react. She fell backward from the onslaught, her back striking the wall. She slid down, curled into a ball, her muffled screams echoing in the confines of the corridor. For a moment, Eddie lost sight of her as The Jester stood over her and continued to slash, its free hand holding onto her while the knife remained a blur.

And then it was done.

The Jester stepped back, its mask covered in a smug expression. Eddie stared at the creature, his own hands half raised, ready to defend himself. Even when The Jester crossed its arms and stared back, its hip cocked to the side, the lifeless black eyes of the mask looking through him, Eddie prepared for the worst. He broke his gaze away from the dead eyes of the mask and kept them focused on the knife in its hand.

A wicked curved blade covered in dried blood.

Dried.

Not a single drop of bright red.

Even as the sound of sobbing reached his ears, Eddie couldn't pull his gaze away from the knife.

"What . . ." Ingrid's voice was distorted. Eddie risked a glance back and found the woman still curled into a ball, arms covering her head. Her body convulsed as great sobs escaped from somewhere underneath the white of her lab coat. A coat frayed and covered by an uncountable number of small cuts. And yet it was devoid of the slightest tint of red.

"What the hell," Eddie rounded on The Jester, his anger blocking out all of the warnings the rest of his mind was screaming at him.

"That's the fear I owe her," The Jester's tone sent a shiver up Eddie's spine. "Except a hundred times over. A million. She owes me a debt that years of her terror couldn't repay. But as long as she follows your direction *and* you live, fear is the only revenge this one will inflict on her. Her life is yours, *friend* Eddie." A look of disgust marred the pale mask as The Jester nodded toward the elevator. "Get her out of this one's sight before Jester's fickle mind decides more fun would be had by exacting more payback now."

Eddie extended a hand toward Ingrid, but his eyes were locked on The Jester. Once he felt her hand in his grip, he pulled the scientist up. He kept a hold of her hand, which trembled beneath his fingers, and led her to the elevator. His eyes on the Horror, he heard her fumble about for a time, and then the soft sound of her keycard swiping through the card reader. Eddie continued to watch The Jester as the audible hum of the elevator grew louder behind him. The Horror stood stock still, its mask a blank expression. He wanted to believe that The Jester was letting them both go, but its outburst, violent but well controlled, had returned all of the tension between them that had begun to melt away as they traveled the halls. It wasn't until the soft signal of the elevator arriving that Eddie finally turned his back on The Jester.

The door opened and for the second time since he had entered the facility, he found the muzzle of a gun inches from his face.

CHAPTER 33

It took Eddie a moment to realize he had closed his eyes after seeing that gun. The sight of the gun barrel, after the roller coaster ride of dealing with The Jester, had just about pushed him over the edge. Funny enough, it was the thought of The Jester that brought him back to reality and made him open his eyes.

Jefferson stood in front of him, the handgun shaking in his grip.

A quick look was all Eddie needed to see that Jefferson was on the edge of cracking. He looked a mess. When they had last been together, Jefferson was the only one on the squad in full tactical armor. All he had left now were his arm guards, his head, chest, and leg protection gone. The simple black shirt he wore now was stained even darker with sweat or worse, a few of the stains surrounding cuts in the material. His face looked like it had gone a few rounds with a boxer; his left eye and cheek were swollen, a gash ran diagonally across his nose, and his lip was split.

It was how the man held himself, though, that made Eddie nervous. Besides the constant trembling in the man's outstretched arm, Jefferson was slouched like a defeated animal. His eyes darted about, not resting on any one person. Which meant despite the fact that The Jester was probably doing who knows what behind him, Jefferson was as worried about Eddie as he was the Horror. Which made the security officer all the more dangerous. The slightest gesture might cause the man to pull the trigger. And the King of Trauma was standing somewhere behind Eddie.

"Jefferson," Eddie spoke slowly and made sure not to make any sudden movements. "It's me, Eddie."

"I know who you are!" The gun shook even more in his hand until Jefferson made a visible effort to steady himself. "I'm not an idiot. Regardless of what you may think."

"Of course." Eddie wasn't about to risk a glance at either The Jester or Ingrid, but he was glad neither had made a move or even spoke. "You can understand my concern, though, with that gun pointed in my face."

"I couldn't give two shits about how concerned you are. You don't have the slightest clue what I've been through, and then I find you down here of all places with that fucking thing." He pointed with his free hand toward The Jester. "Just standing there with a stupid grin on that ugly mask. Maybe you can see why *I* might be concerned."

The man looked more frantic than concerned. Eddie had no idea what he could say to calm him down. "I can explain if you give me the chance."

"Explain why you're in the company of the same Horror that toyed with us and tried to make us kill each other? I doubt you're that good of a bullshitter."

"To be fair," The Jester said from behind Eddie, "I only tried to get your group to kill *one* person. Not really fair to say—"

"SHUT UP!" Jefferson's gun moved so that it was pointing over Eddie's shoulder. "You might be fast, freak, but I doubt you can dodge bullets."

"Maybe." The Jester's voice became devoid of emotion. "But you must know that a simple gun won't kill me."

"It will hurt it, though," Ingrid said. Eddie turned a surprised look in her direction, turning to shock as she took a step onto the elevator. "Put enough bullets in it, and it'll slow it down considerably for a time. Put one in its brain and you'll have a good five to ten minutes before it gets back up."

Jefferson glanced at the woman, then nodded his head toward the back of the elevator. Ingrid went the rest of the way in, placing her back to the wall. She leaned there, hands clasped together at her waist, eyes on the ground.

"Ingrid," Eddie said carefully. The gun might not be pointed at him for the moment, but it would be easy for Jefferson to move it a few inches and put it back in his face. "What are you doing?"

"I'm working with an *actual* security officer," she replied, her gaze still on the elevator floor. "One that realizes that creature is a threat to all of us."

"I never claimed The Jester wasn't a threat. Between it and the cultists, though, it's the one that has at least flipped back and forth between being an enemy and an ally." A question snuck into Eddie's head, the answer of which could mean he was in a lot more danger than he thought. Instead of asking it directly and setting the man off regardless of the answer, Eddie took a more tactful approach.

"Did you see Lizzie? Was she able to escape the cultists as well?"

"The secretary? I don't know. I never saw her."

"He's lying." The offhanded way The Jester said those two words seemed to catch everyone off guard. Eddie glanced back and found the creature leaning casually against the wall. When he returned his gaze forward, Ingrid had finally looked up and was staring wide-eyed at the man. Jefferson looked no more or less flustered than when the elevator door had originally opened.

"Shut up, freak," Jefferson waved the gun toward The Jester, which brought it closer to Eddie's face. "No one asked you."

Eddie pressed a little more. "How did you get away, Jefferson?"

"How do you expect? If a simple janitor was able to fight his way through, obviously someone with my training could handle it. I killed a bunch of them—"

"Lying again," Jester crooned in a singsong tone. "This man is full of lies."

"Why would I lie? I work for Soladyne—"

The Jester clapped his hands together loud enough to make Eddie flinch. "Three lies in three sentences, all as obvious as the white roots of Dr. Westburg's hair."

"You shouldn't be able to tell that. The charm the company gave me . . ." Jefferson clutched at his chest. "Shit," he mumbled. "It was in my armor."

"Ah ha!" The Jester did a little dance, hopping about in place and clapping its hands. "Jester knew something was off about Jefferson! Used a charm to lie and cheat. This one was right about Jefferson's greatest fear. Being buried alive is what you dread, isn't it."

Jefferson was starting to look as flustered as he had looked nervous. "No, I don't . . . you're wrong—"

"Liar, liar, pants on fire," The Jester cackled, continuing its little dance.

"Shut up!"

A sharp pain tore through Eddie's ear as Jefferson's gun went off. It was like a thunderclap right next to Eddie's head, and he gripped his ear as he fell over to the side. At first, he thought the pain came from the bullet ripping across the side of his head, but when he pulled his hand away, he was grateful not to find any of his own blood staining his hand. It didn't make the pain or the overwhelming buzzing sound dissipate though. Fighting through the pain, Eddie twisted on the ground until he could see The Jester.

A red circle bloomed around the black mark where the bullet had entered the Horror's chest. The Jester still stood, the expression on its mask blank.

Another shot rang out, this one muted by the painful effects of the first shot on Eddie's ear.

Then a third.

Followed by a fourth.

The Jester shuddered with each pop, a new black mark followed by a circle of blood similar to the others. Still the Horror stayed standing.

A fifth shot struck The Jester in the face, snapping the creature's head back and finally taking it off its feet.

Eddie struggled to stand, only to find the smoking barrel of Jefferson's gun pointed back at him. The man was shouting at him, but Eddie's focus was scrambled by the ringing in his ear. He raised his hands figuring that was the safest response. The man just kept yelling.

Right up to the point where a small hole erupted out of the middle of the man's neck.

Jefferson looked just as surprised as Eddie when blood spurted from the hole for a few moments then stopped just as fast. The man's head flinched. His eyes rolled back in his head and blood started to run from his nose just before he collapsed to the ground right outside of the elevator.

Ingrid appeared behind where Jefferson had stood just moments before. She took sharp breaths as she stared down at the fallen man, the laser scalpel gripped tightly in her hand. The body at her feet was face down, allowing Eddie to see two scorch marks. A large one was centered in the middle of the man's neck. Another sat at the back of the man's skull, the hair around it still smoking from the intense heat of the scalpel. Eddie took a few steps toward her before speaking.

"Are you ok?"

She continued to stare at the dead man at their feet.

"Ingrid?"

Nothing.

"Ingrid!"

The woman's eyes snapped up, as did the scalpel in her hand. Eddie put his hands up in a reassuring gesture but stopped moving toward her.

"Are you ok?"

She took a few ragged breaths before finally responding. "I've never killed a person before."

It didn't take a psychologist to tell the woman was right at her breaking point. Her arms shook, her eyes were half glazed over, and her face had gone as white as the walls and tiles of the corridor. Eddie worried that the wrong word here could send the woman over the edge. The only thing he could think to do was to keep her focused on anything other than the man she had just killed.

"What made you decide to defend me?" he asked.

For long seconds, Eddie thought he had failed. Ingrid continued to stare at Jefferson's body, a whip of smoke still rising from the burnt hair around the wound in his head. Just when he considered taking a cautious step away from the scientist, she lifted her gaze. A frown painted her lips and she glanced at where The Jester still lay a few feet behind Eddie before responding.

"The Jester doesn't lie about . . . people lying. In all of the years I've observed it, anytime it called a person out for lying, it was telling the truth. And you heard the man. He talked about receiving a charm from *the company*."

Eddie stuck a finger in his injured ear and gently dug around. "And that was enough to change your mind?

"If he was an agent for one of Soladyne's rivals, I have no doubt he would have killed us. It was either him or us."

Hearing the words from her own mouth seemed to help. She released her death grip on her scalpel and returned it to the pocket of her lab coat. Much to Eddie's relief.

"Then you saved both of us, but now the fact that he was some double-agent brings up more questions. Jefferson had already been working here for a few months. Was he somehow part of the cultists plans or did he have orders of his own?"

"No way to tell now." The woman's brisk attitude was slowly returning as she pursed her lips in thought. "Honestly, the threat of infiltrators from our rivals is never ending. Whatever company he worked for could have put him in here to help the cultists or for a dozen other reasons. I doubt he would have been stupid enough to leave any incriminating evidence on him."

"We should probably still check. If nothing else, whatever weapons he has on him would be helpful."

"I'll do that, you don't have to search his corpse."

"Psshhh," she scoffed. "Having to kill was shocking to say the least, but I'm not some weak-willed crybaby. I have no problem searching a corpse, even if it's one I created." She waved him off. "Why don't you check on *your* other friend?"

In the craziness, Eddie had completely forgotten about The Jester. A quick glance found the Horror still lying where it had fallen, its body as still as Jefferson's. Ingrid and The Jester itself had made it clear there was no known way to kill it, but it looked plenty dead to him.

"Are you sure?"

"Yes. When it wakes up, better it sees you than me."

That wasn't the most reassuring thing to hear. Just because the Horror seemed less likely to harm him didn't mean it would be in the same generous mood after being repeatedly shot. On the same token, if showing the least bit concern for The Jester kept Eddie in its good graces, it was an acceptable risk.

At least that's what he kept telling himself as he approached the fallen monster.

Moving to The Jester's side, Eddie took stock of the creature's injuries. Four bullet holes had penetrated the creature's crimson tunic relatively close to each other. Circular patches of dampness surrounded each, slowly expanding. If the creature was supposed to heal itself, it was certainly taking its time. Eddie couldn't find any sign of the final bullet that had brought the Horror down. He was positive he saw it strike The Jester's mask, but the pure white material remained unblemished. It even wore a peaceful expression, thin lines representing closed eyes and a small smile touching its lips.

The rational part of Eddie's brain told him to leave it be. At first. Then that same side of him realized that The Jester might not take it well if it woke up after being shot and realized Eddie and

Ingrid had abandoned it. With how fickle the Horror seemed to be, waking it up seemed to be the safest bet. At the moment, both of its hands were bare, which meant its knives were tucked away somewhere. That was something at least.

Eddie knelt next to the Horror and placed a hand on its shoulder. He gave it a gentle shake. Nothing. Using both hands, he shook the creature a little harder. Still nothing. It remained still, breath not filling its chest or the wounds healing as he had expected. How did the Horror heal anyway? Ingrid would probably know. After all, she was the one that experimented on him the most. When Eddie looked up to ask her for advice, he found Ingrid bent over Jefferson's corpse, combing through his various pockets. She removed something small and rectangular from his belt and deftly placed it inside her lab coat before she realized Eddie was looking at her.

"What is it?" she asked as she moved on to another one of Jefferson's pockets. Eddie didn't know if it was a good or bad thing that she seemed so comfortable searching the dead.

"How do I wake him up?"

Before Ingrid could answer, The Jester's hand shot up and grabbed Eddie's knee.

Which of course caused Eddie to fall backward, emitting a sound that most would consider less than manly.

The Jester's laughter greeted him, succeeding in embarrassing him even more.

"Poor Eddie. So skittish." It sat up, then gave its body a shake. Arms flailed about, its body twisted and turned, and The Jester finished off by rolling its neck. Not only did The Jester's wounds appear to be completely gone, even its garish outfit no longer had the slightest sign of bullet holes or blood. It was as if nothing had happened to the Horror.

"Forgive this one for causing such a fright," The Jester continued. "Jester cannot pass up an opportunity such as that."

"I wasn't that surprised," Eddie replied. He kept his serious demeanor for a moment longer, then let out a sheepish laugh. "Well, maybe I was just a little."

"All in good fun. This one even suspects Dr. Westburg got some enjoyment out of it."

"It was a little funny," Ingrid said with a sniff. She immediately put her hand up to adjust her glasses, but Eddie was almost positive he caught the corner of a smile before her hand blocked it out.

"Were you awake the whole time?" Eddie asked.

"Yes, and Jester heard a funny thing. You called this one *him* and not *it*," The Jester still held a bit of humor in its voice, but there was a touch of something else as well, though Eddie couldn't quite place it.

"Yes, well, you've been acting more human than not. If you ignore all of the murdering."

"Hard to ignore that," The Jester said with a high-pitched laugh, "but Jester is not sure if it takes such a comment as a compliment or an insult. Best to stick with *it*."

"As you wish," Eddie got to his feet and extended a hand to The Jester. It looked at his hand for a moment, then waved him off.

"Let this one rest a bit. Been a while since Jester was shot. Would you say it's been a few years, Dr. Westburg?"

"I shot you after you took Trevor's tongue and you know it," she said with a frown, the last bit of levity disappearing from her face. "Thank you for reminding me."

The Jester put his hands to his mask as a shocked expression appeared on its surface. "That long ago? The days do bleed together when one is locked away in a cell of white with nothing for entertainment."

"If you two are finished, Eddie," Ingrid replied as she moved into the elevator. "I'm relying on the more timid of the two of you to get me to the control room and we're not getting there any faster chatting by the elevator. So grab the dead man's gun—" she gestured to the discarded weapon close to Jefferson's body "—and let's go."

"Sorry," Eddie replied, taking a step in her direction but stopped as Jester grabbed his leg. He was happy that he didn't almost leap out of his skin this time.

"Be safe, friend-Eddie. For one with such high morals, this one still finds you interesting to be around."

"Thanks," Eddie said, not sure how to respond. "You be safe, too."

"Not to worry," The Jester replied as Eddie moved toward the elevator. "Plenty more fun to be had by this one. Jester is sure we'll run into each other again."

As Eddie picked up Jefferson's firearm and got on the elevator, he hoped that The Jester meant what it had said in the friendliest of ways.

"Ready?" Ingrid didn't wait for a response before she pressed the button for the first floor. Eddie checked the weapon in his hand, making sure to put the safety on before placing it in his pocket. The Jester waved to them as the doors closed and then the elevator began to rise, leaving the horror and *the Horror* of the floor behind.

CHAPTER 34

As soon as the elevator closed, Ingrid pulled something out of her lab coat. It was the hand-sized rectangular box he had seen her take off of Jefferson. With everything that had happened recently, Eddie's first instinct was to think it was a weapon she was about to use on him. When she held it out, however, he silently chuckled to himself. Why would the woman have saved him from Jefferson just to turn on him now? Being careful was one thing, but he couldn't let himself get paranoid.

"What is it?" he asked before taking the item. He grew nervous again as the woman pressed the emergency stop button on the elevator, bringing them to a halt.

"A radio. If you have allies in the control room, you might be able to get a hold of them with this. Best to try now while we're in the relative safety of the elevator."

Eddie stared at it a few moments before he shook his head and tried to hand it back. "I don't know how it works. You try."

"Just flip up the switch on the side and press the orange button to speak," she replied with a roll of her eyes. "I've seen that type of walkie-talkie used by the security team. It's set to only work with others of its kind in the facility."

Eddie hesitated. "When I first arrived, it was mentioned that all forms of communications were being blocked. Including radio signals."

"The facility does have the ability to do that." Ingrid put a hand to her chin. "But if the control room was damaged, it's likely that system was shut down or damaged as well. If *I* was part of a security team and the jamming system was still up, that would be one of the first things I'd deactivate as I tried to regain control of the facility. Give it a try. Worse thing that can happen is no one responds."

Eddie thought about it for a moment more, then nodded, flipped the walkie-talkie on, and pressed the button down with his thumb. "Hello?"

Static greeted him. Eddie felt a little foolish, not knowing what to say, but tried again. "This is Eddie. Is anyone there? Hinderlight? Kaga?"

More static. Ingrid shrugged and waved at him to try again. Just as he was about to press the button again, the walkie-talkie came to life.

"Eddie?" Relief washed over him at the sound of Hinderlight's voice. *"That really you?"*

"Yes, sir," Eddie couldn't help the grin that spread across his face. "Alive and relatively well. I have one of the lead scientists from the Living Containment level with me as well."

"Can she be trusted?"

Eddie looked into the woman's eyes and nodded. "Absolutely."

"Glad to hear it. How about we get you both back to the control room for safe keeping."

"Sounds good to me. I can't wait to hear how you took down that Khurobak."

"An excellent story, believe me, although I'm sure you've got stories of your own."

"Plenty. We're on our way to the main elevator now. How much control have you regained over the facility?"

"Limited. Best not to discuss it over the radio. I can send the elevator to whatever level you are on, though. We've got the doors pretty well barricaded, but when I know it's you coming up, we'll clear a path for you."

"Sounds good to me, but there are some things you should know, just in case we don't get there. I overheard who these black robes actually are."

"Excellent. We have access to the company archives. If Soladyne has anything on them, we should be able to look them up. Maybe even figure out what they want so we can go about stopping them. Who are they?"

"They called themselves followers of Voltron."

"What? Like the cartoon?"

"Wait, no, that's not right." Eddie was glad only Ingrid could see the embarrassment painted across his face. "It sounded like Voltron. Vol...Vol..." Eddie was about to smack his head against the wall when it came back to him. "Voltozas. It was Voltozas, I'm positive."

"You sounded positive about Voltron."

"No, it's Voltozas. No doubt about it. And that's not all.

Everything they've been doing has been part of some ritual they are trying to complete."

"All right, hold on. Let me see if I can find anything on them."

As Hinderlight cut off, the crackle of radio static filled the elevator. Eddie glanced over at Ingrid and gave her a reassuring smile. He received a raised eyebrow in return and turned his attention back to the static coming through the radio.

Minutes passed. Ingrid began to tap her toes. Each time Eddie glanced in her direction, the scientist's expression seemed to grow darker. By the fifth time, with the static of the radio mixed with the building tension, Ingrid let out an exasperated breath and moved to release the stop button and get the elevator moving.

Hinderlight's voice returned just in time to make the woman's finger pause inches from the button.

"You're positive they said Voltozas?"

"Yes."

"Shit." Hinderlight's reply was less than reassuring. *"All right. I need you to get to the elevator and get back up here. Just don't expect more than a few minutes of rest. Once we get that scientist of yours settled in, you and I are heading right back out."*

"What? Why?"

"Because, unfortunately, I think we've figured out what they're trying to do, and based on the records I could access, we have the one thing they need."

That sounded less than promising.

"Just believe me when I say we don't want them to succeed."

"Fair enough. We'll get going then. I'll let you know where to send the elevator once we get to it."

"Sounds like a plan. Going to keep off the radio until then. Over and out."

Eddie could barely contain his relief. Not long after he had been left on his own, he had survived a giant spider gotten lost in the air ducts, almost got eaten by an oversized dog with acid slobber, and then traveled with a Horror that could have turned on him at any time. And now he was on his way to safety with a scientist in tow who could possibly help their cause as well. For the first time in a long time, Eddie no longer needed to merely hope for survival. Now, he actually had a decent chance.

Of course, Ingrid was quick to dampen his mood.

"Stop grinning like a fool." She gave him a withering look, then released the stop button and the elevator got moving again. "As far as we know, whatever cultists didn't get eaten or stabbed on the previous floor are all waiting for us on this one."

When the friendly *ding* announcing their arrival filled the elevator, Eddie pictured a mass of black robes waiting on the other side of the door.

Thankfully, that wasn't the case. The doors opened to another sterile white hallway that could have been an exact replica to any of the other corridors in this section of the facility. *See, don't let the negative woman bring you down,* Eddie thought as he stepped out into the hallway. Ingrid followed behind, glancing about as if she expected an ambush despite the lack of even the smallest shadow or piece of furniture in the empty hallway.

"How far away is the main elevator?" Eddie asked.

"Not far. Shouldn't take long to reach it. Unless of course we run into any more surprises."

Ingrid led him down the empty hallway and took a left at the first junction. Despite his mood, the stark white of the floors, ceilings, and walls were starting to wear on Eddie. It was like walking through a snowstorm, except the snow didn't quite reach you and the sun somehow shown through enough to reflect off all the walls just enough to make you squint. How the scientists could spend most of their time here without the faintest hint of color was beyond him.

Ingrid didn't seem to mind. The woman strode along confidently, eyes locked on where they were going. It was hard to get a good read on the red-headed scientist. She kept her expressions to a minimum, except when she threw out her annoyed or condescending glare, and she shared very little. Eddie wanted to think that the woman was more than just a scientist with little regard for her test subjects. She had shown some anger over Trevor's maiming and more so after his death. There had been other cracks in her armor, most often whenever The Jester was involved in some way. But Eddie could only hope there was more to the woman.

When the sounds of their footsteps on the white tile began to grate at him, Eddie decided to pick the scientist's brain and try to get her to open up. After all, they had already been through a great deal and he knew nothing about her.

"Do you have any thoughts about what they might be after?"

"It could be anything." At first, Eddie thought that was all she was going to offer. She stared ahead as they walked, her hands fidgeting at her sides. He was about to change the subject when she let out a breath and spoke. "This facility consists of multiple sections focused on different areas of study, with most having items this cult might be after. There's the inter-dimensional research facility. Another section devoted to sentient objects, and an area focused purely on the occult and what you would probably refer to as 'magic.' And those are just the sections I know about. Curiosity about anything other than your specific field is not exactly encouraged here."

"Sentient objects?" Despite his curiosity about inter-dimensional objects and magical items, for some reason, one item shot into his mind. "Like a toaster that talks to you while it burns your bread?"

Ingrid rolled her eyes in response. "Every time I think we are having a somewhat intelligent conversation, you always disappoint. No, we don't have any *talking toasters* here."

"Then what do you have?"

"I don't know." She shrugged and kept her attention ahead. "Each level has its own teams of scientists. It's very rare for someone from this section of the facility to work with scientists from another section. The company likes to keep us compartmentalized."

"Then technically you could have a talking toaster; you just don't know about it." Eddie did his best not to smile, but he could feel the corners of his mouth twitch.

"You're a child," she replied, but didn't bother to hide her smile. "Yes, I *suppose* there could be a talking toaster somewhere in the facility. More than likely, though, rumors about something like that would have trickled down to my department. Regardless of the strict rules put in place to stop gossiping between departments."

"Well, maybe if we survive this, they'll reward us with a trip down to whatever level they'd keep a marvelous discovery such as that."

"Doubtful." She glanced over at Eddie, her smile waning slightly. "That we'd be given access to another section of the facility, I mean. I'm not as doubtful that we'd survive. Despite my doubts, you have provided the one chance to find some safe ground."

"I'll take that as a compliment," Eddie said with a laugh. He was happy to see Ingrid actually smile. "After all, who would expect a socially awkward custodian to survive more than a few minutes during a crisis involving cults and monsters."

Ingrid stopped walking and stared at him with a skeptical look. "You? Socially awkward? You've barely shut up since you tumbled out of the vents."

"That's true. You know, I used to get really nervous around people. Kept to myself, believe it or not. Even The Jester said interacting with people was my greatest fear. This whole situation seems to have at least lessened that fear." He shook his head. "The funny part is, the company had on record my severe social anxiety. Hinderlight, the man on the other end of the radio, said he'd help me by forcing me to make a speech in front of the whole building. He had been joking at the time, but I've been through much worse than that now, and it seemed to have worked. I guess he had a good idea after all."

"Well, when we reach him, you can be sure to tell him he was right."

"No, the man has enough confidence as it is. No need to add to it."

They turned another corner and Eddie was surprised to find that the hallway opened up a little and the elevator door sat on the opposite side. A light buzzing emanated from the room, but besides that, it seemed fairly innocuous. Despite Eddie's positive mood, with everything that had happened so far, he more than expected to run into some kind of trouble before they reached the elevator. While part of him still expected some monster to drop from the ceiling or the cultists to come running up behind them, he tried to take his good luck in stride.

The buzzing in the room was starting to get annoying, though.

"Do you hear that?"

But Ingrid had already moved toward the elevator door and seemed to not have heard him.

"Look." She motioned toward the lights above the door. The display was counting down.

Five.

Four.

"Did you call your friend and tell him to send the elevator?"

"No." Eddie tried to think but the buzzing was annoying enough to make it difficult. "He said that they had gotten some of the systems working. Maybe he saw us coming on the security cameras."

"What's the buzzing noise?"

It was then that Eddie realized it was coming from the walkie-talkie at his side. Feeling foolish, he grabbed it and thumbed up the volume.

"Eddie! Eddie, respond!"

A knot began to form in Eddie's stomach as he heard the urgency in the man's voice. Fumbling to remove it from his belt, he finally got it to his ear and replied.

"Eddie here. What's wrong? We're just about to get on the elevator."

"I didn't send the elevator anywhere yet. It started moving on its own. Someone else is headed to your—"

Eddie didn't get to hear the rest of it as the elevator door opened to a sea of black robes.

"Shit," Eddie mumbled. He had his hand on the weapon in his pocket but the cultists washed over him before he could get it free. Grabbing hands, dark cowls right in his face, rancid breath assaulting his nose. He struggled against the darkness, right up until a flash of light and ripple of pain surrounded him before the darkness flooded in.

CHAPTER 35

Eddie felt like every muscle in his body had been stomped on. At first, that was all he could focus on, the soreness that touched every inch of him from head to toe. Then his senses started to take in the outside world. The sounds of whimpering and heavy breathing touched his ears. He smelled sterility, like a doctor's office, similar to the hallways on the containment level. His fingers touched cold metal. When he tried to lift them, Eddie realized his wrists were tied down. As were his ankles. The realization brought a sense of urgency crashing down on his consciousness.

At last, he opened his eyes.

Darkness surrounded him, the only light coming from above and extended his view to a circle of a few feet around him. His arms and legs were tied with thick ropes to a plain metal chair. He struggled a few times but didn't manage to loosen them in the slightest. Giving up on escape for the moment, Eddie peered into the darkness. His eyes couldn't pick out even the faintest outline of any one or thing. He could still hear light whimpering from somewhere to his left, which meant someone else was in the room as well. Or some*thing*. He was about to call out, when he remembered exactly where he was. The sound in the darkness could just as easily be a Horror as it could a person. Would the cultists knock him out just to put him in a room to be killed by some monster instead?

A light flashed before his eyes, blinding him and disrupting his thoughts. Just as fast as it had appeared, the light vanished, leaving a bright circle burned into Eddie's vision. He wanted to rub at his eyes, but of course, he was still tied down. All he could do was blink rapidly until the massive spot dissipated. When it did, he found a pale cultist squatting in front of him. The light from above seemed to reflect off his bald head and ran shadows beneath the sharp angles of his face. When he spoke, his gruff voice immediately brought Eddie back to their first interaction when Lizzie and Hugh had been taken.

"Mr. Watson. This is the third time we've been in such close proximity and I have yet the chance to introduce myself. I would say it's poor manners on my part, but each time, the company you were keeping disrupted our conversation with violence."

Eddie's mind raced as he tried to come up with some way to salvage the situation. A useless effort, but it kept him focused instead of afraid. "Well, here is your chance."

"Yes, of course." His mouth opened into a smile of yellow teeth and putrid breath. "I am known among my brethren as Shepherd Yon. You may refer to me as such or simply as Yon. No need to be overly formal, is there, Eddie?"

"I suppose not, seeing as how you have me tied to a chair." What would Hinderlight do in this situation? Eddie paused to look about the dark room and then raise an eyebrow at the man. "Don't you think this is all a little over dramatic? Pitch black room. Sounds of someone whimpering somewhere in the darkness. Blinding me for a moment so you could make a sudden appearance. Seems very campy to me."

"Of course it is, Eddie," the man said with a laugh. His overpowering breath brushed against Eddie's nostrils and made his empty stomach churn. "The backbone of any religion is a strong level of showmanship. Easier to razzle dazzle the simple minded to your cause than to bribe, threaten, or blackmail. Safer as well. Someone who *believes* in your cause is much less likely to turn on you at the most inopportune time."

"So that's what this Voltozas is? Just a front for some phony religion?"

Yon's smile disappeared. He didn't look insulted, but at the same time he certainly didn't look pleased. "Oh, no, no. Voltozas is real. A powerful entity, a god if you will, from a different dimension. Its only desire is to cause change in whatever it touches." The man's eyes began to wander to the side as he appeared to lose himself in some memory or thought. "The great Voltozas can do so many horribly wonderful things to this world with even the smallest breath. Where other religions beg for help from their silent god, Voltozas answers us. Teaches us. Lets us become more than what we are."

"I'm sure plenty of 'prophets' can claim the same thing." Eddie tugged at his bonds, but it was more out of habit now than an actual effort to get free.

"Eddie." Yon moved his head close enough that Eddie actually felt his breath might knock him out. When he spoke, his voice was low as if sharing a wonderful secret. "I wouldn't claim something I couldn't prove."

With his face still inches from Eddie's, the man reached up and placed a single finger up to his own eye. Eddie squirmed but couldn't pull his gaze away as the man pushed his eye back slightly and then pulled down his lower eyelid as if he were peeling the skin from a grape. Instead of the pinky flesh Eddie expected, a hard black chitin, like the back of a cockroach, rested beneath.

"What the hell," Eddie whispered. All of the fake bravado that he had been able to muster was swept away as realization of his situation set in. He was restrained and at the mercy of some man—no, something that was more than a man, or less. He had been able to handle men and women infected by brain spores, psychotic killers straight out of the movies, and monsters out of someone else's nightmares. But now, the concept of other dimensions and the gods that ruled them were being thrown at him. It was more than he could handle. He jerked back as far as he could in his restraints, real fear and awe shaking him to his core.

Yon patted Eddie's cheek, his hand prickly like how Eddie's chin felt after a week without shaving. "There it is. The look when a man living on the surface of the world truly sees how deep and dark things really are beneath him. And how dangerous those depths are.

"Now that you have a true grasp of your situation," Yon continued as he stood, "we can get down to business. While our followers put the finishing touches on the ritual to summon Voltozas, there are some questions I need you to answer, Eddie Watson, master of the philosophical." Yon walked around Eddie's chair until he stood directly behind him. When the man slapped both of his hands on Eddie's shoulders, he couldn't help but flinch. The man's vice-like grip squeezed just enough to make Eddie cringe. "You see, the final part can be quite sensitive. If I were to be completely honest—because I want us to be honest with each other, Eddie—we're not quite sure the exact details of how Voltozas' crossing into our world actually works. We know what to do, but not how it works. So of course, we want the 'what' to run as smoothly as possible, even though not knowing the 'how' doesn't really matter.

"So, as the empathetic person you've shown yourself to be, you can understand my concern that one of your foolish Soladyne flunkies might suddenly show up and disrupt everything we've worked so hard to accomplish. Or worse. Embarrass us in front of the great Voltozas itself. Since I've been so honest with you, I need you to be honest with me. How much do those flunkies know? We heard your little conversation, but you must know more than you said over the radio. I can hardly believe that whatever is left of the security team relied on the bumblings of a simple janitor to retrieve all of their information."

It was unnerving to Eddie that the man seemed to know things about him. Was he even a man? Part man, part bug? Another creature wearing a man suit? And how much more did Yon know that he wasn't letting on? Was he trying to catch Eddie in a lie just to set the tone of the interrogation?

Eddie Watson's Life Rule Number 15: If you have more questions than answers, answer what you can *with* as little as you can.

"They don't know anything more than what you heard. They didn't even know who you were until I told them." It was the truth and Eddie didn't feel it put Hinderlight or Kaga at any kind of disadvantage with the cult.

"Such a quick response. If I knew nothing more about you than that you are some unmotivated janitor with just enough brain matter to get yourself a degree in a useless major, I would believe you. But you're not just that man, are you, Eddie? That man would have died long before he ever made it this far, regardless of whatever help you received along the way. No, you're stronger than you let on. Despite being shaken, I believe you still have some fight in you. I just can't risk everything without being absolutely sure."

Yon clapped his hands. Three lights sprang into existence, similar to the one above him. Each created a circle of vision, shining down on three people sitting in chairs similar to Eddie's with their hands tied behind their backs. Eddie sucked in a breath as he realized who they were.

Hugh was on his left, the man's face beaten and bloody, his black hair and clothes equally a mess. The man's eyes were swollen shut and his head was listed to the side, making it impossible to tell if he was awake, unconscious, or dead. To Eddie's right, Ingrid seemed in better condition. Besides a small cut underneath her left eye, she seemed relatively untouched. She blinked as her eyes adjusted to the light before focusing on Eddie. With his head still a bit fuzzy, it was hard to tell, but he could almost swear she was giving him a condescending stare as if the whole thing was his fault. She probably would have told him as much if she wasn't tightly gagged. He would have given her an annoyed look of his own, but his eyes were drawn to the seat in front of him.

Lizzie sat slumped forward, her auburn hair a mess that covered most of her face but didn't completely hide the bruised skin that peaked out underneath. Her clothes, all but covered in stains of crimson, rose and fell weakly with each breath, a wheeze and a whimper. Despite the futility of it, Eddie strained against his binds as if the sight of three in trouble would somehow give him added strength. It didn't of course. Instead of busting free, all he did was earn a chuckle from Yon.

"Ah, the valiant custodian dismayed by his allies' discomfort." The cultist continued to laugh. "Did you feel your adrenaline spike? Expect to perform some heroic feat? This is not some movie where the down-and-out hero finds a way to surpass his mortal strength and overcome the dire odds. You are *human*. A pure human, with limits. Restrictions. Voltozas will break the binds that limit our human bodies and lift us up above the mortal coil." Again that putrid yellow smile. "By *us*, I mean Voltozas' followers of course. Not you, janitor."

"Let them go." Eddie tried to put some strength in his voice, but couldn't find any. "What are you going to do?"

"Test your resolve, of course." Yon turned his back on Eddie and moved around behind Lizzie's chair. He gripped her shoulder, putting enough pressure to make the woman sit up straight, her eyes snapping open. "I want to see how long you stick to your story as I butcher your allies."

"I told you the truth!" Eddie leaned forward, straining against his bonds. "You don't need to hurt anyone."

Yon shrugged. "We shall see." The cultist began to pace behind all three of his captives, placing his hand on the head of each like some twisted game of duck-duck-goose.

"Now, who should we start with? The feisty scientist?"

Duck.

"The person you've known the longest?" Yon winked at him. "And the possible love interest?"

Eddie cringed. Duck.

"Or the other poor sap that got dragged along into this mess."

The slight hope that poor Hugh would be chosen first crawled into Eddie's chest and quickly turned into shame, like a dog on its belly after being caught pulling apart the trash. It sickened him the moment it appeared and grew worse as he failed to squash it.

"We'll start easy." Yon slapped his hands down on the restrained man's shoulders hard enough that the sound echoed around the room and Hugh came awake with a start. "Hugh it is then."

Goose.

Guilt welled up inside of Eddie. Guilt and shame. "I'm telling you, Yon. The people in the control room don't know anything more than what I told them over the radio. Threatening these people won't change that fact."

Those yellow teeth appeared again as Yon's mouth opened into a smile. He knelt down so that his head was about the same level as Hugh's. "Slow down. When you act so desperately, I know you're acting. I mean, this man was a stranger to you as little as a day ago. But now you're this concerned over him?"

"I don't want to see anyone—"

Yon pulled a slender knife from his robe. The cultist tapped the edge of the blade on his hand, letting the silence fill the room.

It was at that point that Hugh chose to speak.

"Please let me go," he said weakly. "Please."

"Hush, little man," Yon cooed in his ear. "I'm having a conversation with your friend, Eddie."

"Eddie?" Hugh's head perked up and his head moved about as if he was looking for Eddie, despite his eyes being swollen shut. "Help me, Eddie."

Yon pressed the edge of the blade to the side of Hugh's neck, then pressed so that it cut about an inch of his skin. Hugh cried out in pain, struggling against his bonds as Yon held the knife in place.

"Stop it!" Eddie tugged at his wrists. Tried to kick his legs. All he managed to do was make his chair skid forward slightly while crimson starting to run down the blade and Hugh's neck.

"Are you both done with your little outbursts?" Yon asked.

Eddie stopped struggling. Hugh's cries calmed down into whimpers.

"Good," Yon removed the knife from the man's skin. "Now, I'll ask you again, Eddie. What do the remaining security officers know? What plans do they have?"

"I'm telling you the truth. They know as much as you heard." Eddie's mind scrambled as he tried to think of anything else he could tell the man. "They didn't have any kind of plan either. At least not that they told me. If they did, Hinderlight was waiting until I got reached him."

Yon lowered the knife to Hugh's neck again, this time putting the blade perpendicular to the man's Adam's apple.

"It's the truth!"

Yon stared at him, the smile gone, his pale white lips pressed together, revealing nothing.

Hugh continued to whimper.

Eddie held Yon's gaze, willing the man to realize he was telling the truth.

The only sounds in the room were the varied breaths of the five people inside.

The corners of Yon's lips curled downwards.

"Don't—" Eddie began, as Yon started to laugh.

"I believe you," Yon said between chuckles. He removed the knife from Hugh's throat and rested his arm on Hugh's shoulder. "I guess you are the type of person that cares about even a stranger's life. Very interesting."

Yon stood, continuing to laugh. Eddie let himself breathe a little easier. Maybe if he could keep the man talking, keep him from hurting any of them—

The man's laughter continued to fill the room as Yon grabbed Hugh's hair with his free hand and then drove his knife through the man's temple.

"No!" Eddie watched as Hugh stiffened then twitch. Blood flowed down from where the knife was lodged in his head. The poor man continued to twitch against his restraints as Yon yanked the blade free and released his hair.

"You said you believed me!" Eddie croaked, trying his best not to break out in a sob. "Why did you kill him?"

"Oh, Eddie my boy, I do believe you!" He wiped his blade on the shoulder of the still twitching body of Hugh. "The only reason I killed him was because I have two other people to play with and I don't want to waste all of my time with such a boring person."

Eddie felt sick. Wanted to cry. Wanted to scream. He didn't have the energy for any of it. There had been a fair amount of death and gore since the day had begun, but this wasn't just a death. It was the murder of someone unable to defend themself. And there was nothing he could do to protect Lizzie or Ingrid. Eddie had never felt so powerless before, and the worst part was that he had been relieved when Yon had chosen Hugh first.

"You're a monster," Eddie mumbled, but wasn't sure who he was talking about.

"Oh no," Yon replied, waggling a finger in Eddie's direction. "I am entering the next stage of human evolution. When Voltozas arrives, he will complete my transformation and usher in a new age for humanity." He stepped out from behind the now still Hugh. "Don't lump me in with the things this company kept locked away in cages."

"You're right," Eddie replied, which earned a yellow-toothed smile from the man. "You're not like the things they keep here. You're worse." Some strength returned to Eddie's voice, although not much. "The creatures here don't have the morals you and I are born with. It's not an excuse for their actions, but at least—"

Eddie stopped as Yon stepped behind Lizzie.

"Oh please, go on." The cultist waved for him to continue. "I very much want to hear your lessons about morality and philosophy and whatever else your feeble mind feels is important."

Yon tilted his head as if listening to Eddie. The knife in his hand, partially congealed blood still resting in the space between the blade and the hilt where Hugh's shirt hadn't touched, hovering just next to Lizzie's ear. A thousand curses and accusations sat on the tip of Eddie's tongue, but he kept his mouth shut. The effort made his jaw hurt. Half of him desired the man's death, might even drive him far enough to kill him if Eddie ever got free. The more logical side of Eddie, however, feared that it wouldn't take much to drive Yon to kill Lizzie. He would already live with the guilt of Hugh's death on his conscience for as long or short of a life he had left. Eddie couldn't handle adding Lizzie's death to the list.

"Ah, nothing else to say?" Yon waited. Eddie glared at him. "Good, then we can continue."

The cultist leaned down behind Lizzie, his grimy smile just inches from her ear. "How many people are barricaded on the control room floor?"

"Why would I tell you anything if you're just going to kill us all anyway?"

In response, Yon lowered the knife so that it disappeared behind Lizzie's back. He stared straight at Eddie, but Eddie's entire focus was on Lizzie's night-blue eyes.

"What's happening?" she got out just before she began to scream.

Her back arched, her chest coming forward and her legs sliding forward on the chair. Behind her, Yon's shoulder moved as he appeared to dig his weapon into Lizzie's back.

"You bastard!" Eddie was screaming now, his voice mixing in with Lizzie's cries. "You fucking bastard!"

"There are things much worse than the simple death Hugh received." Yon had to yell over the still screaming Lizzie. "I'm surprised with all you must have been through that you haven't learned that yet."

"It's just two people," Eddie yelled.

Lizzie's screams intensified. Yon just scowled. "You came down with more than that. Did you run into any that had escaped our clutches? Did you not find any other reinforcements?"

"It's only two, I swear!" Eddie was caught halfway between yelling and sobbing. The words poured out of his mouth, everything he knew. Anything that might get Lizzie's torture to stop. "The only one I know that escaped was killed." Eddie made sure not to look in Ingrid's direction. "He was a spy that worked for a rival company."

"Ah, Jefferson." Lizzie stopped screaming as Yon brought the knife up and tapped it thoughtfully against his lips. Lizzie slumped down in the chair, sweat pouring down her face as the man

288

continued. "Never met him personally. He was given specific instructions to stay out of the way while we did our work. One of our many followers must have gotten a hold of him and not believed he was working with us. I had hoped he would survive the day. Not a follower of our faith but instrumental in getting us this far.

"But that is neither here nor there. So two people were able to kill the Khurobak? That monster was instrumental in the early stages of our ritual, but then made quite the mess of things. The two men must be proficient warriors. Only two, even as skilled as they, should not be able to cause us any more problems." Yon brought the knife back down so it disappeared behind Lizzie's back.

"Wait!" Eddie stammered. "You don't need to hurt her. I told you everything. I'll tell you anything else you ask if I know it. Just don't hurt her!"

Yon's shoulders shook as he chuckled, continuing whatever he was doing to Lizzie's back. A sharp sawing sound followed, putting horrible images of what mutilation the cultist was causing the poor woman into Eddie's mind.

Except she didn't scream.

Lizzie's head had risen and she shook the hair out of her face. A purple and brown mess of bruises and swollen lumps covered her skin. At first, Eddie thought she must be in shock, the pain of whatever Yon was doing no longer reaching her consciousness. But then she smiled.

The sawing stopped. Yon rose behind Lizzie as she brought her hands forward. She rubbed at her wrists for a few moments before rising as well. That smile still rested among the mass of bruises.

Then, as Eddie's mind struggled to understand what was going on, Lizzie ran a hand down the front of her face. The wounds and bruises vanished as her hand passed. Lizzie's face, a face Eddie had greeted practically every day since he had started working, was restored. Except that her smile, one that he had constantly tried to elicit from the woman, no longer held the warmth that he secretly treasured.

"Thank you, Eddie," she said, her smile widening into a predatory grin. "You've been very helpful to the Church of Voltozas."

CHAPTER 36

"Lizzie?" Eddie's mind reeled. There was no way the person he had seen twice a day for the past three years, the person who had greeted him with a smile and sent him home with one as well, could be working for the cultists. This had to be some kind of trick. Some kind of clever play to give them the opportunity for escape. Except the woman wasn't sending him any subtle winks or some other sign to clue him in. She stood confident in her bloodied button-up shirt and pants, the stains on her ivory teeth doing little to dampen the wide smile she now wore. Not wanting to believe what he saw in front of him, Eddie turned his attention to the person he *knew* was his enemy.

Yon still stood behind Lizzie's chair, his hands clasped together so that they were hidden in the black cloth of his robes. His head was tilted forward, eyes to the floor, the barest hint of his decayed teeth peeking out from behind a thin smile. It wasn't the posture of a man in complete control of another person. It looked more like the supplicant stance of a servant. Which made Lizzie the master.

Eddie's heart sank, but he grasped at whatever straws of hope his mind laid out for him.

"I can understand your confusion, Mr. Watson." Lizzie took a few steps toward him before favoring him with a condoling smile. "But let me make it clear, so that you can settle your mind on what's happening. I'm not the Lizzie McClane you met over three years ago when you first started working for Soladyne. That Lizzie has been dead for quite a while."

Any spark of hope that Eddie had left died. He tried to grasp what the woman was saying. It was a struggle.

"How long?" It was all he could get out.

The imposter Lizzie put a finger to her lip and looked to the ceiling. "A good question. It's been about a year now since I took her appearance, I think. Whenever she was out with—" her smile changed to a smirk "—strep throat. In reality, we had taken her and moved into her apartment while I was transformed into your cute little secretary."

"She's been dead over a year . . ." Eddie felt like he had been repeatedly gut punched. For three years, he thought he was slowly getting to know Lizzie. He had secretly looked forward to seeing her twice a day, despite how nervous she had made him at first. Had finally started getting comfortable around her the past few months. When everything had started falling apart, the stress of it all had actually helped him speak to her like a normal human being.

And it had all been a lie.

"Believe it or not Eddie," the woman continued, "I feel a little bad about being the one to break the news to you. I know she was important to you."

Grief gave way to anger. "What the hell do you know? Just because you look like her doesn't mean you know anything about either of us. You spoke to me for maybe a year, but it was all just one big lie."

The imposter somehow managed to look hurt. "That's not true. Yes, I had to make myself look like her, but changing my appearance wouldn't have been enough. Lizzie saw hundreds of people throughout the day, and any one of them could have seen through my ruse if I had acted the slightest bit different or forgotten a funny anecdote from some random employee. And those are just passing acquaintances. To be able to fool Soladyne, Lizzie's family, and people like you, I had to meld the woman's personality with mine. I literally changed how my own mind worked so that I would be an exact replica of the woman. I took in her memories, her quirks, all of the different sides of her personality that she showed to those she liked and hid from those she didn't. The process involved a great deal of magic and prayer to the great Voltozas and was as long as it was painful. In the end, I was more Lizzie than the person I was before."

"I don't understand. What are you trying to say?"

"That I *do* know how you both felt." The woman that looked like Lizzie fidgeted with her hands and avoided his gaze. "She was fond of you, Eddie. I don't know the extent, but you were someone that crossed her mind more often than the two times you saw her a day. Becoming Lizzie meant I had that same fondness forced into my own mind. At first, I fought it, but it grew tiring holding off the other woman's emotions toward you. And since we're being honest, after a few weeks of speaking to you every day, I understood where her feelings for you had come from."

"Why are you telling me all of this?" Eddie shook his head as if he could cast out the past year of memories of the person he had thought was Lizzie. "Are you trying to make me feel worse than I already do?"

Lizzie had turned to wave Yon off while Eddie spoke, but she turned back around as Eddie finished. The other man vanished into the darkness for a moment, then an audible click was heard. Light flooded the room, revealing a blank space similar to the stark white cells on the Living Containment level, except the walls and ceilings of this one were a royal blue. Yon left out of a door in the back of the room, leaving the imposter alone with Eddie and Ingrid.

"I'm not telling you these things to be cruel," Lizzie replied. "It's the opposite, actually." She gave him a condescending smile, although the rest of her expression looked almost . . . guilty. "I want you to understand why I'm going to let you live. If you want, I'll even spare the scientist."

He could almost believe her, except that the added light of the room just made the wound to Hugh's neck all the more sickening. "And what about Hugh? You didn't think I might want him to live as well? Or were you and Yon having too much fun playing your sick little game with me to consider that?"

"You actually care about that fop?" Eddie had never seen the real Lizzie angry, and even knowing this one was fake, he still shied away from her as she narrowed her eyes and moved close enough to stick a finger in his face. "Are you forgetting how quick he turned on you when The Jester was threatening all of our lives? And what about my pet in the main lobby? I could have easily let it have you, Hinderlight, and Hugh for a snack."

"The bat was yours?" The woman was full of surprises, enough to keep Eddie's mind flipping between anger, grief, and confusion.

"Yes." Her lips turned up in a smug smile. "You think it managed to kill a floor full of people, a good amount of them security personnel, but then couldn't catch four stragglers?

Eddie hadn't bothered to question how they had escaped. After all, it wasn't the first life or death situation he had survived. He had chalked up each survival as a matter of others' skills and a string of good luck. Now, as he tried to recall that hectic run-in with the

292

camouflage bat, he struggled to remember every detail.

"It seemed pretty intent on killing us," he replied, knowing he had no real reason to think she was lying but pushed on anyway. "If we had been a little slower in the elevator, it might have."

She let out a less than friendly laugh. "The whole reason it tried to get in the elevator after us was because it was bred to protect me. The poor thing is probably moping around the lobby as we speak."

Try as he might, he couldn't picture the monstrous bat moping. "So you helped the four of us survive after letting *your pet* feast on a floor full of people? And you expect me to see that as a positive thing?"

"You ungrateful . . . son of a . . ."

The imposter's hands balled into fists and she looked on the verge of striking him, but at that moment Yon returned through the same door he had departed, his eyes alight with excitement.

"High Priestess, everything is set. When you are ready, we can begin."

"Yes," Eddie said between clenched teeth. "You should go, Priestess."

"You can still call me Lizzie. That's who I'll continue to be until the Great Lord decides to change me into something more. I've all but forgotten the name of the woman I was before becoming Lizzie."

"No," Eddie said, not caring how defeated he sounded. "Like you said, Lizzie is dead.

"As you wish." Priestess sighed as she turned to Yon. "I'm going to go and prepare myself for the ritual. Have them brought to the room and tightly secured. They can witness Voltozas' arrival."

"Priestess, are you sure that is wise?" Yon rung his hands together. "Perhaps the other woman's memories are impairing your judgment . . ."

"YOU DARE TO QUESTION ME?" Eddie had thought the woman was angry earlier, but that paled in comparison to the rage she turned on her underling. Her expression twisted into an ugly distortion of Lizzie's cute face, her nostrils flaring as wide as her eyes. Her pale face filled with color, turning pink as every muscle seemed to strain to control the hatred. Yon wilted beneath the heat of her anger and took a step back.

"Of course not, Priestess. Your orders will be followed without further interruption on this fool's part."

The woman's anger seemed on the verge of rising even more but instead it vanished. Lizzie's good-natured smile returning "Good. Then I will see you, and them, in a few moments. I'll send some of our brethren in to assist you."

The high priestess gave a quick glance in Eddie's direction, then strode out of the room. She moved with the confidence of a lion walking among sheep. Nothing like the Lizzie Eddie had knew. Had known. He tore his gaze away from the imposter and looked toward his only ally in the room. Ingrid returned his gaze, her mouth moving against the gag in her mouth.

"Put them to sleep." Yon said with a wave of his hand.

"Wait, what?" Eddie managed to get out before a damp cloth was clamped over his mouth and nose. It smelled sweet, like a well-mixed alcoholic drink. With his arms and legs still tied, Eddie could do little to shake off the cloth and his efforts only caused him to breathe in the tangy smell faster than he intended. After a few breaths, his arms and legs got tired. He forgot why he was even struggling. Too tired to struggle, his eyes slid closed.

***

A sharp smell burned Eddie's noise and caused him to suck in a breath, effectively forcing him awake. A black-robed figure was standing less than a foot away, the cultist pulling something away from Eddie's nose before turning and walking away. Without thinking, Eddie tried to get up but found his arms and legs tied to the same chair. *Again.* This time, his mouth was gagged as well. His thoughts returned faster from the chemical sleep compared to the electrical one. He glanced around the room, ignoring everything else until he found Ingrid. The red-headed scientist was already awake, her mouth still gagged. She returned his gaze for only a moment, but then her eyes quickly moved on to take in everything else.

Which was annoying. If they were going to have any chance to escape and possibly disrupt the ritual, they were going to have to work together. Just because they couldn't speak, didn't mean they couldn't communicate. But they certainly couldn't communicate if she didn't even bother to look at him. Eddie twisted and bobbed his head trying to get her attention but eventually gave up. Fine, he would figure something out on his own and hopefully she would find an opportunity to help. Eddie gripped the anger he felt at being deceived by the high priestess and used it to focus despite his diminished courage. The first thing he had to do was take stock of the room. Ingrid had probably done as much already.

The square room itself was similar to the original one that they had been held in, except twice as large. The walls, ceiling, and floor were all painted the same royal blue as the previous room. Eddie had been placed against the middle of one of the walls, Ingrid at the wall to his left, also in the middle. A single door sat in the wall to his right, but besides that, the walls were devoid of any decoration. Various pieces of scientific equipment took up the perimeter of the room—desks with computers, large and small machines, and several instruments he couldn't identify. Apparently, the cultists had no idea what they were used for either as the two or three dozen spread about the room sat in front of or on top of the equipment, their attention locked on the center of the room.

And when Eddie finally focused on what they were gawking at, the horror of it deflated whatever annoyance he had been feeling toward Ingrid.

Two gray, stone pillars twisted and stretched toward the ceiling, each made of different-sized segments that looked as if they barely fit together. The tops of each ended in points that twirled about each other, forming what looked like a twisted arch. It wasn't the structure that made Eddie's mouth go dry and his arms test the bounds that held him again. It was the men and women that were stretched across its surface and hung down in front of the opening it created, naked and covered in strange purple markings, causing some primordial fear to tug at his mind and paint pictures of their possible ends.

Eddie tried to pull his gaze away from the struggling forms but found he couldn't. Something was drawing his attention to them and the strange structure they were attached to, some force he couldn't explain. He tried to shake it off, turn his attention to Ingrid, the other cultists, anything, but failed. Which only caused his fear to grow.

Sounds began to fill the room, voices in different pitches and timbre coming together in a chorus of words in a language Eddie did not know. The high priestess appeared a moment later, dressed in a plain black robe that mirrored the rest of the cultists' attire, pushing her way through the arch and parting the bodies that hung in front of the opening as if passing through a curtain. She was chanting as well, her voice overtaking the others in the room. Despite the fact Eddie couldn't understand what was being said, the words themselves felt *wrong*. Like a familiar song sung one key off or a curse coming from a child's lips.

As the chanting rose, the pull of the arch grew stronger. Not only did Eddie feel compelled to lock his eyes on its horrible splendor, the strong desire to stand and approach it consumed his thoughts. There were no plans of escape. No sympathy for those tied to the arch. Just a morbid curiosity and desire to place his hands on the gray stone. Eddie was so enthralled that he didn't realize the high priestess had a jagged-edged knife in her hand until she had placed it against the leg of a naked man hung in the exact center of the arch.

Then the blade moved downward.

A pained yell mixed in with chants of the cultists.

Blood began to flow in the knife's wake.

An explosion of air shook the room, the cultists somehow remaining unaffected by it as the force buffeted against Eddie. The shockwave pressed him back against his chair and for the briefest moment, knocked his gaze away from the arch. Somehow, despite the urge to stare at the structure's wonder, he was able to squeeze his eyes shut. The pull diminished even more. Eddie held them closed, not wanting the arch to gain sway over him again. Nor did he want to take in the sight of the men and women being butchered. It didn't block out their begging. Or their screams. Or the disharmony of the cultists chanting words that sounded more like gibberish than an actual language. In the darkness behind his eyelids, Eddie lost track of time as he tried to block out the world. He hoped against hope that he would hear the sound of crashing doors, gunfire, Hinderlight and Kaga letting out battle cries as they stormed the room. He would accept being hit by a stray bullet or two if it meant an end to the ritual.

As the screams and chanting continued to assault his sanity, Eddie tried to think of anything other than what was going on around him. At one point, the sound of a person emptying their stomach reached his ears. It could have been Ingrid, or one of the less devoted cultists. With what little grip Eddie had over his own mind, anything could be happening. For all he knew, *he* might have been the one emptying his stomach, if he had even eaten anything since this whole nightmare had begun.

It wasn't just the sounds that battered against his mind. A pressure was building in the room, its weight pressing down on him like an invisible hand. Every time the cadence of the cultists' chants changed, the pressure seemed to increase. It felt like his head was in a vice while he was riding in a sharply ascending airplane. Any attempt to shut out the horrific noises just made him focus more on the pressure and the pain it caused him. Eddie dug his fingers into the chair, strained against his bonds, tried to cause himself as much discomfort as he could to try and shut out the sounds and ignore the pressure. It was no use. He felt like the combination of everything happening on the other side of his closed eyelids was going to destroy him.

And then the screaming stopped.

The chanting stopped.

The room was silent. Remained silent. Despite every instinct that screamed for him to keep his eyes squeezed shut, despite the fact that every hair on his body felt as if they were standing on end, Eddie couldn't help but open his eyes.

And gaze at an abomination that stood against everything he knew, so immense, his mind wilted from the horror of it all as his understanding of reality was utterly destroyed.

CHAPTER 37

Gone were the bodies from the strange arch, whatever atrocities that had been done to them a mystery that Eddie hoped to never solve. In their place on the gray, twisted stone were swirling red designs that seemed to glow as the light in the room dimmed. The cultists had backed away, their role complete. Between the two twisting pillars, a red sheet of light had appeared, energy crackling along a surface that shimmered and flexed like a ship's sail. Except the surface wasn't opaque like a sail, and it was what Eddie could see through the red haze that threatened to break down what was left of his sanity.

A vast world seemed to open up on the other side. A world of mud, dirt, and stone. A barren, red world that Eddie would have expected to see if he were looking at a live feed from Mars. His brain tried to even label it as such, the shimmering light some special effect that projected a screen showing an old rover video from when studying the red planet had been all the rage. Maybe it was all some great trick, a joke played on him, or some massive reality show where he was the star. Some of the cable channels had caused controversies in the past by putting people in similar situations. Maybe not ones with such graphic violence and gore as he had personally seen, but it was possible.

That thought fled, however, when an enormous entity rolled into view on the other side of the screen. A mass of tanned flesh, as wide as the gate itself, came to a stop on the other side. Its body rippled with life, as if it were breathing from a dozen different spots. It was as awe-inspiring as it was horrific. Sitting on the other side of what Eddie could now only conclude was a gateway to somewhere not on this earth, its very presence poured through like water from a burst dam. Whatever the mass of leathery flesh was on the other side of the pillars, Eddie could feel how ancient it was deep in his bones. The immensity of its mind like a weight on his soul. Nothing natural could impart such overwhelming dominance.

The entity sat unmoving, its skin undulating and its consciousness pressing through the gate. It suddenly jerked forward as if pulled. The rippling along its leathery skin increasing at an exponential rate. Surprise overwhelmed Eddie, followed quickly by a mixture of anger and disbelief that made his head flop back and then roll to the side as he lost all control over his body. He could feel drool trickle down his chin, tears leak from his eyes. He was helpless as his body slumped into the chair as any actual thought fled from the entity's rage. Unfortunately, even with his head lolling to the side, he could still clearly see the entity as it was pulled through the gate.

The massive body shuddered as leathery flesh came in contact with the arch's energy field separating the two worlds. Even mouthless, it somehow let out a scream of pure frustration as it was dragged through. The energy field danced across the mound of flesh, twirling and leaping, leaving small scorch marks in its wake. It raced across the entity's surface as if trying to touch every part of it before leaping off and returning to the gateway.

Once the entity finally pulled completely through, its skin continued to ripple like a disturbed hornet's nest. Wave upon wave of anger and frustration rolled off of it, keeping Eddie in a catatonic state as the force of those emotions beat against his body and invaded his mind. Then, as the rippling of leathery flesh slowed, changing from erratic to a slow, steady rolling, the psychic beating Eddie had been receiving lessened. The entity seemed to calm, its anger and frustration reduced to a rumbling annoyance.

As Eddie's ability to function returned, he was able to pull his gaze away from the mound of abhorrence and see if everyone else in the room had been affected in the same way. Ingrid looked in worse shape than he had felt, her eyes rolled back in her head as she lay slumped in his direction. A tiny trickle of blood dripped from her nose, which Eddie hoped was nothing more than a bloody nose. He had felt the pressure exerted by the entity's will, however, and the darker parts of his mind whispered how being rendered catatonic could be the least amount of damage left behind.

The cultists seemed to have fared no better, much to Eddie's satisfaction. Most lay sprawled about the room on the floor while a few were on top of the scientific equipment or had fallen back into one of the few chairs. Some had the same trail of drool that Eddie felt drying on his chin. For others, it was a red trail that dribbled out of their mouths. The only ones still on their feet were the high priestess and Yon. Neither escaped unscathed, though. The high priestess leaned heavily against a large console while Yon was braced on the back of a sturdy looking chair, his legs wobbling beneath him.

A prickling on the back of his neck made him turn back toward the portal—

Something slammed into Eddie's head, snapping his head back with such force that he was surprised when he realized that his neck hadn't been broken. Even so, it felt like every tendon had been torn. He did his best looking for the source of the new attack without moving his head, but he could see no one in his peripheral vision. A second attack followed a handful of seconds later, this one with only enough force to push his already fuzzy head back. When the pain of the second impact didn't let up, he realized that it hadn't been another blow but instead felt like something had smacked against his forehead and then began to drill. The force twisted through his skull and then scattered throughout his head like a pack of rats in a maze, touching every inch of his mind. Pulling out memories, images, conversations—most of which he had long forgotten—hesitating over them for the briefest of moments and then moving on. This continued for seconds, weeks, years, decades, eternity; all sense and understanding of time vanished as the force probed every inch of his brain.

Then it withdrew. As Eddie struggled to again mend the frayed fragments of his mind, he could see the tightening of Ingrid's face as whatever had touched him moved on to her. Her mouth opened as if to cry out, but then the tension in her face disappeared. A cultist that had been lying prone shot up into a sitting position for a few moments, her back arching as if it were being pushed and pulled apart. Then she was released. Something similar happened to each person in the room, the final intrusion knocking Priestess to her knees. When her body relaxed, she immediately sucked in a sharp breath and pushed herself back to her feet. But it was the movement at the center of the room that snatched Eddie's attention back.

The boulder-sized mound of leathery flesh looked like it was expanding at first, its ambiguous form reaching outward. The longer Eddie forced himself to watch it, however, the faster it dawned on him that the form wasn't expanding. It was growing limbs. Or at least that's what it appeared. Four appendages pushed out from the organic mass, as if they had always been lying underneath and were just now trying to escape. Instead of ripping free, what started as stubby protrusions expanded the skin until four limbs, each as long as a mid-sized car stretched away from the mass at the center. Hands and feet seemed to grow or morph. Arms and legs bent in the middle as joints formed and the leathery mass at the center pushed itself up onto its feet.

Last came the creature's head, its great maw pushing upward from the top of its body, all leathery gums and no teeth, like a baby bird reaching for food. A humanoid head grew out from the creature's neck and mouth, two holes toward the top caving in to form eye sockets and pressing in on its sides to form a sick imitation of ears. Its head looked like something a child would make out of play dough; mouth, eyes, and ears, as if the entity couldn't be bothered with giving itself more than the most basic resemblance of a human. It stood there a moment, eyeless head slowly turning as if to take in the room. When its mouth parted again, it revealed a dark void, as if it could eat entire worlds and never become full. Its voice was a thousand stereos with the bass turned up too high and pounded against the inside of Eddie's skull.

"BEHOLD, THE TRANSFIGURER OF LIFE, THE CATALYST OF EVOLUTION, THE BRINGER OF CHANGE."

The high priestess rose off the ground and moved in front of the new being. She went down to her knees then bowed down, putting her face onto the tile floor. "Change comes from the pain within."

The words chilled Eddie to the bone as he remembered her muttering the exact same thing as the cult had closed in on them on the first floor.

"My lord Voltozas," The high priestess continued, only lifting her head so that she could attempt to gaze up at the entity. "We—"

The blank, leathery face turned to look down on the woman.

"CHILDREN REPEAT WORDS OFTEN WITHOUT UNDERSTANDING THEM. YOU REPLY WITH SOME PLATITUDE YOU FOUND IN A BOOK. WRITTEN BY THOSE THAT WORSHIPED ME CENTURIES AGO. WORSHIPPERS AS IGNORANT TO MY DESIRES AS THOSE THAT STAND

BEFORE ME NOW."

Silence filled the room. The high priestess stayed prone, her head dipping back to the ground. When she finally spoke, Eddie had to strain his ears to hear her whispered words. "Lord, I don't know why you are angry. We only did what we believed you wanted.

"YOU BELIEVED I WOULD WANT TO BE PULLED FROM MY HOME AND FORCED INTO THIS PRIMITIVE DIMENSION?"

"We thought you wanted to rule—"

"RULE? I HAVE NO DESIRE TO RULE ANYTHING. MY ONLY DESIRE IS TO CAUSE CHANGE, NOT RULE. BESIDES YOU FOUL CREATURES THAT CONTROL THIS WORLD, EVERY OTHER SPECIES CONTINUES TO CHANGE. I ALREADY GET ENOUGH PLEASURE WATCHING YOUR KIND TRY AND FAIL TO FIGHT OFF DISEASE AND DEATH. YOU TRY TO FIGHT THE PUREST KIND OF CHANGE. WHY WOULD I WANT TO RULE HUMANS WHEN YOU ARE THE ONLY CREATURES THAT FIGHT CHANGE?"

Eddie would have enjoyed watching the high priestess squirm as she replied if he wasn't filled to the brim with dread. "But . . . if we disappoint you, why do you still grant us boons when we request them? Why do you give us powers above normal men and women?"

"I BELIEVED YOU WERE TRYING TO ELEVATE YOUR SPECIES, MOVE BEYOND YOUR PETTY DESIRES TO LIVE FOREVER. WAS PROUD OF WHAT I *THOUGHT* YOU WERE TRYING TO ACCOMPLISH. AND NOW YOU SHOW HOW FOOLISH A BELIEF THAT WAS.

"We were only trying to serve you." She sounded all but defeated now.

"YOU WISH TO SERVE? SO YOU SHALL."

Voltozas reached down, its giant hand engulfing the high priestess' head. She let out a scream, but it was snuffed out as everything from the neck up became engulfed by the entity's leathery flesh. It lifted her up into the air, legs and arms flailing and beating against the hand that held her tight. It didn't take long until her movements slowed. Then stopped completely. The high priestess' body hung limply in Voltozas' hand before the entity turned her entire body around until she was facing out. Before Eddie could even process the woman's death, Voltozas' fingers bulged out. Priestess-Lizzie's face pushed through the knuckles of the entity, becoming part of the leathery skin, the tip of a nose as pale as it had ever been and slowly growing darker as the skin seemed to mesh with Voltozas's hand.

As horrific as the entire experience was, it was only made worse when the high priestess' mouth opened and she began to speak.

"This one is now a part of Voltozas." It was Lizzie's voice, but flat, lifeless. The entity moved its outstretched arm around so that her lifeless gaze could take in everyone else in the room. "All who played a part in this grave insult must atone."

When the high priestess was pointed at Yon, the man rose and moved forward. "Of course, Great Lord. What must your ignorant servants do to return to your good favor?"

"Join us."

Eddie could see the realization of what that entailed flash across Yon's expression right before Voltozas' other hand streaked out and grabbed the man. Yon let out a small yell as the hand wrapped around his entire body. The yell turned into a horrific scream as the cultist's body began to fold backward into the entity's hand. The sound of ripping skin and breaking bones could be heard as Yon was sucked into Voltozas' hand. He fought against it at first, beating against the hand the gripped him. Unfortunately for the cultist, his resistance was useless. His screams grew weaker as he was slowly sucked in completely by the leathery grip that held him. It wasn't until the screams finally faded away that the rest of the cultists must've realized the situation they had brought upon themselves.

Black robes scattered in every direction. Some waving arms and shouting as they fled blindly in terror. Others dove behind desks and lab equipment. The smartest of the bunch headed straight toward the door. The first few to reach it slammed shoulders into the metal first, trying to force it open. The door held, and that's when Eddie saw the card reader next to the door. Apparently, you needed a security card here to get out as much as you needed one to get in, and the most likely owners of those cards now resided as part of the horrific entity slowly exacting its vengeance.

And Eddie could only watch from his restraints. Watch as Voltozas hunted down each and every cultist in the room. It stomped around, feet crushing then absorbing black robes, its one free hand scooping up cultists and sucking them into itself, or worse, depositing them into its gaping mouth. All the while, the high priestess swung about in Voltozas' grip. Some of the cultists tried to fight back, brandishing whatever scientific equipment in the room they could turn into a makeshift weapon. They struck Voltozas with small microscopes, computer monitors, a few even whipping keyboards and computer mice at the entity, to little effect. They might as well have been gnats assaulting a cow's hide.

The overwhelming contempt that filled the room as Voltozas moved about, ignoring those that attacked him, absorbing whatever target it was focused on first, was clearly aimed at those who had summoned it. The entity could have easily made short work of the cultists, but from Eddie's point of view, it took its time. Chose its next target from those furthest away, sometimes snatching one person up and leaving someone right next to him or her behind as it reached for its next victim on the other side of the room. Only to cross back immediately to claim the person it appeared to miss moments before. Eddie couldn't be sure how long the whole process took, but after the final cultist was sucked into the hand of Voltozas, its attention turned to him.

"You are not one of mine." Lizzie's lifeless voice chilled Eddie to the bone. He was so thrown off by it that he couldn't tell if it was an accusation or a question. The high priestess' hand lifted and pointed toward Ingrid. "Neither is she. Why are you both here?"

Eddie wanted to reply. Wanted to tell this overwhelming presence everything he had been through, not just this past day or so, but his entire life story. Tell it everything he knew, all of the secrets he kept about his past. He opened his mouth, ready to tell the entity everything.

"Mmbaawaa . . ." was the only sound he was able to force out of his mouth.

The entity's eyeless face tilted down toward him. The high priestess' lifeless eyes stared at him. Eddie felt as good as dead.

"This one knows," the high priestess said after a pause that felt like a millennia. "A simple human. Fooled by the one that speaks now for Voltozas. Put in situations that should have killed a human of greater physical prowess than yourself. Yet you survive."

It might have been Eddie's desperate hope for survival showing him something that wasn't actually there, but he thought that a smile touched the high priestess' lips for the briefest of moments.

"Maybe." Voltozas paused, leaving the high priestess' mouth hanging open for a moment before continuing. "Maybe something even greater than me keeps you alive. Or perhaps you have survived on luck alone. Either way, I will not be the one to strike you down."

Relief flooded into Eddie. Relief for himself and concern for the only other person left alive in the room. The combination was somehow enough to allow his lips to finally work.

"What about her?" he stuttered while nodding toward Ingrid.

"That one is not so innocent. You wish her life spared as well?"

"Yes." Eddie found it much easier to get out a simple word.

"Very well," Voltozas continued, "but it comes with a price."

Before Eddie could respond, Voltozas extended the hand that wasn't holding the Priestess toward him. Still tied to the chair, Eddie could only watch as a single, leathery finger, longer and thicker than his own leg, reached out to him. Every instinct in his body screamed for him to rip through his bonds, topple the chair over, basically do anything to avoid the entity's touch. But even if he could get out of the way, it would more than likely lead to Ingrid's death.

So Eddie faced whatever price Voltozas was going to exact and reassured himself that at least he *and* Ingrid were going to survive. This situation, at least.

Voltozas's finger felt coarse as its tip pressed against Eddie's forehead. All Eddie felt was the slightest tingle, like walking through a single strand of a spider's web. It continued to caress his mind even after the entity pulled away. Eddie waited for something to happen. A horn to sprout from his head. Start speaking in tongues. Anything strange that a deity focused on change might force on him. When Voltozas silently turned and started walking toward the gate, the high priestess still in hand, Eddie couldn't contain the combination of worry and curiosity that shook his mind a great deal more than the small tingling the entity left behind.

"What is going to happen to me?"

Voltozas didn't bother to turn. "You will see."

"See what?"

All at once a pressure began to build in the center of Eddie's head. It pushed and pulled at the same time, compressing his brain while it tried to break out of his skull. It felt like a black hole had just opened up in the center of his head. His mind was being filled and emptied all at the same time. Every emotion possible assaulted his consciousness: fear, anger, hope, sadness, pleasure, happiness. It was too much. Blackness began to creep into his vision, encircling the world in front of him as it slowly closed in.

Eddie held on long enough to watch Voltozas step back through the portal before utter darkness embraced him like an old friend.

CHAPTER 38

Consciousness returned to Eddie at a crawl. The first thought to cross his mind was that he had enough of being electrocuted, drugged, and having his mind overwhelmed to the point of passing out. He had no defense against whatever Voltozas had done to him, but the fact he had survived multiple Horrors just for a few people in black robes to get the better of him not once, but twice, grated on his nerves. On the other hand, the fact that he had woken up each time was certainly a plus.

The second thing Eddie noticed was that he was relatively comfortable. His head was propped up on something soft. Hopefully, a pillow. Worst case, some new monster he would have to deal with. In case it was the latter, Eddie stayed perfectly still. Something with the softness of silk covered his hands while something else cold was wrapped snuggly around both of his wrists. His ears picked up a steady beeping sound and the low hum of machinery at work. Those sounds and everything Eddie felt was more intriguing than threatening, but he couldn't imagine where he might be now. His slight headache and drowsy feeling told him that at least he wasn't dead.

All right, he thought, *time to open my eyes and see what mess I've gotten myself into now.*

Bright white light blinded him and he was forced to squint until his eyes could adjust. When he could open them enough to see without pain, he found a clean white ceiling above him with a single vent at its center. He tried to turn his head to take in the rest of his surroundings but couldn't get his muscles to move even an inch. As panic started to set in, a movement to Eddie's left caught his attention.

"Hey." Hinderlight's friendly face leaned into Eddie's sight. "Welcome back to the land of the living."

"I can't move," Eddie mumbled. His lips felt heavy but at least he could move them enough to speak. "What's wrong with me?"

Hinderlight moved out of his line of his vision before replying. "Probably just some side effect of all the medicine they've got you on. Hold on a sec, they showed me how to decrease the dosages if you—" he let out a weak laugh "—I mean, *when* you woke. Give me a second."

What else could Eddie do? He lay there, waiting for Hinderlight to do whatever it was he needed to do. The other man moved about to his left, the sounds of buttons being pressed and dials being worked mixing with the steady beep that Eddie had heard earlier.

"Just so you know," Hinderlight's voice said over the noisy clatter, "Soladyne has full control over the facility and the high rise above it again. They saved as many of the infected as they could in the main building, those that the spores hadn't infected past the point of no return, then went on to contain all of the subjects that got out of their cells, and rounded up what remained of the cultists. Basically, everything around here is back to normal. These people seem so used to death and destruction that I bet most of them will be walking around like nothing happened in another week or two."

"They accomplished all of that while I was unconscious?" Whatever Hinderlight was doing, it was working. Eddie no longer felt like he was trying to speak with a mouthful of honey and he could move his arms and legs again, even if just an inch or two. He could even turn his head enough to watch what Hinderlight was doing. The broad man was standing in front of three different machines, the slow beep coming from a heart monitor, although the rest were lost on him. IV lines and wires ran from the machines to Eddie's bed and disappeared under the sheets that covered most of his body. From what Hinderlight had said, at least some of the instruments the man was working with controlled the medicine Eddie had received.

"Well," Hinderlight said, his full attention on the machines in front of him. Then he hesitated for a moment, the usually confident man paused what he was doing and seemed to struggle with his thoughts as his shoulders slumped. Whatever bothered him, it didn't take him long to shrug it off and continue. "You've been out for around two weeks."

"Two weeks?" Eddie would have shot up in surprise if his body had been working properly.

"About that, yes. We weren't really sure if you would wake up, after what that scientist, Ingrid, said in her debriefing."

"She's ok then?" A sense of relief began to trickle into Eddie's stomach but the loss of two weeks and the fear of what had been done to him quickly soured it. "What did she say?"

"Some pretty crazy stuff. Most of which I wouldn't have believed a month ago, even with everything I already knew about this place. There, that should do it," Hinderlight said as he turned one more dial. He moved away from the machines and took a seat at Eddie's side. "How do you feel?"

"Like my whole body is covered in tar. I can move now but not much."

Hinderlight reached over and put a reassuring hand on Eddie's shoulder. "From what I was told, now that I've switched off the medicines you were receiving, that should pass fairly quick. While we wait until you're back to fighting condition, why don't you tell me what really happened? Like I said, Ingrid told us a great deal—you dropping out of a vent and pretending to be a security officer to get them going, fleeing cultists and devil dogs, getting an escort by The Jester." Hinderlight shook his head with a laugh. "Which I still won't believe until you confirm it yourself. And then getting captured and having front row seats to the arrival of the cultists' deity."

"All of it was true," Eddie replied, able to laugh a bit over the ridiculousness of it all now that the actual danger of it was two weeks in the past. "Traveling with The Jester, even if just around one of the floors, felt like having a viper strapped to my back. A viper that continued to whisper in your ear how it was your friend, which only reminds you that its fangs are that much closer to your neck. If I was being honest, though, part of me actually felt a bit bad about how it had been experimented on. It might be classified as a Horror, like The Reaper, but it certainly seemed much more human."

Hinderlight let out a nervous chuckle. "Yeah, well, I wouldn't go telling too many people you have sympathy for one of the monsters they keep." Eddie must have looked nervous, as Hinderlight quickly added, "But you'll receive no judgment from me. At the least, The Jester was a tool you somehow used to stay alive. Nothing wrong with that, in my mind."

"Thank you," Eddie replied. He felt some of the tension start to evaporate. It felt good to be back in Hinderlight's company. The two had been through a great deal, and although Eddie had found some strength and confidence while he was separated from the man, he still felt more sure of himself knowing the other man was there to back him up. He felt the sudden urge to shake the man's hand, and with some of the control of his body returned, he attempted to sit up.

Which he succeeded in. Partially. On sitting up, Eddie realized the fact that both of his wrists were restrained. He shook himself until the sheet covering dropped and he found that besides the IV lines and monitors attached to various points on his body, both of his wrists were handcuffed to the bed's guardrails.

""What the hell?" Eddie moved his arms enough to rattle the cuffs against the metal rail.

For the first time since Eddie had met the man, he caught a flash of guilt in Hinderlight's expression. Only a flash. "You have to understand, Eddie. What happened here was quite the big deal. Cults infiltrating the most secure facility the company owned. Civilians infected by dangerous spores. Horrors running about murdering *most* people they come across. A gate to another dimension actually being opened." He paused for a moment, seeming to struggle internally with something. With a sigh, Hinderlight pressed on. "A custodian being touched by something powerful enough to be considered a god. It's made a lot of people very nervous."

"They think that because Voltozas spared me, I've been secretly working for the cult."

"Voltozas. The Jester. Who knows how many other monsters. You have to admit, if you were someone that hadn't been through everything we have, some of it could look a little suspicious. And that's not even taking into consideration what Voltozas might have done to you. Ingrid didn't hide the fact that Voltozas didn't just spare you. He said Ingrid's life came with a price that you accepted. Who knows what that price might be."

That's when it dawned on him. Plain white room, nothing else occupying it besides his bed and the machines hooked up to him. A single grate in the ceiling and the memory of looking down a similar one as he crawled around in the vents.

"I'm in one of the containment cells! You were keeping me

drugged. That's why I couldn't move."

"Of course you're in a cell." At least Hinderlight didn't bother to deny it. "And the higher-ups had no idea what you would be like when you finally woke. The numbing drugs were just a precaution. One that I quickly eliminated after only a few moments of speaking with you, I might add."

A dark thought crossed Eddie's mind. "And what if, while speaking to me, you thought I might be dangerous?"

"Then a different set of dials would have pumped enough drugs into your system to put you back out." Hinderlight paused for a moment, then shook his head. "Or kill you. They left it to my discretion."

Eddie didn't bother to hide the vitriol in his voice. "Well, I'm glad then I passed your little interrogation."

"Eddie." Hinderlight's tone straddled the line between being condescending and consoling. "You were touched by something from *outside our own dimension*. Besides inter-dimensional beings and deities being way out of my pay grade, from what little I've been able to pry from those under my limited authority down here and trick out of those above me, there have only been *three* attempts at opening gateways and communicating with entities in other dimensions before your experience two weeks ago. One ended with that dog creature you encountered crossing over and killing a team of scientists before it was captured. The second created a vortex that sucked in three scientists before they managed to get it closed again. And the third—" he shook his head "—even the mention of the third around those that seem to know anything about it cause faces to go pale before the person practically flees my presence.

"Meanwhile," he continued, "you and Ingrid are the sole survivors of an incident where not only was there a successful gateway opened, something with immense power crossed over and back. If Voltozas was some all-powerful deity as the cultists believed, it could have done hundreds of things to you that might have put the entire planet in danger. And a hundred more that we might not even be able to think of. It makes sense for the higher-ups to want to play it safe. If anything, you should be thankful they put someone you know, and hopefully trust, in charge of your fate and not some lab coat still on edge from everything else that happened two weeks ago."

He was right, of course, but it only took some of the edge off the fact that Eddie might have been murdered for something he had zero control over. "What exactly were you looking—"

The sound of a door sliding open caught both of their attention. Eddie abandoned what he had been about to say and turned his attention across the room where the single door, the *cell door*, had opened and a man in an expensive looking suit tentatively stepped inside.

"Mr. Hinderlight?" The man bit at the inside of his lip, making his next words a little difficult to understand. *"He's* ordered you and Mr. Watson to see him at once."

"What?" A mixture of surprise and anger laced Hinderlight's voice. "How the hell did anyone know Eddie was awake?"

"I don't know, sir. He was very insistent over the radio, however, that you not dally. Someone should be coming right behind me with a wheelchair for Mr. Watson."

"Wonderful," Hinderlight ran a hand over his face. "Thank you, Erik. Wait outside for a moment so I can speak with Mr. Watson. Keep whoever is bringing the wheelchair out until I let him in as well."

"Yes, sir."

Hinderlight watched the man go, then shook his head as he turned to address Eddie. "Alright, we don't have much time—"

"Wait, was that the same Erik that escorted you into the building? The one that you made perform my duties while I followed you?"

"What?" Hinderlight blinked a few times, then waved off the question. "Yes. Same one. Apparently whatever floor he was working on when everything went to shit didn't have any of the infected on it. Thinks I'm the reason he lucked out. Incredibly loyal to me now. But that's all beside the point. We have to talk about the man we're going to see."

"Who is he?"

"Well, to be honest I don't know. All I was told was that someone from higher up in the company was coming to question us both. Higher than me could mean a lot of different things. No

312

matter what they ask, you have to tell the truth. Don't try to cover for me in any way or embellish things. Stick to the facts. More likely than not, at the very least, this person has some kind of psychic power, and if he catches us in even the smallest lie, it could mean horrible things for us."

"Horrible things?"

"I'll just say that it would be a shame that both of us survived just to end up being murdered by an employee of the company."

"They would do that?"

"Eddie, you've seen enough to know the full extent of what this company is capable of doing."

"True."

"So just be honest, and hopefully we will just get a pat on the back for our service or maybe even a nice bonus."

Hinderlight stood and cracked his knuckles. "But in case things go south, I'd be ready for one more desperate fight."

CHAPTER 39

Eddie and Hinderlight sat in silence until the man with the wheelchair arrived a few moments later. An average man in a lab coat, he didn't even bother to give his name as he parked the chair next to the bed and removed the health monitors and IV lines from Eddie's body. To Eddie's credit, enough of his strength had returned that he was able to maneuver himself off the bed and into the chair on his own. Hinderlight hovered next to him the whole time. When the orderly tried to take the handles of the wheel chair, Hinderlight brushed him off and took them himself.

"You just lead the way," he said as he waved the man off. "I'm sure he would rather I push him than some stranger."

The orderly shrugged and rolled his eyes as if the whole experience was below him. He led them out into the familiar white hallway to the maze of corridors and cell doors that lined each. The memories of Eddie's flight from the Hound and cultists and then his time with The Jester popped into his mind as they moved. It all seemed like they had happened hours ago, not weeks. And even with Hinderlight pushing him along, from what the man had said, it didn't sound like he was completely safe yet. In fact, with the fight-or-flight adrenaline long gone, he was more nervous now walking into a situation where he had no idea what to expect.

Eddie was annoyed to find himself completely in the dark once again. He didn't even know which of the four floors he was actually on. Were any of the creatures he had faced behind one of those doors? He could do without *ever* seeing The Reaper again, that was for sure. But The Jester had been an ally for a time, even if Eddie could have become its next victim with any sudden shift in the Horror's mood. With The Jester, Eddie had known how dangerous the monster could be and the risks involved in working with him. Now, as he was pushed steadily forward, Eddie had no idea what this company man would think. Or do. Hinderlight didn't even know who the man was, and Hinderlight was much higher on the corporate food chain than Eddie was.

It was more than likely that Hinderlight would receive a slap on the wrist at worst. Eddie, meanwhile, could end right back in the cell he had woken up in. Or worse, one of the other cells that was already occupied.

Well, he wouldn't go easy. Eddie tested his legs, pushing his hips up so that he barely came off the seat. It was tiring, but it felt like he might be able to stand. His arms felt stronger. Might be able to throw a few punches. Make it back to the wheel chair and roll his way out of wherever they were going. After that, he pretty much had zero chance of escaping the vast underground facility. But at least he wouldn't just take whatever fate the company tried to hand him.

As subtle as Eddie was trying to be, Hinderlight must have caught the little movements Eddie made as he tested himself.

"Don't do anything crazy," Hinderlight whispered. A hand squeezed his shoulder. "At least not until I say so."

Eddie couldn't decide if he was reassured that Hinderlight was ready for a fight as well, or if it made him more nervous that the man expected one. It didn't help when the man that was leading them stopped in front of one of the cell doors instead of continuing on to the offices and labs closer to the elevator.

"What's this?" Hinderlight asked, mirroring Eddie's concerns.

"The liaison from the company has set up a small office here." The man shrugged. "He said he wanted a quiet place away from the other employees."

"If you say so," Hinderlight replied. He sounded less than convinced, but still wheeled Eddie forward as the other man worked the control panel and opened the door. Eddie braced himself for a desperate leap as he was wheeled into the room, just in case.

As they entered the cell, Eddie didn't bother to hide his relief as he noticed a makeshift office set up inside and not some terrible monster. An ornate desk sat in the center of the room, intricate carvings wound up the legs and around the edges of the dark wood, adding the appearance of both age and significance to the piece of furniture. A large wooden chair, more ornate than the desk and made of an even darker wood, sat with its back to them on the other side of the desk. A single chair, its plain design even more conspicuous among such ornate furniture, sat on their side of the desk. Besides that, the room was as bare as all of the other cells Eddie had seen.

Hinderlight wheeled Eddie further into the room, and as if on cue, the ornate chair behind the desk turned, revealing the man seated in it. A pale man stared back at them from behind a pair of circular glasses, his eyes hidden behind darkened lenses. He was clothed all in crimson, from the bowler hat on top of his head, past the Italian three-piece suit, down to his wing-tipped dress shoes that Eddie could see peeking out from beneath the desk. Beside the mass of red, the man wore a tight-lipped smile that was far from genuine. When he spoke, his words carried a lisp that sounded more like the hiss of a snake as opposed to a speach impediment.

"Mr. Watson, so good to see you awake after your harrowing ordeal. And Mr. Hinderlight, a pleasure to finally make your acquaintance as well." The man paused for a moment, his smile widening as it turned into a sneer. "Mr. Hinderlight, I would hate for there to be any misunderstandings. I would suggest removing your hand from the gun tucked into your belt. We both know that would be quite useless against me."

Eddie turned in the chair to find Hinderlight tense behind him, one hand still on the handle of the wheel chair, the other hidden behind his back.

"I've heard differently," Hinderlight replied through grit teeth. His hand stayed positioned behind his back.

The red-suited man let out a laugh that had the hair on the back of Eddie's neck standing on end. "You were misinformed. But not to worry. If the company wanted you dead, they wouldn't have waited for Mr. Watson to wake up. In fact, Mr. Watson *never would have woken up.*"

No need to wonder what the company was capable of anymore.

Hinderlight stepped out from behind Eddie, moving to his side. The man looked ready to pounce. "That may be true, but it doesn't explain why they would send one of *you*—" Hinderlight spat the word out like a curse "—instead of some other company lacky. The Red Suits aren't known among my rung on the corporate ladder as peaceful tools of The Board."

"Which just shows how little you know. Understandable, considering '*your rung on the corporate ladder.*'" The Red Suit turned up a palm as if expecting an acknowledgment of his point. When Hinderlight remained silent, the other man let out a huff of

316

breath. "My particular section of the company is utilized in a number of ways, all of which involve stressing how important it is for those that see us to know that our words come directly from The Board. That does not always mean the message needs to be one of pure violence."

"I've never heard of an appearance by one of you that wasn't followed by death, usually of the gruesome variety."

"Because those we don't greet with violence are sworn to secrecy to begin with. If we are that feared, then surely if we told a person not to speak of a meeting with us, they wouldn't even tell the one person closest to them. Let alone some other corporate employee that may turn around and betray them just to curry favor with The Board."

Hinderlight didn't acknowledge any of the man's points, but when he brought an empty hand from behind his back, it seemed to appease Red Suit.

"Now," Red Suit continued. "If you could position Mr. Watson in front of the desk and take the other seat, we can get down to business, so to speak."

"And what should we call you?" Hinderlight asked as he pushed Eddie's chair into the spot that the other man had indicated.

"Mr. Red will be fine."

"How unoriginal," Hinderlight mumbled as he took a seat. "All right, Red. Why are you here?"

"To inform you both about what the company has planned for you from this point forward. Seeing as how there is a vast gap between your positions and you played two distinctly different roles in the events that occurred, The Board has come to separate conclusions for your future."

Hinderlight leaned over and placed both of his hands on the desk. "Enough dragging this out. Just tells us what has been decided."

"Very well. Since you seem so intent on rushing things, we can start with you. The Board acknowledges the vast amount of effort you put into restoring control to the company's most valuable asset. With what little information someone with your clearance is given, you were able fight your way to the heart of the facility, secure the control room, and organize with those still trapped inside and the

317

company's external assets the reclamation of the entire facility in a matter of weeks. While others played key roles, Mr. Watson here being one of them, the testimonies of the surviving members of the security teams, scientists, and containment teams all agree that you were the keystone that held the entire operation together."

Eddie let himself relax. Why had Hinderlight gotten himself, and Eddie, all wound up when it was clear that he had been the main influence in securing the building? Of course his accomplishments were going to be rewarded. Even with the appearance of the off-putting Mr. Red, Hinderlight had to know the company would appreciate everything he had done.

By the way Hinderlight kept his palms pressed firmly against the top of the desk, though, he still didn't seem convinced. "Then they sent you to reward me? With what? A promotion? Some sort of bonus?"

"You also—" Mr. Red acted as if he hadn't heard the man "—brought unauthorized employees from the above-ground business down into the company's highest security facility. One being a useless office dreg, the second being a lowly custodian, and the third a simple secretary." Mr. Red shook his head. "Except the secretary turned out to be the high ranking cult member behind the entire excursion that almost brought down the facility to begin with."

Eddie ignored the slight directed his way and immediately jumped to Hinderlight's defense. "The imposter had taken the identity of a well-known employee, fooling everyone for close to a year. She had some kind of magical charm that prevented even the company's advanced forms of detection from catching her deception. Bragged about it to my face. You can't possibly blame Hinderlight for falling for it when everyone else did as well. Plus—" Eddie leaned forward.

"Which would be a valid argument," Mr. Red replied, "except that if he hadn't broken company policy, she never would have gotten into the facility to begin with. My investigation indicated that at the time Mr. Hinderlight brought your little group down into the facility and joined with the members of Squad K, the cultists had lost control of the facility. It was only through Mr. Hinderlight's actions that the cult's leader was able to not only enter the facility, but get past the last remaining security team in the process."

"Still—" Eddie began, but to his surprise it was Hinderlight that cut him off.

"Don't waste your breath." Hinderlight visibly deflated. His shoulders slumped as he leaned forward on the desk, his arms stretched out in front of him on the thick wood. "You can't argue or reason with a Red Suit, Eddie. They don't make decisions; they just follow orders. Whatever The Board has decided, it's better to just accept it and move on."

Seeing the usually confident man give up so easily took some of the wind out of Eddie's sails as well. A small smile touched Mr. Red's lips.

"An excellent observation." Mr. Red stood and gave a respectful nod in Hinderlight's direction. "Often a great deal of time is wasted with arguments and pleading. It's a pleasure to deal with an employee that knows his place and accepts the decisions The Board passes down to him."

There was no warning.

One moment Mr. Red was speaking, the next he had a machete in his hand as long as his forearm. The blade rose and fell before Eddie could even suck in a surprised breath. Blood erupted as the edge sliced through Hinderlight's right arm, just below the elbow, the force enough to cut flesh and bone, even into the thick wood of the desk. The large man fell to the side with a cry, his remaining hand going to the wound as if it could stop the blood flowing freely from it. Crimson flowed across the wooden desk, painting the walls, blending in with Mr. Red, who stared down at Hinderlight, his expression blank, eyes still hidden behind his glasses, all while Hinderlight curled into a ball around his mangled arm.

Eddie used what little strength he had to launch himself out of the wheel chair to the other man's defense. To his credit, Eddie was able to push himself across the top of the desk. Papers scattered everywhere in his wake. A sense of triumph filled him as Mr. Red's eyebrows rose in surprise above his glasses as Eddie slid across the desk toward him.

Unfortunately, that surprise did not mean Mr. Red wasn't able to defend himself. As Eddie attempted to grab the man, Mr. Red casually stepped aside. Eddie couldn't stop his own momentum at that point and found himself sliding right off the desk. As he fell off the wood surface, it was Eddie's turn to be surprised as a vice-like grip snatched him by the throat. His neck strained as he came to a sudden stop, his breath cut off as he was lifted into the air.

"Don't interrupt." Mr. Red didn't sound angry or even annoyed. "I'll get to you in a moment."

The man held Eddie aloft with impossible strength, then tossed him back across the desk with as much ease as if Eddie had been a tennis ball. His hip struck the edge of the solid desk before he tumbled to the ground. Both impacts hurt like hell, but no worse than any of the other bumps and bruises he had experienced during his ordeal a few weeks ago. His small burst of energy expended, all Eddie could do in his current condition was roll to his side so he could at least see how Hinderlight was fairing.

Which was not well.

Blood stained his clothes and had begun to pool in front of him. Most of the color had already drained from his face. His eyes were shut tight against a pain that Eddie didn't even want to imagine.

Forcing his body to move, Eddie began to crawl toward the injured man. A custodian might have very little medical expertise but he was smart enough to know that if he didn't find a way to stop Hinderlight from bleeding out, and fast, he wouldn't survive for very much longer. Eddie was able to get himself as far as the side of the desk before his arms gave out. On the other side, Mr. Red was moving.

The man in the crimson suit pulled something from a drawer on his side of the desk and moved to Hinderlight. Eddie tried to grab his leg but his outstretched arm was easily kicked away. Mr. Red squatted down next to Hinderlight and grabbed him by the shirt. He flipped the man onto his back with little effort and grabbed the wounded arm. Despite Hinderlight's effort to keep the bleeding stump pressed tight against his chest, the red suited man yanked it free and pulled it straight.

Even more blood than Eddie thought possible spurted onto his suit, blending in with the color of the material. Eddie was about to try and stop the man again but froze. The blood not only blended into the suit, it seemed to be drawn in and absorbed by the fabric.

"What the hell are you," Eddie whispered.

Mr. Red ignored him. While he held Hinderlight's arm with one hand, he pressed whatever he had pulled from the desk onto the wound. When he pulled his hand back, Hinderlight's wound was covered in a light blue membrane, like an elastic sheet pulled tight over the man's stump. It was fastened to his arm by a silver ring, held tight an inch or so above his elbow. Whatever Mr. Red had placed on him had stopped the bleeding. Despite Hinderlight's face being as pale as a ghost, his eyes were open and his breaths seemed to be slowing.

Mr. Red stood and looked down on the injured man. "The medicloth should be numbing your pain enough so that you can hopefully understand me. Now that your punishment has been administered, despite the multiple serious breaches in protocol that you are guilty of, I have been authorized to offer you a promotion. Your exemplary work in the past two weeks has impressed The Board and they wish to offer you the position of building administrator here at the company's headquarters. You would be in charge of both the legitimate business dealings of the main building as well as all of the research and development that occurs down here in the facility. Perks include a very generous increase to your wages, the ability to make your own hours, and of course, access to the company's more advanced medical programs." He waved a casual hand toward Hinderlight's damaged arm. "Something you can take advantage of as soon as all the paperwork is completed. But for now, all that's required is a verbal commitment on your part."

Hinderlight groaned and gave a slight nod of his head.

"Excellent. I'll let you remain there on the floor to let all of this sink in. When I've completed the rest of my duties here, we can have one of *your* employees assist you with your injury."

Hinderlight groaned again. Seeming satisfied, Mr. Red left him and turned toward Eddie. Before Eddie could do anything, Mr. Red grabbed his collar and hoisted him back up into the wheelchair.

"All right, Mr. Watson. Now that my business with Mr. Hinderlight is concluded, we can discuss your future with the company."

EPILOGUE

"Greetings, employees of Soladyne. This announcement marks the end of the 12:30 to 1 pm lunch shift. All employees assigned to this shift should be reporting back to work. Those on the 1 to 1:30 lunch shift may now report to their designated break rooms."

Eddie stuffed the last of his Italian wrap into his mouth, chewing it up as fast as he could as he got out of his seat. Around him, other employees did the same, finishing off bottles of water or grabbing one last chip before tossing their garbage into one of the nearby trash cans. There were only four other people in the break room that day, each dressed in whatever they considered to be comfortable clothes; t-shirts with the band logos, video games, or whatever else held their interest, jeans or sweats, sneakers, a pair of sandals. Eddie would have loved to be able to dress in comfortable clothes instead of his plain white jumper.

Eddie had been working in his new position for over a month now, and even though he had been nervous about taking the job offered by Mr. Red, he had enjoyed the switch. It wasn't that his responsibilities had changed that much. In fact they had mostly remained the same. He just felt a greater sense of purpose in the mundane work he did as a custodian. Well, maybe not in the cleaning of the bathrooms or the emptying of the garbage. Those jobs still provided him with a form of contentment, but it was the extra responsibilities, the added freedoms he was afforded, that gave him a new sense of purpose.

"Eddie Watson. Please report to room 8HH immediately."

"Not again," Eddie groaned. This was the third time in the past two weeks that he had been called down to room 8HH. Probably another one of the newer employees doing something foolish or making a mess of things. There had been an increasing influx of new employess to supplement the ones that hadn't survived what many were calling "The Incident."

"Best to hurry," one of the other employees said. Eddie thought his name was Chris. "If you take too long, whatever the problem is this time, it can only get worse, not better."

"I know."

The other man gave him a knowing nod, then grabbed his lab coat and put it on before leaving the break room. The other three people in the room followed shortly behind.

Eddie gave himself another moment or two to collect his thoughts before walking out into the hallway. His cart was waiting for him, filled with its cleaning supplies, trash bags, retractable mop, and various other tools he required for his more tedious tasks. He left it behind as he began making his way down the pristine white hall. Pale white doors sat on either side of him as he moved through the corridors he now knew like the back of his hand. As he left the rooms meant for the employees and entered into the twisting maze of hallways meant for things not human, a small chill crept up his spine. As it always did.

A month's time did little to cast a haze over his first memories of this place. The blood, horror, and death. He still found some of the blood during his work, dark, crusty stains that he had to scratch off the walls and floor. But each time he cleaned away one of those stains, he found the chill bothered him a little less. That wasn't to say that it had less of an impact. It was just that he grew more accustomed to the feel of it, like an old injury, always there, becoming as familiar as an intake of breath or his own beating heart. Eddie hoped that over time, that chill would only serve to remind him of the dangers locked behind many of the doors he now passed.

And if not, the first person he saw as he rounded one of the many corners in the detention area would do the job instead.

Kaga looked as intimidating as ever, a scowl cutting across his face like a fresh scar and his bare arms covered in a tapestry of tattoos. His face darkened even more as he caught sight of Eddie. Thankfully, he wasn't the only one waiting outside of room 8HH. Bukowski leaned against the wall, his massive girth busting out of the full body armor he wore. Hafiz was there as well, his face grim as he listened to a scientist making erratic gestures as he spoke. When Eddie had first heard that both men had somehow not only survived The Reaper but also took it down and contained it, he hadn't believed it. When the two showed up with Kaga during the first incident in 8HH, it had still been a shock. Despite seeing them a few more times after that, though, he had never been able to get out of them how they had taken The Reaper down.

Of course, he had tried asking the normally friendly Bukowski but he wouldn't budge. Kaga had made it overly clear he had no desire to talk to Eddie unless it was work-related. And Hafiz, well, the man was even more intimidating than Kaga.

"Eddie," Hafiz said in his usual grim tone. "Hurry up. I want this taken care of quickly so that I can get back to more important matters."

"More important?" The scientist with him practically screamed. The man seemed to become more erratic as Eddie approached. "What could be more important than the safety of one of my team members?"

Hafiz rounded on the man. He didn't say a word, just stared the scientist down until the other man lowered his gaze and squirm.

"If *your* team member had been properly trained, he wouldn't have gotten himself into this mess to begin with."

"We're doing the best we can! We lost over eighty percent of our scientific team during The Incident. The company has been pressing new recruits on us faster than we can train them. Despite not having the decades of experience of their predecessors, the company expects us to be right back to where we were before everything happened."

"Well, maybe you should worry more about training your employees than your quota, otherwise they might not be as lucky as this one."

"Lucky? How could you call his situation lucky?"

Hafiz rolled his eyes. "Your scientist will be fine. It's just doing this for attention."

"It's already got my attention—"

"Not yours." Hafiz gave a dismissive wave toward Eddie. "His."

"Why—" But Hafiz had already turned away from the scientist.

"You ready to go in?" Hafiz asked, annoyance lacing his voice as he addressed Eddie.

"Yes."

"Good. Try to hurry this along."

Hafiz reached over and pressed a few buttons on the control panel next to the cell door. A moment later, the thick door slid upward into the wall. The scientist stumbled away from the door, fear painting his face. Bukowski gave Eddie a reassuring smile while Kaga and Hafiz shared the same bored expression. Steeling himself against whatever scene he would find inside, Eddie stepped through the door.

The cell room was typical of every other one on all four floors of the Living Containment levels: plain, bright white walls, floor, and ceiling, devoid of any kind of furniture. A single ventilation grate rested in the center of the ceiling a good two floors above the ground. And in the middle of the room, a single lab tech stood. A pair of safety goggles covered most of his face but couldn't hide the man's trembling lips. From behind the man, a faded multicolored sleeve reached around and held a scalpel to his throat.

"Jester." Eddie kept his voice steady and calm, despite the fact that one wrong word or move could lead to the scientist's death.

"Friend Eddie!" The Jester let out a little giggle and poked his head out from behind the man. "So nice of you to visit!"

"Jester, you need to stop doing this." Eddie took a few more steps into the room. "Let that man go."

The Jester's mask took on a wicked expression. "But there are so many fun things Jester could do to him with this little knife. Remove a few digits. Peel him open like shedding an apple skin, this one could even—"

"Enough. You're scaring the poor man."

"*Fiiiiiinnnnne.*" The Jester's mask took on a petulant look as he moved the scalpel away from the man's throat. "Ruin all of Jester's fun." He gave the scientist a push. "Go on, little rabbit. Get out of here."

The scientist hesitated for a moment, which of course The Jester exploited.

"BOO!" it yelled, causing the man to jump and rush forward. Eddie grabbed the man's arm as he tried to hurry past him.

"You got lucky today. A mistake like this with one of the other detainees and you could end up dead before you even know you are in danger. Do I make myself clear?"

A quick nod from a pale face was enough for Eddie and he let the man go. Eddie watched as the man fled out the door before turning to face The Jester again. He had taken a seat on the ground and was juggling the scalpel from one gloved hand to the other. The mask he wore had a large smile and squinted eyes as he waited for Eddie to approach. To Eddie's surprise, the strange mask and the many faces it wore no longer instilled the slightest bit of fear into him.

Which was a good thing, as long as he never forgot what the creature was truly capable of doing.

"You know you have to give the scalpel back," Eddie said, taking a few steps toward him, his hand outstretched. He was happy to see that it didn't shake in the least.

"Of course, of course." The Jester tossed the small blade high into the air. It tumbled about, almost striking the ceiling before falling back down. He caught it by the blade and continued to juggle it back and forth between his hands. "After you stay and visit. The scientists are such a bore. All they're interested in is performing their horrid little tests on this one."

"You can't just take a hostage every time you want to have a chat."

"Oh?" The Jester tilted his head to the side. "Is Eddie Watson offering to visit without outside motivations?"

Eddie only took a moment to consider it. "Yes. If you can refrain from hurting any more scientists."

The Jester's mask took on an embarrassed expression. "This one only knicked that first little man. By accident, of course. It only took Eddie a few minutes to clean up what little blood was spilt."

"Well, if you can stop getting into situations where scientists are having accidents, I'll come and speak to you when I can. I promise."

The Jester flipped the scalpel up again before snatching it out of the air and twirled it between its fingers. Faster and faster it went until it was just a blur. Then it was gone entirely. "Friend Eddie should not make promises he cannot keep. It's a rotten thing to do."

"I'm sure if it will keep others safe, Hafiz or whoever else can grant me access to see you. So how about returning the scalpel and we can sit and talk for a bit."

"Very well." A quick twist of his wrist and the blade appeared again in his hand. The Jester placed it on the floor and slid it across to Eddie's feet.

Eddie kicked the blade toward the door. It smacked into the wall a few feet from the opening. At least he hadn't been that far off. A few moments later Hafiz stepped into the room long enough to pick up the scalpel, shoot a questioning look at Eddie, and left again when Eddie returned a nod. The door closed behind him, locking Eddie inside.

"See." Eddie moved over and sat down in front of The Jester. "They got the weapon back and still let me stay."

A slanted smile appeared on The Jester's mask. "Jester supposes you are correct. So what shall we talk about today, Friend Eddie? Philosophy? Monsters? Murder?" He shrugged as Eddie shot him a look. "Have you learned any good jokes lately? This one's humor tends to lean more toward the darker side. Some fresh, lighter material would be more than welcome."

Which is how Eddie found himself sitting on the floor of a cell designed to contain the worst horrors of the world, deep underground in a secret facility run by a morally questionable company, trading jokes with a monster. A monster, dressed as a Jester, that could kill him easily enough without any weapon. And yet, instead of feeling fear, Eddie felt comfortable. And for the first time in his life, friendship.

Eddie Watson's Life Rule Number #6: It is much easier to accept change than it is to fight it.

And to think, after everything Eddie had been through, this would only be a minor change compared to what was to come.